Praise for the thrillers of Robert W. Walker

Pure Instinct

The "Queen of Hearts" killer is stalking New Orleans. And the Police Commissioner has requested—by name—Dr. Jessica Coran...

"WALKER TAKES YOU into a world of suspense, thrills, and psychological gamesmanship."
—*Daytona Beach News-Journal*

Primal Instinct

No killer in Dr. Jessica Coran's past can compare to the relentless, psychotic "Trade Winds Killer" lurking deep within the underbelly of Hawaii...

"EVERY BIT AS EXCITING as the chase is Coran's rigorous examination of the evidence."   —*Publishers Weekly*

"*FATAL INSTINCT* AND *KILLER INSTINCT* showed Walker at the top of his form. With *Primal Instinct*, he has arrived. [It is] a multilevel novel packed with detective work and an interesting look at the Hawaii that exists beyond beachfront hotels."   —*Daytona Beach News-Journal*

Killer Instinct

Dr. Jessica Coran tracks a blood-drinking "Vampire Killer" deep into the heartland of America...

"CHILLING AND UNFLINCHING...technical without being heavy-handed, and brutal without glorifying violence or murder."   —*Fort Lauderdale Sun-Sentinel*

Fatal Instinct

Jessica Coran is summoned to New York City to find a cunning, modern-day Jack the Ripper nicknamed "The Claw"...

"A TAUT, DENSE THRILLER. An immensely entertaining novel filled with surprises, clever twists, and wonderfully drawn characters."   —*Daytona Beach News-Journal*

Titles by Robert W. Walker

DARKEST INSTINCT

ROBERT W. WALKER

JOVE BOOKS, NEW YORK

DARKEST INSTINCT

A Jove Book / published by arrangement with
the author

PRINTING HISTORY
Jove edition / May 1996

All rights reserved.
Copyright © 1996 by Robert W. Walker.
This book may not be reproduced in whole
or in part, by mimeograph or any other means,
without permission. For information address:
The Berkley Publishing Group, 200 Madison Avenue,
New York, New York 10016.

The Putnam Berkley World Wide Web site address is
http://www.berkley.com

ISBN: 0-515-11856-7

A JOVE BOOK®
Jove Books are published by The Berkley Publishing Group,
200 Madison Avenue, New York, New York 10016.
JOVE and the "J" design are trademarks
belonging to Jove Publications, Inc.

PRINTED IN THE UNITED STATES OF AMERICA

10 9 8 7 6 5 4 3 2 1

This book is affectionately dedicated
to some great people who know me well:
Georgine and Richard Walker and their son,
Ricky Walker, Jr., all of Chicago.

ACKNOWLEDGMENTS

My thanks to Andrea McNichol and Jeffrey A. Nelson for a completely absorbing book, *Handwriting Analysis: Putting It to Work for You.* My thanks also to *Fodor's Miami Guidebook,* and the American Booksellers Association Convention of May 29–June 1, 1993, for giving me an opportunity to combine business with pleasure in getting to know the city of Miami far better than I had. As for dark poet e. j. hellering, I have only my own dementia to thank, along with inspiration from e. e. cummings. Hellering is a figment of my imagination and cannot be found in ancient British volumes lost in dusty castles, so waste not your time in pursuit of him.

DARKEST INSTINCT

· PROLOGUE ·

She left the web, she left the loom.
She made three paces thro' the room,
She saw the water lily bloom,
She saw the helmet and the plume,
She looked down to Camelot.
Out flew the web and floated wide;
The mirror cracked from side to side.
—ALFRED, LORD TENNYSON

Off Key Biscayne, Florida, in Biscayne Bay
April 2, 1996

The powerful beam from the Cape Florida Lighthouse came some distance over the water, once a beacon of warning to sailors, now just for show. Still, it told Tammy that they had sailed out to the tip end of Biscayne Bay and were fast approaching the open sea. Tammy Sue Sheppard watched the light as she would a star, watched it blink on and off, on and off, on and off again, actually going around in a circular motion, spinning, like her head, racing like her pulse when he took her in his arms.

Patric smelled of a tangy, spicy aftershave here in the ocean breeze. He'd been so attentive, and now he was tantalizing her with his gentle caress, the soft touch of his tongue in her ear as they danced again about the deck of the beautiful, large sailboat. It was better than any schoolgirl's dream.

He now gently asked her patience as he returned to the controls and paused the ship here at the southern tip of Biscayne Bay, skirting the northern tier of the famous underwater Biscayne National Park, where coral reefs and sunken ships beckoned thousands upon thousands of recreational divers each year. But all that activity, even by night, was far to the south. The area around Cape Florida Lighthouse Point was long since deserted, save for a handful of passing boats, each with its own running lights reflecting off the water ahead of them, each mirroring in Tammy's mind the image of how she and Patric's boat must look from across the bay aboard these other ships.

One of the other boats was large and not a sailboat, however, storming by at some distance like a rhino rather than a bird like the soft others. The big boat had disturbed the water, sending an enormous wave across to where they had moored, causing the sailboat, as large as it was, to shake and shiver violently from side to side, disturbing their romantic moment, causing Patric to stare after the cutter for a long time, as if he were fighting the darkness in his effort to read the numbers on the Coast Guard cutter, wishing to report it. Tammy soothingly asked him to come back to the dance.

And he did so, turning to her with the widest, welcomingest smile she'd ever known.

Now, peace restored, Patric Allain was doing it again. He made her feel so feminine, so alive, so vibrant all over. He began to kiss and caress her, making her quiver in the most pleasant manner she'd ever experienced. The promise was as enormous as the sailboat, and at the moment, she didn't care whether it was a rental or it belonged to him.

Her best friend, Judy Templar, had whispered a whiskey-laden warning in her ear earlier in the evening, before Tammy had disappeared with Patric: *Don't believe a word he tells you, girl . . . and that boat's likely not his to begin with.* In his arms now, feeling overwhelmed with passion, she almost hated Judy for suggesting what she had. Judy and Cyn were both just jealous, because Patric had picked her out of the trio tonight.

She wanted to believe Patric, every word he'd said about himself, his boat, his plans and his feelings. It all seemed so wonderful. In fact, having had a great deal to drink tonight, everything seemed wonderful and anything seemed possible—especially love.

It seemed that all life lay at Tammy's beck and call now; it seemed, with such a stunning-looking man actually on his knees to her, now slipping off her shoes, massaging her feet, teasing her toes with his tongue, deliciously tickling her, that anything was possible. It was beautiful out on the large, open bay where the blinking lights of Miami winked at them like some enormous campfire where people huddled, afraid to come into the darkness where they could see the moonglow and the firmament so obliterated by the city lights. Here all of the black void of space was held back while her soul was cuddled and rocked into a safe place by Patric, who'd created this moment: the rhythmic, friendly sound of water lapping at the boat, gently rocking this big cradle into which she had nestled; the beauty of the restored lighthouse; the warmth of the music, soft and in harmony with the wafting sea breezes; a nurturing ocean, teeming with life. And then there was also Patric's gentle, sweet touch, his rich, sonorous voice, filling her with expectations of delight and sensual pangs.

His hands moved along the contours of her body now as he regained his feet; towering over her now, he took her in his arms now, his tongue finding and jousting with her own now, his body heat flowing into hers now. All now; everything, all life focused on the now. Certainly every fiber of her being was focused on the now.

His passionate tongue next found her ear, his sensual overtures continuing to happily chill her.

Doesn't he know he has turned me to putty? she wondered.

Then his hands turned from gentle to rough, all in a careless instant, and she looked up into his eyes, only to find the eyes of another person—wide, crazed, lascivious, indigo eyes that spoke of evil and bestiality.

He tore at her clothing, ripping her blouse as she tried to pull away. He slammed her to the deck, and the soothing sounds of the bay were drowned by the terror raging now in her ears as he rammed her forehead into the deck several times, knocking her into submission and oblivion.

When she awoke—she thought it moments later—it was to her own coughing and retching and gasping for air, her windpipe in pain. He had long since torn away her remaining clothing. She lay naked and raped there on the deck, seemingly alone. She could not make him out in the darkness. An eerie fog had enveloped the boat; there was no lighthouse anymore, no sign of shore, and it didn't feel as if the boat were moored any longer either. In fact, they seemed far, far from shore, and now she was shivering from pain and nudity, shame and the awful taste and smell of her own blood where he had slammed and bruised her, cutting her lip as well as her forehead. There was considerable pain the entire length of her throat, and she continued to gasp for air. Aside from the water hitting the side of the boat, her gasps were the only sounds to be heard.

Tammy Sue, get a hold of yourself, figure a way out of this, she silently berated herself. She tried to assess the damage, finding most of the pain lodging in and about her throat and her private parts. She had no doubt that he'd strangled her near to death—and enjoyed his sex rough, no doubt—and she was as yet dazed and confused by the encounter. Apparently, he could only enjoy sex by taking it—and the rougher the better—while she had nothing but pain from the encounter.

"Sonofabitch bastard," she moaned aloud.

From somewhere behind the fog, like a man behind a mirror, just out of her vision, came his voice, but it, too, had changed. "Pirates never were the romantic figures Hollywood made them into, my dear little mother." His accent now sounded ugly to her ears—and why was he calling her a mother?

She began to weep and think. She thought of her own mother, her little sister, her father, home. She wished with all her heart to be home again—not her lonely little apartment, but her childhood home. She wondered if she would ever see home again. She wondered if Patric meant to kill her.

She reached up to touch the bruised, painful area about her Adam's apple. It was so tender, she could hardly touch it. He truly had choked her so roughly that she'd been near dead.

"Be of good cheer, child," he said cruelly, still standing back of the mist, where she could hardly make out his form.

"For while you once were a nobody, I am going to make you a somebody, someone important."

She begged, "No, no . . . please, Patric. I just want to go home . . . I just want to go home. Please?"

He mimicked her words, and followed with a taunting laugh. He stepped into her line of vision, looking like some sort of monster, huge and hulking. "Your friends there"— he pointed as if he were on a stage, reading lines from a script he'd memorized—"what were their names? Julie and Cynthia? They will read about you in the papers, Tammy. Isn't that nice? You'd like that, wouldn't you?"

"Don't . . . hurt me, please . . . Please, if you'll just let me go, I won't tell anyone, not a thing. I . . . I promise . . . I swear. I know I led you on. It wasn't your fault, Patric. Please, please, just let me go." Her words trailed off in a keening, animal whine which further excited him, bringing him to his knees over her, bringing him to begin to trace his finger along her naked thigh, sending dread throughout her body.

"I'll let you go . . . when I'm finished with you."

Where was this maniac coming from? What did he want of her? Why had he done this to her? The Patric she'd wanted to love was here but not here, a phantom somewhere in the air around her while this evil twin kept them both in its awful clutches.

"Patric!" she screamed.

He clamped both hands over her throat, drowning out her cry. Subdued, certain now he meant to kill her, she again fell silent, wide-eyed and fearful. More than anything, she feared fainting. She feared that if she lost consciousness again, she would not awake a second time. He suddenly released his stranglehold on her and cruelly latched on to her hair, then dragged her to the back of the boat, kicking and screaming. It had become obvious that they were far out in the middle of the ocean. No one could hear her screams.

"I want to show you something, sweetheart." He pushed her aside and began tugging on a thick, black nylon rope which hung taut over the stern. He pulled at what was a great weight at the other end. For a time, she thought he'd be unable to lift whatever was on the other end, but soon the rope and its hoard were hoisted up.

She expected to see a large fish perhaps, but instead she found herself staring into the dead eyes of a completely waterlogged dead girl near her own age and similar in general appearance, her hair like seaweed, her skin drained of color, only the shell of life remaining. Tammy screamed, causing Patric to laugh delightedly and push her head into the dead girl's now mushy countenance, some of the skin peeling off and adhering to Tammy's forehead and cheek.

"Like looking into the future, into a mirror that reflects back your own future, Tammy, don't you see? I didn't want to lie to you another second."

He pushed her down, where she feebly grabbed on to his legs, pleading.

"Now that you know, it's . . . well, out of the way. It's good now that you know exactly what's going to happen here."

While Tammy began to whimper and blubber, he stared fixedly into the eyes of the dead girl he'd placed at the end of the nylon rope. "Her name was Allison. She's been in the water for a long time. See?"

He snatched up the dead girl's right arm to reveal that it had been severed at the forearm. "Sometimes I feed the sharks, you know, bits and pieces . . ."

Tammy's scream wafted across the great expanse of the Atlantic. He dropped Allison's body back into the depths and yanked in succession at two other ropes that hung over the stern. "Mary Ellen and Carrie Beth," he named each rope. Then he tugged at a fourth rope that gave easily, looping about his hands. "This one's for Tammy."

"Ahhhhh! Oh, no, no, please!"

"Shut up!" He slapped her hard across the face and she fell to the deck.

"Why? Why?" she pleaded. "What did I ever do to you?"

"Nothing and everything. You were born to be mine.

You're a perfect victim.'' He dug his thumbs into her throat again, registering the life's blood of her pulsating heart there. He easily, helplessly choked and choked her, enjoying the pleasure of it all, feeding himself on the life as it was given up from her a second time.

She fell again, eyes bulging wide, into unconsciousness. As he continued to squeeze, he felt the life draining from her, rising into his fingertips, into his hands, along his forearms and toward his heart and head. It was a feeling that gave him a sense of incredible power, a sense of identity and purpose and freedom from the mundane world.

"Thanks to you, Tammy, I'm no longer bored," he told the unconscious woman.

While she was out, he tied the thick nylon rope in a sailor's knot about her throat and bound her hands with a leather thong.

"When she returns to consciousness, Tauto," he spoke to himself and the cosmos, "we'll put her in the water and she'll be all yours to enjoy, hey?"

Then he set about fulfilling his perverted sexual needs on the near-dead victim for a second time this night, baying at the moon as he did so.

· ONE ·

We wove a web in childhood,
A web of sunny air.
                    —CHARLOTTE BRONTË

The flight to Miami from Quantico, Virginia, played un-relenting hell with Chief Eriq Santiva and the tourists, but it delighted the innocent children and Jessica Coran, since she and they reveled in a ride through rough waters—in this case air pockets, shifting thermals that rocked the air-boat like crashing waves from every direction while it cruised at 30,000 feet. The pilot, either by design or in-ability, seemed unable to get above or below the distur-bance. But it made Jessica feel something, and that was the rush, because for some time now she had been without feelings or emotions. The flight provided an adrenaline rush she hadn't felt for a long time, proving—at least in her case—that fear was sometimes better than no emotion whatsoever. Some people, even those she counted as friends—without voicing it, unable to put it into words—worried nowadays that she was perhaps beyond what others might consider the everyday, normal, rational fears and anxieties, and maybe she was. Maybe it was the legacy left her by Mad Matthew Matisak and other such monsters she'd hunted down and destroyed.

True or not, she considered going down with the plane in a storm a small fear. After all, she'd faced down New Orleans's Queen of Hearts serial killer the year before, and compared with dying as one of that monster's victims, a plane crash seemed an almost pleasurable end.

Below their airplane, the entire Eastern seaboard remained blanketed in an ocean-thick, roiling, bubbling, gargantuan glacier of gray-white cloud, and below this the continent was under attack by an arsenal of thunder, lightning, sleet, snow and hail, the world pounded by an unfeeling, killer storm. But *unfeeling* was hardly the right word. What natural phenomenon of raw power had feelings? Jessica thought it foolish of newscasters to call a storm cruel or heartless or evil, or to give it any human characteristic whatsoever or bestow the feminine personal pronoun *she* on it, since it had not a whit of human emotion about it. Like a sociopathic criminal on the loose, a storm destroyed life and limb without any more emotion than was felt by the sea or the void of outer space. None of these acts of nature or acts of God or abominations experienced any feelings one way or another toward human suffering. Yet some lamebrain newspeople insisted on calling this the cruelest storm in recent history, perhaps the meanest in a decade, and on reporting that *she* meant to torture the mid-Atlantic and Eastern states for days, playing out *her* unkind work until *she* might finally exhaust *her* evil self over the very land *she* ravished. And it further infuriated Jessica that storms were always characterized as female fury, unleashed feminine emotion. *May as well read a Harlequin romance novel as listen to the weather report these days,* she thought.

Jessica had seen on the Channel 2 TV newscast how the computer rendition of the storm appeared, and how on the forecaster's maps and screens, it was given an unreal, cartoonlike quality, making it look like a swirling mass of harmless, honeycombed whip cream, friendly in every aspect. A cotton candy apparition hunkered over thousands of miles of territory.

In reality this blanket of deadly white had killed over a hundred people along its zigzag path across the U.S., its subzero and snow-related deaths racking up sizable numbers from Wichita, Kansas, to Pittsburgh. The unkind storm had crept across from northern Canada, through the Great Plains, up again toward the Midwest, scourging Chicago and Buffalo, causing catastrophic problems for some, death for others, across Indiana, Michigan, Ohio, New York,

Pennsylvania and West Virginia, and now working on a downward spiral in its mad rush toward the Atlantic. The ride over this storm front was indeed calamitous, riotous and heart-pumping.

Still, it was good to feel that long-silent heart in her chest pounding again; Jessica was only sorry that it was at the expense of so many other passengers. She'd gone numb on December 2, 1995, the day she had left James Parry and Hawaii for a second time. They had made such a perfect pair, and his showing her the return of the glorious, spawning humpback whales in Maui's steamy, warm-water bays was an unforgettable experience which she would cherish forever, just as she cherished her moments alone with Jim. But they had both felt the rest of the world crushing in by November's end; they were both committed to their work, their careers once more conspiring against all happiness.

Still, on returning to the mainland, she'd put in for a transfer to the islands, telling headquarters that she wanted to make the move a permanent one. But D.C. wasn't in any mood to play Cupid for Jim and her, and there had appeared no real solution to the dilemma. Then things had changed quickly and drastically.

Jessica found herself in that daydreaming-again-about-Jim territory of her mind here now on American flight 312 when she was shaken from her reverie by the first of Eriq Santiva's deafening groans. She stared at him on her left, watching him turn to Jell-O with sound effects. His reeling head and dizziness, along with his stomach pains, were as real as his fear of flying, and those double-decker flapjacks he'd had just before takeoff had come to life, jumping up and over again.

Eriq Santiva wanted her here, on this special case which didn't involve Hawaii. In fact, it appeared it might lead in an entirely different direction, that of London, by way of Miami, and the Keys, perhaps.

A string of brutal murders along the Intracoastal Waterway between Key West and Miami had left local authorities guessing and ghost-chasing. The phantom killer seemed to come and go on the tropical wind, seemed capable of complete deception and near invisibility. And he had quite a knack for making his victims vanish as well. It was as if these young women were abducted by some sort of spectral visitor from another planet who floated in, dazzled them with pixie dust and then *poof!*—all gone but the remains, which washed ashore out of an uncaring ocean some twenty to thirty days later.

What the killer did with the bodies in the interim was anyone's guess, and at the moment, Jessica wasn't sure she wanted to look under that rock. That kind of peek into the pit would come soon enough, she knew.

The killer left no trail, no clues, no sign of himself, no killing ground, and his victims averaged one a month—*a far greater number than those of the heart-taking killer of New Orleans*—all eventually washing up on lonely, deserted Florida beaches, and on occasion, at one of the classier private beaches of a prestigious hotel, where guests would wade in the water with the floater until someone recognized it for what it was, usually by the gruesome gashes taken out of the body by passing sharks.

One victim had washed up outside a plate-glass window at a seaside restaurant where patrons were dining on native grouper and other delicacies of the sea. The most recent floater washed up just behind a house in South Miami Beach. The outline of the story read like a dark, perverse, reverse fairy tale without a happy ending: That bright morning the wife drew the curtains and stared out on her stretch of beach to see a glorious sunrise and what she believed to be the remains of the largest jellyfish she'd ever seen. It proved to be the fish-eaten, flesh-gone-slick torso of a missing seventeen-year-old named Allison Norris. . . .

Forensics estimated her time in the water at about the same number of days as she'd gone missing, which was just over a month. What remained was hardly human, save the superstructure of bone below the clinging gelatin.

No one in the medical or police profession knew how a floater—a body in the water—could take thirty days to wash ashore. The body had to have been anchored in some manner below the water, since it was determined by the local M.E. to have expired between twenty-five and thirty days before—a difficult call with any floater. So the thinking was that the body had been moored somehow below the surface, but had somehow worked loose. Yet there were no chains or ropes attached, although there was evidence to indicate that the girl's wrists had been burned and bruised by ropes or handcuffs or a combination thereof. Her throat also showed severe signs of rope burn, as well as manual strangulation, as if she'd been hung by her neck, or so said the M.E.'s protocol.

Cause of death was listed as strangulation-drowning, as if the two had curiously occurred simultaneously.

Eriq Santiva, sitting the entire flight in the aisle seat beside Jessica, was still struggling with his half-digested breakfast. Beside Eriq in the aisle, and on the floor on her rump, sat a tall, leggy stewardess who'd been flirting with the dark-eyed Eriq, whose natural good looks made him a kind of Latin George Clooney. The stewardess had simply plopped, unable to in any way gracefully return to her seat to buckle in, when turbulence had struck a third time, this time with a vengeance, and as if on cue with Jessica's rising dislike of the other woman.

The stewardesses had only just finished serving what American Airlines referred to as a "Continental Breakfast" and was about to clean away trays and cups when the seat belt light dinged on for the third time, at which time the curvaceous woman had simply given up trying to maneuver on the wild ride.

"You okay, Chief?" Jessica felt compelled by common courtesy to ask after her boss's discomfort.

Santiva swiped at his face again with the damp towel he'd specifically asked the stewardess for. She had obliged and had been cooing over the "poor man" ever since. At least he had been wise enough to decline any coffee or Danish, and for good reason. He'd had enough trouble just watching Jessica scarf down her own.

Breathing heavily, he said, "Never was a comfortable flyer, but I've never gotten into anything quite like this before."

She patted his hand and with a smile said, "No need to apologize, Chief."

"This goddamn seat feels like it's on a gyrating compass."

"Who knows," she replied, fighting back a gasp with the updrafts. "Might make you"—she grasped hard onto the sides of her seat when the plane was yanked to one side by unseen but powerful forces outside the aircraft—"a more comfortable . . . flyer in the end."

"Just wish the turbulence would end."

"Ultimately, it will."

"That doesn't sound exactly reassuring, Dr. Coran."

"Perhaps if we went over some of the particulars of the case, it might take your mind off of it?"

Santiva was a bronze-skinned man with dark, piercing eyes and a rakish grin when he wasn't reeling from nausea. He'd made a number of changes back at Quantico, one being to replace Paul Zanek with his own, more trusted man, and he made it clear that on the more important cases where profiling techniques and handwriting analysis were being used, he might well be along for the ride. He had built a reputation on solving cases through the use of handwriting analysis.

Santiva had also instated the use of psychic detection within the Behavioral Science Division, wisely giving full credit for its introduction into formal FBI channels to the departing Paul Zanek, who had been made bureau chief in Puerto Rico, having finally gotten that island paradise job he'd always fantasized about. This innovation had not come without controversy, and at great personal and professional costs to Santiva's own safety and well-being, primarily in the loss of points with the big guys overhead, who were all extremely conservative and old-fashioned—the Hooverites, they were called in the ranks. But no one could argue with the results in New Orleans the year before, when Dr. Kim Faith Desinor proved the extreme value of psychic detection in a major-profile case, the baffling, bizarre instance of the infamous Queen of Hearts Killer, a dreaded monster who literally preyed on the still-beating hearts of young transvestites in the French Quarter district of New Orleans. But Dr. Desinor had a history with Miami-Dade which was not conducive to good relations, so she was not to be directly involved in this case, although she might be contacted at any time with material evidence and asked to run her sensitive hands over it to see what might surface.

Kim Desinor had remained in touch with Alex Sincebaugh of the NOPD, and Jessica cheered them on in their ongoing love affair. Sincebaugh had left New Orleans and had found a detective's job in Baltimore to be closer to Kim. Jessica silently cursed Jim Parry for not having made such a move; if he had, everything would have been different. But he hadn't, and now she often felt completely alone in this world.

Chief Santiva interrupted her thoughts of Jim a second time, this time with a Cuban curse, something about his ill luck at having failed to get one of the FBI's Lear jets, or at least one of the military transports out of the Marine base at Quantico. But she informed him again that no aircraft would be comfortable in this storm. She'd continued her own flying lessons whenever she could find a moment, and she knew that none but the craziest, most thrill-seeking pilot cared to fly in such weather.

Lightning flashed outside the windows, and she thoughtfully closed the shield so that Eriq didn't have to look any longer. Santiva was slightly taller than Jessica, and he sported a roguish Venetian-styled beard, something that called to mind the players in a Shakespearean play set in Italy. And the man was so polite and well-mannered that she didn't know quite what to think of him. He was intelligent, quick, keen, hardworking and driven to do his very best, and far more interested in results than in lip service or politicking, so far as she'd judged. All qualities she had in common, all qualities she liked in a man. He was quite the opposite of Paul Zanek, the consummate diplomat and politician who seldom, if ever, left the side of his phone.

Santiva began to get his mind off the turbulence by looking over the file Jessica handed him. It was the Norris girl's file, faxes mostly, sent up from Miami-Dade PD. He lifted the file and began scanning it, even as it bobbed along with his knees on the roiling plane.

"Peculiar how long the body was in the water, wouldn't you say, Dr. Coran?"

"Please, call me Jessica. It's going to be a long trip if you continue to call me Doctor the entire way."

"Eriq then," he immediately countered.

"That medicinal patch I gave you? Did you put it behind your ear like I told you, or did you eat it?"

"Yes, no . . . I did like the doctor told me."

"Is it helping any?"

"Some . . . and thanks for the concern."

Even as she spoke of different things, Jessica gave thought to what he'd asked, about the peculiarity of Allison Norris's body being in the water so long. She said, "Strange thing about a body, any body, Chief . . . Eriq . . ."

"Oh, what's that?"

Jessica didn't readily answer, noticing that the flight attendant beside Eriq had leaned in to listen in on their talk. The pilot, crew and flight attendants on the plane had earlier been privately instructed that they were FBI so that there would be no undue concern over their weapons.

Jessica took this as her cue to gross the nosy woman out by flashing one of the crime scene photos and adding, "A body . . . well, it wants out. It wants to be seen, wants help, wants to give up its identity. Sometimes it screams."

"Screams?" asked the stewardess, whose name tag read Tawny.

Santiva frowned. "Wants out . . . wants to be seen? Screams?"

"For instance, how often do you hear of a body at a huge city dump, say in New York City, being discovered?"

"All the time, unfortunately."

"That's what I mean. The bad guys bury the bodies in places you'd think no one could possibly sniff them out, right?"

"Right with you, so far."

"Given the stench of the place on any given day, who'd ever find the body in a New York City dump?"

Eriq held back his breakfast, flashing on a mental picture of a bloated body at a dump site.

Jessica continued. "And it's not just confined to dump sites, this phenomenon." Jessica was warming to her audience, having them on.

"Oh, really?"

"Killers are notoriously resourceful. Killers place bodies in cement lockers and bury them below the earth, but still the body *leaks* information. The Jimmy Hoffa scenario is actually quite rare."

"Leaks information, huh? Stinks up the place, you mean?"

"By hook or by crook, the body screams, 'I want outta here!' Put it in a trunk and throw the trunk into the ocean, you think you've got it made, but the body works its way out like Houdini, or the trunk floats not out to sea but onto shore, and no one can stroll by such a 'treasure' without opening it up."

Santiva laughed now, and it did him good. His mind was taken off the flight, if only momentarily. "You really think the body's got some kinda power to, you know, influence the ocean swells? I mean the Norris body in Florida?"

She smiled a faint and mysterious smile, shook her head and laughed lightly, thinking about what she'd just said, realizing she meant every word, before replying. "All I know is that even if the body's been put in acid, its skeleton finds a way out."

He nervously laughed again, and Tawny nervously joined him while Jessica kept talking. "Put your dirty dead deed in the ocean, and it wants above the waves. If you bury it below ground, it wants above ground. If you cut it up into fifty little pieces, all the pieces want to find one another. If you stuff all the pieces into a drainage pipe, they all come out at or near the same location. If you burn the body, it will sit up and grin and wave, because in its mouth it holds firm to its identity, and its identity will hang you. If you drink the blood of the corpse, you'll spill enough to mark a trail to you. If you chop it into pieces and feed it to the sharks, some guy in a research facility hundreds of miles away will discover it in his laboratory when he goes to dissect a shark for its secrets. In other words, dead men have a way of plotting their revenge and pointing accusing fingers at their killers.''

He nodded appreciatively. ''You ought to know, Doc— Jessica.''

''I'm telling you only what every decent M.E. in the country knows, that the most immovable, inanimate and inert object on God's green earth—a body—will find a way out. It will simply find a way out, a way to move or a way to point a finger, either literally or in blood and body fluids, hair samples or fibers. It might take the help of a sensitive nose, a hunter's dog who likes to dig away at the grossest odors, a fisherman's hook, a dogged medical examiner or obsessed detective, but like life itself, always finding a way to evolve and grow, death remains intractable in its desire to evolve and, if not grow, mutate, and it is in that mutation that the body sends out signals, tugs at its moorings or surroundings, bloats and floats and finally pulls away in search of us, Eriq.''

''You think that Allison Norris was looking for us?''

''I have to.''

Santiva and the stewardess exchanged a glance, the woman lowering her eyes to her lap, a bit embarrassed at having listened in, or simply wishing she hadn't. Santiva returned to Allison Norris's file, likely sizing it up in relation to what Jessica had said, trying to determine if there were indeed a fatalism at work here, perhaps one that began when victim and killer spoke their first words to one another.

Jessica's own thoughts again turned to James in Hawaii. They'd made superficial, perhaps frivolous preparations to have Jessica return to Hawaii a third time; to shed everything she owned, all that she was, give it all up to be with him in Hawaii even if the FBI could not see its way clear to a transfer, since he simply could not leave Hawaii. Even if the FBI did see its way clear, she'd have to take a lesser position, become a field operative at the state level. She'd still be working cases, but her work would be confined to the Hawaiian island state. "Not exactly the worst wall to have your back against," Jim had kept reminding her of her choices.

It was a major life and career change, and she and Jim had a great deal of thinking to do before lunging ahead. Still, she recalled those precious days on Maui where she had spent the most wonderful moments of her adult life. Jim had been so vibrant, so loving and good for her. James and Hawaii had rejuvenated her, had conspired to make her whole again, and in Hawaii you could almost believe that evil no longer had a depressingly powerful foothold in the world.

Finally, at one point she'd sworn to Jim, and any of her friends kind enough to listen, that she'd return to D.C. only once more, to make all necessary arrangements to return to Paradise for good and all. Jim and she had talked of taking their romance to the next stage. And she'd made up her mind that either the FBI would grant her a full-time arrangement on the islands, so that she and Jim could be together, or she would seek a civilian job outside the agency, go back into pathology work with one of the hospitals in Oahu . . . maybe.

Jim and she were talking marriage, a home together, stability and *someday—somedays* for an array of milestones awaiting them, among them *someday* children. Her closest and dearest friends—Donna LeMonte, Kim Desinor, J. T., even Paul Zanek—were happy for her, and her life's work quickly became how best to get the hell out of the D.C. area and back to Jim. She began by divesting herself of the many worldly possessions she would have had absolutely no need of in Hawaii, from heavy winter coats, hats and gloves to woolen blankets and rain slickers and boots. In Hawaii people went barefoot in the rain.

She had also begun to rid herself of binding arrangements here, from her job to her apartment and money matters, looking into electronically moving her money into a bank in Oahu, and she was discreetly saying her good-byes when she got the wake-up call that, while she was gutting her own world, James Parry was actually unwilling to give up anything for the relationship. She was uprooting and changing everything so that her life might fit into his life, while James had forfeited nothing. She had leapt into love's crevasse, while he stood yet at the cliff, looking on. All these impossibly huge life changes she'd made without the slightest guarantee, and it suddenly dawned bright that it wasn't fair. Then her friend, psychiatrist Donna LeMonte, had kindly and cleanly cut her up into little pieces with the truth, that this perceived lack of sacrifice on Jim's part was all the excuse and rationale she'd secretly, subconsciously been waiting for, so she might escape the terrifying stress and equally terrifying idea of commitment and devotion, for which she would have to relinquish so much of herself, her hard-won identity.

Donna had reminded Jessica that there were never any assurances in the best of relationships. But Jim had made no assurances whatsoever, and for Jessica, the signals she was basing her new life on suddenly crumbled like stale cookies, forcefully alerting her to the kind of fool she'd become. And next she began to question her and Jim's motives. Was Jim worth turning her entire life inside out for? Maybe yes, but he might've at least shown some of the class Alex Sincebaugh had in giving up his beloved New Orleans for the woman he loved. Whether right or wrong, Jessica decided at the thirteenth hour that neither Jim nor Hawaii was going to back her into any corners.

She had desperately tried to explain her newfound well of concerns to Jim, but his typical male response had infuriated her. He'd complicated the issue with his ego; had dared complain that he had already placed his house up for sale and had been searching for a beach house, a place for the two of them. He had finished with a lame joke, some nonsense about how much Jessica was going to be underfoot. She heard it as how she had "put him out."

"Wrong answer," she had told him, hanging up on him. She hadn't heard from him now in several days.

Depressed, she had closed in on herself after that, closed off her feelings, like blinds closed against the light. She had not taken time to mourn the loss of their phantom future life together; instead, she'd thrown herself back into her work, even as Donna argued that this was not the full extent of who she was. Pretending for the time being that nothing mattered but her profession, she had asked for an assignment, any assignment. So now she was on her way to Miami with Chief Eriq Santiva, who had the day before forwarded to her a strange telephone call from a shark research facility in the Florida Keys. She'd spoken to a Dr. Joel Wainwright about some interesting specimens found upon dissection of sharks at his facility—female human body parts. A map of the area showed that, as the shark flies, there was not a lot of distance between Key Largo, where the sharks were caught, and Greater Miami.

Together now, Jessica Coran and Eriq Santiva had joined forces on a true fishing expedition, on what seemed a convoluted trail that might lead to a madman who was drowning his defenseless young female victims after sexually molesting them.

"You think the water has any significance to the killer?" asked Eriq.

"Damned straight it does. Could mean anything from the amniotic fluid in the womb to the salt of the earth to this guy. Look at the letter he wrote to the *Miami Herald*."

He fished among the papers for the handwritten, faxed copy of the purported letter from the Night Crawler, as the press had dubbed the killer.

Chief Santiva had already scanned the Night Crawler's scrawl several times. Now his patient eyes played over the loops and swirls of the killer's feral handwriting once more.

Santiva, of course, had wanted and had screamed for the original handwritten note attributed to the Night Crawler, but the local police wouldn't or couldn't provide the document; something was even said about its having gotten lost in the "cage," cop talk for the Evidence Lockup Room. Thank God it had been faxed before it was completely lost, if it were indeed from the killer.

Meanwhile an Interpol communiqué, forwarded to the FBI via Scotland Yard by an Inspector Nigel Moyler, had mentioned a similar outbreak of killings occurring along

the Thames River in London the previous year, killings
which had gone unsolved. He had forwarded a handful of
letters written by the Thames River Killer when Santiva
had shown an interest. The two cases seemed to have some
similarities, and Santiva had seen some immediate similarities in the handwriting, but there were also differences.
Many of the most salient differences, according to Eriq,
could be attributed to a growing neurosis which was reflected in the letters from overseas.

Eriq had made no outright promises, but he had mentioned the possibility that since Moyler was pursuing a similar course with a similar monster on the other side of the
Atlantic, Eriq or Jessica might go over to see what sort of
joint efforts could be made. "In the name of cooperation,
should the handwriting of the two killers match up," Santiva had teased Jessica, believing that she would jump at
the chance to visit London and the famous Scotland Yard.

Santiva continued to study the faxed document, scanning
it for perhaps the twentieth time, reading again the purported
lines of the man Jessica had half-jokingly called the Bible
Belt Beast. Like Jessica, Santiva had already memorized the
dark, sinister little note, a poem actually—the lines spoke of
a disturbed individual who held a fathomless hatred for
women. Each time he read the lines through, he seemed to
get something new from them, gathering in the larger context, the innuendos, the slings and arrows the monster had
endured, and the slips, slits and chinks in the madman's ar-
mor.

The interested stewardess had now disappeared, the jolt-
ing of the plane having slackened.

"The maniac's words are almost eloquent in places,"
Eriq said.

Eloquent wasn't quite the word that had jumped out at
her when she'd first read the killer's remarks. In fact, *eloquent* was the last word she would have used to describe
the bastard. Still, Santiva had a point. Like the missives of
Jack the Ripper, the note was brief, concise and eloquently
simple. In business parlance, it was to the point. "Well, I
give him one thing," she conceded.

He looked askance at her. "What's that?"

"He has a good command of the King's English, wouldn't you agree?" she asked.

Santiva nodded, managing a half grin of thoughtful reflection. "Right, he's certainly no slacker with regard to grammatical correctness and construction. Bet Mrs. Higgins would give him an A for that alone."

"Mrs. who?"

"Oh, just a spicy old English teacher of mine when I was in grade school. She'd bust your chops for confusing the use of the personal pronoun *I* with *me* or vice versa, and God forbid you use a possessive pronoun incorrectly. She'd hold you up to public ridicule." He fell silent a moment longer, his expression telling her that he remembered Mrs. Higgins with more fondness than annoyance. When he spoke again, he said, "You know what we've got here, don't you, Jessica?" He waved the copy of the killer's note.

"Yeah, 'fraid I do. He's the most dangerous animal on the planet—an educated lunatic."

"Did you notice the British spellings? On the words *caliber* and *theater*?"

She admitted that she hadn't noticed the transversed letters E and R. She'd have to analyze more carefully, she told herself. What would Mrs. Higgins say of her carelessness?

The turbulence outside the plane settled somewhat, and this settled the unrest inside the plane to some degree, but most people remained cautious, ready to expel yet another gasp if it came to that, and it did. The momentary lull in the turbulence only resulted in a new wave of shocks to the system, the force of the assault seeming to double, sending many people to the altar of the vomit bag. This was all Santiva needed to see and hear. The stewardess who'd sat alongside Eriq was returning to check on him and had to quickly move out of his way as he snapped off his seat belt and raced for the lavatory, too polite a man to vomit in Jessica's presence. She liked that.

· TWO ·

Art is myself; Science is ourselves.
—CLAUDE BERNARD

Islamorada Key, Florida, April 13, 1996

The yellow made-over Ryder truck, equipped with an on-again, off-again freezer compartment, wasn't truly large enough to be called, in trucker lingo, a reefer, but it was fully functional when it worked. It rode low to the ground with the weight of its five thousand pound cargo, and now the frozen cargo was being backed up along a concrete ramp at the University of Florida's Abbott Marine Research Laboratory on Islamorada Key. At the top of the ramp stood two massive doors and a conveyor belt, beside which waited two strange looking scientists in hip boots and protective gear more suited to the river than the laboratory.

Lynette Harris and Aron Porter, to whom all the scut work naturally fell, stood poised in bulky clothing and chaps, prepared to enter the truck from the rear, to wade in and slide about in their hip boots, protective clothing, thick rubber gloves and goggles. A pair of student trainees at the high-tech marine research center, each now resignedly climbed aboard, despite Aron's bitching, to begin the struggle with the dead beasts within: some twenty-five recently deceased sharks of various size and species.

The protective wear was as much to guard against cuts and bruises as to avoid possible infectious viruses the sharks might easily pass to the humans. Aron marveled at the enormity of the workload that lay ahead of them now that they'd traveled back from Key Largo, and he didn't appreciate Lynette's shoving him and nagging, saying, "Let's have at it. The work won't get done standing here staring at it. Come on, Aron . . ."

Aron was already tired, and he was hungry. He moved slowly, as if his muscles were atrophied.

Lynette, by comparison, seemed full of energy at all times. She was anxious to have the job behind her. Whenever they might finish downloading their third shipment onto the ramp, there would be upward of ten thousand pounds of shark flesh in the holding tanks, which were filled with a saline solution and kept at a constant thirty-two degrees Celsius for preservation purposes. The sharks would be processed, not for canning or freezing or selling to the local eating establishments, but for study of the reproductive cycles of the species in order to help determine if the U.S. government—the EPA in particular—really wanted to get involved in controlling fishing rights over sharks in Florida's coastal waters.

The trainees knew that their work here was important, that overfishing of sharks, according to Dr. Insley's projections, would mean a lethal break in the food chain, creating an imbalance that might subject all fish to extinction if the next link in the food chain were to suddenly have a population explosion. But according to Dr. Wainwright, an even more important reason for gathering the shark specimens at Islamorada was so that other research facilities across the nation would have ample biological samples for cancer research, for studies of the immune system with possible application to AIDS research, for cornea implants, and for a supply of skin for burn victims, not to mention for ongoing research into shark repellents.

Dr. Lois Insley's major concern, however, was to determine if free-for-all fishing of sharks up and down the Keys and Florida would or would not lead to the extinction of certain species.

Ironically, the institute had for several years now sponsored the Shark Research Fishing Tournament in order to gain enough sharks for research purposes to enable Insley's extinction theory experiments to continue. This year, they had solicited and obtained dual sponsorship of the popular tournament with SunFin Boats Incorporated, and this made their mother institution, the University of Florida, extremely pleased.

Now, the third and final day of the tournament had come and gone, Aron and Lynette the night before having weighed and marked each specimen for identification—and, of course, the inevitable photos with the winners in each class having been all taken, before a crowd of curious tourists fascinated by the thirty-odd fishermen, the gathered scientists and the grand prize winner, a 317-pound monster hammerhead which lay now in the back of what passed for a freezer truck at the Islamorada scientific facility.

The truck, its cargo and the weary lab workers had long since been ready for the tournament's end, and an end to the grueling effort required to transport the bestial cargo from Key Largo to here.

This was the final trip this year for the unmarked yellow truck, which had traveled from the southernmost tip of Key Largo; the battered old machine was showing signs of wear and beginning to smell like a slaughterhouse, despite the frigid air compartment. Both Lynette and Aron had come to accept the stench along with their strenuous duty. Later on, they could do what they'd come here for: dissect and study the inner workings of the incredible animals which had netted the contestants in the tournament some fifteen thousand dollars in secondary prize money and an incredible twenty-nine-foot SunFin flybridge boat as grand prize. It was a sleek sportfisherman's speedboat with choice of gas or diesel power, twin Crusader 350 or 200-hp Volvos—also winner's choice.

The folks out of Fort Lauderdale really knew how to spruce up a tournament. Getting SunFin Inc. to come on board had been the work of Dr. Joel Wainwright, and it proved an ingenious move.

As for the institute's prize, it now had a supply of specimens of various sharks to carry it through another year and a half of research, possibly two, not to mention the profits from selling off the parts to other research labs across the states.

Inside the mammoth facility, which had been designed to blend in with the surrounding palms and palmetto brush—even the brick was a sand hue to match the white-shell sands of the Keys—research into man's amazing cousin, the predatory sharks of the Florida coast, was always ongoing. And it was the kind of research that necessitated a great number of shark corpses.

Each ponderous shark body was now shoved onto a conveyor belt—each going down into the hold like so much luggage, thought Lynette Harris, except that this luggage had eyes that simultaneously appeared as lifeless as large glass beads and so hypnotic as to appear alive. Life and death mirrored in the milky cornea of a magnificent animal laid waste to. She felt the need for science and the need for life both at once, but as she had many times before, she shoved the thought to the back of her mind in order to carry on with the work at hand. And the work was considerable. They could use both Insley's and Wainwright's help, but God forbid the doctors should get their hands dirty at this stage.

The sharks were incredible, even the smaller species; the average weighed in at or near two hundred fifty pounds. It took some strain and effort to move the lifeless animals from their frigid moorings in the back of the truck to the conveyor belt. The work was cold, hard and thankless.

"Grab 'im by the dorsal and tail fin! Yank and I'll push," Aron instructed Lynette from where he stood at the head of a particularly huge monster.

"Aren't you going about this bass-ackwards, Aron? Why not turn 'im around, then you grab the dorsal and tail? Then you push and I'll pull 'im by the jaw with my hook." Lynette held up a huge meat hook, and given her protective wear, she looked like the creature from the remake of *The Thing*.

"You sure you weren't a longshoreman in another life?"

She stifled a laugh. "Just do it my way, okay? It'll be less strain on us both."

"Stop squabbling, you two!" came a voice from around

the truck. It was Dr. Lois Insley, head of the institute, keeper of the keys and a demanding boss who insisted on blind obedience and deference to her arrogance. She'd even been angry with Wainwright for bringing in the SunFin people as sponsors, at least at first. Aron had told Lynette that it was because Lois hadn't thought of it herself.

"Have either of you seen Dr. Wainwright about?" Dr. Insley asked, her nervous eye twitch back like a bad rash.

"Think he's in his lab, Doctor," replied Lynette, her gloves already slick with the juices exuded by dead fish, her toes and fingers freezing.

"I'm so furious with that man," announced Dr. Insley.

"But why?" asked Aron. "Hell, this-sis-been one hell of a tournament, thanks to Dr. Wainwright."

Lynette immediately agreed, smiling behind her protective wear. "We've got all the specimens we need, and it didn't cost the institute or the university a dime. I think Dr. W. is a . . . well, a genius." Lynette knew Aron and Dr. Insley must know how she felt about Dr. Wainwright, that she had an uncontrollable crush on the older man.

"Getting SunFin to put up the prize was certainly a stroke of *marketing* genius," Aron quickly added, knowing it needled the frumpy Dr. Insley to tell her that anyone but Her Majesty had any genius. He hoped that the use of the word *marketing* to qualify Dr. W.'s genius would keep Insley on an even keel.

"The damned fool has called in outsiders about . . . about what we've been seeing in the lab."

"The human body parts, you mean?" Lynette unnecessarily asked, recalling vividly how several days before, with the first onrush of new specimens, Dr. Wainwright, with her and Dr. Insley beside him, had uncovered yet another stash of undigested human body parts and bones amid the usual stomach contents. There were some gruesome intact parts, from toes and fingers to whole hands and feet. And while this wasn't totally unusual, the sheer amount, from the very first specimens opened up, gave everyone in the lab a chilled pause.

"Keep unloading and don't stop till you've emptied the truck. We're paying that driver for his time as well, you know. I want him back on the road for the final cache and back here by tomorrow this time. So, move!"

"But, Dr. Insley, this is the third and last load," Aron corrected as gently as he could. Dr. Insley, however, had angrily waddled away, in search of Dr. Wainwright.

Lynette and Aron exchanged a long look from behind their goggles, Aron finally shrugging and Lynette saying, "She may know how to work with data and statistics and her computer program, but she hasn't got a clue about the real world, does she?"

"Know what gets me?"

"What's that, Aron?" Lynette worked as she talked, but Aron took a break with each word.

"How she ever got in charge of this place in the first place."

"Wrote a grant, and grant money speaks volumes in academia. Anyhow, all you've got to know is that she *is* in charge."

"She's in charge . . . but she's not in control. . . ."

Lynette watched the older woman, with her no-nonsense step and severely arranged hair, storm into the building, wondering what Lois ever did for fun, for frolic . . . for sex.

Inside the spacious facility of the laboratories, Dr. Insley found Wainwright studying the latest human body part to fall from the gut of a great white.

"How dare you disobey me, Doctor?" she stormed at him. "To go over my head to the board members, and to call in the FBI after I assured you that there was no necessity here to do so, that these human body fragments are par for the course in our research and that—"

"I tried reasoning with you, Dr. Insley," Wainwright calmly replied, his body language rigid, unable to completely ignore his so-called superior. Still, he kept his eyes glued to the human bone and tissue specimen he was studying through the wide lens of the powerful magnifying glass, which he now swung away from himself, the glass careening away on its swivel arm, trying its best to strike Dr. Insley.

Finally, he could no longer ignore the woman, who stood like a pillar of salt before him in her white lab coat. Meeting her eyes, he said, "These parts are extremely fresh, and the sheer number indicates an anomaly at best. You have to concede that much. Don't you read the papers?"

"What papers?"

"The newspapers."

"I have enough to read just keeping up with the literature in the field."

"The *Miami Herald* and even the Keys papers have been filled with missing persons cases lately, and some freak has been claiming responsibility, writing letters to the authorities about how he hates women, and all these parts appear to be petite . . . female parts? Get it, Doctor? I mean you have to concede that—"

"*Concede*? I don't have to concede a damned thing to you, Dr. Wainwright. In fact, you can pack your belongings and find the door. Your dubious services are no longer required."

"I'll fight you on this, Lois."

"Goddamn you, Joel, do you really think that you can come in here and unseat me, a person of my standing, with my record and years?"

"I don't intend walking out of here without a fight, if that's what you mean."

She stared icily at Wainwright, a tall, imposing man with prematurely graying hair. She held her stare, as if hoping her eyes alone might destroy him.

Joel Wainwright looked back at Dr. Insley's fleshy jowls and pink complexion, thinking again how unbecoming a woman she was, and how powerful she remained. Precisely why she had been given so much authority here was beyond Wainwright's comprehension, but he had obviously won her wrath this time, regardless of how successful the Shark Research Fishing Tournament had been. It had been successful in large part thanks to him, but Dr. Insley didn't wish to deal with reality, that they had twice the amount of specimens as last year; nor did she want to deal with the fact of the human body parts in the back freezer stacked like wrapped raw steaks from a deli—hands, arms, legs, shoulder bones, pieces of flesh that hadn't yet been digested by the shark's slow metabolic juices, they were that fresh. Neither had the body parts been properly categorized by the scientists on Islamorada, because everyone here majored in shark, not human, anatomy.

So Wainwright had begun to collect the human anatomical parts, after at first simply discarding the occasional piece as "expected remnants of shark attacks" which occurred up and down the coast of Florida every season. Dr. Insley had made inane assurances that most victims of shark aggression, while scarred for life, lived past such attacks, but then the number of body parts became too high—and the sheer size of those parts too large—to ignore a moment longer. *Ignore it and it will go away* seemed Lois Insley's management style, her modus operandi. Meanwhile, an entire pelvic section dropped from one shark, and there were twenty-five more sharks now being dumped in the cold tanks, forty-seven in all, some ten thousand pounds. How many more human parts might they expect, he wondered and calculated, his prediction frightful.

As for the FBI, who else was he going to call? The frigging EPA? The coast guard? His phone call was put through to the FBI's forensic laboratories the day before, and he found himself talking to a charming voice on the other end which turned out to be that of Dr. Jessica Coran, who was immediately curious and interested in what they had found.

"Dr. Insley," Wainwright began slowly now, deliberate in his every word, "you might well ignore this heinous, unpleasant side effect of our tournament if you wish; you may have no problem concentrating on the prize for Florida's Abbott School of Marine and Atmospheric Science laboratory, on the plentiful specimens, more than we possibly know what to do with, but God bless it, woman, I'm a simple man with simple ethics, and I am not willing to ignore the obvious—at least not in this case.''

''Show me what is so obvious, Doctor!''

He took firm hold of her and moved her to and through the freezer doors, where a vaporous cloud engulfed them, then fought past them to escape into the lab.

Inside the freezer, Wainwright pointed at shelves stacked with body parts and bones. ''Look, look closely, Dr. Insley. Do you need the problem put on a string and tied about your neck? This is an uncommon phenomenon, an incredibly high incidence of human parts found in a relatively small, concentrated shark population. It's neither incidental nor anything less than an abhorrent anomaly. Something had to be done about it. This information could not stay inside these walls. And that's what I intend to put in my report to the board of governors.'' The threat was clearly unveiled.

Checking his now frozen watch, he added, ''So, I expect that something will be done when Dr. Coran of the FBI arrives, and I expect that will be soon now.''

''I cannot believe that you invited FBI operatives into this facility.''

''Just what're you afraid of, Doctor? This is the U.S. Government, their official police arm.''

''I'm afraid of nothing. I . . . I detest military and paramilitary types of any sort.''

''They're coming to see if there's any connection between our discovery and those missing young women, that's all.''

''Suppose they want records? Copies of our work here?''

''I can't believe the level of your paranoia, Doctor.''

She clenched her teeth and glared up at him. ''Our work here must remain secret. Do you know how many others are desperate for our research?'' Insley spat her words at him, and as she stormed from the cooler, Wainwright thought he sensed in the cold gloom of the place a warming trend. And rightly so, he thought, the place having rid itself of the woman. He wondered how he might rid himself and the institute of her. She was right to feel a threat, but not from the outside.

Jessica Coran stared out through the thick bubble of the helicopter at a world so far removed from D.C.—and civilization as she knew it—that the place emerged in her sifting mind as a primordial playground set in a time warp. The chopper was generally following the Overseas Highway, built to connect the string of Florida Keys that snaked out into the Gulf on the one side, the Atlantic on the other. The gleaming white strip of sand, concrete and steel that marked bridges and roadways looked, from up here, to be a string of spaghetti, a tenuous connection of palm-sprouting island hideaways without Kmarts and superstores, only the sporadic shell shop for unique Florida collectibles might be found alongside Texaco signs and near-deserted strip malls at which the bare necessities—bait and beer, tackle and bread, buckets and bologna—could be bought.

There was no want of traffic, however, along the single lanes going north and south, and the sheer expanse of the bridges over the greenest, purest-looking water she'd ever seen was in itself amazing. The bridges were thin connective tissue between the islands, long and narrow and sizzling beneath an unmercifully hot sun.

For as far as Jessica could see, there were dozens upon dozens of low mangrove islands floating on the luminous green mirror of the sea. Above and around the islands, ancient gulls and egrets, pelicans and white-winged ibises played, cartwheeling through the primitive sky—the same birds as had flown here a thousand years before, she imagined. The endless blue-green panorama conspired to make the beating helicopter and the pulsing cars on the highway below seem like just so many reverse anachronisms, things out of sync, out of time and out of place.

By some uncanny miracle, the development wars had left the land here between Key Largo and Key West virtually untouched; there were no Hiltons, Marriotts, Holiday Inns or other resorts, not a single gleaming monument to man save the occasional house, shack, marina and dive shop.

The pilot called it the "backcountry" and nailed his estimation of the place with a few choice phrases: "devoid of fresh water"; "not suitable for housing"; "a breeding ground for mosquitoes the size of my mother-in-law"; "a dumping ground for gator-baiters and drunken fishermen."

"Says on the map it's a protected wilderness," she replied into her headphone set.

"That's right. Great fishing and bird-watching, but most casual boaters wouldn't risk it. Waters are extremely shallow and channels are narrower'n Heaven's Gate. Only the locals can safely navigate here."

"Good fishing, though, you say?" asked Eriq Santiva, who sat opposite Jessica and only occasionally looked down over their destination.

"The best, but a man's got to be solemn quiet. I mean it's so quiet here, the fish can hear you breathing from ten feet off."

Jessica lifted her polarized sunglasses so that nothing rested between her naked eye and the natural beauty. "I can almost imagine dinosaurs roaming here," she commented.

"Well, they did once, according to the experts, especially sloths. I'd say a few sloths still exist, but now they're called bubbas. I tell you, the area is so swamp-ridden, you couldn't even get a good paramilitary group together down here."

Jake Sloane, the helicopter pilot, was something of a character. He was a born Floridian, a "rarity" in these parts, he'd said. And since he was a native, he felt comfortable running down the area and the other natives.

As the helicopter dipped and moved in closer, Jessica made out an oyster bar hidden below vegetation at the terminus of a dirt road, beside which were a handful of broken-down skimmers—lightweight boats with outboard motors used by local fishermen. "I suppose Jimmy Buffet passes for Christ here," she muttered to Sloane, garnering a laugh from Santiva and the pilot, a man who preferred the name of Spider Sloane. The Miami Police Department had guaranteed the FBI agents that not only was Spider certified as one of the best charter pilots to this area, but he'd flown in Desert Storm.

"There it is, folks! W-e-i-r-d place. Locals got a name for it; call it Frankenstein's Castle," said Spider, a mock grin playing about his bearded jowls. Spider flew small jets as well as helicopters in and out of the Keys and to the Bahamas, daring the Bermuda Triangle to someday swallow him up.

Jessica Coran leaned into the bubble window to stare down over the well-masked, camouflaged-from-the-world buildings belonging to the University of Florida. It was neither easy to see the facility nor simple to determine its size, as all the angles blended in with surrounding flora and white sand. The place could easily be missed, created as it was to be a part of its natural surroundings, and this gave it an illusory effect, both disturbing and interesting at once, for it had a kind of otherworldly, alien appearance to it; a space station in a mangrove field—like the bizarre photographs of modern photographer Jerry Uelsmann.

The grounds all round were neatly kept and cultivated, the building high-tech and eco-conscious, making the awkward yellow pachyderm of a made-over Ryder truck appear out of place, like a brightly painted elephant squatting at a baby shower.

Beside Jessica, Chief Eriq Santiva, anxious for a landing, leaned over to see what the other two were gazing at. He was not a good flyer, and this showed only too grimly now on his jaundiced face.

"There's a helipad for their regular deliveries from the university," explained the pilot through the headphones.

Jessica pointed out the pad to Santiva, adding, "There now, see? Not long now."

Spider piped in with, "Yeah, we'll be on the ground in a few minutes, Mr. Santa-va, so just remain calm, okay?"

"San-T-va; the name's Santiva," Eriq corrected the burly, gray-bearded pilot, a stand-in for Papa Hemingway.

"Sorry, sir."

Jessica stifled a laugh.

As the chopper rounded the research facility, someone at the Ryder truck waved at them. Jessica pointed, but saw that Eriq was preoccupied with his knotted stomach. She watched Eriq swallow hard, struggling to hold back the natural want, recalling just how awful the plane ride to Miami had been. This was the last leg of their shared journey.

"This better be all that this Dr. Wayne—"

"Wainwright," she corrected Eriq.

"—Wainwright, right . . . better be all that he's cracked it up to be. That's all I've got to say, and it better have something to do with matters other than fish."

"We'll know that soon enough. And, Chief . . ."

"What?"

"Sharks are not fish."

"They look like fish, swim like fish, and it's a damn sure bet they taste and smell like fish." He was instantly sorry about conjuring up the aromas. Jessica felt compassion for Santiva. He had, truth be known, gone through hell to get this far.

The helicopter was putting down, sending up a storm cloud of white rain—sand pellets which created a milky veil all around the scientific laboratory buildings.

Jessica saw the two figures at the rear of the yellow truck, each in protective gear but one a full-figured young woman and the other a tall, broad-shouldered young man. It took her a moment to make out the cargo they were unloading onto a conveyor belt—a truckload of dead sharks—that then efficiently lowered the bodies into some subterranean chamber. The young people were sweltering in the tropical heat, as was a bored driver, who—smoking and hacking away—stood nearby. The three of them were far enough from the helicopter that they received only a cool, probably well-wished-for breeze from its noisy rotor blades. The trio at the truck all now halted their lives and watched the chopper's descent in rapt attention, as if here were the event of the year on Islamorada Key. And, under usual circumstances, it probably would have been.

Santiva was the first to deboard the chopper. Jessica thought he was going to kneel and kiss the ground, but instead he stumbled toward the front entry doors to the research facility, anxiously wondering if there might be a lavatory within the laboratory. Jessica grabbed her black medical valise and followed, automatically ducking below the rotor blades, which were still grinding overhead.

The chopper pilot had cut his engines, but the blades continued to circle like unruly children, slow to wind down, until Jessica reached the building, where she and Santiva were met by a stern-eyed woman and a younger man with a toothy but pleasant smile, both in white lab coats. The man's lab coat was filthy with blood and secretions, giving him the appearance of a butcher, while the woman's coat was spotless. The man quickly extended a hand to Santiva and introduced himself.

"Dr. Coran, Chief Santiva? Joel Wainwright. I'm the one who made the call to you people."

He manfully grabbed Eriq's hand and shook it, then took Jessica's hand and shook it vigorously as well.

"Lois, won't you say hello to our guests?" he asked his associate, but the woman merely frowned like a mother angry with her child.

"Aron will see to any bags you have, but there truly are no guest facilities here, I'm afraid," she said, her voice stiff and cold.

Neither the woman's hand nor her eyes were set on greeting Jessica; instead, she soundlessly ground both Jessica and a cigarette butt she'd snatched from Wainwright's mouth into the white-sand dust before turning and entering the facility ahead of the others—as if hoping to tidy her room a bit before anyone should see it. Wainwright limply shrugged and pointed the way, ushering the two strangers into the building.

"What is it precisely you do here?" Jessica asked him.

"We cut sharks—open them up, study them intensely, you might say."

"So it's primarily a shark research facility?"

"Well, it didn't start out that way, but yes . . . that's what it's become over the years, despite the lip service given other areas of study that go on here." Entering the facility, Wainwright joked about its being a perfect setting for an *X-Files* episode since it was home to unspeakable experimentation on eels and other marine life. Inside, much of the light was natural, filtering in through broad overhead skylights. The place otherwise looked and felt like a large factory or hangar.

Dr. Insley stood in the downpour of light from one of the skylights. "*Doctor* Wainwright enjoys a bit of humor now and again," she said, finally introducing herself. "I am the head of the institute, Dr. Lois Insley."

"Well, let's have a look at what you've got here, Doctors," said Santiva. "Just as soon, that is, as I can find a place to . . . to freshen up?"

Wainwright showed Santiva to a nearby men's room while Jessica was left alone with the frost lady, who, still flooded in light, looked made of ice.

After an uncomfortable silence, Insley said, "Dr. Wainwright's action in calling you all the way here, I fear, will prove foolish." She seemed to be speaking without moving a muscle.

"Our understanding is that during your shark dissections here lately, you've found more of them to be holding human body parts than is normal. Is that correct, Dr. Insley?"

"Dr. Wainwright would like nothing better than to be on *Good Morning America*." She laughed nervously at her remark.

"Are you saying he's exaggerated the situation here, and that his motives are suspect?" Jessica moved about, examining photos hung on the walls, realizing they were in a corridor, still being held at bay. "We've come an awful long way for fun and games, Dr. Insley."

"You may judge for yourself. Yes, there's been a curious increase in the number of human body parts we see, but there's nothing abnormal in that alone. Statistically speaking, we might not see another body part for months on end. It's just that our sample was so large this year. The tournament was a big success.''

"Dr. Insley, I'd like to see what you do have. Is that possible?" *Is it?* Jessica secretly wondered, glad that Santiva hadn't heard Insley's remarks.

"Yes, of course. Dr. Wainwright has some specimens laid out for you.''

"Chief Santiva and I are engaged in a manhunt for a serial killer whose victims have been held underwater for a period of time, and whose bodies have been partially eaten by sea life.''

"I see your problem is great, most assuredly . . . Dr. Coran, is it? Still, my . . . our interests here are fairly specific, well-defined research areas, and we . . . study specifically what is in the sharks' digestive tracts, you understand, and certainly, we aren't in any sort of search for incriminating evidence in your . . . in a murder investigation.''

"I understand that.'' Jessica knew she had to put the woman at as much ease as possible, but this lady had some recoil factor. Their coming into her domain like this had obviously unsettled her. "Look, Dr. Insley, we're going to be in and out of here, doing our job as discreetly and as quickly as possible, truly. We have the helicopter waiting outside. It's just that several bodies that have washed ashore along the Florida coast in the past several months have had obvious shark injuries. And if we can pinpoint the geography of the sharks, this might well help us with the geography of the crimes.''

"Geography of the crimes. My . . . I've never heard such a phrase before. But if a shark attacked and killed someone, then its pack would likely have eaten more or less the entire body,'' she countered.

"We believe the victim was dead before the shark bites were made.''

"So, you surmise a lack of blood, and therefore no feeding frenzy?''

"This has appeared evident by the lack of blood around the wounds, along with a lack of any vital—"

"You needn't say another word. I understand, but still, sharks feed in groups. If a floating body were attacked by one, it'd be attacked by all; there'd be nothing left to wash ashore."

Jessica frowned. "Well, that little mystery will have to await further information, I suppose. But for now, we're interested in finding out what we can from the pieces . . . the parts you and Dr. Wainwright have uncovered."

"And continue to uncover," said Wainwright, returning to them now. "There's one in particular I'd like you to see, Dr. Coran. Come this way."

Wainwright led Jessica into a lab, a room filled with many more workstations, microscopes, Bunsen burners and trays filled with test tubes than there were students to work them. Jessica wondered if Insley wanted it that way, or if marine biology had fallen off as a subject of interest for the young, or if so few students were being serviced here due to funding.

At the center of the room, a cranelike device was lowered, and hanging from it was the opened, gutted carcass of a huge, lackluster white and gray shark.

"This one came damn near to winning the tournament," said Joel Wainwright. "It's a great white. Perfectly beautiful creature, older than time itself. You know they date back two hundred million years? To the Triassic period, when all that separated Florida from the coast of Africa was an ocean the size of a wide river. They lived before the dinosaurs appeared, right alongside the crocodiles, and they're so plentiful now in the seas that we run lotteries to catch them so that we can study them under our scopes."

"He is beautiful . . . or was," Jessica commented, her eyes riveted to the once sleek exterior of the gray and white carcass, ignoring for the moment the huge rent to the underbelly. Then she saw the sac and fetal tissue that had been carefully placed in a nearby tank.

"*She*—this time of year, we don't take too many females, as they're spawning, but Dr. Insley's work requires a full study of the reproductive system and habits of the females and the males, so—''

''Oh, do get on with it, Joel,'' Dr. Insley insisted.

''Anyway,'' Wainwright continued as Santiva entered the semidarkened room, ''she coughed up this.'' Wainwright lifted a small, feminine forearm from a medical cooler, the sort of cooler which kept organ donations fresh. ''It was lodged in her small intestine, which makes it fairly fresh.''

Jessica inched closer to the awful sight. The hand and most of the fingers were still intact, though green now with brown spots, and a golden wristband, embedded in a nasty gash, would have been invisible had it not mirrored the light with its metallic reflection. Wainwright had placed the entire thing under glass.

For a long moment everyone remained silent, staring, giving hushed homage to what this mangled piece of human flesh mirrored for each of them—their own mortality and connection with the dead.

''I didn't want to touch it—scientifically speaking—until you got here, Dr. Coran,'' Wainwright explained.

''Let's put this under a bright light,'' she calmly replied while her insides readjusted to what lay before her.

Soon the others were watching Jessica meticulously retrieve the thin, gold wristband from the gnarled flesh. It had been dented, gnashed and chewed as it was sifted through the shark's powerful, razorlike teeth, before being swallowed whole like a chunky cashew.

Jessica turned the gold beneath the light now and read a single word inscribed there: ''Precious.''

''What?'' came a chorus of curious onlookers around Jessica. The two young students who'd been at the truck, having shed their outer protective gear, now joined the others inside.

''There's an inscription here, on the bracelet,'' Jessica explained.

''An inscription?'' asked Aron Porter.

"What kind of inscription?" asked Lynette Harris.

"What does it say?" asked Insley.

"It reads *Precious*."

Santiva's response was quick. "Who killed Precious?"

· THREE ·

"Just how many more body parts do you have on ice, Dr. Wainwright?" Jessica asked.

"Quite a stack, actually. A couple of leg fragments, part of another arm, some feet and a cache of bones."

Jessica turned to Santiva and said, "Tell the helicopter pilot to take off, but to remain on standby for our call. And Eriq—tip him well. And since we're going to be here for some time, maybe a couple of days, you may want to get a rental car and rooms for us." She turned to Wainwright and asked where the nearest hotel might be.

"Two days, you estimate?" asked Santiva.

"Hotels, around here? Sorry," replied Wainwright. "Closest thing I might call a hotel around here is our dormitory, but it's pretty stark. No room service, but you could dine with us."

The prospect wasn't particularly appealing. These people reminded her of the Addams Family for some reason.

"Do you really figure it'll take so long, Jess?" Santiva repeated.

"Long enough so you can get that fishing trip in you'd hoped for, since you are in the Keys, after all. Go for it. But do like Spider said: Get a local guide."

"Now *that* I can help you with," Wainwright proudly piped up.

"Know one, do you?"

"We know and use several, but Jabez Reiley, he's the best, though expensive."

"Never mind the expense. Where can we get in touch with Mr. Reiley?" Jessica asked.

Eriq put up a cautionary hand to her, taking her aside and whispering, "But Jessica, won't you need help around here, maybe to keep that dragon lady off your back?"

She returned the whisper. "I can handle the crone, and you'd just be in the way." She then turned to Dr. Wainwright, telling him, "I want to see every single body part your people have discovered."

"No problem."

"And I want each one photographed from every conceivable angle; have you a good man for that?"

"Aron Porter here is an excellent photographer. One of his gifts."

"Good . . . good . . . Then I'll want some, if not all, of the body parts collected, boxed and protected with your best absorbent material, okay? I'll want to take everything back to Miami with us."

Dr. Lois Insley had gone white by this time and had found a stool upon which to perch; she now leaned against one wall, making the noises of one about to hyperventilate. Jessica quickly approached the older woman and offered her a brown paper bag to breathe into, from a supply she kept in her black valise for reasons other than sickness. Brown bags were useful for certain types of evidence gathering, items such as blood spatters on cloth, items you didn't want to smear or to have drying out in too rapid a fashion.

Dr. Insley graciously accepted the bag, opened it wide and began breathing from it, inhaling deeply, gathering herself up. No one in the place seemed the least concerned or helpful, Jessica thought as she returned to Wainwright and said, "You want to take care of Dr. Insley first?"

"Sure . . . sure . . . although I'd rather get Reiley on the phone for you." But instead he went over to Dr. Insley, placed a hand on her shoulder and marched her down a corridor, where, presumably, he had her lie down to rest.

Jessica hadn't time to wonder long about their obviously strained relationship. She rocked on the balls of her feet before what remained of Precious, her attention riveted on the torn and ugly limb and the bracelet beside it.

From down the hall, a gentle sobbing welled up from the woman named Insley. Jessica thought the woman on the verge of a nervous breakdown; she'd certainly overreacted to their intrusion on her private little world here—or had Precious simply gotten to her?

While Eriq did a cursory stroll about the facility, Jessica continued her examination of the would-be evidence, the two students curiously watching her.

Soon Wainwright appeared and assured Jessica that the other woman was quite all right. "Mood swings, a hormonal thing," he whispered in Jessica's ear—the archetypal male response to any female emotional venting too complicated for the male mind, Jessica irritatedly thought. She wondered how much plotting and politicking went on in this little research hothouse. With their lives so wrapped up in this place, so focused on their jobs that their identities—*who they were*—had long since become inextricably mixed up with what they did. It was obvious the work was everything to them, with their whole world and worldview shaped by it. Jessica gave a thought to what Donna LeMonte so often warned her about, that she should not obsessively become Jessica Coran, FBI, ME. She worried momentarily that she might have a lot more in common with Dr. Lois Insley than she cared to admit.

Jessica had seen a look of animal fear in Dr. Insley's eyes when they'd arrived. She had also seen the sudden loss of color in the woman's face, replaced by a doughy pallor which reminded Jessica of how Santiva's naturally dark, Cuban skin had gone two shades lighter by the time he'd returned to his plane seat over North Carolina on the long journey coming down.

And now, as Wainwright began bringing out the accumulated body parts, each tagged and dated, and as Jessica rolled up her sleeves to go to work over each errant body part collected by Wainwright, she thought back to the plane trip down. With her hands, eyes and mind busy at her current task, she considered just how her relationship with Santiva was shaping up, even as her mind wandered back to what they knew of the killer they'd come in pursuit of.

She recalled now the killer's taunting note to the authorities and what Eriq had revealed to her about it through the handwriting analysis—a kind of magic—he performed.

The note was written out in lean but large and hard strokes, the aggressive longhand having a character of its own, and it read:

Son of t
feeds the soul
of woman
in The theatre
in the theatre
of want
and sacrifice,
whilof to strikes
out for the highest
calibre of moment
when breath
and life are one,
each sacrificed unto f

as he deems

all the whores to be

When Jessica had looked up from the note, Santiva began working with her, explaining, spending great effort in carefully filling her in on what hidden and subconscious messages the killer had given them. "Notice he signs in the name of his god, not unlike the Zodiac Killers we've seen over the years."

She nodded. "Yeah, he's from a long line of upstanding killers. Hell, it's easy to kill if you can pass the buck along to some demonic force within you which you conveniently have no control over. Lets you and your murderous hands off the hook, so to speak. Gives you reason and motive, and removes all personal guilt. That's my personal favorite. What a bastard."

"The big excuse," Santiva agreed, the plane having finally leveled out above the storm. "Takes away your inhibitions. Greatest excuse in the world."

"Ranks right up there with 'a woman made me do it,' 'the Devil made me do it' and 'God talks to me.' Sonofabitch."

"You see these little clubs at the end of each long letter, the L here, and F here and here?" Santiva pointed to each letter he mentioned.

Jessica quick-studied them, knowing he had come up through the ranks as a documents and handwriting analysis expert.

"Yeah, I see them."

"See the thin tight lines? A lot of letters you and I would loop, he makes straight up and down. See here, the G? And notice the force with which he crosses his Ts? The long extension across the page?"

"Yeah, I see." The lines were overlong, overdone, overwhelming, thrusting forward like lances.

Eriq continued, "The drive behind any line going forward can show excitement, energy or a lack of energy. In our man's case, we see energy in the extreme—not a positive sign of energy, but rather in this case aggressive and unrestrained energy, sexually motivated, potent energy, even hostility, rage."

Jessica immediately felt the truth of what Santiva was saying and sensed that Eriq was indeed a gifted handwriting analyst and interpreter, although she didn't have much firsthand evidence to base this conclusion on. Still, she was hoping to learn more about this interesting "science" that had years ago been adopted by military authorities, police agencies and the FBI. She believed that Eriq could teach her a great deal about what he called "graphology" as they worked this case together.

"It is a rare murderer who writes notes, letters or poetry to the press, although a surprising number do write to authorities: the Zodiac Killers, both the New York and the California one; the Son of Sam; and Jack the Ripper, to name a few," Eriq continued. "They do so for a simple reason: they must convey their feelings about their kills—conquests—to someone. Is it safer to vent such feelings in a bar with buddies or to write authorities and taunt police? Either way, the phenomenon reveals the killer's need to tell the world what he has done, to validate it, because he craves validation, and in this perverse validation there comes a twisted absolution. It underscores the killer's original need to first control and then destroy other living beings, in order to convince himself and the world that he is better than the role life has meted out for him, that he isn't a hapless nobody, that he is in fact *somebody*, somebody with an identity. The killing becomes a vicious circle so as to cyclically codify and warrant his own bloody identity: *I kill... therefore I am. I kill therefore I am a killer... therefore I kill... thus, I become a more efficient killer... therefore I kill again... and again kill...*

"Law enforcement authorities count on this need for self-actualization, which causes men locked in cells to spill their guts to strangers in lockup with them. Writing letters that claim responsibility for brutal murders is another cry, not so much for help in most cases as a cry for recognition, a cry that shouts, 'Look at me! I did it, and I'm somebody important for having done it.' "

Jessica, nodding the whole time, agreed. "The thinking isn't far removed from that of an assassin who kills merely for the purpose of seeing a picture of himself in the newspapers, or to be able to say that he's become one with his god as a result of fulfilling his god's wish." Because of Jessica's keen understanding of this and the killing mind, she squarely sided with the prosecution whenever the blood and DNA evidence was overwhelming.

Given the Night Crawler's liking for the pen, and Eriq Santiva's genius, Jessica looked forward to a case which might prove extremely interesting while also proving or disproving some of Santiva's theories regarding "handreading," as he liked to call it.

Santiva reached from his seat to take her hand in his, guiding her fingers to one of the letters on the killer's words. "Touch it. Feel it. See it?"

"See what, exactly?"

"The small clubs at the ends of many of the letters. See here and here, at the bottoms and tops of the long letters."

"What exactly do you mean, clubs?"

"The little caveman clubs."

"Oh, you mean how the author has allowed the ink to swell into a bulb at each end?"

"Yes, precisely what I'm driving at—like the bulb at the root of a hair follicle. You see, this man... this supposed killer didn't passively allow the ink to run there. It wasn't passive. His hand pressed hard as hell at those points. This indicates great aggression, pent-up anger, rage released through the ink and pen. See here and here, and over here?''

Suddenly she saw little clubs all over the page where before she hadn't noticed. He continued, guiding her forefinger like a marker on a Ouija board. ''Take a close look at his lowercase Ds.''

Together they located a number of lowercase Ds. ''What's so remarkable about his Ds?'' she wondered aloud.

''Well, you do see the pattern, the similarity between every lowercase D, don't you?''

''Yeah, they all slant drastically far to the right. But what's the significance?''

''It's what we call the 'maniac D.' See how violently slanted they are, leaning at an acute right angle toward the next word? See how far to the right it goes from the center line of the words on the sentence plane?''

He had told her about center, top and lower lines, saying each was a plane. Everyone's handwriting followed a center line; some people dipped below their personal center diagonal excessively, and those with wild, swooping lower-plane letters, while not necessarily sexual deviants, were highly charged sexual beings. Those who spent most of their writing energy in upper regions, above the center line, were more interested in mental games, money, domination and winning. Aberrant behavior was shown in shaky, enigmatic loops and swirls on letters at either upper or lower regions. Those who maintained an even keel, staying close to the center diagonal at all times, were both better at control and more even-tempered and rule-conscious, and perhaps less sexually inclined. A shaky hand which had no control or patterns whatsoever might be that of a madman or a seriously ill person, or a person suffering from cerebral palsy or some other nervous disorder. He demonstrated via a quick forgery of Richard Nixon's handwriting when he was at the pinnacle of his career how ''in charge'' and brash the man was; showed her a forgery of his name during his near impeachment that demonstrated how incredibly deteriorated the handwriting had become; and ended with a reconstructed, steadier Nixon signature upon his becoming an unofficial delegate to China. The emotional differences were startling and revealing.

It appeared the Night Crawler was all over the scale, swooping high, showing intelligence and creativity, and then dipping low below the center line, showing deviances of all sorts, his hand sometimes erratic, sometimes calm and controlled but always aggressive, harsh, brutal.

"Whoa, you're losing me a bit here," she complained now and again as Eriq painted a picture of both the value of the analysis and the character of the killer as seen through his writing, saying that handwriting clearly mirrored the condition of the mind, that it was as good as or better than having a look into a man's soul through the eyes.

Jessica began to see the pattern Eriq called the maniac D. "Oh, yeah . . . I see what you mean by the Ds now. Each D leans or points directly across at the word following?"

"Like a spear, an attack, isn't it?"

" 'Maniac D.' Just how scientific is that term, Chief?"

"Jack the Ripper, in his notes to the White Chapel Vigilante Committee and authorities in 1888, used clubs and the maniac D. That's how scientific it is. And we see it time and again with violent offenders behind bars."

She looked again at the clubbed ends and the strange, violent Ds. "I take your point. What else does his handwriting tell you, Eriq?"

"Tells me he's a jumble, a complex SOB. Creative, ingenious perhaps, certainly an above-average IQ, which—"

"Suggests a Ted Bundy type? Suave, smooth, lures his victim in and snares her in that instant when her guard is completely down?"

"Could well be, but if so, it's an act; likely a well-rehearsed and polished act, but an act all the same. This guy's full of phobias and problems. Likely the product of a broken home; likely a failure at most everything he's touched; likely working at some menial job somewhere which he regards as far below his natural talents."

"You can tell all that from his handwriting?" She could

not completely keep the skepticism from filtering into her voice.

"Well, I combine the handwriting analysis with what we also know of profiling, of course. It's in the combination that I sometimes get startlingly lucky results."

"Sometimes?" she replied sarcastically. Much of Santiva's work was chronicled, much of it now standard reading for FBI Academy personnel. His work in both document investigation and handwriting analysis had caused his star to rise meteorically, due to his extraordinary success rate at pinpointing killers through trace evidence and profiling techniques which were applied to victim and killer alike to create a matrix for murder.

Santiva coined an interesting line to explain what it was that his profiling team did, telling the press once, "We create a vector of character, personality, physical traits, even habits of both the victim and the killer."

By studying the victim or victims, as well as by studying the killer, Santiva and the profiling team to which Jessica now belonged could put together a total picture of what occurred, and sometimes from that why it occurred. Before getting on the plane, they had already put together a complex picture of the man the press had dubbed the Night Crawler, but Jessica had not been in on sessions directly related to the handwritten document the killer had felt compelled to forward to authorities.

There at thirty thousand feet, Jessica had next concentrated on the ME's report on Allison Norris. A capable man, this Miami M.E. named Coudriet demonstrated his own smaller, neater, nearly pinched handwriting, which Eriq called controlled, conservative, careful. "He's likely to hold his cards extremely close to his chest," Eriq said, sizing the man up in much the same terms as Jessica had. Even the corrections he'd made on the page told her that he was a guarded man. There was that element of purposeful equivocation in his language. He'd likely been prodded and rushed to turn over a report which he was not entirely happy with; he likely had wanted much more time to find the truth than people and agencies around him wanted him to take, from insurance companies to the Miami Police Department to the FBI. In Dr. Coudriet's couched tones, bruises about the wrists *might* indicate handcuffs or possibly tightly tied ropes. Strangulation about the neck *perhaps might* indicate use of rope or cord, *and/or likelihood* of the killer's hands. Strangulation death *may have* occurred before seawater entered the lungs, and this *may indicate* death before drowning. The man's tentativeness was a sure sign the autopsy was a slapdash job, that he was attempting to cover his ass in the event questions arose later, at which time he could simply say, "I never said that . . ."

"What do you know about Dr. Andrew Coudriet?" Santiva had suddenly asked, as if reading her mind.

"Not much, save by reputation."

"Good, bad, indifferent?"

"Highly regarded, well respected. He's always on someone's dais."

"Someone's what?"

"You know, giving speeches on the latest technologies used in crime detection. Speaks anywhere and everywhere they'll pay his fee."

"Which is?"

"Astronomically high—five, six figures, I'd assume."

"Sounds lucrative. Why aren't you on the talk circuit?"

"Doing's better'n telling? I haven't given it much thought. Not that I haven't had offers, but who has the time?"

"Obviously Coudriet does," he replied, but beneath his words, he was running a thought—trying to figure out just how to take her last remark about having had offers, she guessed.

She tilted the photo of Allison Norris's body in his direction, a mushroomed body that had exploded with gases after having been picked over by sea life. In the photo, sand crabs were still making a meal of the dead girl, who was missing a chunk of flesh from her upper left thigh, a right femur and a right arm up to the elbow, where, obviously, sharks had taken more than a passing nibble.

"Whoever did this to Allison Norris wants for power,

craves control of the ultimate—life itself. He kills to show that he has the power in his hands to do so,'' Jessica said.

"He takes their *manna*, their being," Santiva agreed. "At least, he thinks he does, and so long as he believes he does, he'll continue to kill."

"He takes their power away from them, takes power from another living creature and claims all that power for himself. I've seen it before."

"I know you have. That's why you're here on the case with me. Now, if you don't mind . . ." He indicated the picture, his queasiness threatening a return.

She closed the file jacket, leaned back in her cushioned chair and rode out the remainder of the storm.

Forty-nine minutes later, below a silver spray of rain shimmering in bright sunlight, they landed on a newly blackened, rain-slicked, glassy runway at Miami International. A smoother landing Jessica had never experienced, and when the captain came on the intercom to give himself a cheer, saying that after twenty-seven years of flying he'd finally made the perfect landing, everyone offered a spirited hand-clapping and hooting reply—at least those who were able to.

After this and the taxiing to the airline terminal, the usual deplaning chaos ensued. Everyone wanted off as quickly as possible, wanted to feel their feet on the solid construction of the airport walkways. But one man was forcing his way onto the plane, holding up a gold shield and shouting Santiva's name.

Santiva waved the heavyset, middle-aged man with the balding head and Gene Hackman features forward. As the passengers thinned out, the Miami-Dade homicide detective managed to shuffle down the aisle and come alongside the patient FBI team he'd come to welcome to Miami.

"You're Eriq Santiva," he said, smiling, extending his hand, the gregarious grin remaining on his face even as he vigorously shook Santiva's hand and then exchanged it for Jessica's. "And you must be Dr. Coran. What a pleasure, an honor, really, to meet you both. I'm Detective Charles Quincey, MPD. Just call me Quince. Everybody does. I was sent ahead with Mark, my partner''—he indicated a man in a gray suit who'd held back at the exit—''you know, to kinda escort you out of here and onto the waiting helicopter for Islamorada, or if you prefer to take a little time, freshen up; we can arrange that as well.''

Santiva turned to Jessica and muttered, ''Helicopter . . . isn't there any other way to this Isma-whatever-Key?''

She stifled an urge to smile. ''Not if we're going to make time, no.''

Eriq's frown brought the enthused MPD detective down. ''Escort away,'' Eriq told him, ''and as for taking a little time, yes, by all means, and thank you, Detective.''

Jessica grabbed her carry-on and the round Detective Quincey made a grab for it.

''No thanks, Detective. This one stays with me.''

He realized that it was her professional black bag. ''Ahh, yes, Dr. Coran, and may I say on behalf of the MPD, we're extremely glad to have you on the case.''

''That would be a refreshing attitude,'' she replied.

''It's true, Doctor. We're at wit's end and we know it. This makes the ninth victim in the state to wash ashore in as many months. I mean this bastard's doing 'em on average of one a month, maybe more. We've had a lotta strange disappearances.''

''The disappearances outnumber the bodies, I understand,'' she replied.

'' 'Fraid so, yes ma'am . . . er, Doctor.''

Outside the plane but inside the exit ramp, which was like a sauna in Miami in the springtime, they met Charles Quincey's partner, a well-proportioned, tanned and tall man with piercing blue eyes and the rugged good looks of an outdoorsman, perhaps a fisherman or maybe just someone who spent a lot of hours playing volleyball at South Miami Beach. The younger man's level of enthusiasm was nil, contrasting sharply with Quincey's attitude. Obviously, Quincey's partner did not share his appreciation for having the Feds come in on the case, for this detective offered no handshakes, nor could he be bothered to open his mouth, more or less groaning his name, Detective Mark Samernow.

Jessica thought that Samernow looked as if he'd slept in his clothes; perhaps he'd pulled an all-night stakeout, or simply an all-nighter.

Samernow was disheveled, whereas Quincey had obviously put some hair gel and some thought into their meeting. Quince was together, perhaps for the first time in his career as a detective, his hair slicked down, his tie in a knot around a neck that didn't easily take to it, reddening and swelling and about to burst; even cuff links showed at his wrists. Samernow, by comparison, had a wild shock of dark hair lying over his forehead and one eye, his tie snatched viciously away from his neck, a short-sleeved white shirt with a jacket carelessly tossed over his shoulder, making Jessica wonder where his gun was.

Samernow began kidding Quince about how his thick neck looked like ten pounds of sausage in a five-pound bag, and how, when it burst, the buttons were going to go like shotgun pellets. Samernow warned Jessica and Santiva to duck when the thing blew and then laughed at his own joke.

Quince told his partner to shut up.

Now the two detectives warned of the press just ahead, and they weren't kidding. Along the corridor, there was a retinue of police uniforms and authorities in suits, all waiting along with a small army of newspeople with notepads, recorders and huge microphones extended on lances, their cameras held overhead like loaded cannon flashing the fire of battle.

"I guess things are kinda slow in Miami these days," commented Jessica.

"Looks like we're tomorrow's headline."

They stopped long enough to assure the reporters and the people of Miami and south Florida that the FBI was making the Night Crawler case a number one priority. Cameras flashed in their faces as they fielded a handful of questions, each one of which required more assurances.

Quince parted the sea before them and led them to a private room in the airport, where Santiva composed himself and Jessica lingered at a window, staring down at a helicopter waiting below to take them to Islamorada Key.

For a time, Jessica wondered if she would ever get Eriq on board the helicopter, telling him at one point that he should stay behind and get familiar with the case from Miami's point of view, and that she would rejoin him as soon as she could. But he proved too stubborn to leap at the opportunity she extended him, begging another Dramamine patch instead.

And now finally, here they were, at the shark research facility that had tipped them off to what appeared to be quite a cache of body parts, the pathological evidence they had come for. To Jessica, it appeared a kind of dark gold mine.

"Precious is a nickname given Allison Norris by her father," said Eriq, just returning from a hurried phone call. "That's according to Quince in Miami. Quince will call to confirm if Allison wore a bracelet inscribed with the name, but it seems an almost foregone conclusion, given the circumstances."

Jessica paused in her work over another body part. "Still, a tissue match will be necessary to verify the fact beyond a mirrored shadow . . . to lay solid foundation against the man who fed Allison to the sharks."

"Well, sure . . . just thought you'd like to know."

She nodded. "Thanks." Jessica would also have to return with any and all other body parts which Wainwright and company had unearthed here, and tests would have to be run on each, with an eye to matching them to other bodies that had incongruously washed ashore along Florida's blindingly bright, pastel-colored, idyllic-looking coastal waterways.

Wainwright came to her with yet another bundle of body parts. "There're a few more small pieces in the freezer, but you've got the bulk of it now, at least till we continue our work on the sharks again maybe . . ."

"I want to see everything you have, Dr. Wainwright, every specimen, all of it," she announced. "And I'll need a larger area in which to work, if you don't mind."

"That'd have to be our main lab, where we do most of the sharks."

"You can't use it," said Insley suddenly. She'd obviously gotten hold of herself and had returned from her bed. "That would disrupt our entire operation."

"I believe, Dr. Insley, that your entire operation here has already been interrupted," countered Jessica. "I'll need the space for at least the next twenty-four hours, and if your people discover more human tissue or bones, I'll want you to turn these over to us as well."

"Then I did the right thing, calling you in?" asked Wainwright, solely for Insley's benefit.

Jessica nodded solemnly. "That you did, Dr. Wainwright . . . that you did."

· FOUR ·

It was a miracle of rare device,
A sunny pleasure dome with caves of ice!
                    —SAMUEL TAYLOR COLERIDGE

Razzles on the River
South Miami Beach, Florida, 11 P.M.

Once again Kathy Marie Harmon glanced up and into Patric's alluring, azure eyes ... *once again.* They were the eyes of dreamy miracle within a house of crystal and aquablue mirrors—where a girl could get lost and giddy and not care if her head were spinning; they were the eyes of cool, blue ocean swells into which she could so easily splash. He spoke with such assurance and confidence, yet without the arrogance of other men Kathy had met in and around the bar scene in South Miami's Biscayne Bay area.

Kathy had come to Razzles in the company of two girlfriends, all of them looking for Mr. Right, Mr. Good, Mr. Solid. Usually, they wound up with Mr. Jell-O, a spineless creature with one thing on its mind—satisfying horny urges through unadulterated self-gratification. And most were in fact engaged in some base form of "adulterating" self-gratification, many turning out to be married.

Most of the guys hanging out at bars like this just wanted someone to stick it to, to feel warm flesh against their privates, to "get inside" a woman.

She hadn't wanted to come out tonight. She was going to sit at home, do her hair, watch an old movie, maybe pop some corn, curl up with a Vincent Courtney or a Geoffrey Caine horror novel and read her brains out, maybe. But the tug and pull of her two girlfriends was too strong. Melissa and Cherylene could not be denied. They, like Kathy herself, believed in rainbows and lotteries and love and romance, all under a full moon, and tonight there hung at least a crescent moon, aglow in the sultry Miami night, rocking like a stellar cradle over the City of Dreams, Oz South.

Perhaps it'd been the moon that had tipped the scales to bring her here tonight. Whatever it was, sitting across from Patric Allain, she was eternally grateful, while her two best friends had turned a resonant shade of chartreuse that shone through the purple-blue Art Deco lights of the evening world of Key Biscayne.

The live band did their best imitation of Jimmy Buffet, Dylan and Bob Marley tunes all evening long while she and Patric sipped piña coladas and munched on curly cheese Cajun fries below the moon out on the ocean deck, where beautiful Biscayne Bay met the incoming swells of the Atlantic on picture-postcard Key Biscayne. Over one shoulder blinked the moon, over the other the colored lights of the Sheraton Royal Biscayne. Stretched before them were the milky white sands of Sonista Beach on one side, Harbor Drive and the Harbor Drive Wharf on the other. The night was enchantedly lit, the ocean breeze like a lover's caress, and Kathy's dreams had all come alive.

Patric had arrived by boat—his boat, an incredible seventy-footer, all wood and sail and lovely, and all his, bought and paid for. He must be rich beyond rich, Kathy surmised. Maybe Patric was the one. Who knew? Life was a gamble, an exquisite dice game, and love and heartache formed the soft felt playing field of white lines, numbers, colors, rules and order. If you remained on the rail, outside the borders, afraid to toss the dice, nothing happened, all was nil . . . If she hadn't shown up here tonight, if Cherylene and Melissa had come here without her, it might have been one of them sitting now across from Patric instead of her—Melissa most likely, since she was so much prettier than Cherylene—and if so, it'd be Melissa's eyes all dreamy and swimming with handsome Patric's at this moment . . . But it was as if Patric had come on the wind of fate for her alone, as if she had heard the enchanted, holy wind call her name so that she might meet the one eternal lover for whom she had longed her entire life.

He sat across from her now.

She didn't stop to analyze her thoughts or doubts, whether Patric would simply have found Melissa instead had she come to Razzles without Kathy, nor what this said about him. There was no time for analyzing. There'd be more than enough time for going over the details tomorrow when Cherylene and Melissa came sniffing around to find out what happened.

So, thanks to lovely, intricate destiny, chance, fortune, circumstance, karma, kismet—all stepping in at once to play Cupids—this time it was Kathy Harmon's turn to shine instead of Melissa's or Cherylene's. Yes, this time it was her time, her fortune, and Patric was the treasure of a lifetime, meant only for her, fated. And what a treasure, looking as if he'd stepped off the cover of a romance novel or magazine cover. And the way he'd picked her out from among her friends, just as if he'd come directly here from some exotic port of call for her and her alone; just as if he had sailed across the Atlantic to find her, and with that dreamy accent—British maybe, or perhaps Australian— maybe she wasn't far wrong. He obviously had money, and didn't mind spending it, either. And he hadn't gotten the least annoyed when she'd been unable to finish her veal parmigiana dinner across the street at the Sheraton, where he had insisted on taking her.

''We've wasted so much time, Kathleen,'' he suddenly said. No one ever called her Kathleen. ''I have been to many places, I have done many things and I have loved many women, but tonight, it is as if my life has been one long search.''

''Search?'' she squeaked.

''A search for you, of course . . . and it has taken so awfully long.''

Sure it sounded like a line, but by now she didn't care. ''A search for me?''

''I've dreamed dreams about you.''

"That's just ridiculous. How could you? You don't—didn't even know me until tonight."

"No, it is true. Dreams are like mirrors held up to the soul, and you are the one in my dreams, and I want now to show you my virtual soul, my other love which allows me the freedom of the seaman's life."

"Virtual reality I've heard of, but virtual soul?" she asked, looking out beyond the riggings of the many boats and ships in harbor. "Is that like some new rock band?"

He pointed toward his sailing vessel. "It is where my other self resides, where I am free, unencumbered . . ."

"Oh, I'll bet." She tried to laugh, but something in his eyes told her not to. "I mean, I bet you can do just about anything you want with that kind of a . . . a ship. So what kind of weed or pill is this virtual soul? Or are we talking PCPs? I don't do needles."

"No, you misunderstand. It is not a drug. It is my life."

"Sorry, I didn't mean to make it sound gross or anything."

"It is where my Tauto lives."

"Your tattoo? Lives?"

"No, not tattoo, dear. Certainly you've heard of the Tau cross?"

"Tau cross? That sounds like a good name for a boat, but what's a Tau cross?"

"The T-cross. It is an essential element of nature. Where two lives cross, such as our lives are crossing tonight, now . . . below this moon."

"Is that like what you mean by virtual soul? Or is that just what you call your boat?"

"Never mind," he replied, pointing toward his boat, which was lost amid the forest of others. "Isn't she beautiful? All I need now is someone like you to share her with."

"How did you get . . . I mean, how can you afford such a boat?"

"It was an inheritance. One of many."

She could hardly believe her luck. "What do you do, besides sail, I mean?"

"I write."

"Really? What kind of writing?"

"You will laugh."

"No, no I won't. I think it's romantic, that you write."

"I write stories, mysteries, romances. I earn some from that, and as I said, I have an inheritance."

"You're independently wealthy?"

"Well-off, let's say. Now, will you come aboard? We can take her out, and you can enjoy the river from a whole new and exciting perspective."

"Sure . . . sure, why not? Let me just say good-bye to my friends. You'll drive me home after we dock?"

"Oh, of course, absolutely."

There again was that divine English accent. *Dreamy,* she thought. "Be right back, then."

"Meet me at the boat."

It took all of ten seconds to tell her friends not to bother waiting for her, that she had scored big time. They were full of questions, which tumbled forth with their giggling; they were anxious to know more about the handsome, sun-painted god that Kathy had cornered.

"All I know is he's European or something with a nice accent, and his name is Patric without a K. Talks with an English accent, I think, like Pierce Brosnan as James Bond, and he's loaded as well as handsome. So, girls, have a nice night. Ciao . . ."

It was the last image—her friends smiling and waving—which Kathy Marie Harmon recalled when once again the brutal, sadistic bastard brought her around to consciousness. He wouldn't let her die so easily, wouldn't let her find the peace she had moments ago accepted. She was too weak to fight him any longer, and he placed her, naked, into the water alongside the other dead girls. That's exactly what she was now: a dead girl . . .

She felt the stranglehold of the noose about her neck and the tearing ropes at her wrists; she heard the powerful jets of the motor as he revved it up, and in a moment her glazed eyes made out the back of the boat, the big letters spelling

out the T-cross; then the stalwart, potent rush of the seawater slammed into her and her entire body was dragged
paper-doll fashion, a puppet on a string to bring him
perverted-beyond-satanic kicks.

She herself was beyond tears, beyond pain actually. She
felt a languishing, uncaring feeling wash over her on the
wave created when he powered up the boat for faster speed,
dragging her form through the now ugly, dark sea that had
until so recently been a beautiful, romantic setting for her
and the man she thought he was.

She'd been so wrong.

His every word to her had been a lie.

He had orchestrated a trap.

She had stepped willingly, blindly into his trap, into the
trap of the Night Crawler's tangled and perverted net.

Then the boat slowed and the monster who called himself
Patric brought it to a stuttering halt, her cold body slamming hard into the bow, pressed in by the other dead girls
dangling there with her, and he returned to the bow to look
out over the side to taunt her, saying, "Life is death, death
is life, and now you go to a greater glory . . . the glory of
Tauto, the god of all things which are indivisible. Now you
travel to the virtual soul . . ."

Seeing that she remained yet alive, he returned to the
controls and dragged her farther out to sea.

*Two Days Later, Miami-Dade Police Department Crime
Lab and Morgue, Evening*

Jessica was relieved to learn that Dr. Andrew Coudriet was
involved all day in courtroom testimony, giving evidence
on a Mafia-linked killing, and had become too fatigued to
meet with her until the following day. Meanwhile, he'd left
word that his offices were at her disposal, and that she had
carte blanche with respect to the physical evidence already
logged and remaining. This meant she had full access to
the most recent victim's body as well. She and Santiva had
flown back to Miami earlier in the day, having finally finished up in the Keys.

They'd returned with what she trusted was enough evidence to bury the Night Crawler several times over when and if they ever caught the bastard.

She'd learned that there was a positive ID on the bracelet, and although continuing to match the tissue and blood seemed a footnote to the truth, she ordered the tests just the same. She had also put a team of experts to work on the photos from the crime scenes and the photos of missing parts found inside the sharks that had been caught off the coast of Key Largo. They had to work from photos because, save for Allison Norris, all the victims had by now been either buried or cremated, and any exhumations appeared at this point out of the question for several reasons, not the least being the costs, in both financial and emotional terms.

The photo expert teams must attempt to match up, as if they were placing jigsaw pieces into a puzzle, the various parts with the parts missing from victims who'd come before Allison Norris. If they had any additional matches, this could speak volumes about the killer. From there, further study would go forward and decisions regarding exhumations made. They hoped such measures could be avoided.

After suiting up, Jessica had gone straight for the freezer cabinet housing what remained of Allison Norris, and now the body, such as it was, lay before her. Two assisting physicians, internists who'd aided Dr. Coudriet in the initial autopsy, were at Jessica's disposal. The two men stood nearby, ready to assist in any way possible, or so she'd been told.

What she hoped to gain by a second examination, she didn't herself know, so explaining it to the two internists wasn't particularly successful. She merely stated—in an effort to cool the two anxious interns and their inquiring minds—''I see no reason for a second full-fledged autopsy.''

''Good,'' one responded in knee-jerk fashion.

''We'll call my examination merely a routine check, for the record and my FBI protocol.'' She said this for the microphone as well as for the worried pair, who had donned surgical masks and garb, as had Jessica.

One of the men seemed to buy it. She was as cursory as possible, sensing that both Drs. Thorn and Powers were anxious and appeared to have been coached into a reticent silence.

Coudriet's two men, Theodore Thorn and Owen Powers, both capable young interns, explained that they had felt duty-bound to be on hand. Still, she had little doubt that *duty-bound*, properly translated, meant that Coudriet had ordered them to be there.

All was routine until Jessica questioned the findings on the throat and the single wrist of the girl. She saw the ligature marks just as Coudriet and his associates had before her—ugly discoloration scars about the neck, indicating that the girl was strangled. Of this, there was no doubt. But the ligature marks were soft compared with the thumb tracks embedded in the tissue at the larynx. Some things even the ocean couldn't completely wipe away, such as a broken hyoid bone.

Jessica reached up and turned off the camera that was taping the secondary autopsy; she did so lavishly enough to tell the two men that what she was about to say was off the record. "This monster so thrusted his thumbs into the girl's throat that it scarred and dented tissue far below the surface, so far below that it's clear even after several layers of skin have sloughed away and nearly a week has gone by since discovery of the body; and it's estimated that the body's time in the water was an astounding three and a half to four weeks. Doesn't that strike anyone as odd, that it took so long for the body to surface?"

Coudriet's men remained silent, one of them nodding.

Seeing they had no comment, she switched the TV camera back on in just as ceremonious a fashion as before, a bit angry at the two crows who stood across from her. Now on the record, she continued, "The killer rammed his large thumbs deep into her throat. A closer look tells me that the girl's entire pharynx was bruised and swollen before death."

The pharynx is the tubelike structure that acts as both the digestive tract and the breathing hose. It also works in speech, changing shape to allow a person to form vowel sounds. Jessica momentarily wondered what kind of sounds Allison might have emitted under such brute force applied to the muscle and cartilage and membrane. The entire structure divides into three distinct regions, the second being the oropharynx, which extends from the soft palate to the level of the hyoid bone just below the lower jaw.

It was this area that Jessica took great time and care in examining, causing Thorn and Powers to stare and sweat beneath their surgical gowns. She asked for one of them to grab the Polaroid nearby and snap close-ups of the area she had opened with her scalpel. After Powers snapped three shots, Jessica asked Thorn to hold up a sterile tray to receive the small samplings she now sliced from the larynx tissue.

"I thought this was going to be a cursory exam," said Powers.

Jessica shot back, "It is."

Thorn abruptly said, "Dr. Coudriet was aware of the condition of the throat."

"But he chose to examine it only externally?"

"He examined it by hand, coming up from the breastplate after the Y-cut was made below. He knew she'd been choked to death before she drowned, if that's what you're . . . wondering. And besides, there was pressure on to do as little as possible and still call it an autopsy. Allison Norris's father's a very influential man."

"Yes, well, if that's the case, why wasn't it reported as a strangulation death?"

"It was, eventually."

She bit her lip and nodded. "I see." Coudriet was no doubt under some pressure at the time and saw little difference in whether the dead girl was strangled by rope or by hand or drowned, since all had the same result. This explained his qualifying language in the report.

Jessica next repeated her procedure for the laryngopharynx, which extends from the base of the hyoid bone to the esophagus. The entire region, up and down, was badly bruised, not simply from the ugly blemish caused by the attempt to mask rope burns, but from powerful hands, the hands of a sociopath who had killed many times before until the routine and habit of his killing had begun to actually bore him, so that now he slowly and lastingly strangled his victims, no doubt in a controlled fashion, in controlled time and in a controlled space—his space—where he felt most comfortable and had a great deal of time to carry out a lingering murder. He then obviously dumped the body into the ocean—but where, to keep it from surfacing for so long?

Thorn and Powers exhibited signs of boredom themselves now. They'd been up and down this territory before, no doubt wondering what volumes of information she hoped to locate in the larynx, or voice box.

"The hyoid bone," she said, as if to allay any doubts, "while fractured, remains very much intact, indicating some sort of controlled strangulation, in which the killer took his evil time with the strangulation process. Patient, composed, self-possessed strangulation. The killer shows all the characteristics of an organized murderer who had likely fantasized killing for years before he ever attempted it, and who, once he did attempt the thing, began to meticulously work out the particulars in cool and cunning detail."

"You got all that from looking at the throat?" asked a befuddled-looking Thorn, his eyeglasses slipping to the end of his nose.

She ignored his question and continued, "Now that he has any number of killings behind him, it has become a ritualized killing sport, each step as important as the next, and nothing left to chance or forgetfulness."

She explored the wounds further, no simple task given the bloated condition of the skin; but the freezer had at least held the decay in check. She used a stainless-steel probe and handheld magnifying glass. "He's devised the perfect murders, so far as he is concerned. And in conceiving such murders and carrying them out, he's given over his soul to whatever demons drive him."

Yes, the hyoid bone was fractured—as was reported in

the original autopsy—indicative of strangulation, but she'd seen many a crushed hyoid bone, and this one was far from crushed. In fact, it was near intact. She so noted this fact for the record, which disquieted Thorn and Powers a bit. Jessica was used to posing questions and scenarios as she worked; it had become part of her modus operandi.

She didn't bother now with asking Thorn or Powers anything further, but she did ask the microphone and camera, "Could the victim have been alive yet after the fracture of the hyoid? It was quite certain that she was, since the lungs, too, were full of water when the body was discovered, although in and of itself this fact does not prove death by drowning. Clearly, more tests need to be run, but my most educated guess is running along the lines of a torture murder of the sort the FBI rates on a scale of one to ten, Mad Matthew Matisak having been a Tort. 9. This fiend, if he is slowly strangling the life from his victims, only to allow them to resurface from death as it were, only to put them through the torment again, and repeatedly, ranks right up there with the blood-drinking vampire killer. While he does not appear to have cannibalized or drunk his victim's blood, he obviously breathes in their suffering to empower himself."

Thorn, even while shaking his head and pushing aside Powers's restraining hand, asked, "What're you saying, Dr. Coran?"

"I'm saying this murdering . . . fiend first incapacitates his victim with repeated strangulations and then drowns them, that this evil being, whoever or whatever he is, has turned back down the evolutionary trail, allowing his most base, animal desires to overtake him."

"But why repeatedly kill someone?"

"He obviously gains great pleasure at watching an Allison Norris struggle and suffer, and he too much enjoys watching his victim languish and agonize to allow her a quick death. He wants long hours to pass before he allows her to go."

"But why?"

"He wants to control the clock, hold back time and death

itself, to send her soul across a high wire of tension, with himself at the controls; he wants to control death itself.''

If memory served Jessica, Dr. Andrew Coudriet had not questioned the method in which the throat had been brutalized and the bone splintered, as opposed to crushed or mangled. He had taken it at face value that the strangulation was the result of a tightly wound rope about the neck; he'd described it as a hangman's noose, due to the angle of the ligature marks. And he was definitely correct in that assumption. A hangman's noose burned the back of the neck at the base of the brain far more than it did across the Adam's apple and throat. She had noted this in her report.

Yes, Coudriet was right about the rope burns, but before the rope burns, the girl had been strangled by hand, and strangled badly, repeatedly. The question remained, was she choked to death so far as the killer *knew*—an important distinction in determining the level and duration of torture heaped upon the victim—before or after she was lynched? Also, was she dead before he threw her into the water, or had she been choked repeatedly first and then, while still alive, thrown into the water, where exhaustion and blackout would do the rest? Jessica asked the questions aloud after formulating them. Articulating the horrid questions proved too much for Powers, who suddenly reached up and shut off the camera and audio.

He stood staring across at Jessica now, the body lying between them. ''Dr. Coudriet's report had the lungs full with water, so the woman was alive when she swallowed the ocean.''

''That may well be,'' Jessica agreed, knowing that as far as many forensics experts were concerned that was the only way for the lungs to be filled with water. But Jessica wasn't so sure. Water was a force that could find its way into the lungs of even a dead person, particularly if that force were guided. It didn't have to be inhaled in to find its way into the lungs.

''All right, let's speculate on why the bodies are always found so far from the victim's last known sighting. Hundreds of miles, in some cases.''

Thorn said, ''We found her lungs bursting with water,

so we know she was alive at the time of drowning.''

"You ever hear of a pump?'' she replied more sarcastically than she'd meant to. Still, she wondered at his use of the term *bursting*. It sounded like an exaggeration.

"What?'' Thorn replied.

"The kind of monster we're after, gentlemen, would be capable of killing her with his bare hands and then, using a mechanical device, pump her lungs full of water just to throw us off.''

Powers's eyebrows rose appreciably as he asked, "Really?''

"I know—I've hunted this type before.''

"Do you really think—'' began Thorn, but Powers put a hand against his chest, reminding him to keep his mouth shut.

Powers then sarcastically added, "If Dr. Coudriet says she was drowned, then she was drowned. He's only handled ninety-two drownings this year. Do you really want to call his judgment into question?''

"Killers sometimes mask their moves. You . . . we . . . can't be too careful.''

"The autopsy report faxed to you at Quantico was premature, but that wasn't our fault; there wasn't time,'' explained Powers, his hands in the air.

"Your superiors were on our necks,'' added Thorn.

"So it was a hurried report?''

"Well, yes. It was hurried, I'm afraid. At the request of your FBI field office chief here—DeVries?''

DeVries was the first man to alert Eriq Santiva to the trouble brewing in Florida. Plagued by health problems, he'd since taken an extended leave. "Dr. Coudriet had wanted more time with the victim, but this one's red hot, politically speaking.''

"Understood—a senator's girl.'' And she did understand. She'd been in the same predicament on several occasions.

She stared closely again at the force-injury at the throat. She brought a more powerful magnifying glass on a swivel arm to bear on the wound, and found only collaboration for what she had originally theorized. "She was repeatedly strangled, gentlemen."

"Repeatedly?" asked Thorn, his eyeglasses bobbing.

"Whoever did this took his own sweet time with her. Brought her to near death with his hands more than once before he threw her into the water. My guess? The rope burns came afterwards, and it's also my guess that she was in the water when the rope burns did their work on her neck. She drowned from exhaustion in the water, possibly from blacking out and going under repeatedly—after considerable strangulation by hand."

Thorn tore off his glasses and wiped his brow with a cloth; Powers, though more stoical, looked perturbed by this news as well. Each of them, Jessica included, tried to picture the type of killing ground—liquid, it appeared—that the killer worked out of. It had to be controlled; it had to be all his for the long hours he needed it.

Still Powers defended his boss, saying, "Dr. Coudriet must've wished to spare us the details."

"I'm sure," she replied. "Look, what we've got here is a high-level torture victim, gentlemen: a young woman who didn't go quietly into that gentle night . . ."

Thorn and Powers looked across at one another, most likely still unconverted by Jessica's version of the truth, disbelieving that Dr. Coran or anyone else could deduce so much from so little.

She didn't mind their skepticism, half expected it; furthermore, Jessica Coran didn't care. What they thought mattered little. She had to tell Santiva what she had, but she wanted time to run some tests, to be certain of her deductions and to have some science to back her up. She wasn't Kim Desinor, the psychic detective. No one was going to take her "vision/version" of the crime at face value, especially one so horrible as the image that now threatened to make her as ill as Thorn looked to be.

She intended to send some items connected to the various bodies and crime scenes back to headquarters at Quantico for Kim Desinor's special brand of inspection, but what was there to send? Like Allison Norris's partially dismembered body, all the others were without clothing, or rings, chains or bracelets. They wouldn't have had Allison's bracelet either if a certain shark hadn't taken a certain tournament fisherman's hooked bait below a certain boat off Key Largo some forty nautical miles south of Miami during a once-a-year fishing event sponsored by the very people who crusade to save the sharks.

She had reminded Santiva of what she'd said on the plane coming down about murder victims stamping their wills on the evidence, how a body placed in the ocean would find a way to shore, by hook or by crook. Now, with the message stamped clearly in the metal artifact found inside a dissected shark, Santiva had appreciatively agreed with her. What better evidence of this strange phenomenon than the bizarre fate of Allison Norris's engraved bracelet. Had she, before death, hidden the bracelet away somewhere and somehow on her nude body, say in her mouth, only to later replace it? Or had the killer intended to send another "poetic" message by way of the bracelet, allowing it to remain on Allison's wrist? Either way, the story of Precious had made a believer out of Eriq Santiva.

It may well have been that the killer was in such a state of excitement that he had somehow overlooked the bracelet. No doubt he had collected many such items of jewelry from his victims, likely used the trinket to fondle and to place around his genitals, to reanimate the lost moments leading up to the victim's horrid death again and again, or until he struck again, taking another life, adding to his head count and the grisly paraphernalia of his murderer's museum. "Find that museum," Jessica had told Santiva on the helicopter ride back to Miami, "and you have his head on a platter."

But for now, Jessica wondered what she might send back to Quantico for Kim Desinor's inspection. A goddamn tissue culture, a strip of DNA? A hair sample, what little was left of the arm? Forget about the girl's nails or fingerprints—there weren't any, as nothing was left of them, the epidermal layer of skin and nails having long since sloughed off into the ocean along with the lower layers of skin. The body had to have been in the water at least three and a half to four weeks. So where in the ocean had it slumbered in the meantime? she continued to wonder.

She momentarily wondered what Kim, her colleague and friend at the Psychic Detection Unit of the FBI, would think of her forwarding a package of samples and body parts; wondered if Kim wouldn't be better off with one of the internal organs, or at least a sliver of the heart. Kim had done wonders with the hearts in New Orleans the previous year when they'd tracked down the Queen of Hearts Killer, the maniac who terrorized the French Quarter and ripped the hearts from victims.

Jessica doubted that such forensic matter as organ tissue from the victims of the Night Crawler would be of any use to the psychic in this case. Would it not be better to fly Kim down, to provide her with the means to perform one of her patented psychometric readings over the body itself? Maybe the magician—sorceress—could pull something out of the collective and to-date bare hat.

Jessica made a mental note to discuss the possibilities with Santiva.

"How can you be certain she was strangled more than once?" asked an interested Thorn, breaking into her thoughts, his beaked nose twitching.

She frowned at first, then clicked the recording camera and audio back on before she began to explain. "Look closely here at the center of the wound. The way he did her, well, it's certain that it was done with a direct, blunt force, and not as the result of a cord or rope about the neck. But there are two distinct circular marks as well, so he used a favored cord or rope during part of his party time—before he got to the larger, thicker rope that was the last to be tied about her neck. The wider strip, if you look closely, is actually newer, fresher than the smaller choking device used. In fact, the wider strip is the freshest mark on the entire body except for those cuts and slashes which were determined to be from the coral reef as her body drifted toward shore."

"We looked at those cuts carefully, yes," agreed Powers, "and they didn't fit the contours of any knife blade. They were all the doing of Mother Nature."

"I guess if there's anything to be grateful for—and believe me, there's not much here—it's that this creep doesn't get off on blood. Frankly, gentlemen, I'm sick to death of butchers who have some craving for mutilating dead bodies into unrecognizable cuts of meat."

"What're you thinking?" asked Thorn. "You think this guy is some sort of gentleman killer who doesn't want to destroy the beauty of the bodily form? If so, think again. He just lets the sea do his dirty work for him."

Owen Powers snapped off his gloves and, nodding his agreement, added, "I think this bastard's a momma's boy, afraid of the sight of blood, afraid to get his hands really dirty. He probably vomits at the sight of blood. So he chokes and drowns them instead."

"You may be right, but I'm not so sure he doesn't just prefer that their deaths be more lingering and painful. A single knife wound can send a victim into paralysis and shock and the fun's over. I think this guy just likes to have long-lasting fun." Jessica stared across at Thorn, who looked the picture of Buddy Holly minus the guitar, his studious air and overbite marking him as having been a sure whipping boy for bullies during his childhood. Powers, by comparison, was muscular and handsome, sporting a full beard and deep-set, penetrating eyes. He hadn't totally ignored Jessica's conjecture, although he pretended otherwise.

"So, whoever this guy is, he likes to use his hands," Powers now said.

"Rather than a meat cleaver," agreed Thorn, pushing his glasses back up on his nose with his rubbered fingers and looking away from the body, regaining his composure again.

Jessica pushed the swivel-arm magniscope out of her way and replied, "The bastard also likes rope, and plenty of it. He enjoys trussing up his victims. He likes to touch his victims, a hands-on kind of guy. And while he's not particularly fond of blood, it's only because it doesn't excite his libido.''

A booming voice through a magnified electronic filter made them all jump. ''Are you saying he gets off on this, sexually?'' asked Dr. Andrew Coudriet from over her shoulder and above, looking down on the scene from a viewing tower where students usually gathered to watch an autopsy. He spoke through an intercom, and Jessica wondered just how eccentric the red-haired M.E. had become over the ensuing years since she'd last seen him lecturing on a stage at George Washington State University.

One thing was obvious—the world hadn't been particularly kind to Coudriet. Besides the white-gray pallor of his skin and the thinned-out patch of red hair dusting his cranium, there was a decided limp and arthritic gait as he found the stairs and came toward her.

She decided to answer the man. ''What excites this bastard is the draining, the feel of death as it moves through his fingertips, as death washes over his chosen victim. In fact, he likes it so damned much that once is not enough for this SOB. He wants to feel her life drain from her once, twice, three times, maybe four before the night and the fun comes to an end. And I'll tell you something else, Dr. Coudriet . . . gentlemen . . . this body's been stashed in the water somehow for just about as long as this young woman has gone missing.''

''So I gathered,'' Coudriet replied, his amplified voice like that of God, his eyes daring her. ''Makes you wonder where the cadaver has been all this time; you suppose our killer maintains a Davy Jones locker somewhere out there at sea?''

She'd wondered the same thing—how was this creep keeping the bodies from surfacing sooner?

Thorn muttered across at his male colleague, ''I tried to tell you that, Owen.''

Powers bridled at this, as if the other man had slapped him with a pair of wet, heavy gloves, showing him up in front of a woman. ''I've never worked with floaters before, Ted. So what do I know.''

"There are ligature marks on each ankle where I surmise ankle weights were used, the marks having been caused by metal as you might see with handcuffs, but no such weights came in with the body—or any of the earlier bodies either, Dr. Coran," the Miami M.E. stated.

"And as for the ligature marks about the wrists?"

"Well, I'm inclined to believe they're due to rope and not metal as in cuffs."

She hadn't yet gotten to the marks on the ankles, but she took a cursory look and replied, "I must agree, Dr. Coudriet."

"Bravo!" pealed the booming voice of Dr. Coudriet. "But, still, the cuts from both the weights and the ropes are so deep, like knife wounds." Coudriet pushed through the door now and entered the autopsy room, with Jessica wondering just how long he'd been standing overhead. The older man, sporting an Armani suit, continued speaking. "It's as if the rope grew tighter and tighter around the skin over a period of days, weeks even. How do you account for that?"

"Leather thongs," she suggested.

"Possibly . . ."

"But you don't think so?"

"No more than you."

Coudriet moved closer, extending his hand to her, and they shook, with smiles all around. "Lotta pressure on those wrists and the neck, and a great deal of moisture buildup in those wounds, too. The single intact wrist was near severed as a result."

"Not unlike the neck," concurred Jessica.

"Well, it does sound as if we're pretty much in agreement as to how this unfortunate young woman came to be in this state."

"We are," she replied, liking Coudriet instantly.

"So do you wish me to tell you, or will you tell me what we have here?"

"I would like very much for you to tell me whatever suspicions you harbor about our killer, Dr. Coudriet. I think you've already heard my own theories."

Coudriet looked at each of his assistants in turn, took a deep breath and paced before her, saying, "They were all dragged."

"Dragged?" asked Powers.

"Maliciously, through the water, at relatively high speeds," Coudriet continued.

Jessica nodded her agreement, saying, "Frankly, Doctor, I was beginning to suspect as much."

"Wanted verification, did you? That's quite understandable," he said, nodding. "Intelligent, I daresay. It's what I want, too."

"Thank you, Doctor." She said it both for the compliment and for the implication that he wanted full cooperation and give-and-take to reign here. She just wasn't certain she could trust him to actually carry through on such promises.

"You realize that we've all heard about your exploits, Dr. Coran, especially with respect to one Mad Matthew Matisak, and your daring on Hawaii with the Kowona case, not to mention the heart-taker—in New Orleans, was it?" Now Coudriet went to the monitor and shut down the camera and audio.

"Yes, well, thank you. I do my best, and I'm sure we can work together, Doctor. I have the utmost respect for your work. I've read every paper you've ever presented at the Forensics Institute for Medical Advancement and in the *Medical Examiner's Eye.*"

The mention of the newsletter for the Medical Examiner's International Association brought a smile to Andrew Coudriet's broad, passionate lips, and well it should have. Only the top men in the field were published in the prestigious and eclectic newsletter. But the old M.E.'s smile was quickly extinguished and replaced with a grim frown when Jessica turned to Owen Powers and asked, "Dr. Powers, can you get a close-up shot of the wrist? Follow that up with a close-up of the severed wrist. I know we have some, but the lighting here is far superior to what we had in Islamorada."

Powers momentarily looked to Dr. Coudriet as if for permission, then snapped to it. "Ahh . . . yes, certainly, Dr. Coran."

"These close-ups of the wrists and throat will be helpful. I want to compare them to what we found in Islamorada."

"But Powers has already done a full set of photos," protested Ted Thorn. "They're in Dr. Coudriet's portfolio on the corpse."

"I'm starting my own FBI collection, for the record." She looked over to Dr. Coudriet now and added, "I believe we're done here, Doctor."

"Good, and thank you . . ." he impishly replied.

"For what?"

"Showing my boys here a good time, and teaching them something in the bargain, Doctor."

"Well . . . thank you," she replied, surprised at his courteous remark, and knowing also that her having further disfigured the body by opening up the throat took him off the hook with the senator from Florida, Allison's bereaved father. She sensed that the elder M.E. would have no difficulty in passing information along to the senator. No wonder he'd worked it so that he would not even be in the room when she took to the body.

Coudriet walked her toward the changing room. "You'll have to pardon my young assistants. We're all on edge for many reasons, not the least being that we've had to stare into the bowels of a demon the likes of which no one truly wants to deal with, yet we are in no position to walk away, either."

"I can appreciate that." She started to push through the door, but he quickly grabbed it and held it open for her.

"I have since heard about what was found at the shark research center in the Keys. You will share what you have found there with us?"

"Absolutely, and not to worry about Thorn and Powers. Floaters are the worst kinds of corpses to work on, even worse than burn victims. I understand their reluctance to work on the same floater twice," Jessica tried to assure him. "Kinda like double jeopardy in the emotions department."

"And dealing with this floater on this table was particularly difficult work, because the Norris girl is . . . was, rather, the granddaughter of Congressman Bill Norris, and the niece of a former governor of the state as well as . . . well, you already know all that, now don't you."

Actually, she had not known the girl was quite so well-connected; still, beyond this indisputably political fact, the corpse was so damnably mannequinlike in appearance that it no longer resembled anything human, but rather a gelatin mold in places, a slick of albino tar in others. Strong political ties could no longer help her.

Coudriet laughed mildly at some deep inner thought.

"You wish to share something funny, Doctor? I could use a laugh," she said, unable to fathom what could possibly be funny in this affair.

"No, not at all. It's just that this is more than just a case of a simple floating victim perturbing my boys. The two of them see this as an opportunity to advance their careers, if they can impress the former governor and Congressman Norris, or the senator, you see."

"But you don't?"

He laughed further, more uproariously now. "Me? What can a congressman or a senator do for this old shell? No, my dear, I believe you could do more for me and my libido than all of the congressmen in all the states combined, thank you." He laughed more—an infectious laugh—and this time Jessica joined him. Maybe she was wrong about him, she thought now.

Still, she thought the use of the term *boys* for Thorn and Powers spoke volumes, and she wondered if the doctors were some sort of threesome outside the office, say golfing buddies. But she rather doubted that. Coudriet likely simply thought of them as his underling children.

"In a way, I'd rather work on a faceless, featureless corpse than the other extreme," he said, confiding what she thought to be an odd statement, even for a medical examiner.

"Really?" she replied, pulling wide another door and stepping into the closet where she could strip away her surgical garb and dump it into a basket.

He'd followed her in after taking a long, lingering look at her backside. "A floater like this isn't near so bad as a victim with identifiable features," he continued, trying to convince her of his sincerity but unable to fully do so. He was mostly talking to hear himself, she gathered. "Especially when the corpse has a familiar face, say that of an acquaintance. Ever happen to you, Coran?"

"Once or twice, yes."

"Then you know what I mean. Good. Experience shows in you. Now, with this Norris girl's cadaver here, unless you saw the pictures in the papers of this young woman before this happened to her, you could just treat her like a mannequin, like one of those corpses we had in medical school, right, Doctor?" He looked to Jessica for affirmation, but Jessica didn't give him the satisfaction. He took another long, lingering look to admire her form as she removed the green gown, displaying her crisp, white blouse and beige slacks beneath. In the other room, she could hear the click-click-click of Powers's Polaroid at work.

"But if they've got looks, these sweet features," continued Coudriet, coming around to face her, "well, it's just harder for me, personally. I'm a grandfather now, three times over, and I look into those innocent eyes and faces, and I think if God ever put one of those innocent little sweethearts of mine on my slab, I'd run out of here screaming. Be right off to the loony farm. Felt the same way when I saw those little baby children blown to bloody shards in Oklahoma City. What's so frightening about it all is that in today's world, I have a one-in-five chance of seeing one of my grandchildren violently killed before I die."

She mentally questioned his statistics but had to agree that he wasn't far off. He was a half inch or so taller than she, his eyes a burnt umber, the brown orbs shining orange under the dim light of the dressing area. The little orange flecks glowing in his eyes matched his limitless freckles and augmented what was left of his red hair. In his time he'd been a powerfully built, handsome man, and he still managed to bring together enough stage presence to make others curiously jealous of him. His eyebrows were bushy across a thick ridge of forehead. He was a genius and he knew it, and he wasn't certain he wanted Jessica's competition on the case. His little display of first trying to make her feel uncomfortable and threatened, then the mild form of sexual innuendo, followed by ruminations about his grandchildren and their vulnerability, meant that *he* felt vulnerable. The Night Crawler cases had so escalated as to eclipse any and all others his department was working on— or had ever worked on during his twenty-nine-year reign as chief medical examiner for the city of Miami.

She guessed that he might've retired with an outstanding record, but then this had come up, and he felt duty-bound to see it through, like the president of a failing business trying desperately to see black again before retirement. She both respected and disliked his stubborn Irish. And she realized that he was understandably feeling like a man under a microscope, the intense heat of which could burn away a lifetime career.

She did her best to allow for this.

"I guess I know what you mean," she said, humoring him regarding his preference for a corpse without a face to one that possessed fine, comparatively healthy features.

He suddenly took her by the arm and escorted her back into the autopsy room, where he stood and pointed at the bloated, fishy creation of the sea that lay across the slab. Powers was just finishing his snapshots.

The senior medical man began a new diatribe. "She has no hue in her bloated eyelids, no eyebrows, lashes or color; this girl has neither a pointed nor a flat nose, no ears jutting out or lying back in feline majesty; no moles, fissures, pockmarks, overbites, underbites; the lips are neither dark nor light, thick nor thin, nor meaningful, since you can't say where they begin or end; and as for the eyes . . . God, were they ever so deep-set in life as now when they are missing altogether, pecked out by crabs and microscopic sea life?"

"Dr. Coudriet," said Powers, taking hold of his boss's arm.

But Coudriet shook off the other man's touch, continuing, "Is that her brow or that of a Cyclops? If she had eyes, brows, a large or small forehead, at least she'd be somebody, even in death."

"I think I've seen enough for one night," Jessica firmly told Coudriet, anxious now to step away from Allison Norris's remains for the last time, angry with Coudriet's having put her so near the girl and so far from her main objective.

But he continued on, waving his hands as he spoke, a professor repeating a favored lecture to a student. "With this kind of bloated corpse, every minuscule pore and cell is saline-swelled, burying the facial characteristics in pulpy flesh, so there is no recognizing Allison for Allison."

Now Dr. Thorn tried to intervene, using a kind word. "Doctor Coudriet, it's late, and you must be exhausted. . . ."

Still he continued on as if he were alone with the corpse. "With Allison Norris, even the distinguishing birthmark on her hip—used along with dental and medical records to ID her—was so ballooned up as to be three times its normal size. She—it—had no identity left, not to speak of, no fingernails or prints, eyebrows or lashes . . ."

Jessica easily and quickly acknowledged all this as true enough. The sea had been merciless, unaffected actually, uncaring and unforgiving—like a storm—leaving Allison's body a blank, a mold upon which nothing had been stamped. All color was bleached white to an albino finish, a waxy white lather painted on with a huge brush to create the patina of death. Her auburn hair, once quite close to Jessica's own in appearance, was bleached from the intense Florida sun. And even this hinted at a horrid truth, Jessica realized. The body had floated atop the water for at least two and perhaps three weeks before discovery. But where and how could it have without being seen by someone somewhere? And if dragged through the water, wouldn't it have had to be by boat? And if by boat, could not the killing ground have been the sea, the entirety of the ocean itself? If so, this explained a great deal.

Coudriet, like some bad actor now, was still working on his monologue. "Without the birthmark and the dental records, Allison's body could never have been identified. The quivering mass of flesh remaining was like an empty slate, and decay had even blemished this when the abdomen, due to a buildup of noxious gases, had erupted and ruptured. A hell of a lot of fish had dined on her after that.''

As if on cue, a globule of flesh, now at room temperature, first separated itself from the body like a piece of living clay and then spattered onto the white-tiled morgue floor, where it promptly seeped like thick syrup through a grate over a drain below the slab, following the water seeping from a hose that ran continuously to keep the area clean. Pieces of Allison were disappearing before Jessica's eyes, Jessica thought just as Coudriet, being careless, still wearing his ''civvy'' shoes, slipped on a second globule off the dripping dead woman, going to one knee. Powers quickly helped the older man back up. Coudriet's face was flushed red now, and Jessica realized for the first time that he'd been drinking.

There wasn't much hope of learning anything further from Allison tonight, but at this rate, Jessica wondered how much more Allison's corpse could tell anyone, including Jessica Coran or even the impatient and obsessed Dr. Coudriet.

Jessica made a few additional quick assumptions about the killer and his modus operandi, but she wisely kept these to herself for the time being. It was late, and Coudriet was being a tad more than strange and eccentric now. When he signaled with a slight nod that he was finished, Ted Thorn took charge to remove the body.

Jessica thanked Coudriet for his opinion and his time, adding that she was tired and thought she'd go back to the hotel to get some rest, in order to return refreshed in the morning.

''Yes, of course,'' Coudriet agreed as if coming out of a trance. She wondered if, besides the booze she now smelled on his breath, he were on something—perhaps medication for an ailment.

"Well, good night to you all. I'll likely see you tomorrow."

She quickly exited, noticing the embarrassment on the faces of the two junior men in the room. Perhaps their mentor was slipping in more ways than one.

· FIVE ·

Fair is foul, and foul is fair.
Hover through the fog and filthy air.
    —WILLIAM SHAKESPEARE

Jessica stared momentarily at her watch as she made her way from the bowels of the teaching hospital's morgue and back toward Miami-Dade Central Police Headquarters through a series of tunnels, stairwells and twists and turns that eventually brought her to ground level. She wondered why morgues were always located below ground, as if in constructing them a kind of subconsciously created perdition was ever the aim, but she also knew two truths which led architects and builders to place morgues at the base of modern buildings. First, like their Egyptian counterparts who placed their most distinguished dead in secret chambers where cavernous mazes terminated, modern builders utilized the principles of cold storage, and nature provided the first refrigerator in the earth itself; and second, everybody knew that no one really wanted to be reminded of the dead on a daily basis, even if those dead were frozen or mummified. Out of sight, out of mind. Nowhere was that truer than in modern America.

Jessica had made arrangements to have dinner with Eriq Santiva, so she located Detective Quincey to take her back to the hotel. Quincey didn't know how to be subtle. In the car on the way to the hotel, he wanted to know her and Santiva's relationship; wanted to know the outcome of the trip to the Keys; wanted to know the outcome of the second autopsy performed on Allison Norris; wanted to know if Dr. Coran had a dinner companion for the evening.

She managed to dodge all his questions with the vague generalities she had come to rely on in the early stages of investigations, knowing he'd hear soon enough through Thorn, Powers and possibly Coudriet her views on the crime. She managed to keep the detective happy and satisfied that she was cooperating on the case, yet confused enough to think she might still have some answers forthcoming.

"Then there is a connection with some of the body parts found in Islamorada?" he pressed. "And not just the Allison Norris/Precious connection?"

She conceded this, saying, "It appears so, but it's too soon to be a hundred percent, Detective."

"Quince . . . you can call me Quince, Dr. Coran. How much more percentage do you need? I mean, the word *Precious* on that bracelet turning out to be the girl's nickname, an endearment from her father?"

"I take it her father's whole life is politics, like her grandfather's and uncle's?"

"No, no . . . not entirely."

"What else does he do?"

"Owns a string of boat lots, yachts and sailboats."

"Boat lots?"

"He sells sails—sailboats. You name it. Sales, repairs, outfitting, but he's never there any more than he was at home."

She wondered if there might be some connection between Allison Norris's disappearance and her father's connection with boats.

"Why? Whataya thinking?"

"Did Allison perhaps work for her father?"

"Yeah, out of the Biscayne sales office, as a matter of fact. But we covered all her boyfriends."

"She had more than one?"

"Hey, she was a hot property, quite well-off by most standards."

"During your inquiries, did anyone see her get on a boat with any of these boyfriends—before she disappeared, I mean?"

"Nothing like that surfaced. You think she was killed on a boat?"

"I'm beginning to think so, yes. Why don't you and your partner—what's his name?—Samer . . ."

"Samernow—Sam, I call 'im."

"Why don't you revisit the boatyard, ask around about any recent flame, someone who might've brought a boat in for repair or had recently purchased a boat and was hitting on her."

"What kind of boat?"

"Anybody's guess at this point."

"I hear you."

If nothing else, this line of investigation might get Quincey off her back, she thought when she saw in a flashing light that reflected off the darkened windshield that the detective was grimacing. "That is, if you think it's worth the effort, Quince," she qualified her request to make it more palatable to the male of the species.

"No, no, that's no problem."

"What is it, then?"

"Sorry, but I'm afraid the smell of the morgue has attached itself to you, Doctor. Sorry I'm so crude."

"I'm sorry. I would've showered at the lab, but I was a little uncomfortable doing so with certain *live* stiffs around."

Quincey laughed appreciatively, knowing that she was referring to Dr. Coudriet. "Then you met Doc C? He never was one for bashfulness, and he has a keen eye for the ladies."

"Yes, I made his acquaintance, and we'd best leave it at that, Quince."

"He likes the ladies," continued Quince. "But in your case, it's probably purely professional, Dr. Coran, although I could understand why . . . I mean, how . . ."

"Quince, let me suggest that we leave this subject alone."

"You got it, Doctor."

She was never so glad to see her room before, to shut

out the world. Once behind closed doors, she freshened up, scrubbing away the smell of the morgue, she prayed.

Jessica met Santiva in the Blue Piano Room, a restaurant fashioned around a baby blue grand piano. A talented pianist was playing some Yanni as if it were his own, the melody hauntingly filtering its way through Jessica's entire being and somehow relaxing her. The entire atmosphere was perfect—a fitting place for Jessica Coran to remove herself from her professional life, she mused.

She spied Eriq at the bar, throwing back a shot of what appeared to be either bourbon or brandy. She guessed it to be bourbon, and she guessed from the look of him that Eriq had spent as frustrating and dismal a day in Miami as she had, that he had not seen any of the renowned sugar-white beaches or any girls in bikinis, but rather only the inside of an institutional-gray or -green room, swapping leftover information with Quincey and his reluctant partner. He could probably match her item for item on distressing moments, despite the fact that she'd spent her day with a revolting corpse and a peculiarly male bastion of doctors whose leader was a kind of modern-day failing Genghis Khan. No doubt Eriq had spent his day with a revolting pack of local politicos and press harpies calling for someone's head.

She waved across the room when he looked up in search of her. He returned the salutation and came across the floor to greet her, commenting on how different she appeared tonight.

"Different? What's that supposed to mean?" she asked.

"I don't know, so *Cosmo* and beautiful. It must be that stunning dress."

The way the compliment was phrased, she wasn't sure whether to thank him or slap him, but she chalked it up to male stupidity and let it go at that.

After showering and splashing herself down with jasmine, she had slipped into her best dress, a sleeveless, strapless black affair, only because Eriq had booked them into the most prestigious hotel in the city, the Fontainebleau. Santiva obviously liked his accommodations first-class.

"This place is a palace," she said to him, thinking the prices were going to be astronomically high. "Paul Zanek would've blown his stack if I'd ever dared put in a voucher for this."

"As it is, the accountants're going to be screaming," he agreed, hefting a half-empty glass.

"But since you are the boss . . ."

"Quit worrying," he advised. "We may as well be decadently comfortable. After all, our days are filled with so much . . ."

"Shit. Say it, Eriq, but tell me, which is it to be? Decadent or comfortable? I think that's what we call an oxymoron. The two don't go hand in hand. Comfortable is Holiday Inn, comfortable is Best Western, comfortable is—"

"This business we're getting ourselves into is going to become more and more horrendous as we go on. But of course, we both knew that going in, didn't we?" From the tone of his voice, she'd been absolutely right about the bourbon and his day. Eriq had his own monkey on his back.

He located a table, a waiter and menus, all in one fell swoop. Seated now, enjoying the lovely music and delightful atmosphere, Jessica tried to forget for the moment the reason they were in the tropical city of golden sunsets—the Gold Coast, it was called, nestled as it was on an enormous blindingly white-and-yellow sand bay where cruise ships formed a large part of the skyline.

"So, how'd it go in your sector today?" Santiva's question felt like a tentative probe, and no doubt he both needed and wanted answers; his tone also conveyed the tenor of his day, and it didn't sound upbeat.

She shrugged, saying, "Ahh, all right . . . Got my feet wet with the boys."

"Three against one, huh? Some odds. Can't say that I fared much better."

"Well, Coudriet found some excuse to be away for most of the time I was there, but I later found him eavesdropping, if you can believe it. But mostly I just had the two assistants, Thorn and Powers, to deal with until the last twenty or thirty minutes. Coudriet's gotten rather colorful since the last time I saw him speak.''

''That makes him better or worse?''

''Different.'' She used Coudriet's word against him.

''Hmmmmm.'' Eriq didn't know quite what to make of the assessment, so he asked another question altogether. ''His staying out of your way, how's that? Good or bad for our case, I mean.''

''Better would be my guess.'' She glanced about the room, allowing the live music to continue its path over her mind, to soothe her frayed nerves. She was still wondering about Coudriet when she asked Eriq, ''How about you? You get your feet as wet as your throat?''

''Drenched, actually. Damned fools. Near as I can tell, they've been dragging their asses on this for some time, letting this SOB work freely up and down the coast from here to the Keys without once putting it together.''

''That's not atypical of local jurisdictions,'' she said while glancing about, people-watching.

''Too many little jurisdictions all along the seaboard and damned little in the way of cooperation or coordination of effort. You'd think Miami could get it together, but—''

''But somebody obviously did put it together,'' she interrupted.

''Coudriet, actually, the M.E.''

''Really?'' She was both curious and impressed with Dr. Coudriet all over again.

''Seems he was on vacation, a fishing trip down in the Keys—Sugarloaf Key, about a hundred twenty miles south of here, when a floater came ashore in the same condition as two others he'd seen earlier. He put two and three together, put out a call to all PDs along the coastal cities, asked for any information on similar cases, placed all the information in his Hewlett-Packard and voilà!''

''The similarities were, as they say, too close for comfort . . . too close to ignore.'' Her tone made it clear she didn't question it in the least. ''So Andrew Coudriet next contacted all the pathologists and detectives along the waterways.''

"He already tell you all this himself, did he?"

She shook her head firmly. "No, he didn't. Quite self-effacing of him. He didn't tell me any of this. Maybe he's more modest than I'd given him credit for. I don't quite know what to make of him."

"Did he tell you that there's an entire highway of water—the Intracoastal Waterway—which sweeps from Key West north to Jacksonville and beyond?"

"Which all experienced seamen and weekend warriors use regularly, I'm sure."

"You suppose right. Traffic is as heavy here as on the damned Mississippi River, but here most of it's pleasure craft."

They had expensive appetizers and wine before ordering dinner, and Eriq talked about his day with the deputy mayor, the police commissioner and William DeVries, the Miami FBI field chief who'd met with him despite his being in a recuperative condition, something to do with surgery to the small intestine, all in the company of Quincey and Mark Samernow, the two chief detectives for Miami. "Good man, Will," Eriq commented of DeVries. "Been on top of this thing from the moment he learned of it, saw the serial nature of it. Gave me some good insights into what's been going on down here, politically, that is. . . . Nobody can say precisely what's actually going on with the killer."

Jessica had heard DeVries's name in connection with the case before. It was Will DeVries who'd first alerted Santiva to the situation brewing in Florida, and when Jessica had gone to Eriq to give him the particulars of the strange phone call she'd taken from Islamorada, Santiva had surprised her with his instantaneous response—a single curse word suggesting both exasperation and procreation. His next response had been a question: "How soon can you be packed to leave for Florida?"

"We haven't left yet?" she'd countered that day in his office at Quantico. Later, on the plane, he'd confessed to having put the call from Islamorada through to her. Her involvement in the case had been carefully orchestrated.

Now, here in Miami, she wanted to know, "Why didn't DeVries's men meet us at the airport when we first arrived? Why MPD detectives?"

"Every agency in the entire state is antsy and sensitive at the same time over this one. There isn't a jurisdiction along the entire Eastern seaboard of the state that isn't missing some little girl. And as you know, the latest victim, the Norris girl, was highly connected, so it's become a real bone of contention as to who exactly is in charge, and Will's become disenchanted with the local authorities."

"Pissed off, you mean? So everybody's scrambling and watching his own ass?"

"Something like that."

She bit her lower lip and added, "Meanwhile it's all to the killer's advantage that law enforcement can't get its collective act together."

"Enjoy your appetizer," he told her, his tone still that of the boss and dictator. It was his show now, no mistaking that. "Will didn't want any sort of scene between the MPD and his guys out at the airport, not with so many cameras around."

"What's the connection with London?" she asked.

"DeVries has a friend at Scotland Yard. I mentioned him to you earlier, Nigel Moyler? Anyhow, they've worked a few international cases together. I've got a few contacts in the mother country myself, but these two guys realized that what happened a year ago in London was being duplicated here—or so it seemed to Moyler. But I believe he's not quite seeing this with twenty-twenty vision."

"Something's cast doubt on the connection?"

"Not something—me. I pointed out some glaring differences in the two cases, and the single fingerprint they have is a partial and is practically useless, and the notes they were supposed to've forwarded haven't arrived yet, so who knows."

"Glaring differences? Like what?" she asked while enjoying the fried zucchini appetizer.

"Well, I can sympathize with Moyler. The London murders were never solved, but the victims there were all of a type wholly different from our own.''

''Wholly different? Were they men?''

''No, no . . . they were all women,'' he conceded.

''Were they all strangled?''

He nodded. ''All strangled and—''

''—their bodies all thrown into the water?'' she finished for him.

''They were all determined by authorities there to've been drowned after repeated strangulation, yes.''

''Really?'' She kept her counsel.

''But there are more dissimilarities than similarities, I'm afraid.''

''For instance?'' she asked between bites and sips of wine.

''No poems to the authorities, for one.''

She nodded. ''Go on.''

Santiva's eyes were busy. They followed people about the room. ''Our victims are young women, hardly out of their teens. So far as I can tell, the English victims were all a good deal older, all with similar facial characteristics and body builds. Ours are younger, sweeter, more naive, thinner and a great deal more upscale.''

''Well, you may well be right, Eriq, about there being no British tie-in here.'' She watched his eyebrows take an inquisitive leap.

''What're you saying?''

''Hold on to your modus operandi theories, Eriq, because Allison Norris was definitely choked, but not to death; she drowned after having been repeatedly choked by hand and by rope. But she was alive when she hit the water. Does that sound like our British killer, Eriq?''

''They've listed them all as having drowned after repeated strangulation, yes, but I thought Coudriet's report said she'd been strangled and the body discarded in the ocean,'' replied Eriq.

''Actually, if you read Coudriet's report carefully, you'll note he fudged on whether she was dead or alive when she hit the water. I think since then he has amended his reports to certify that she was alive when she inhaled all that water. At least that's what I got from the team tonight. The report sent to us was a rushed job, corrected later. She was alive in the water, her lungs filled to bursting with microscopic sea life and saline. There's also evidence pointing to the killer's having dragged her bodily through the water.'' Jessica finished her drink and sucked on an ice cube.

"Damn, that puts a different color on things. Dragged her through the water? That means he used a boat of some sort, and that's how he moves in and out so quickly and easily. Think of it—a floating lair, a floating kill scene. Little wonder we have so damned few clues to go on.''

She dropped her gaze. "It's made him brash, cocksure. He travels with his incriminating evidence, keeps it close to him. It makes him feel safe to know where it all is, so safe he sends us word to tell us so . . .''

Eriq seemed caught up in an image building in his mind. "Imagine this bastard hauling them through the water like so much garbage.''

"What did you mean that the London victims were upscale?'' she asked.

"No, I said that our victims were upscale compared with those found in England.''

"Ahh . . . meaning?'' Jessica asked, her eyes fixed on him, alert and waiting for his answer.

He shuffled uncomfortably in his seat, finding some modicum of repose. "So far our victims haven't been prostitutes.''

"I see.''

"Most of the London victims were rough street girls, women actually . . . like I said, average age thirty, thirty-five. Our girls here are ten, twelve years younger on average with no history of prostitution, no more promiscuous than most. There was one arrest of a prostitute who claimed to've been a near victim of the Night Crawler early on in the case, but she was kicked loose for want of verifiable evidence.''

"Averages can be misleading, Eriq. Suppose the killer's taste in victims has changed over time.''

"An evolving fantasy?" asked Santiva. "I guess we might consider it, but the British connection seems tenuous at best even so, and it could lead to a dead end and a great waste of time and effort."

"So, your mentioning a possible British connection earlier was just to get me interested?"

He shook his head. "Not entirely, no . . ."

She let it drop. "So, tell me more about your day," she suggested, a waiter now clearing away their dishware and providing more wine.

Eriq told her how he'd spent much of the day walking through police reports with various homicide detectives working the cases, explained that Samernow and Quincey were but two of some thirty detectives from fifteen different municipalities dotting the coast who were all interested in the case, all with their own separate lists of missing persons, and he further informed her that they had all come to the city to see what the FBI could do for them.

"So what have we done for them lately, Chief?"

Santiva exaggeratedly scratched behind his ear and said, "Duuuh . . . well . . . ahh . . . hmmmm."

"I hope you didn't use that line with them!" She was now laughing.

He shook his head, smiling, playing with the lit candle in the bottle that was their centerpiece. "No, that's what I told the press."

They laughed together now.

"You can bet I talked you up, Jess. They were cheered to have our forensics capabilities, and I promised that our Behavioral Science Division profile of both killer and victim type would be circulated among them all. I strongly urged, called for, pleaded for a central clearinghouse and a task force to be put together in which FBI, state and local officials would cooperate, sharing and pooling information."

"And how'd that go over?"

"The PR cop liked the idea. . . ."

She laughed and knowingly nodded.

"Said it was something they could feed the press, show

the outside that the MPD was doing something constructive. Said the *Herald*'s been raking their rocks . . . raking *them* over the coals.''

They ordered and ate a wonderful meal, Jessica enjoying the native grouper, sautéed in garlic and butter. Santiva, the philistine, had filet mignon, despite her protest that he could get steak in D.C.

"I can get fish in D.C., too."

"Not fish native to these waters," she countered.

"Don't tell me how to eat, okay?" His Latin blood had been fired up by the idea that some woman was telling him what to order.

After dinner, Santiva, who was part Cuban and who knew Miami well, showed her some of the nightlife, taking her to South Beach Street, Cocowalk in Coconut Grove, showing off the Art Deco regions and Little Havana. In Little Havana, she learned why Miami was called the Capital of Latin America. It was wild, raw and romantic all at once, their trip punctuated by perpetual stops all along the way for small cups of café Cubano. They visited Ayestaran, El Meson Catellano, Malaga and Casa Juancho, all in that order, and she had to keep up with Eriq. Some of the furnishing and the Art Deco seemed out of time, as if 1950 still held sway here.

Miami was every bit the wild, raucous city that it was purported to be—a multifaceted city, a place of dizzying, dancing lights, too many signs, too many twisting, confusing streets and other more sinister mysteries. It was an international city, filled as it was with the fashions, foods and faces of many nationalities, but the Cuban influence—at least in the circles Santiva took her—was most strongly evident at every turn.

One place where they had drinks appeared to be full of Mafia types who suspiciously eyed them the whole time. Santiva left her alone for a moment and bullied right up to the head man of this ''tribe,'' flashing his badge, talking loudly and holding back nothing, explaining why he was in the city. Soon he and the others were talking like old friends, with Eriq repeatedly pointing at Jessica as if she were some prize he'd won in a raffle.

He's just playing his part, getting on their good side, she kept telling herself, but she didn't care for being made to feel like a piece of merchandise. She had read a line once from the Pulitzer Prize–winning author Edna Buchanan of the *Miami Herald* that called Miami home to big-league football, basketball, baseball and motorists who'd kill for a parking space or simply to prove *quien es más macho*. She wondered if that wasn't exactly what Santiva was trying to prove here tonight, just what a tough guy he was, or if there wasn't some other hidden agenda. The strangers wanted to know where Eriq and his family had originated, what part of Cuba. Eriq didn't tell them that he was born in Sioux City, Iowa, but rather bullshitted his way through, having learned Cuban geography long ago.

By the time Eriq returned to Jessica, where she sat all alone at her table, Jessica had had enough of bar-hopping and dancing, but he insisted they have one last dance.

"For *mis amigos*," he said, pointing. He then turned back and said conspiratorially, "Make me look good in their eyes. It's *importante*."

She shook her head, sighed heavily and stood, replying, "This better produce something, Eriq. I've been on my feet all day."

He swept her up in his arms and moved her about the dance floor with a grace and panache she didn't know he possessed. The Latin in him had surfaced fully, and she found herself twirling and dancing to a fast-paced mamba that steadily increased in tempo as the music from a live band threatened to blow out the walls. When the music finally came to an abrupt halt, Jessica felt as if she ought to have a rose between her teeth, but the "hombres" didn't seem to mind the omission as they roared their approval, some high-fiving others.

Eriq waved to them as he and Jessica made for the door.

"What was that all about?"

"They know every fishing fleet, cutter and pleasure craft that comes and goes from the ports here, and how a manifest is doctored and who gets paid off and—"

"I thought we had the Port Authority Police for that."

"—and if we can get them on our side . . . well, let me put it this way: They have more eyes than do the police."

Both Eriq and Jessica knew that the majority of victims had last been seen at one of the countless oyster bars and pier restaurants around the state, and that the killer might well be coming and going via the waterways. "Well, the more the merrier," Jessica finally conceded.

"If this guy is using a boat as his killing ground, maybe someone in the Cuban community has seen something odd somewhere along the line."

"I get the picture, but Eriq, I'm beat and I have to get an early start tomorrow with the MPD guys and the M.E. so—"

"Coudriet, yes. Don't be intimidated by him." Eriq handed the valet his car tag and the young man in white jacket and tie rushed off for their car, leaving them standing before the Havana Tocador nightclub.

"Me, intimidated by the M.E.?" A light sea breeze lifted Jessica's now damp hair from her brow. The night air felt deliciously cool.

"Yes, well, I understand he's something of a giant, physically."

"He's no taller than you, Eriq, and he vaguely resembles Andy Griffith when he was sheriff of Mayberry, and he's about as folksy, and he has freckles."

"All that and red hair. I can picture it, but what I meant was his professional stature. Don't let his professional stature—"

"Influence me? Not to worry, Eriq." She then asked, "What does it mean, Tocador?"

"Good move regarding Coudriet, but he's very good at what he does. He's your senior by fifteen years, and he is used to being looked up to, or so I'm told."

"Most tall people are. What does the name of the nightclub mean? Havana Tocador?" she repeated.

The car shot to a halt in front of them, and Eriq opened her door for her, tipped the valet and off they drove. "Tocador. It means one of two things."

"Yes?"

"Boudoir, but it has also a sexual connotation as *dessert*."

She looked askance at him, her eyes asking before her mouth, "No lie?"

"Yeah," he confessed, "I'm just teasing. Hey, before going back to our separate, lonely hotel cells, how about maybe—"

"Cells? You call those rooms cells?"

"—how about a walk on beautiful Miami Beach?"

"Eriq, Eriq . . . don't you ever run out of steam? Whataya got, a sleep disorder or something? Insomnia or something?"

"Something," he muttered in return.

"'Cause that I can understand, but Eriq, it's past two A.M., and I have to be in early tomorrow if I'm going to be in any kind of shape to duke it out again with the big guys, to stay ahead of Coudriet and company."

"All right, then . . . I will escort you back to your hotel and say good night like a decent fellow."

His slight tone of irritation sounded both sweet and sophomoric at once, she thought, wondering just what was on his mind. He certainly had had enough to drink. "I did have a . . . an interesting time, Eriq, and I do appreciate your having shown me a side of the city I would not have seen otherwise."

"Don't mention it. I had a good time, too."

"Frankly, in this town, I'm lost."

"So are several million others."

A light sprinkle began, like the spray from a partially opened nozzle, and suddenly the streets were slick with water, reflecting car, billboard and neon lights, painting Miami in the fluid rainbow hues of quicksilver and mercury. Headlights flashed by them like speeding ghosts, and the dark interior of the car grew smaller, denser—an enclave against the artificial light of this place.

Eriq turned on both the radio and the defrost, clearing the fogged-up windows to the beat of a mellow Johnny Mathis song, a welcome respite after the noisy restaurant music.

Jessica laid her head back, trying to empty it of all

thought, all pain, when out of nowhere Santiva said, "Look, I don't think I've expressed my deep regret about your recent loss, Jessica, and I want to now." He had had too much to drink. He was getting schmaltzy, his voice slurred, and she hadn't any idea in the world what the hell he was talking about. "I'm extremely very sorry that Parry took that bullet."

"What the hell are you talking about, Eriq?"

"I was told that this guy you were seeing, that you were going to chuck everything for, was shot in the line of duty, killed."

"When? When did you hear this?"

"Two weeks ago. It was going around Quantico."

"That's the craziest piece of bullshit I've heard in a year."

"Then it didn't happen? But I was under the impression you were . . . that you two were . . . and then suddenly you're back as if nothing had happened, so I asked around and somebody said—"

"Somebody's full of shit, Eriq." She gulped back the rest of her reply, not knowing what it ought to be, and she fought back hot tears. "It's rather old news now, Eriq, but we simply broke up. Nobody . . . no one was shot. At least no one that I love . . . not this year . . ." She imagined that someone had somehow scrambled the story of Otto Boutine's death with the story of her recent breakup with James Parry, and that somehow Parry's obituary had been written. As Mark Twain would've said, the reports of Parry's death were greatly exaggerated. "Can we now get back to the hotel, please?" she asked.

He drove on, saying something inane about having to use a rental, that the dummies in the bureau hadn't been organized enough to get him a radio car, "but that's going to change tomorrow!"

After this, the silence between them was like lead inside glass.

When they got back to the beautifully lit palace of the Fontainebleau, he parked the car and grabbed her hand. "In the interest of doing a good job down here, I'm going to support you in every way possible, Jess.''

"Thanks, Eriq. You're doing fine.'' She wondered what he meant by *in every way possible*.

"Jess, I'm faxing all we have first thing tomorrow. Anything else I can use in the report back to Quantico?''

"I can't be certain, Eriq but . . .'' She hesitated.

"Go on, what?''

"They were strangled, that's certain, but I have a sixth sense about this guy.''

"Whataya mean?''

"I have to run some tests on the Norris body first, but I've got a sensation that this guy is very controlled, and that he wouldn't be satisfied to just kill his victim by strangulation or drowning. Not this guy.''

"What're you getting at?''

"I think—and it's just conjecture until I can run some tissue samples, check out the lungs, that sort of thing—but it's just possible that he watches his victims drown, to get a full charge; you know, watching their struggles in the water.''

"Can you prove that? Damn, if you could prove that, once we get this sicko-scumbag-bastard into custody, it'd go a long way toward the death penalty with a Florida jury.''

"I think I can prove it, yes.''

They walked from the lot to the hotel foyer, where Jessica said good night.

Eriq again apologized. "I'm sorry about my blunder earlier, for my error regarding Jim Parry.''

"Forget it, Eriq, and get some rest. You're going to need all the rest you can get for this case.'' She started straight for the elevator and her room.

Once alone, Jessica kicked off her shoes and tore away her clothes, anxious for a shower and rest. She walked to the bath, where she and ran the hot water, catching a glimpse of her slim body in the quickly fogging mirror. She watched the smooth film of condensation create a mosaic of the mirror—lines, veins, arteries of condensation forming nectarlike before her body, erasing her, making a ghost of her before her own eyes. She gave a thought to Allison Norris's last involuntary pose before the camera; somewhere in the thick protocol and information on the victim, Jessica had read that she was a part-time model, so she had worked as daddy's little girl in the boat sales show-room, just waiting to be discovered by Hollywood East— Orlando. Sadly, her final photographs taken on this earth found her the victim of a cruel death which robbed her of beauty and dignity, her backdrop the Miami city morgue.

Now all that Jessica could see in the fog-laden mirror were her hands reflecting back at her where she reached out to touch the intangible image of herself lost inside that mirror. She wondered how lost Allison Norris must have felt the night she died.

Jessica tore herself from the mirror and stepped toward the shower. She tried to shake off the dark, dreary images by recalling to mind her lover, Jim Parry. She gave Jim a long and thoughtful moment, recalling the warmth, the gentleness they had shared, the explosive sex that was beyond any lovemaking she had ever known. She arched her body toward his memory, the memory of his touch. In her waking dream, she pressed her lips to his and all of an instant, she was making passionate love to him again. It was a deep, abiding love which rivaled the Hawaiian trade winds in sheer intensity and duration.

She recalled how deliciously their lovemaking had progressed, gaining momentum, getting better, better, better each time she found herself in his naked embrace. The loving went in measured point-counterpoint fashion, an unfolding melodic composition, a choir of rising and falling crescendo with the ebb and flow of the midnight-blue waters on the black-sand beaches of Maui. For a brief moment, she recalled how she and Jim had become one out there on the beach, not only with one another but with their primeval setting, and how they had flown together, having become the very air they breathed in and out of one another.

That morning on the beach, she'd awakened and begun

to tease, saying, "Now that's the way to welcome a girl to paradise, James Parry."

He had laughed lightly, taking her again in his arms and kissing her in response. Then he'd said, "I've loved every moment of our time together, Jess."

Looking around at the empty little room she now stood in, Jessica wondered if she'd been wrong to stay away from Jim's recently arranged and fully bogus funeral, the one the gossipmongers had created for the gullible likes of Santiva. Perhaps she ought to've hopped a jet for Hawaii, shown up unexpectedly with a wreath and a bottle of cognac so they could toast his demise. With Jim ostensibly dead, their lovers' quarrel might have evaporated.

She laughed at the idea. Then she stepped into the shower and felt the warm spray drain the excesses of the day from her bones.

No doubt there was talk about what kind of woman she was to've not attended James Parry's funeral. She wondered if he'd been cremated, his ashes dropped over Mount Haleakala on Maui from a police helicopter, or if his body had simply been laid out in the bottom of an outrigger canoe and cast off into the cradling arms of the forever sea. Either way, she had missed the romantic ceremony and was, no doubt, being crucified for her stony heart.

She wondered if Jim knew he was dead; wondered if he'd seen or heard his obituary reported, and if so if he would immediately call her to allay any concerns she might have? Most likely he'd get a good howling laugh out of the entire matter, she told herself as she lathered her hair and body with soap. Perhaps he could no more deal with the greatly exaggerated reports of his death than she. On the other hand, it gave him a damned good excuse to contact her, so why hadn't he?

Perhaps there was a guiding hand in all the world's frenetic activity and business—maybe. A hand reaching down into the lives of individuals like herself, a hand that kept turning her in this single-minded direction; a hand directing her, telling her that she was meant for this one path, this single road, and that she must travel it alone. That there was no room for Jim; no room for her personal happiness and peace of mind.

Perhaps her star, the one she was born under, made of her some sort of crusader of right and justice, perhaps even divine vengeance, or at least intervention. But maybe that was sheer and absolute nonsense, like all else; certainly it was stretching a point to call it *divine*, but there did seem to be a hand that sometimes not so gently forced her back to her never-ending toil as an FBI medical examiner, forced her onto the trail of the most brutal monsters roaming the darkest corners of the planet.

So here she was again ... showering, toweling off, readying for bed at the moment, yet readying also for an arduous search for a sadistic, unfeeling sociopath with a fixation on young women and his own brutal, ritualistic game of destruction; a psycho who believed in his heart and brain that he was placed on this earth for the sole purpose of meting out a brand of justice all of his own creation, an evil passed on to him by some demonic force that controlled his intentions, his actions and his perverted pleasure-seeking. He, like her, was on a mission; he created her mission as he wreaked death on others.

Allison Norris had not stood a chance against such a foul creature as stalked her, at least not while she was alive; but maybe, ironically, she stood a chance against the monster now that she was dead. Allison had come to them—to Jessica in particular—washing up on South Beach that bleached-white morning here in Miami, followed by her missing part, deposited before Dr. Wainwright's astonished gaze from the gut of a shark some forty miles south of the city.

Allison had somehow demanded to be seen, to be ignored no longer. She demanded it here and in Islamorada. She demanded justice, and in her death, she held up a dirtied, bloodied and opaque-looking glass through which Jessica must now step.

But for now, weary and needful of sleep, it took all Jessica could do to step from the shower, towel off and find her bed. She stretched out, her body pleading for REM sleep. However, Jessica's mind, helplessly driven, played over the events of the day, and Allison in particular.

Allison's body—such as it remained—on ice at the MPD morgue, had spoken its death song to Jessica Coran. Why else was Jessica here, why else than to take up this young woman's haunting cause? Allison Norris deserved to rest in peace. She didn't deserve to waft about in some ethereal purgatory, to remain so much flotsam to haunt those left in the wake of her sadistic murder. But the sheer duration and intensity of Allison's suffering wouldn't allow anything but a purgatory at this point, and nothing would change that—not until her killer was brought down. Only in some measure of justice might Allison and her family find peace, along with other victims who'd suffered at the hands of the Night Crawler, or Tidewater Killer as the phantom trawler of souls was also being called—not to mention future and potential victims of this fiend: young women who might otherwise live long, fruitful lives if this monster were caught, put away or put out of his primeval misery.

It was up to Jessica Coran to put an end to this monster's patterned, ritualistic assassinations.

And on this troubled thought, her eyelids firmly but independently closed, her brain seeking out and finding slumber, her soul patiently waiting like a Nostradamus come to dream visions from the fabric of moonlight, mist, smoke and mirrors.

· SIX ·

Here are a few of the unpleasant'st words
That ever blotted paper.
　　　　　　　　　　　—WILLIAM SHAKESPEARE

The Following Day

C. David Eddings looked once again over the obituary news of the day, the page for which he was responsible. All looked well except for the column on George T. Flagler, a descendent of the great Flagler who had brought the railroad to Florida when Miami was just a trading post on the great waterway, a speck on the map. It was hardly enough space for a relative of this great man who had opened up a wilderness to the outside world, the wilderness which was Florida in the late 1800s. True, from what he read of the reporter's notes, the third-generation Flagler had done little to distinguish himself in his own lifetime, living off the fortunes won by his forebears. All the same, some show of respect was required and the young reporter, Dabney, hadn't understood the importance of the history behind the man's name, that this man's ancestor had brought the first tentative signs of civilization to Ormond Beach, Fort Lauderdale, Miami and even Key West with his railroad. For his part, Junior had sold shares in a fledgling and faltering land development company, so maybe placing the man's obit at the top, first column on the page, smacked a bit of the "old boy" syndrome the South was already so well-known for. But Eddings didn't think so.

"Be damned if C. David Eddings'll ever add to that total fabrication by bowing to it! I'm not in the business of fostering misconceptions or carrying on stereotypes, no,'' he mumbled to himself, as was his habit while he worked.

The habit was so well-worn now that only the greenest of office workers and reporters might stare; everyone else took it in stride, along with the noise of several hundred computer monitors, all humming their chorus of meaningless gibberish.

C. David Eddings was the obit page editor and the last man to be called into an editorial board meeting, but today he looked up to see that Merrick, the editor in chief of the *Miami Herald*, was gesturing him to follow the pack into the boardroom.

''Wonder what's up,'' he said to himself, checking the wall clock and seeing that it'd just turned 8:06 A.M.

''We got another sweetheart letter from this freak who's killing girls up and down the goddamn coast,'' said Bill Lawrence as he whizzed by. ''Come on, Eddings, you don't wanna miss this.''

There was something ugly and unsettling, yet terribly exciting about what was going on with this serial killer everyone was calling the Night Crawler. *Unsettling* was the best word for it, like someone had taken a cold, coarse, rusty pair of pliers and reached into Eddings's stomach and torn at the core of him, at the soul of his being, rocking his world on its axis—mainly because he found that he enjoyed the excitement of it; something like a strange, prurient interest had hold of him, and since the paper had begun reporting the disappearances and the subsequent discoveries of the bodies, he found himself unable really to get enough. This fact and his reflection over it disturbed him greatly. It was a side of himself he had not known existed. He found himself sitting up nights, wondering what the killer was like, who he was, where he was at that moment, why he was doing it, how he did it—curious about each gory detail. He dared not share his newfound fascination with anyone, but keeping it bottled within had become more and more difficult.

He saw death every day in his obits, dealt with it as a sausage grinder might sausage, but there was something so titillating, so invitingly dirty about this whole Night Crawler affair that it must be like what was at the heart of most illicit love affairs, he guessed. Yet this was far different, at the other end of the spectrum of emotions, he reasoned, and it had continued to confuse and agitate him, this dangerous, pseudonymous side of himself that he'd discovered, this sick interest he had taken both in the case of the Night Crawler and in the monster himself, as well as in what he did to the women. What kind of man was he? Was he of the same species as Eddings? The same race? How could he do such terrible and vicious things to lovely young women? What did it do for him? Did it make him forget who he was? Did it make him feel taller, larger, stronger, immortal—what? And why was he sending newsy little tidbits about himself to the *Herald*?

The short, stubby obit page editor snatched at the loops on his suspenders and straightened his pants, hitching them up before he threw on his coat and stepped toward the big boardroom. He was conscious of the stares and the chattering going on all around the bull pen. Word had leaked, as it always does across a newsroom floor, and everyone knew what the emergency meeting was all about. Eddings felt like a snoop, a prurient meddler, his guilt rising as he moved from his desk to the juicy information which awaited him inside the newspaper boardroom.

C. David Eddings, no matter what his small stable of reporters called him behind his back, would be at that meeting, just as he'd been involved in the first such meeting. He'd be there because death was involved, and death reporting was very much a part of what he did; he and the city desk editor were in constant contact, because today's headline, *Youth Shot in Drive-by on US1*, was tomorrow's obituary column. As Merrick was fond of saying, "One hand's gotta know what the other's doing at all times." Eddings routinely countered with, "One foot in the grave had to know where the other foot was at, at all times," after which he'd snort and laugh. Perhaps it was for this reason that other journalists considered him a ghoul, an undertaker who used words rather than a shovel.

Still, he was *in*. In on the biggest, breakingest story to come along in years. How many others could say they were on the inside of the biggest manhunt in the history of the city?

Instinct, however, had told him to again, like the last time, keep his mouth shut and his eyes open during the meeting. The letter from the killer was passed through everyone's hands that last time—even the cooking and accent page editors—before it had finally reached C. David Eddings's fingertips. He didn't expect any change in the pecking order today. Still, he was in; he was part of it all. How many men in Miami could say that?

As he filed into the room behind the other editors, C. David Eddings saw that Glenn Merrick's secretary, Sally Hodges, a busty, middle-aged woman for whom Eddings had nursed a crush since coming to the paper, stood in back of Merrick with an overhead projector, replacing a blown light, it appeared. And next Eddings noted that there were strangers among them—very stern and serious looking customers, a dark-skinned handsome man and a strikingly interesting woman with silky auburn hair which created a fishnet and lattice effect about her shoulders, hooding a pair of dark, alluring eyes.

Sally looked up from what she was doing to give Eddings one of her bejeweled smiles. Eddings wondered if she was smiling out of politeness or genuine interest. He'd never gotten up the nerve to find out.

Merrick began by introducing their guests: Eriq Santiva, chief investigator for the FBI, and Dr. Jessica Coran, M.E., FBI. Merrick informed them all that Santiva and Coran were now spearheading the manhunt for the Night Crawler.

" 'Bout time we got some clout in on this."

"Damn sure not going to see any results from the Miami morons in uniform," said another.

"Welcome to our city," said the lone female editor. "I hope you don't judge us by what's going on out there in the streets, or by what's said in this room."

"Of course not," Santiva said, nodding and smiling at the assembled editors. "I wish to thank you all, and especially your editor-in-chief, Mr. Merrick, for showing such civic duty, calling me the moment anything having to do with the killer broke.''

Even Eddings got the underlying message, that Santiva and Merrick had had a serious talk at some previous point, and that Merrick dare not screw around with Santiva on this matter.

Jessica Coran quickly added, ''Without your cooperation, gentlemen, catching this fiend will be far more difficult.''

''What're the chances he'll be stopped?''

''Just how far along are you in the investigation?''

''Got any suspects? Anyone good?''

The questions were like live ammo coming at the FBI people.

''We're not here for a news briefing, gentlemen!'' shouted Glenn Merrick over his people.

Nancy Yoder, the accent page editor, replied with an explosive, ''Oh, pooh!''

Merrick next announced what they all already knew, then asked that Jessica hold up the note from the killer for all to see.

She reached into her black valise and pulled forth a plate of glass which had been sealed to a second plate. Between the two plates lay the now flattened communiqué, the second to have been sent to the *Herald* by the Night Crawler. The ridges where it had been folded and stuffed into an envelope could still be seen. Jessica held up a cellophane bag which housed the envelope. The editors studied both the note and the envelope from their seats.

The killer's note was on ordinary white bond typing paper; nothing special or of particular importance there, and certainly no helpful, easy or telltale clues such as a mast or letterhead, though the postage seal on the envelope told them it had been forwarded from Key Biscayne, extremely close to the location of the last two missing girls believed to have fallen prey to the killer, a girl by the name of Tammy Sue Sheppard and another named Kathy Harmon.

''This time we don't piss off the authorities, right, Agent

Santiva?'' suggested Merrick. ''We work with you, in full cooperation, not against you.'' He eyeballed his people and added, ''That means we keep our goddamned mitts off the note, and—''

''Whataya getting in return for our—'' began Lawrence, who was instantly cut off by Merrick.

''And there's no time lapse between when one of these damned notes appears on the city desk and when we contact Agent Santiva here. Understood, gentlemen? This is how we react to a city emergency. Understood, everyone?''

''We get an exclusive, Glenn? I mean when the case is solved, right?'' asked Lee Blake, the city desk editor.

''We have had assurances to that effect, and I'm not going to jeopardize that in any way. That means no leaks from here, either. I mean you don't tell your wives, your lovers, your mothers, your fathers, your priests or your bookies; you got that?'' Merrick fairly screamed the order.

''What're they saying, Glenn? That it's somehow our fault this creep's still at large? Screw that shit,'' muttered Blake from around his cigarette, his small eyes sunken amid the heavy face and leathery skin.

''Wasn't your fault that last time, Glenn,'' soothed Lawrence. ''None of us had any reason to believe the authenticity of that first letter when it arrived on Blake's desk that day.''

''Are we any surer of the authenticity of this one?'' asked Nancy Yoder, her hands rising skyward.

''Well, it's definitely the same handwriting; we've had an expert—Santiva here—tell us so, and since the cops and the FBI are operating as if the first communiqué is indeed from the Night Crawler, we're doing the same here,'' explained Merrick.

''Why not copy the damned thing so we can all have a working copy, Glenn?'' asked city editor Blake.

''Yeah,'' agreed some of the others.

''What's with you people?'' Merrick barked. ''Do I have to paint a picture for you?''

''That might help,'' replied a belligerent Blake. ''It's our story, Glenn.''

"G'dam'it to hell, I don't want copies of this thing getting all over the freakin' building and finding its way over to the bloody *Times* like the other bastard thing did *before* we're given the go-ahead from Agent Santiva to print it, all right, Lee? And God save the sonofabitch who's selling us out if I ever catch 'im."

"Paranoia becomes you, Glenn."

"It's got me this far."

"Where's the letter postmarked from?" asked Nancy Yoder.

"Yeah," agreed Lawrence. "Last one was from goddamn Palm Coast."

"This one's in our backyard—actually, our front yard, if you want the truth," replied Merrick.

"Where, damnit?"

"Key Biscayne, across the bridge." Merrick's blunt reply sobered the editors. The bridge was right outside their window.

"Christ," muttered Lawrence.

Yoder took a deep breath, grabbed for her water glass and gulped.

Blake began to grind his teeth, gnashing like an angry woodchuck before saying, "Isn't that where that teen disappeared from the other night, Key Biscayne, out at Razzles?"

"That's right. We're speaking to witnesses on that situation now," Santiva assured them.

"Eyewitnesses?"

"Anyone actually see this guy?"

"Can we talk to the witnesses?"

The reporters' questions rifled anew.

"We haven't as yet determined the reliability of those involved; they're emotionally involved—young friends of the missing girl," Santiva explained, holding his hands up as if under arrest. "But as soon as we know something worthwhile . . . useful, that is . . . we promise to cooperate with you as you have cooperated so generously with us."

"That's our deal, gentlemen, lady," said Merrick to his people.

While the chatter continued, Jessica carefully resettled the glassed-in note into her black valise along with the cellophane bag holding the envelope.

It was earmarked to travel, within the hour and by jet, to Quantico, where the psychic fingertips of Dr. Desinor would pass over the physically and psychically "clean" document before it was to be turned over to the Documents Division for further graphoanalysis and scientific analysis. Santiva had taken extreme care in his preliminary and cursory viewing of the note to establish its genuine nature, keeping it under glass the whole time. It was duplicated through the glass for Merrick's secretary Sally, who'd created a single opaque replica.

Sally now closed the curtains, dimmed the lights and flicked on an overhead projector, the beam creating a square window of light against the north wall. She next placed the opaque replica of the letter onto the overhead and the alleged words of the killer were beamed against the wall. It read:

whilst t feeds on
those hungry
for touch,
t requires little much:
Your sweet jasmine
gone sour,
Your sweet belle
gone dully silent

in her last hour
~~sacrifices twice~~
and thrice
and given power
in her final breath
as t deems
all the whores to be

"Whataya all make of it?" asked Merrick.

Lee Blake studied it and sighed heavily before pronouncing the little ditty, as he called it, in incredibly bad taste, "and even worse poetry."

"Looks like something maybe Jeffrey Dahmer might've penned before he was wasted in prison last year," suggested Nancy Yoder. "'Cept he'd have said boys instead of whores."

"Wrong," muttered Eddings, unable to keep silent a moment longer. "I know this poem, and the killer's use of it is really quite . . . quite . . . ingenious."

But Eddings was being talked over by the others, ignored by the others. Bill Lawrence had been visibly shivering in reaction to what he'd read across the beige wall. Merrick looked for responses from each of the three additional editors around the table, but none were speaking in sentences, just a lot of grunts and "jeezes." Each followed suit until Merrick was left again to look to C. David Eddings, a man he'd been trying to build a case against so he might fire the twerp before any chance of a pension kicked in.

"Well, damnit, what're you trying to say, Eddings? Eddings?" pressed Merrick while he smelled blood. Eddings took a moment for a second glance at the enlarged document on the wall. Even Jessica and Santiva, outsiders, could sense the tension between Merrick and Eddings.

Bill Hynek, the sports editor, attempted to reprieve Eddings by clearing his throat and saying, "Looks like the guy's a loony, Glenn, a real crazoid, if you ask me."

"You mean the author of this trash or Eddings?" teased Merrick in a cold and irreverent manner.

Eddings mouthed the words off the wall a third time, ending with, "I know these words . . . this poem. I know it, Glenn. It's familiar to me . . ."

Merrick's voice filled with venomous rancor now. "What in hell're you talking about, Eddings?"

"Hellering," replied the small, balding man.

The others instantly attacked the little man.

"Who's hell-raising?"

"What's a hellering?"

"Is that anything like a herring?"

"A red herring in this case, no doubt."

Lee nervously laughed and said, "Eddings is a hell-raiser, aren't you, C. David? Eddings, you got to lay off those liquid breakfasts."

"What would you know about herrings?" Nancy Yoder nastily remarked, causing more laughter.

"Hellering," he repeated. "I'm telling you this is a poem, circa something like 1938 and written by e. j. hellering, who was first to use no capitals, even before our American counterpart, e. e. cummings, did it. He was what you might call a little-understood, little-read English poet, but in his day, he had a large underground following. His poetry was not considered fit for polite society."

"I can see why," replied Hynek as the others stared down the long table at C. David Eddings.

"A little-known English poet," chanted Lawrence and Yoder together.

"Oh, yeah," chimed another as if he'd known all along.

Merrick said, "You mean this guy can't even be original? He's copying a poem out of a book?"

"All I know is that it's from an entirely lowercase poem by e. j. hellering, one I think entitled 'all sacrifice to the stars.'"

Jessica and Eriq were instantly interested in what C. David Eddings had to say, each on edge now, Jessica asking Eddings to continue.

"Well . . . what I remember of it . . ." Eddings caught the look of pride in Sally's eyes, glinting in the semidarkened room. "I mean, I believe it has four verses, maybe five."

"You think you can get your hands on a copy?" asked Santiva.

"Sure . . . sure, the library's full of hellering."

Nancy Yoder twittered again at this.

Merrick ordered, "Do it then, now."

"Try the Internet, Eddings," suggested Blake. "It's the quickest way to information."

"Not bloody likely," replied C. David. "If they've got any of hellering listed, it'd probably be his more-favored poems. This one's fairly arcane and a little too strange for even the ditto heads—the Internet dudes and dudettes."

Eddings stiffly stood and marched from the room, daring only a quick glance back at Sally as Santiva and Jessica followed the little round man out, Jessica wondering if the romance was just blossoming or if it had been kindled earlier.

"I was a student of e. j. hellering's work and dark style when I was at the university," explained Eddings.

"Oh, and where was that?"

"Northwestern, just north of Chicago . . . very elitist, snobbish place really, unless you happened to be in a fraternity or sorority, neither of which I qualified for, of course. At any rate, I studied modern British literature, which meant anything after 1899. Hellering falls under that umbrella, and I became quite enamored with the man's poignant ability with words; quite lovely, really, and I suppose the use of the lower-case letters—which he'd come to be known for—piqued my curiosity.''

Jessica nodded, saying, ''I remember now . . . e. j. hellering.''

''Wasn't at all hellering's idea, you know. . . .''

''What's that?'' asked Eriq.

''Using lower-case letters throughout his poetry.''

''Really?'' Jessica explained to Eriq that e. j. hellering had used lower-case letters in his signature as well as throughout his poetry as a kind of trademark, the same way that e. e. cummings had.

''It was a publisher's idea, something to put a spark into a dying art form—or rather to gather in more sales,'' explained Eddings. ''Same publisher, two sides of the Atlantic.''

They were inside the mammoth Miami Public Library, where the solemnity of the place was at direct odds with the bright, even blinding sunshine pouring through overhead skylights. The architecture reminded her of the airport. The large, open area at the center of the library was filled with palmetto plants and palm trees, basking beneath the skylights. People going about their interests created a tapestry of tap-dancing noises along the marble floor.

Eddings went directly for the nearest unoccupied computer terminal. He brought up the screen he wanted and began his search through the mammoth archives for the long-forgotten poet. Jessica held her breath for a moment, believing hellering would have so much dust on him, there would be no way he could be brought to light.

But in the next instant, with C. David Eddings pounding rapidly from one key to the next, his mouse going at lightning speed, he announced, ''Aha! Ahh, here it is.''

Eddings was obviously enjoying his sudden and surprising celebrity as the poetry guru or Obi Wan Kenobi of the moment. He gathered the call numbers with his Citizen pen, scrawling them down on a scrap of paper, and again they were off, this time for the basement and the stacks.

Eddings went directly to the book, as if this entire moment had been choreographed many times over. He smiled up at them as he flattened out the book of poems, and went right to the exact page to reveal the full poem and its title. Jessica and Eriq stared for a full five minutes at the complete poem, entitled "to breathe as 't'."

"This is incredible. Let's make a copy," suggested Santiva.

Jessica, annoyed, trying to read the verses, shushed him and returned to the poem. It read:

to breathe as 't'
by
e. j. hellering

son of t	whilst t feeds on
feeds the soul	those hungry
of woman	for touch,
in the theatre . . .	t requires little much:
in the theatre	your sweet jasmine
of want	gone sour,
and sacrifice,	your sweet belle
whilst t strikes	gone dully silent
out for the highest	in her last hour
calibre of moment:	sacrificed twice
when breath	and thrice
and life are one,	and given power
each sacrificed unto t	in her final breath
as he deems	as t deems
all the whores to be . . .	all the whores to be . . .
t gives back	t tenderly floats
all the little girls	all the little girls
in the sea	in the sea
an opportunity . . .	as opportunity . . .
opportunity to be	opportunity to be
if only for a singular	if only for one
magnificent moment	inclusive moment
the daughter of t	the daughter of t
and to breathe as he . . .	and to breathe as he . . .

> when audience cries,
> lungs full with venom
> and foam and lies,
> moments before she dies,
> an applause, a bow, arise!
> for t smiles down
> from taurus's distant eyes!
> as t deems them all to be
> flush with his breath,
> so washed by his empowering
> hand they will be flowering
> and cleansed.

"Jeez, and you say this was written in 1930?" asked Jessica.

"Late thirties, thirty-seven or -eight."

"Here I thought sheer hatred toward women was a more modern development, along with gang rapes, wife battering and nasty lyrics out of rap groups like 2 Live Crew," Jessica confessed.

"A man ahead of his time, perhaps," suggested Eriq.

"Oh, no . . . no . . . no, hellering was a gentle man, a kindhearted man. This hardly reflects his feelings, but rather is a lament of twisted souls which he simply crystallized in a moment of artistry."

"You're saying he could write this stuff objectively? That he didn't feel the rage that he wrote about? Or that he was in control of that rage?"

"I'm saying all of the above." Eddings nervously wiped sweat from his brow. "Warm in here, isn't it?"

"Yes, it is uncomfortable," Jessica agreed.

"You're a very lovely woman, Dr. Coran," he near-whispered.

"Tell me more about this guy hellering."

"He was a small man in stature, extremely bookish, not . . . not unlike myself; thin, however. A quiet man, no doubt, extremely controlled—tightly wired, as they say . . . but he had fun, his own brand of fun . . ."

"Really? Then you see this poem as an exception to his major work?"

"Oh, quite certainly. Although no doubt every man feels some rage toward women, as every woman feels some rage against men—and deservedly so, wouldn't you say?"

The remark caught Jessica's breath as she contemplated Jim Parry, how much she both loved and hated him at the moment. "Yes, I suppose I might say as much."

"But you are in control of your faculties, and you would not murder a man because of the arrogance or stupidity of his sex, am I right?"

"Agreed."

"Like the artist, you do something constructive with the rage," Eddings continued, going to a nearby copy machine to make duplicates of the poem.

She followed while Eriq, tiring of the little obit man, began to wander the lush stacks and stare at the old pictures on the walls.

Jessica shadowed Eddings and asked, "Do you mean then that the artist releases his anger in the process of, say, sculpting, painting, writing?"

"The true artist works with his emotions—all of them, the entire cascade of feelings, don't you see? Both light and dark are released through and reflected in his art."

"Released . . . reflected?"

"Yes . . . placed through a prism, released out into the world and out of himself, perhaps to save or at least hold on to his sanity."

She nodded and probed further. "And you're saying this is a healthy exercise?"

"Oh, extremely . . . like writing out one's anger or fears for the purpose of releasing the demons. Excellent and cheap therapy, if only people knew."

She thought of her sessions with Dr. Donna LeMonte, which had come to an abrupt end when Donna decided that seeing her any longer would only turn the psychiatrist's couch into a crutch. At first Jessica had been infuriated, but it had actually proven beneficial when they struck a compromise and Donna began accepting her letters as therapy, an outpouring of all her grief, guilt, remorse and anger over the years since she'd become an FBI agent.

"The criminally insane, however, don't know what to do with art; they must have a real time forum, a tangible medium, something other than clay to carve on, is that it?" she asked.

"Uncontrolled, unfettered madmen make poor music, the Mozarts and the van Goghs notwithstanding. The criminally insane take artistic license beyond sanity."

"And therefore are no longer involved in pure art but in a tainted, compromised *danse macabre* wherein victim becomes medium, weapons tools and materials to reach not creation but destruction?"

"Creation is turned inside out, yes; destruction becomes the demented means to creation, and that is why he is no longer a true artist, for now he is working less with art and the stuff of dream and nightmare to mirror his soul as he is with real time and real victims, and art becomes skewered on the lance of insanity."

"You've given a lot of thought to this, haven't you?" she asked.

"I have . . ." He hesitated. "Since these killings began, yes, I have."

"So, if I'm understanding you . . . the artist on a subconscious level may feel, for instance, that his mother was a victim to his father all his life, and this incenses him as much toward his mother as his father?"

The final copy Eddings needed required another dime, but he didn't have it. Jessica fished in her purse for change and came up with a quarter, which the machine gobbled down.

"Every monster has to have a willing victim," Eddings agreed. "The artist has a powerful sense of justice"—the hum and flash of the Minolta copier punctuated his words—"and the fact that the monster's mother, the creature who brought him into this world, nurtured or neglected him, the fact that she allows herself to be humiliated and whipped like a dog all the child's life then leads him to ambivalence, yes. By the same token, a parent, mother or father, who physically or sexually abuses a child sows the same sort of seeds of hatred, which in later years spring forth full-blown as rage.''

She wondered how much Eddings was speaking of their phantom killer and how much of himself. He seemed turned inward for the moment, as if searching in some secret looking glass of his own.

''By ambivalence, you mean he finds himself in the unenviable position of having to both protect and cherish his mother right alongside detesting and hating her?''

''She asks for it! She steps right up to it; she allows herself to be a victim, and this feeds his rage toward all women.''

''I see, I think . . .''

''Instead of going out to victimize other women as some men would do, the artistic-minded among us resolve the conflict in more creative endeavors, from building a business to writing a poem—creativity is born of pain, no matter the pleasure it gives . . .''

''Do you write poetry, Mr. Eddings?''

''I don't, no, but I have a novel I've been shopping around for years.''

''By fashioning a world or a poem inside which women are brutalized, you're saying no harm but rather good comes?''

''In the fictive world, we are in constant control of the props, the staging, the curtains, all the strings, my dear, so that it is safe to unleash these passions, however evil, however bleak and destructive or raw to the bone, perhaps so that we do not act on these same impulses in the real world as the Night Crawler obviously has.''

So this explains the little man's interest in the killer, she thought. ''And you think all men have such ingrained feelings toward women?''

''Given our genes? Given our race, our heredity, our primal instincts or that leftover-from-another millennium beginner's brain we all started with and still carry around inside here like a ticking bomb?'' He ended by poking his cranium. ''Yes, I'm afraid so. Even those of us who deny it in both appearance and deed are saddled with it, yes.''

''So you are yourself a writer, other than at the newspaper, I mean?'' she asked.

''I'm working on my second novel, yes. Working toward publication.''

''Oh, really? And what's it about?''

''It's something of a nasty little mystery coiled around the newspaper business, the spiraling injustices one young reporter faces at the hands of his superiors, one of whom is a woman not unlike the owner of the *Herald*'s rival paper, for which I used to work. If it ever sees the light of day, I'm through in this town, certainly at the *Herald*, you can bet on that.''

She wondered just how deep his anger toward this woman ran. ''But the writing keeps you sane?''

''Precisely.''

She momentarily wondered who was the real victim here in this little obit man's world, where he had squirreled away his hatred and anger only to resolve it amid black ink markings hidden like glyphs in an undiscovered cavern, an unpublished book, a poem like hellering's. Or was the true victim the target of C. David Eddings's venom, the mystery woman he mentioned? She further wondered if Eddings was sleeping with the woman he hated so much, and if so, what made him so full of rage. Her control over him? His need for her? Or the fact that he was the leak at the *Herald*, giving away the trust of his current bosses, and perhaps that of a woman he truly loved? In any case, he seemed a walking basket of nerves strolling along a needlepoint of stress as a result, all in the name of love, or hate.

In that moment she caught a glint in his eye that told her he had seen the understanding in her eye, and in that instant, she saw a reserve of anger leaving a trail just for her.

Santiva noisily rejoined them, remarking on how nudity in paintings by the old masters like Rubens was perfectly acceptable in libraries like this, but that a brown paper wrapper had to go around the cover of *Penthouse*. He got no response from either Jessica or Eddings, who instead extended a sheaf of paper to him. Santiva accepted a copy of the hellering poem. "Ahh, good," he crooned. "Now each of us is armed with words which we share with the killer . . ."

"And thoughts and emotions, Eriq," she replied as Eddings reached for her change at the bottom of the copier.

Eddings had gone silent. He extended fifteen cents to Jessica, and in the exchange she felt a well of emotions firing the little man's spirit.

"Do you think the Night Crawler is insane then, because he acts on his hatred?" she asked Eddings.

Eddings removed his glasses, cleaned them with a handkerchief and nodded. "Yes, I do."

"Then he's no artist."

"No doubt in my mind. He may think of himself as an artist; he may have once been an artist, but once the killing started in this world, the artist in him no longer existed, you see. If Picasso were ever to have killed anyone before he painted out his bare emotions of slaughter and rage in *Guernica*, then the depiction of raw murder and carnage of that awful war would have fallen flat. As it is, it moves anyone who sees it. Why? Because he emptied the vessel from which the emotions flowed directly into the painting, and not into a world without a frame. . . . Had he gone out and killed someone in retaliation for the real Guernica debacle, he could not have brought the passion to bear on a world both confined and radiated by form."

"How did we get to Picasso?" asked Eriq.

Eddings ignored Eriq. "Art both confines passion and crystallizes it. So neither a van Gogh, a Picasso, a Michelangelo, a Kipling or a Sartre, nor a Twain or a hellering, could ever have proved murderers . . . Look through the history of the world, the history of murder in particular— and being an obituary man, I know something of murder. How many true artists have been murderers? There have been far more doctors who've become murderers than writers and painters, I assure you."

Eddings's voice had risen on the final words as he warmed to his subject, and this brought a snarling librarian from behind the counter to ask them to please be quiet. Santiva nudged Jessica and said, "Let's get out of here, shall we? This place is giving me a case of indigestion."

"Everything gives you indigestion."

"I was the kid in school who always got caught talking in the library and sent to the principal's office for talking back to the librarian."

"I'll bet, and you were always talking about books, too, right?"

"You got me . . . girls."

"That would figure."

"I like a good figure . . ."

Jessica realized only now that like many men, Santiva saw little use for poetry, that it was about as significant to his life as was a little man like C. David Eddings. Eriq showed his boredom in his face; it appeared he felt the direction they had taken was costing them too much time and energy for whatever dividend they might reap. For this reason, Eriq had already stepped away from Eddings once, and now he wanted farther away from the round obituary editor, without even fully knowing why. Jessica, too, wanted away from the small man at her side whose dream of becoming a satirical novelist revealed an ambiguous creature filled with copious, venomous and passionate secrets all of his own making. He had in effect told her that so long as he regarded himself as an artist, he would remain sane, but that should that self-image ever be shattered, he, rightly or wrongly, would blame others—specifically female others; he had told Jessica that one day she could well be hunting him. She wondered how many other men balanced their sanity on such a flimsy, egoistic scale. Then she thought of Adolf Hitler, the failed painter, and Manson, the failed performer.

Jessica and Eddings followed Eriq toward the huge entryway and foyer of the library, but Eddings stopped at the desk, whipped out his library card and asked for assistance in checking out the book from which he'd made copies.

"What's he doing now?" asked Eriq, who had found himself going through the checkout gate alone and having to return to Jessica. As she stared across at Eddings, he asked, "Is it me, or does this guy give you the creeps, too?"

"He reminds me of Burgess Meredith in that old *Twilight Zone* episode—you know, he's the last man on earth, surrounded by books, but he breaks his prescription glasses."

Eriq only guffawed and said, "Let's get some air."

They waited just outside at the Grecian columns and the huge stone staircase, a place where Charlton Heston in robe and sandals might have played a scene out of *Ben Hur* if only the traffic noise, the overhead airplanes and the constant buzz of city construction and electricity could be silenced.

"Here you are," said Eddings when he joined them.

Jessica looked up to see that he was offering hellering's book of poems to her. "I'm not sure—"

"There's two weeks on it. Return it to me when you can. I'll pay any late fees." He was adamant. "Who knows, you might learn something valuable—something that might help you with the case, I mean."

"Thank you, Mr. Eddings."

"If anything comes of it, you can thank me then."

Just what she'd hoped to avoid, she thought—ever seeing him again. He obviously wanted it otherwise, however.

They parted company back at the newspaper, the original note from the killer safely tucked away in Jessica's valise. From there, they drove to FBI Headquarters in Miami, where Jessica ceremoniously turned over the evidence to Eriq.

"You'll make sure, then, that Kim Desinor sees this immediately? Are we agreed?"

"Consider it done. I read all about how she helped you in N'awlins last year."

"You have no idea."

"I have every confidence that our psychic sector will flourish in the coming years. Say, Jessica, do you think that Eddings was any help? He sure was a sad sack."

"Yeah, something melancholy about him, that's for sure, Eriq. As for being a help, who knows. Although in a sense, he's predicted for us what the Night Crawler's next love note will contain."

"The second stanza?"

She nodded, a chill running up her spine.

"Spooky, huh? And the guy was kinda spooky, too. You don't suppose he's the Night Crawler, do you? That would tie in with the *Herald* connection."

"Sure, he chooses to send his murder messages to his own paper, then identifies the source for us. No, I don't think so."

"Strange little guy in a way, kind of a mix between Peter Lorre, Wally Cox and Bela Lugosi, wouldn't you say?"

This made her laugh, which felt good. There hadn't been much to laugh about in a long time.

"Did I hear him say something about writing a book?" Eriq asked between laughs.

"As a matter of fact—"

"What could a guy like that have to say that anyone would want to hear?"

"Well, it takes a certain amount of arrogance on the part of anybody to write a book, to believe they have enough to say to the world and that people—strangers to them— are going to actually be riveted to ink markings on a page. But you've got to admit, he was the only one in that room who knew about hellering's bizarre little poem, if you remember," she defended, not knowing why.

"Yeah, yeah . . . I stand corrected. He wasn't like, you know, hitting on you, was he?"

"And what is it with you men who feel threatened by a little man like Eddings, or . . . or a woman with a brain, anyway?"

"Threatened? Who feels threatened?" Eriq threw up his hands.

"Forget it. Just get me back to Miami Crime Lab; I've got lots to do there. You promise now to get the killer's note, the original, off to Kim as—"

"Like I said"—he was annoyed—"consider it done."

· SEVEN ·

*When, on the road to Thebes, Oedipus met the
Sphinx, who asked him her riddle, his answer
was:* Man. *This simple word destroyed the monster.
We have many monsters to destroy. Let us think of
Oedipus' answer.*

— GIORGOS SEFERIADES

The Following Morning

Morning came to Miami as if all of nature's most peaceful
and warm and beckoning best had come knocking at the
door of mankind's most striking artifices—the towers of
the modern city. A brilliant, blinding Florida sun omni-
sciently and without struggle won the battle for hierarchy
here, alongside an equally rich and stunning blue sky, a sky
which acted the foil for the creamiest, whitest clouds Jessica had ever seen in any place other than Hawaii, all vying
for attention amid a lush cityscape of skyscrapers and man-
made spirals and pinnacles. For a moment, looking out over
the pearl-white sand beaches, she thought that she was back
in the paradise which she and Jim Parry had shared; imagined for a moment that he would step out onto the wrap-
around balcony here with her. A part of her soul went out
to him. He had to be feeling her, even from this quantum
distance.

But she stood alone on the Fontainebleau balcony overlooking a fresh, new paradise which was compromised once
again by the stain of human passions, and unable to answer
her own questioning heart, she wondered anew why she
had chosen to be so alone. Was there some truth in what
C. David Eddings had communicated to her, all that about
male/female roles and how you could no more escape the
hatred and contempt than you could escape the allure and

fascination, unless you were a bona fide third sex maybe? She imagined it might be called a UNIX—a completely combined mix of the female and male sides of the species coming together as in some bizarre and wonderful Clifford Simak science fiction tale.

Perhaps that was what she was—what she'd become over the years, so that she was unfit company for either male or female friends; but if so, why did she still feel so much anger from her encounter with Jim Parry, as if all the misunderstanding was his fault alone?

She nestled into a chair at a small table on the balcony, nursed a cup of coffee and nibbled at a croissant sent up from room service. Miami was a beautiful lady, but she was also an ugly lady, unfeeling with an unadorned growth across her belly. Like all American cities, Chicago, New York, New Orleans, L.A., Honolulu, Miami ate its young.

Jessica stared long and longingly out over the pristine, sun-dappled, sea-splashed, ever-renewing bay, and from this distance it created a magnificent still life; she found the ocean an immense cradle which both supported and destroyed life, its white-tipped waves beckoning and constant, and the horizon above the sea a fresco of thunderheads poised in a moment of time, painted there by some artist of colossal size, his brush and palette beyond all human proportion. It made her think of what Eddings had said about creation and destruction, giving life and taking life.

"If the Artist of creation cannot kill," she prayerfully whispered to the wind as it rushed around her on the balcony, "then God does not kill; so then God is not synonymous with nature or mankind, for both nature and mankind kill indiscriminately. Therefore, God is without guilt."

Believing the syllogism she had just created might assuage some of the pain she had stored up over the years, since her first encounter with her first serial killer in 1992, she had begun to pursue this notion when her peace was shattered by the telephone.

She reached the phone on the fourth ring, hesitant to answer, wishing for a little more time with the blue, the stark white and the brilliant pinks and yellows of the Miami morning. Still, she acted.

"Yes. Jessica Coran. Can I help you?"

Detective Quincey's overwrought voice fired back, "Dr. Coran, you gotta come right away. I can pick you up in five, maybe ten minutes. There's been another killing. The body's washed into Silver Bay, near Virginia Key."

"Give me time to dress. I'll meet you in the lobby. Have you notified Santiva?"

"I'll do that now."

"Good." She hung up and dressed quickly, glad that she'd showered the night before. She knew she'd be wading in water, so she pulled on a pair of lightweight jeans and a loose-fitting shirt. She didn't have time for makeup, but she brushed out her hair, grabbed her bag and was in the lobby before Quincey arrived. Standing on the street corner just outside was Santiva, who had also hastily dressed. But she liked the fedora. He was going native, it seemed.

The standing order to all law enforcement that they be notified immediately of anything smacking of the work of the Night Crawler was obviously being observed. It was 7:03 A.M. when Charles Quincey and his partner, Mark Samernow, pulled up to the hotel lobby.

Santiva had had his car brought around. "You ride with the detectives. Find out whatever you can about the circumstances of discovery and make sure they're—"

"—following our request that nobody touch the body before I get at it," Jessica finished for him. "Right, I know, Chief. See you at the scene."

"You all right, Jess?"

"Yeah, I'm . . . I'm fine, Chief. Just that sometimes . . ."

"Sometimes what, Jess?"

"You ever feel like a ghoul? What we do, I mean . . . sit around knowing there's going to be another victim, knowing and waiting, knowing and being unable to stop it, knowing and being unable to do anything."

"Get control, Agent Coran," he firmly said. "See you at the scene."

She climbed into the backseat of Quincey's departmental

car, and once again noted how dull and bored the man's partner was with the whole undertaking. She mentally made note of the fact that Samernow smelled of liquor from the night before and that he looked as if he'd slept in his clothes. Perhaps the case was taking a toll on the younger man.

Quincey seemed to know what she was thinking, having gazed up into the rearview mirror. "Mark's going through a tough divorce," Quincey said, covering for his partner. "It's his first."

"Oh, I'm sorry to hear that, Detective."

"Still, if the captain sees you in this condition, Mark, it'll be hell to pay."

Samernow scowled. "Mind your own damned business!" He sat sullen for the duration of the trip to Silver Bay.

"Anything you can tell me, Detective Quincey, about how the body was discovered that might help me now?"

"Same as the others, really. Naked, same signs of wear and tear, as if in the water for a long time. It's bad, from what we've been told."

"Think I'm going to be sick, Charlie," announced Samernow in a near whisper. "Pull over."

"We can't pull over, Mark! We're on our way to a crime scene."

"Then let me the hell out!"

"What?"

"You heard me, damnit! Either pull over and let me puke or let me outta the damned car."

Quincey, exasperated, pulled hard into the curb, hitting it and jarring them all. He ordered, "Get out, partner! Go on!"

"Just hold on a minute," Samernow replied.

"Get the fuck outta the car, Mark!" He glanced back at Jessica and added, "Pardon me, Dr. Coran, but lately all Mark responds to is cusswords."

Samernow slammed the door hard and Quincey burned rubber, leaving his partner to alternately shake a fist at him and double over to vomit in the grass. Again Quincey was apologizing to Dr. Coran and blinking back at her image in the mirror.

"Sometimes we all make asses of ourselves, Quince," she assured him. "Not to worry on my behalf, Detective, really . . . I understand. The job takes a toll."

"Between Mark's divorce and this case, he's . . . well, he's just stretched to the limit is all. I hope it . . . well, I hope you don't have to say anything about this to anybody."

"You have my word."

"Maybe the captain'll believe one more excuse . . ."

"But you doubt it, right?"

"So, you read minds, too?"

"Not exactly."

"Experience, huh? Some teacher."

"The mother of all teachers."

They passed over a beautiful, spiraling causeway, the water shimmering, even blinding in the morning rays, which danced like splattering nickels and dimes atop the water's glimmering surface.

"Here's our turnoff just ahead. I'll have you there in a jiffy."

"Part of me wishes I'd gotten out of the car with your partner back there, Detective," she darkly joked.

"Yeah, I know what you mean."

"So, who discovered the body?"

"Some young couple on bikes, out for a predawn ride. Honeymooners, I hear."

"Uhgggg . . ."

"Anyway, they rushed to the nearest phone and dialed 911; the paramedics and a couple of cruisers got there about the same time. The paramedics started toward the body, you know, to check it out, but one of the cops, a veteran, saw it for what it was and wouldn't let them proceed. They got into a shouting match, but we got lucky and the veteran cop stood his ground, a guy named Frank Lombardi who's seen a lot, used to be a cop in New York City. Anyway, he knew about the FBI request to leave floaters who've been in the water for any length of time alone until you guys passed on 'em. So, here we go.''

He swung the car into an area where a Medivac van and several police cruisers stood silent sentinel over a stretch of palm trees and crescent beach. Already a mob of on-lookers was at the scene, and police had snaked a yellow and black banner, flimsy in the wind, between the palm trees, daring anyone to cross the line.

At the back of the Medivac van a young couple, each in spandex wear, their English touring bicycles beside them, the woman weeping, held on to one another, speaking to each other in British accents. They looked up at Jessica, wondering about her as she snatched a lab coat from her black valise and kicked off her shoes, placing them in the back of Charles Quincey's car. She prepared to go barefoot across the sand and to wade out to the body in the surf.

Santiva had pulled in alongside them, and he called out to Jessica that he would speak to the first on-scene cops and anyone who might shed any light on the situation. She went for the sand and the water and the body.

Jessica had done this before, trawling out into water with her black valise on a float-table for a close examination of the body before anyone else got their hands on it; the fear of allowing others to drag the body to shore, tumble it onto sand, lift it into a waiting body bag, then hoist it into an ambulance to be whisked away, was the fear of losing vital information and possible evidence which might not other-wise be had, as floaters were known to drop evidence all along the path of transportation. Waterlogged, the body was literally coming unglued cell by weakening cell.

Jessica was followed out to the body by a handful of curious seagulls and a crotchety old pelican, all wondering what she had in her bag that might be of interest to them. One or two of the seagulls dipped to the body to examine it, but knowing by some instinct that it wasn't for them, they immediately fled back to the relative safety of buzzing about Jessica's head as she continued toward the corpse, wading farther out into the hip-deep water, her lab coat floating around her now like a white Christmas tree skirt.

The body had come up against a jetty of jagged stones, where it washed like flotsam in a gentle, rocking tide. The situation was similar to an earlier floater case she'd supervised in D.C., but this time she didn't need hip boots, a flashlight or a raincoat. This time the sun beat down on the awful waste and the waters surrounding her lapped against her skin with a warm tongue. In the earlier instance, the water had been frigid and black.

She recalled the other floater, a young teenager whose death had at first appeared the result of drugs and a stumbling accident. It was before her FBI days when she was chief of pathology for Washington Memorial, and it certainly hadn't been her last floater case—as much as she would have liked for it to be. But an M.E. always remembered her first floater . . .

Jessica had proven the cause of death in fact to be a blow to the back of the head which had sent the teen into the water, causing his death by drowning—he had drowned while unconscious. Armed with this knowledge, the WPD stepped up their investigation and learned that the boy's so-called friends had attacked him and left him to drown, all over an argument involving a pair of sneakers— the only article of clothing missing from the body. Life, she mused, was as cheap today on the streets of America as it was in Hitler's Germany or in the time of the Romans, who fed on the carnage of Christians thrown into the lions' dens in their sporting arenas. While technology and weaponry had stepped into futuristic vistas, man himself had changed very little since the days of his caveman ancestor, who picked up the first femur to use as a club to strike down his neighbor.

This floater and everything around the victim was different. This floater—basking beneath bright sunlight on the lip of a vast, aquamarine and lush velvet horizon of sky and water—was altogether different from the starfishlike little boy found in that filthy, stagnant stone quarry in Washington, D.C., so many years before. The boy had died in a dark little hole, a watery cemetery; he'd felt no pain after the initial blow to the head which had rendered him unconscious. He hadn't felt a thing after his school buddies had attacked.

But today's corpse, this body on this bright Florida morning, lay in stark contrast here to the screaming life all around her, both above and below the water. Both killings were unconscionable; perhaps all killings were unconscionable, she reminded herself now, but in the light of so much life, this one seemed doubly so.

The others onshore stood watching her approach the victim. A second and enormous pelican with more life in its webbed step than the first perched on the jetty rocks, squeaked and walked back and forth in anticipation that she'd feed it. The old pelican seemed resigned simply to stare at Jessica's advance. She gave neither the men behind her nor the fowl ahead of her any mind, but she could hear the muttering men at her back, and she could sense their absolute discomfort at having to stand idly by while a woman did their work for them.

Reaching the body, she found what appeared to be a pair of black serpents swimming lazily about a bloated, jellyfish version of a large rubber doll, slick and ballooned up. She instantly realized that the black asps coiled near the body were in fact lengths of hefty nylon rope, one coiled tightly about the neck, the other wound about the wrists, which Jessica could only surmise since she could not see the wrists. The corpse floated facedown, on its stomach, the hands somewhere below. She'd either have to fish for them or tug on the detestable rope that had been used to kill the victim.

She instantly saw that the body had been in the water from two to possibly three weeks, and she was grateful both that it hadn't been there longer and that the corpse lay facedown for now.

There appeared to be no superficial gashes to indicate shark attack. Even as a child, Jessica had been both horrified and shockingly fascinated by the sort of quick death the powerful jaws of a shark might bring, like the mindless devastation of a lightning strike or a blow from a speeding truck. She had always been interested in the myriad shapes and convolutions taken by the Grim Reaper to ply His trade of finality. This eerie predilection had led her to push and push her father for details about his time in the war, what he had seen, experienced and done as a medical officer. For many years, he ignored her requests, denying her any such information, not wanting to relive the horrors of the war, but when he realized that she was serious about going into medicine, about following in his footsteps to become a medical examiner, he began to come around. He began to tell her the truth, quoting Antoine de Saint-Exupéry, saying, "Horror really can't be talked about because it's alive, because it's mute and goes on growing: Memory-wounding pain drips by day, drips in sleep." When she continued to prove her genuine interest, he had told her that he had seen every kind of wound imaginable, had seen bodies without limbs or heads; but the bodies which disturbed his sleep the most, he had confessed, were the floaters. He had been in both Korea and Vietnam, where he was part of a M.A.S.H. team, and he'd seen the result of many a battle; he had also seen many a man whose body had gone waiting for attention as the war raged on, many dying in rivers and lagoons deep in the jungle, a world from anywhere.

Here in sun-drenched Miami Beach, there were no long, dark lagoon shadows beneath which to bury the floating corpse, and the water was warm and alive—teeming with life. It saturated Jessica's jeans and wrapped itself about her, catlike, filling her pores with its touch, this living saline ocean surf which foamed about her waist now where she stood. It wanted to be friends.

It also wanted to revive the dead girl, this life-asserting cradle she was nestled atop in a mockery of the fetal position, this amniotic fluid. That was why it kept lapping at this dead parcel, kept caressing it, licking at it like a favored pet anxious over its master. Yet this seemingly concerned licking was removing small parts of the deceased in infinitesimal increments with each incoming and outgoing tide. Neither time nor the tide was on Jessica's side.

Jessica stared down at the body again, leaned in over it and tried to work, steeling herself against the awful appearance death had sculpted here. The saltwater had preserved the body to some degree, and this did cut down on the stench, which would otherwise have been overwhelming. Small favor, she mused as she set to work, first studying the hands, which she'd had to tug free from below. There had been a strange reluctance, as if something was weighing the hands down and didn't want them revealed, but this inertia was followed by the equally unnerving ease with which, once freed, the hands began to float in her direction. She saw them as huge, white blowfish coming at her now.

Settling her nerves, Jessica saw that only two nails remained on the right hand, one on the left. All the other nails had popped from the combined pressure of expanding flesh and moving water. Even the few nails remaining, however, had been washed entirely clean by the ocean, and were rather useless as a result. Even if Jane Doe had fought her attacker and taken scrapings from his face or arms, the skin tissue and hair was long ago lost. But she did note that both remaining nails were jagged, torn and split, as if the victim had attempted to bare-handedly rip her way free from a stone hole, or quite possibly to pull her way up alongside the hull of a boat, obviously without success.

"Poor young devil," Jessica lamented, giving thought to who she was, what her dreams and aspirations might have been, who loved her and why.

Jessica took the two remaining nails from the right hand, and as she did so, one was caught by the tide pool and whisked into invisibility. "Damnit, God . . . give me something to work with here," she mournfully cursed.

With the extreme care that comes only of long experience, she carefully, gently twirled the body so that it floated closer to her and away from the jagged rocks abutting the victim's left side. She now examined more closely the left hand nail. There was only the one remaining, the sea having peeled away the others. This one, like the other two on the right hand, was broken and jagged.

She carefully grabbed hold with her tweezers and with a quick pull, the sun-and-water-bleached nail silently, easily came away from the rippled skin at the fingertip. This time, Jessica lifted it out of reach of the nipping surf.

Each of the victim's fingers now resembled a bloated snake, the fat thumbs like turtles. Little wonder a shark, even a small one, might find such parts of the floater an appealing strike. The hands were like pillow-sized jellyfish, squishy to the touch.

Jessica mentally placed the time in the water at between twenty and twenty-five days, something shorter than that of earlier victims, and she wondered about the difference, whether it was significant or simply a fluke. Jessica stowed away the second of the two nails she'd recovered into a vial which contained a pink gel fixative. She placed this deep into her valise and felt the pontoon platform bang against her ribs, as if the sea were upset with her for taking that which belonged to it.

She considered the stroke of luck she'd had when the right cop had come along and kept the gung-ho Rescue 911 paramedics from wading out here and dragging the unfortunate victim to shore. All her nails would've been gone had that taken place, not to mention another layer of skin. She alone would give the body the care and attention required, like a marine archeologist with an ancient artifact.

Jessica heard someone shouting from behind onshore, and this noise made her look over her shoulder. She saw Santiva arguing with one of the medics, on the verge of a fistfight, it appeared, when suddenly the medic's partner intervened and pulled his coworker away, the two of them backing off like a giant crab, kicking up sugar-white sand as they danced together until the first man finally threw up his hands in what Jessica understood to be part of that male sign language that meant control had been regained.

No doubt Eriq was protecting her honor, she thought; no doubt the medic had called Jessica a witchy ghoul woman, but in far more unappealing language. No doubt she presented a strange picture to the people ashore, to curious onlookers from hotel windows and joggers who'd stopped to stare, what with her out here performing some sort of weird travesty of a baptism to send the deceased over to the other side.

But baptisms were celebrations of life, not death. Here the recipient of the baptism was the color and texture of Styrofoam, bloodless in appearance. At the slightest touch pieces of it—pieces of her—sloughed off, floated away, marrying with the sea, dissolving, and with it precious evidence was lost. But evidence of what? she wondered while staring into the intricate pattern created against the water by the woman's floating strands of hair.

Still, Jessica's medical examination, this antibaptismal ritual, was absolutely necessary. Even so, few could realize or understand that such an indignant Eucharist might be needed. Something in people wanted to protect the body from the foul elements—including foul people—to snatch it from the water's grasp, shade it from the sun's glare, cover it with a blanket to give the corpse some semblance of modesty and dignity and consecration. She understood the impulse, but she also knew that in a capital case such as this, with a repeat offender on the loose, people like herself were rare and must be allowed to do their jobs.

She turned her entire attention back to the body. The corpse was like a plank gone pulpy with water, like plasterboard after flood damage. However, Jessica had come to the body prepared, her vials, fixatives, tweezers, bags, pliers, scalpel and more at her disposal on the floating minibarge attached to her arm. It was a contraption she had developed with her mentor, Dr. Asa Holecraft, many years before for just such occasions as this. Beneath the still platform upon which her valise rested was a swivel that took the brunt of the mild surf here in the protected bay, and beneath the entire structure, which measured sixteen by sixteen inches, were two small pontoons.

Knowing that the victim had been in the water for as long as she had told Jessica that not one moment's delay could be tolerated for certain tests. She drew a sample of the victim's blood here and now. She took a splotch of skin, a swatch of hair. DNA testing could begin immediately on these samples alone, along with tests for blood alcohol level at the time of death and for whether or not certain poisons could be ruled out. Any delay now could mean that Jessica might not be able to exact from the body who she was, precisely how old she was, and if she had been drugged or abused either physically or sexually or both before her death.

"How old is the kid?" someone from shore called. It was one of the cops, and from the size of his gut and the mileage on his weary and worn face, she guessed him to be the man who had preserved her evidence, such as it was.

When she didn't readily answer, he said, "We got a missing persons report on a thirteen-year-old runaway. Any chance it's her?"

"Rest easy, officer," Jessica replied. "This one's in her late teens, maybe early twenties. More suitable to our profile than yours."

He waved a thanks and returned to the ranks of others waiting for Jessica to finish so that they could do their jobs. She saw that Santiva had stripped off his shoes and had rolled up his pants and was preparing to join her. The jetty had seen some erosion and a large barricade had been erected where it met land, so no one could safely come out along the rocks.

Santiva waded toward her, his pants and pockets and shirt filling with water, the weave of the fabric drinking it in. When Eriq got to her, he looked over the body and watched Jessica's hands at work, curiously silent for the moment.

Jessica could not help but have the impression he was sent out by the others to report on what she was doing. Either that or he couldn't stand being with the others another second and actually preferred the company of the body and the M.E. to those ashore.

He finally asked, "How's it coming, Jess?"

"The natives getting restless?"

"I think Quincey's going to chew his fingers off. His captain's chewed his head off already over his partner's being a no-show and—"

"Yeah, well . . . some things can't be helped. But where

the hell's Coudriet and his boys?''

''What exactly happened with Samernow?'' he stubbornly pressed. ''I saw Quincey pull over and put him out. Started to pick him up myself, but decided I'd best steer clear of that one.''

''I'd say the case is . . . has gotten to him . . .''

''Quincey or Samernow? Or both?''

''Samernow for certain.''

''Doesn't surprise me.''

''A case like this, Eriq . . . it's enough to get to anybody, so go easy on him.''

''None of my concern until it gets in the way.''

''Far more important, where in hell's Coudriet's brigade? I'd expected him to come sloshing out to me a good twenty or thirty minutes ago.''

''There was another call, Jess.''

''Another call. Well, that figures, a city the size of Miami . . .'' She continued to work over the body, snipping at loose tissue and filling vials.

Santiva was having a hard time of it now, looking at the body, turning a shade of green to rival the waters.

''I mean another call's come in on another floater . . .''

''Another floater?''

''Yeah, what are the odds, huh?''

Jessica continued to work. ''Well, this is water country . . .''

''It was in another section of beach south of here. In fact, there've been two additional bodies located, three in all this morning.''

She looked up at him from her work and found Eriq's eyes now pinned on the open sea and horizon, his mouth mumbling something about how each of the bodies must have come in from a northwesterly direction, this one having gotten caught up on the jetty, the other two released elsewhere, but all within close proximity and along a straight line with the coast. As he mumbled, she kept repeating the single-word question: ''Three? Three?''

''Fraid so.''

''Are you telling me—''

"All quite possibly related, yes."

"Three . . . He gives us three in one bloody day?"

"Coudriet is overseeing one of the others and his two assistants are taking care of number three. It would appear that our man has stepped up his timetable considerably."

She nodded her dismayed agreement, cursing the monster under her breath.

Eriq turned, stared into her eyes and then at the corpse over Jessica's shoulder and said, "He's decided to really rub our faces in it, hasn't he?"

"You sure you want to be this close to the corpse, Eriq?" she asked. "I'm going to need help any minute now to roll the body. You want to get those medics out here?"

Santiva shook his head and donned a smug look that told her he was macho enough to take whatever she could. He looked down once more at the blowfish corpse and suddenly Eriq's large chest heaved like a machine, pulsating in staccato rhythm to the pump that was now in control of his stomach and spewing forth bile into his throat. He lurched away and vomited into the ocean.

"Aww, damnit, Eriq, can't I take you anywhere?" she asked, half smiling. "Maybe you had better wait onshore with the others. I'm near about done here, anyway. You can tell the others to come ahead with their ropes and nets."

"I'm all right, damnit. Whatever assistance you need . . ."

"Eriq, you ever roll a floater before?"

"One or two . . ."

"This long in the water?"

"No, but it's time I got my hands wet, so to speak. Let's get on with it, Doctor."

"Got a bit more here to finish up on first, so hold on, Eriq."

"Do you know any more than when you began?" he wondered aloud.

"Will I ever know all the answers you seek, Eriq?" She bagged and labeled a strand of soggy hair. "Yes, I'd say so."

"How much longer, Jess? Out here like this, I mean?"

She breathed in the sea air. "I want enough for my collection, Eriq."

"Cute . . ."

"I'll be done in five, maybe ten minutes. Takes time collecting fibers, skin, embedded minerals, chemicals, trace elements, all that good stuff."

Eriq guffawed, repeating her words. "Good stuff . . ."

"I don't exactly have time to train you in the ways of forensic medicine here and now, Chief."

Eriq pointed to the body and said, "Look at this . . . It's like a parade balloon. How can you tell the age from this?"

"I'd like to get a look at her throat and face now, Eriq, if that's possible. Will you gently help me to turn her in the water onto her back?"

His mortified expression said, *Jesus, Jess . . . I didn't come out here for this, but if it'll help speed up matters*, while his voice said, "That's what I'm here for . . ."

"Good, it'll speed up matters."

He extended his hands in a gesture to indicate they were there for her bidding. "Just tell me what to do."

"Just follow my lead; grab on to her right forearm, not the wrist, and her right ankle. With her hands still tied, that's going to help turn her. I'll keep her steady."

He tentatively touched the spongy flesh until it was no longer quite so disturbing to him, but this took some time.

"Got hold?" she asked.

"Some date," he muttered.

"Now begin to turn her with the tide on my count. One, two . . . three and go."

Each layer of skin was like a soggy pastry crust, more water than flesh. Tissue came off the bloated corpse like cream at the top of curdled milk as the dead girl was twirled in the water, and now the FBI agents looked into a pair of empty eye sockets, like mirrors removed from frames, the soft tissue of the eyes having been first to disintegrate or become a meal for feeding microbes, fish, crabs and the like. Nose, chin, cheeks, ears and forehead had all congealed into one puffy, featureless putty mask. No one could safely or routinely identify what the sea had sculpted from flesh. Santiva looked as if he were ready again to lose it, but he obviously had nothing left to chuck.

"The body has had long exposure to the air as well as the water," she informed him. "If it'd remained underwater, at some depth, the decay would have been forestalled to a greater degree than we see here, pressure at greater depths being equal on all sides. The flesh would've remained firmer, more intact. As it is, with the slightest touch, the skin sloughs off."

Santiva watched as a piece of the dead girl curled away with the outgoing tide, like oil spilling into the water. "What does that say . . . ahh, tell you about the body, about how it came to be here like this?"

It was a good question. "Come back at me with that one when I know more, will you, Eriq?" she asked.

"Can't get over what water does to flesh," he said, even his words creep-crawling as he spoke.

"Kinda like centuries-old books," Jessica replied. "You know, how they crumble at the slightest touch, even at the threat of a touch," she added, both fascinated and pitying at once.

"How can you be so damned clinical?" he said, and immediately regretted it, apologized and fell silent again.

She shrugged both the remark and the apology off, searching the bloated rolls of skin about the throat and trying a peek below the rope for what she might find there.

Santiva, perhaps in an attempt to further mask his earlier remark, now asked, "How can you be so sure of the age, or even the sex for that matter?" The woman's torso, stomach to sternum, was one large blimp, swallowing the breasts in bloated mimicry of the female form. The crotch area, too, was inflated beyond recognition. What they had was hardly human.

Jessica dared not, at this time and place, attempt to remove the tightly twisted rope from the bloated neck to reveal what awful bruises lived beneath.

"The other bodies before Jane Doe here were discovered without rope around their necks."

Santiva blinked and nodded. "That's exactly right."

"Did Coudriet say anything about ropes on his victim of this morning?"

"No, no . . . but that doesn't mean there wasn't any. I'll check when we get back ashore."

Jessica loosened the rope about the neck with some care, looking to find the bruises she had come to expect about the Adam's apple, the thumb impressions of the murderer. They were clearly present, and so she mystified Santiva once again by saying, "This is no copycat killing, Eriq. This is the real thing; all the marks of our boy."

"You're sure of that?"

"I am."

"Then why the ropes left on the neck and why'd he leave the hands tied? You think he did on the others, too, maybe, but then the rope came loose and was claimed by the sea?"

Her most doubtful glance told him she didn't believe that theory for a moment.

Santiva tried to salvage the question. "Or do you think the bastard is taunting us with the rope?"

"Probably . . . yes, I'd guess he intentionally left the rope for us to find."

"Then he damned sure is starting to play games with us. Three bodies in one day, intentional clues left behind. He's grown bored with the game as it was being played and has changed the rules, hasn't he?"

She quietly said, "I put my fingers in her mouth."

"What?"

"You asked me how I can be sure of her age."

"You can tell by putting your fingers in her mouth?"

"Earlier, I placed my fingers into what's left of her mouth; actually, it's easier to do with her face down if you want the top molars. I felt out the dental work."

"And?"

"She's got a full set of wisdom teeth, very few caps and fewer spaces. She's a young woman, in her late teens or early twenties."

"Wisdom teeth, huh?"

"They usually emerge between sixteen and seventeen

years of age. It follows that since hers are fully formed
that—''

''All right. . . . I get it . . .''

''I can also tell by the skeletal size and makeup, but this
is all guesswork, as you know. It'll take a complete autopsy
to be certain of anything.''

''She looks much older . . . so damned large.''

''How many floaters have you seen, Eriq?'' she asked
again.

''I confess . . . not many who've been in the water this
long, obviously.''

''The tissues expand far beyond normal.''

The skin tone was bleached, stark, bloodless, albino in
nature. Santiva couldn't rise above the awful hue, the bloating, the sloughing away of skin, as if the sea owned her
now and was not willing to allow her to be taken, at least
not wholly.

Jessica began helping Eriq understand what was going
through his mind. ''It's the glue . . . the bond between the
outermost layer of flesh and the corium below. It has weak-
ened so much that the blood has seeped out through the
corium, escaping a trace bit at a time.''

Eriq shivered in the blistering sun and the warm water.
''You mean like osmosis?''

She nodded. ''Precisely, osmosis and diffusion . . . just
like in a high school chemistry class experiment, except
this one's due to murder.''

''You just enjoy grossing me out, don't you, Jess?''

She managed a wane smile. ''Let's say you make it too
easy for me, Eriq.''

''I need a drink.''

''You'd only spew it up, Eriq.''

''I hope you're not forgetting that I am your superior,
Agent Coran. Talk like that could get you into trouble. No
Cuban can be told he can't hold his liquor.''

''A thousand pardons, Chief.''

''How much longer?'' he asked again.

''Okay . . . Okay, you win. Let's get her bagged, but
please, please see to it that those clowns on shore don't

drag her out using the damned ropes or her hair, so her hands or her head doesn't pop off.''

"They'll take every precaution. I'll see to that.''

"I mean it. The ropes have cut and burned their way near through the wrists and neck, and there's really not much holding them on.''

"I'll make them apprised of it.''

She stopped him with a hand on his forearm. "Eriq, this bastard takes delight in dragging his victims' bodies through the water at high speeds.''

Eriq gulped at the image this notion once again caused inside his head. "I recall you saying as much the other night over dinner.''

"It's pure conjecture, but I think one, maybe two of the victims weren't so much victims of shark attack as victims of the ropes, which cut off their heads and hands, allowing them to pull free of their moorings unbeknownst even to the killer. I think that's why some have come undone, as it were.''

"But these ropes didn't come loose from anywhere?''

She held up the end of the rope that trailed from the dead girl's throat. "No, no . . . This was cut with a knife.''

"Don't worry, I'll make sure the medics know the score.''

"Without giving too much away?''

"Right. Of course.'' They both knew they had to keep some information about the killer and his private moments with his victims a complete secret from the press and public. How else to know *him* when they were standing across from him in an interrogation room?

"And make sure they take her to the right morgue, Eriq, and—''

"All right, I get it.'' Eriq didn't need a second telling. He was now quickly wading toward shore, solid ground and the other men. He looked back only once, when he heard Jessica saying a prayer over the dead.

Jessica felt his eyes on her as she finished what few words she could muster for the deceased young woman, for now Jane Doe. The brilliant sun reflecting off the water was blinding, burning, hateful to the eyes, which she had kept protected with her sunglasses all the while she worked. The polarized lenses didn't distort colors like other glasses, so they had served her well here while she'd labored over the body, the lenses also cutting down on the awful glare, so much so that she could see the trail of lively, excitable minnows nipping at her feet below the surface. The miniature fish also tried to nip at the rest of the corpse, wanting it in death to give over to them continued life.

· EIGHT ·

The Churchyard *abounds with images*
which find a mirror in every mind, and with
sentiments to which every bosom returns an echo.
—SAMUEL JOHNSON

Rainbow Heaven Beach Resort

Dr. Andrew Coudriet, like Jessica Coran before him, stood
now in an alcove of the cathedral of the saltwater Atlantic,
up to his calves after having removed shoes and socks and
rolled up his pants. His own near-alabaster skin was not so
far removed from that of the corpse, and the sight before
him was beginning to be too damned common, angering as
well as disgusting him. Neither statistical data on suicides
nor accidental drownings could account for the sheer number of bodies washing up on Florida shores this season.

And all this bleached-white death was so damnably stark
by contrast to this brilliant, lovely morning with its heady
sea breeze that whispered tales of immortality in the air.
The ocean swells were mere curious creatures this morning,
rising only a soft few inches in this estuary where the land
developers had placed their pinnacle of a resort, which
shone in the sun like something out of Oz, but the swells,
like persistent, hungry dogs, kept up a constant begging at
his calves, soaking the fabric of his pants in ever-higher
increments, even as the water cradled the body in a rocking,
back-and-forth fashion.

"To and fro, lullaby and good night," he murmured to
the dead as the next swell hit and then moved away from
him, trying to take the too-heavy body back with it.

He had taken most of what he wanted from the dead girl

as other officials waited to do their jobs, each looking on from afar. One of the hotel guests, looking down from his window, had that morning stepped from his shower to a balcony and spotted the corpse as it washed ashore here. He'd immediately dialed 911 and everyone was put on alert. Coudriet was on his way to another crime scene when he was diverted here by the call.

The slightest pressure on the water-soaked corpse stripped off such vital portions as the nails and epidermal skin layer, some of which had miraculously held. He believed that if he were extremely careful fingerprints could be had from one or both hands, since the next layer of skin below the epidermis had miraculously remained intact—soupy, but intact. If he could cut away the fingertips and drop them into a preservative now, he'd have them. But it would take everything he had and another pair of hands. Unfortunately, his two assistants were on yet a third drowning victim call, likely just that—a drowning victim. Perhaps even the body which Coran and Santiva had surrounded was a simple drowning victim. He dared not think that they had three murder victims in one bright morning here. He knew for certain that door number two—this victim—was like those murdered before her. The rope burns about the wrists and neck would no doubt become evident when, back at the crime lab, Coudriet removed the ropes which still clung to the deceased, trailing ribbons of torture and abuse.

He had at first considered this a copycat killing because of the thick nylon ropes dangling about the body's throat and tied hands, but closer examination had determined this to be the work of the Night Crawler. Of this, he was certain.

The tail ends of the ropes at both neck and hands floated in serpentine loops, two trapped black vipers.

Removing the ropes here and now would only cause a further loss of tissue, and coloration with it, to the water. Best to leave well enough alone. Still, the cause of death was as evident to him as the glare of the sun over the water's sparkling surface, despite the bloating and the folds of tissue which worked so hard at masking the features and the facts.

"I'll need another man here!" he shouted over his shoulder. "A volunteer, someone experienced and capable." Even as he shouted it, he wondered who was experienced in such horror.

One of the paramedics didn't hesitate, wading out into the water in a pair of boots she'd donned earlier, announcing, "I'm your woman, Dr. Coudriet."

Coudriet found himself staring back at a woman who looked like a housewife in a Pillsbury doughboy ad, her plump form and chubby cheeks offset by the stern and steely gaze of a woman who meant business despite her pleasant, white-toothed smile. "Serena Hoytler, Dr. Coudriet. I've hauled a few corpses to you over the years. I'll be happy to assist in any way I can."

He didn't recognize her, but then he seldom mixed with the paramedics, and certainly not a woman paramedic, although he wondered how he had not noticed her before. Then again, at a distance, given her dress, she looked like a heavyset male paramedic. Still, she had a grace about her, the way she carried her weight, and how her eyes sparkled, he thought now.

"You see these surgical scissors?"

"Yes, sir."

"I want you to know what you're in for. We can have no mistake here."

"Yes, sir."

"I'm about to cut off her—the fingertips at the joint."

Serena swallowed hard but simply nodded.

He was delighted that she didn't ask him why he was going to take the fingertips.

"They will pop free and the water will eat them up if we don't do this correctly," he continued.

"Just tell me what to do, sir."

He stared at her, nodding, saying, "Good . . . good. Now just take one of the large plastic bags from my right coat pocket and hold it around the woman's hands."

Serena saw that the dead girl's hands were tied together

with thick, black nylon rope in what appeared an unyielding knot. Saying nothing, she reached into Coudriet's lab coat pocket, jerked out one of the large plastic bags and pried open its lip. She next cautiously took the dead girl's hands without the slightest recoil and slipped them into the polyurethane bag.

Coudriet closely watched the paramedic's hands, and saw that Serena Hoytler was not trembling in the slightest. "I'll make the cuts inside the bag. That way, we catch what we need, you understand?"

"Affirmative, sir."

"Good . . . good . . ." He had to hand it to her. She had grit, unlike many of the other paramedics—male and female—he'd employed over the years.

They went to work, Serena looking away whenever the scissors closed around a joint; but she couldn't close her ears to the little crunch each cut made, and she could feel the weight in the bag around the bloated hand increase with each cut.

"There, done," he finally said. "We have them all."

"Do we do the other hand now?" she asked, her voice steady.

"You lost count. I've done both hands; I've got all the useful tips I'll be taking. What few are left would prove a useless exercise."

Serena Hoytler breathed in her relief. "Glad I could help, Doctor."

"I couldn't've done it without you. Thank you, Mrs. Hotler."

"Hoytler, sir, Miss . . . Ms., actually. I divorced my husband six years ago, returned to school, got my two-year degree, finished the medic program at State, and I've been working the meat wagon ever since."

Coudriet saw that she was pretty, despite her size; her eyes were filled with a radiance he hadn't seen in a woman in a long time, and this radiance seemed to be for him, directed at him. Now, staring at her, he found her reddening up, actually blushing.

As he worked to place the dismembered little pieces of

the victim into small vials of a preservative which the sales-man had called WonderPlus Glow 19, Coudriet said, "I've been a widower for about as long as you've been single. And how old are you, if you don't mind my asking."

"I'll be twenty-nine soon enough."

"I'm old enough to be your father."

"Yes, sir, Doctor. I know, but personally I . . . I like older men."

He looked up from what he was doing to see that she was blushing even more, yet staring deeply into his eyes. He managed a smile and was instantly kicked at the same time by the body so near—as if it were vying for his full attention—the water having heaved it into his leg. His wife of so many years was gone now; still, he was a grandfather, an old buzzard, set in his ways. What could this . . . this child see in him? *Is that why you so readily volunteered to wade out here and hold hands with a corpse for me?* he wondered but dared not ask. Flirting here like this, over the body, was wrong, he told himself. He opted for what he felt was a soft joke instead. "Where does it say in your job description that you have to help cut off fingers?" He'd had outrageous thoughts all his life come full-blown and unbidden into his head, but this . . . thoughts of making a date with the paramedic over the body: No, he couldn't, he told himself now.

"My job is to assist my superiors and officials of this city as best I can, where I can and when I can, sir, and I would never, ever allow my personal life to get in the way of that, sir."

He smiled, enjoying her now immensely, loving her paramilitary bearing and speech. "Tell you what, Ms. Hoyt—Hoytler, is it?"

"Serena, yes."

"Serena, a lovely name . . . Listen, how would you like to have dinner with me tonight?"

She smiled now, the sunlight dimming amid clouds as if on cue. She was so cheery, so delightful . . . perhaps just what he needed, he silently told himself, although a deep-seated voice also said, *No fool like an old fool*, and then a third voice interceded, saying, *Nobody's a fool like the fool who lets her get away . . .*

"You just tell me when and where to be, Doctor."

"Andrew . . . call me, Andrew."

"All right, Andrew. You don't know how long I've wanted to speak your name aloud to you."

"That's . . . that's sweet," he replied, thinking that it was also a bit extreme. He wondered just how intense she might become, welcoming her intensity, and a bit fearful of it as well.

"Do you need me for anything else, Ann-drew?" A fresh twinkle shimmered in her strikingly green eyes.

"Sure, sure . . . yes, help me bring the body onto shore."

"Well, I've got my partner for that. We'll take it from here, sir. Around the others, I'll continue to call you sir and Doctor, sir."

"Thank you very much, Serena, and if you'll leave me your number, I'll call you later and we'll get together."

She whipped out a card with her address and telephone number clearly printed, handed it to him and said, "Funny, huh . . . How an ugly, awful thing like these brutal killings can bring two people together. Oh, I'm sorry. I shouldn't've called her ugly." She indicated the bloated body bobbing inches from them. "It's just so . . . so ghastly to see . . ."

"The one kind of death they don't even like to discuss in medical school, even in M.E. training, my dear Serena, is the floater. A floater is an ugly travesty of the human form. Don't feel ashamed."

"But it's so horrible that I should gain from so tragic a loss . . ."

"Just be thankful you still have feelings at all. In our business, it's hard to hold on to honest feelings, believe me."

She instantly agreed with a nod. "I know drivers, paramedics like me, who're so burned out. Why this one guy, Stover—" She realized she was carrying on too long for here and now, so she closed down.

Coudriet turned and waded back to shore as Serena's burly partner came out toward the body, the two men nodding vigorously to one another as they exchanged elements.

Coudriet clutched the small medical pouch, stuffed now with the evidence of the crime, where it dangled about his neck on leather thongs. He had all the evidence the body could give him here in the field. The rest would have to wait for a thorough examination in the morgue, in dry conditions, below bright lights and under the microscope in his lab, where he might turn for a warm cup of coffee and listen to classical music as he worked, anything to lessen the abomination of the moment.

"Take love when and where you can find it," Coudriet muttered to himself when he had arrived ashore. He turned to watch how Serena manfully hauled the body toward land, her partner hardly helping or keeping abreast. She appeared to be quite a woman, perhaps too much of a woman for him. She was intriguing, but he worried about what might become of them if they were to get involved. Perhaps it'd been wrong of him to encourage the young woman, but something in Serena stirred him even now, as he watched her wade ashore. Something deep within told him it was a feeling he should pursue, if for no other reason than to experience some much-needed excitement in his life, to feel again. It seemed a selfish reason, but he was too old anymore to fall back on falsities, to deny that he was selfish.

"There's a call for you, Dr. Coudriet," said a uniformed cop in his ear, bringing the M.E. out of his reverie. "You can take it in my unit. Follow me."

Coudriet climbed into the front seat of the man's squad car and took up the nicely contoured, modern police receiver, barking into it, "Coudriet here. What is it?"

"It's me, Dr. Coudriet, Powers."

"Oh, yes, Owen, good of you to call. Now tell me, what've you and Thorn got out at Lighthouse Point?" Coudriet pictured the lively little Coconut Grove park where the historical monument—one of Florida's most ancient and prestigious lighthouses—looked out over luscious palmettos, native cacti and other vegetation along the riverside, and the sugar-sand beach, cerulean waters and distant Atlantic horizon on the other. There was also nearby

Peacock Park and the oldest building in Miami, the Barnacle, an historic home built in 1908 which had long since become a museum offering a glimpse into Florida's past, the grounds overlooking the ocean, ideal for strolling and spotting the occasional native armadillo and raccoon. He imagined how crowded the entire area would be even at an early hour, it being a favorite haunt of both locals and tourists, with cafe, gift shop and beach all in one place. The red-brick lighthouse, while no longer operational, still acted as a beacon, a magnet, for people to come and visit, whether it was to climb her 320-odd spiraling steps or to party amid the seascape.

What an awful foil against which to examine a body in the water, he thought, even worse than doing so below the thousand or so windows of the Flamingo Hilton Beach Resort. At the lighthouse, there would be little children about, dogs and Frisbees, sand castles and sea urchins to chase. But looking around now, he saw children already locating the pool at the resort while others impatiently waited with sand buckets and colorful shovels in hand so they might hit the beach.

"So, tell me . . . what exactly do you have out there, Owen?"

He silently prayed for a stabbing victim, a drowned surfer, anything but another sampling of the work of the Night Crawler.

"Ted and I both concur, sir, that it's the work of the Night Crawler."

"Goddamn it all! Are you absolutely certain?"

"Absolutely, yes. Unfortunately, all the signs, sir."

"Were the hands bound in front with a black nylon boating rope?"

"As a matter of fact, they were, and the same rope was tied about her throat."

"Sounds like we've got the makings of a . . . a hat trick . . ."

"A hat trick, sir?"

"Hockey, Doctor . . . You remember hockey, don't you? I'm talking about mass murder, possibly three victims in a single day, if Coran's victim is also one of his."

"Oh, yeah, ice hockey . . . hat trick, sure . . . gotcha, Dr. Coudriet."

"Damn . . . damn . . ."

"So your victim, sir . . . was a bound female, nude except for the ropes with the same ligature marks, same time in the water, sir?"

"One and the same, but not so long in the water as previous victims, no . . ."

"That is unusual, isn't it?" Powers was a master of the obvious.

"Two victims, a possible third, all given to us on the same day, yes, Powers, damn you . . . damned unusual. Have you gotten what you may from the body at this point?"

"Wasn't really much to get. The usual samples were impossible to take, but yes, sir, we did what we could with what little we had."

"How're you doing with it, Powers?"

"Sir?" He sounded confused.

"Are you and Thorn holding up?"

"Well . . . yes, sir, but I gotta tell you, I really hate these floater bodies, sir, and Thorn about came unglued when we turned her in the water."

"Get everything into the lab; I'll see both of you back there. Tell the press nothing at this point, and especially nothing about the ropes, do you understand? This will have to be handled delicately. Leave it to our PR guys." He cut off communication with the younger doctor and asked the waiting officer just outside the car if he'd call in and have him patched through to the first crime scene. "I want that FBI guru, Jessica Coran, or her boss, Santiva."

The officer got him patched through to Santiva. "What's the word there, Agent Santiva? Does Coran think it's the work of the Night Crawler?" Coudriet feared the answer.

"She does indeed. And your location? What's going on there?"

"I'd say we're being courted by this bastard, Santiva. I mean, we're given three *gifts* from the bastard, Santiva . . . three all at once. He's like a fucking cat now, bringing his dead to us as prizes for show."

"Three? And that's a lock? We're sure that all three are victims of the same killer?"

"Think he's trying to tell us something?"

News of the triple-sightings of bodies by civilians and the confirmed triple-slaying by the Night Crawler, all along Miami's seashore resorts, left a burning trail of curiosity-seekers and media sharks from one end of the city to the other, one insensitive radio talk show host likening it to "beached whales—only now we got beached babes!" He didn't seem to care that the victims' families might be listening. The Chamber of Commerce, the mayor and his deputies were hastily applying Band-Aid measures to shore up the image of their beautiful city, but too late. The damage was done.

TV and newsprint media saturated viewers and readers with whatever few details had made it past the police PR team assigned to minimize the deaths and maximize the appearance that everything humanly possible was being done to end the nasty little career of the Night Crawler.

The triple murder was being analyzed by psychiatrists across the city as a throwing down of the gauntlet, as a slap to the collective face of law enforcement and Police Commissioner Orlando Everette. Jessica and others working the case were hounded and harassed and bombarded with microphones, cameras and inane questions at every turn and down every corridor.

"What're the police doing?"

"How're you FBI people helping?"

"Why isn't anything being done?"

"Who's responsible for this?"

"Will he strike again, soon?"

"Where will he strike again?"

"Is it true that one of the bodies was a copycat killing, maybe two of them?"

"Is it true that one of the bodies hadn't been in the water as long as the other two?"

Jessica and Santiva plowed through with "no comments," geysering forth until they came to a door which was off limits to press, closing it behind them, knowing how foolish they would look on the six and eleven o'clock broadcasts.

They were led through another door and down a passageway to Dr. Coudriet's Crime Lab Unit, with its adjacent morgue. Jessica still had to log in the evidence she was carrying from her seawater crime scene. Here it would be logged by date, tag number and item description and then she would have to sign off on it. This done, she could begin her lab work and analysis of the evidence—such as it was.

They soon located the evidence lockup and Jessica filled in forms which indicated every piece of evidence she had collected, each item now logged in on a manifest. This took some time, so Eriq located a nearby coffee machine and brought back a Styrofoam cup filled with the black liquid for Jessica. She hadn't had any breakfast, so the coffee was welcomed.

"What kind of monster is behind this?" she asked Santiva as she finished up the necessary paperwork, not expecting an answer. "The damned reporters want to know if and when and where it will continue—stupid questions."

"Well, it's not like we can read minds or look into the future," he replied, "but on the other hand, we are the experts. Who else're they going to come to for answers?"

"Then maybe we'd best work with the press, the *Herald* at least, as we promised?" She gulped down the remainder of her coffee, which had gone lukewarm.

"Leave that to me. You concentrate on the lab evidence."

The uniformed officer at the "cage," where the evidence was finally and completely logged, now thanked Jessica and told her everything appeared in order. She returned the thanks, tossed away her empty coffee cup and indicated to Santiva to follow her and they'd locate the morgue from here.

Eriq's request that she focus on the lab work and leave the press to him sounded like an order, so she said no more on the subject, but it seemed that Santiva felt a need to explain himself further. He looked over at her as they continued down the institutional-gray corridor and said, "People are rightfully upset, and I'd be more worried if they weren't. Hell, it's a goddamn mystery, and they want some goddamn answers, and we'd better begin to provide some or we'll be crucified along with Commissioner Everette and his guys."

She nodded in agreement, still in jeans and shirt stained with saltwater, her hair pulled back and in a ponytail. "People need to know why this is happening, why here, why now . . . to them. Only problem is, so far, God alone knows the answer to that one. But you know, Eriq, I'm wondering if anything like this has happened before, if this case can be linked to any earlier bizarre outbreaks elsewhere."

"Where multiple victims have been dumped at once?"

She brightened a bit, hopeful. "Has the computer told you anything along those lines?"

"Nothing quite like this, no. Like I said, London thinks there could be a connection, but I don't see it."

"What do you think he's trying to tell us, Eriq, sending us three bodies at once?"

Eriq shrugged and pushed a door open for her. "Your guess is as good as mine. But I would hazard a guess that he's not quite as in control of himself as he was earlier."

"He's getting careless; that's for sure."

"Not so much careless as uncaring, perhaps."

"Which could be made to work in our favor, if we work swiftly." She stopped him in his tracks and looked deeply into his eyes, asking, "He's become bored with the game that he's played thus far, hasn't he? That's what you're driving at, isn't it?"

"Let's say he's altering the routine of his fantasy. If it holds true that all three of this morning's victims were his to give up to us whenever he chose, its clear that he's become more interested in . . . well, in us . . ."

"Good Christ, you don't suppose he's stepped up his killing spree as a direct result of reading about our coming in on the case, giving the case a high profile, do you? So he plays to the press even more than ever, which means he steps up his killing agenda?"

"It is a distinct possibility, Jess."

She dropped her gaze. "God . . . so, he jazzes it up a bit. To what end?"

"To make it that much more challenging, exciting, dangerous maybe."

She nodded, relenting. "Yeah, I can see that."

They continued along the corridor, coming to the Miami-Dade Crime Lab, one of the finest in the nation, where Coudriet had already made arrangements for Jessica to view the additional two bodies that'd washed ashore that morning.

She had instantly wanted to know more about the freshest of the three kills as soon as she'd learned of the three-in-one deal allotted them by the murdering Night Crawler. That body had turned out to be the one Coudriet had attended to. The most recent kill could quite possibly tell them far more than any other body turned up thus far.

"I've had an opportunity to reexamine my corpse from the Flamingo Hilton Beach Resort," Dr. Coudriet told them. "She hasn't been in the water for longer than a week and a half, maybe ten, twelve days at the outside, but she had a condition as a child which medication has over the years stabilized—Addison's, which bloats the skin. Without her medication, bloating set in, along with the natural expansion of the tissues by the water. It's how and why I was able to get fingerprints from her." He held up a single vial with a tiny lump of flesh in a preservative gel. "It's one of Tammy Sheppard's fingertips. It was enough to ID her with a missing persons report. You want a witness list?"

Thorn hung back, but Powers rushed them with a long-bone X ray, the left femur and knee. "It's from our victim. She once had a compound fracture. You can see it here, just below the knee; and just above, here, you also see a simple spiral fracture," he said, pointing with a ballpoint pen. "It has gone a long way in IDing Jane Doe number three."

Thorn momentarily joined them, piping in with, "As for your victim, Dr. Coran, we found absolutely nothing to distinguish her. Her insides are as clean a slate as her outsides."

"And all three were strangled, repeatedly?" she asked. "The water in the lungs—"

"Lungs full to bursting, but yes, signs of multiple lacerations and strangling," added Thorn.

"—about the throat and wrists, just like the others, and that information was not released to the press," added Powers.

"So, there's little chance any one of these was a copycat killing," surmised Santiva.

"Virtually none . . ." Coudriet put aside the little vial he'd been tightly holding, a dark shadow coloring his features.

"Parents of the IDed Jane are on their way." Jessica only half heard Powers's last remark as she stepped into the autopsy rooms, where all three victims lay beneath sheets, well within view of one another, separated only by glass partitions. The three bodies looked like an endless trail of reflected images here, as if a mirror were being held up at each end.

Three in one, one after the other; the bastard had cut them loose close enough to shore to insure that they would float straight into the hands of authorities. Had the SOB learned via TV or newsprint of her and Santiva's arrival and the organization of a task force? Was that the cause of his sudden rage? Either way, all three victims had been long dead *before* their arrival. It was like stepping into a dark theater in the midst of a play about insanely vented evil. She stood silent vigil over the bodies for a moment, looking into each room from where she stood, realizing anew the enormity of the moment. In each death room lay a separate victim of the Night Crawler, three young women who had most likely not one thing in common before now, and who now had everything in common.

"If they could only talk," whispered Coudriet in her ear.

Peeling back the sheet in the first room, Jessica recognized the remains of the young woman she had earlier examined in the field. She went next to the second room and looked into the bloated face of another victim, this one with features still adhering. This one was Coudriet's subject, the young woman he was calling Tammy Sue Sheppard. Jessica lingered, looking over the remains and instantly agreeing that this woman's body was in far better shape than the one she had examined.

Thorn and Powers, like children anxious to show off a favorite pet or toy, led her to the third body, the one they had taken charge of in the field. "Want to show you this," announced Powers, his glasses bobbing as he tore away the sheet covering the swollen, draining body. There was a terrible gash in this one's left side, just below the rib cage.

"Looks like another shark bite," said Thorn.

"Measures up rather shallow for a large shark, but a small one might've done the damage," Powers instantly added.

Jessica's mind worked over the possibilities: auto crash wounds sometimes looked bad, but seldom was so large a section of flesh missing from the torso; she'd seen hatchet-type weapons such as meat cleavers do as much, but the cut would be clean—cleaved in two. "It's more than a simple fall or collision," she agreed. "And the edges of the wound *are* really quite jagged."

"In keeping with a shark bite, I'd say," Thorn quickly defended, as if his reputation were on the line.

"Try an outboard motor," said Dr. Coudriet. "I've seen outboard motor cuts a lot down here; somebody, or something like a manatee, gets tangled in one of those things, it can take out a hell of a chunk of flesh."

"Along with the sailor's rope and knot, it all points back to a boat being the killing ground," suggested Santiva.

"The bodies may've traveled a good distance across the channel, too, in which case a speeding boat may've hit her," cautioned Coudriet.

Jessica agreed but did not say so. "We have lots of work to do here, Eriq. I'll see what I can learn from the Sheppard body in particular."

Eriq nodded as he said, "Word's come down that her parents are on their way to ID the body, so I wouldn't do any carving until—"

"A little late for that," said Coudriet, recalling his bag of fingertips, "but not to worry. We'll have her presentable at the window."

"I'll go talk to the parents," Eriq said, "and I understand

there were a couple of young ladies with her the night of her disappearance. I'm seeing them today; see what they can give us. Touch base with you later.''

''Right, and good luck.''

Eriq nodded and disappeared through a corridor, led by Powers to where civilians, and parents in particular, awaited officialdom.

''No doubt having the FBI on the case will do wonders putting the concerns of the victims's relatives on hold,'' Coudriet mocked.

''We have released enough information that we can hope for some help in learning the identities of the other two girls,'' Jessica told Coudriet. ''It may take some time, but we have television and the news media on our side for the time being—''

''Don't count on that lasting very long.''

''All three of them died in the exact same manner as Allison Norris, and I suspect there will be more.''

''Shall we go to work, Doctor?''

She nodded, then went for a surgical gown and gloves. She superstitiously located her own scalpel from her bag as well, the scalpel her father had given her so many years before, the scalpel she'd used to foil Matthew Matisak's ugly plans in Chicago. She knew she'd need all the luck and skill she could muster to end the career of the heartless Night Crawler.

The autopsies on the two as-yet-unidentified young women only corroborated what they already knew, that each had died in the same manner, at the hands of the same killer. Tammy Sue Sheppard died in identical fashion, the fantasy-murder ritual precisely the same.

But it took seven hours of intensive lab work to prove it beyond any doubt, so Jessica was seven hours on her feet as they performed three autopsies simultaneously, each M.E. in communication with the other. By the time it was over, all the doctors were exhausted.

It was after six P.M. when suddenly Santiva showed up and said, ''I've got something for you to see, and there's someone I want you to meet right away.''

"Eriq, I'm beat. Can't this wait until tomorrow?" Jessica pleaded.

"There's been another letter from the killer."

She was tearing away the rubber gloves she'd used during the autopsy, tossing them into a trash bin, thinking how stupid it was to expect anyone to replace rubber gloves at every single step of an autopsy or evidence-gathering. "As we expected there would be," she said far more calmly than her heart was beating.

"Here's a copy. Read it, then meet me in the corridor. The eyewitness hasn't been exactly forthcoming with us. I thought perhaps if she talked to you, another woman, it might be productive of something."

She waved her hands in the air. "Jesus, Eriq, at least let me change and scrub and throw some water in my face, and while I'm doing that, do you think you could find me a nice garden salad?"

"Jess, this is important."

She took in a deep breath as she tore away her surgical garb and deposited it in a gurney. She then took the copy of the killer's note in hand and walked into a nearby locker room where female internists and lab technicians changed. Coudriet and the other doctors had disappeared after the triple-autopsy like scattering rats, leaving the technicians to find freezer space for the bodies.

Santiva stormed into the women's locker room behind her, saying, "I know you've been on your feet and you're stretched to the max, Jess, but I think you'll want to talk to Tammy Sue Sheppard's girlfriend. The girl remembers something of the man Tammy Sue disappeared with the night she didn't come home."

A female lab assistant stepped in from the shower, placing a towel about herself as she did so. Seeing Santiva, she gasped and shouted for him to get out. Jessica joined in the chorus of expletives, driving Eriq from the room.

"Pervert! Get outta here!" Jessica ordered, feeling good about doing so. She then sat down and stared at the strange note from the killer. Just as Eddings had predicted, the sequel verse in the e. j. hellering poem was continued. It read:

to gives back
all the little girls
in the sea
an opportunity...
opportunity to be
if only for a singular
magnificent moment
the daughter of t
and to breathe as he

· NINE ·

*Has anyone ever seen
a stranger moral fervor?
You who dirty the mirror
cry that it isn't clean.*
—JUANA INÉS DE LA CRUZ

Santiva had somehow come up with a garden salad in a plastic container, a peace offering there in the hallway. "Will you talk to the girl? Judy Templar's her name. She's told police everything she remembers twice over, but she's holding back, says she can't remember the features of the man whom Tammy Sheppard was last seen with. It's like she wants to but she's blocked it out, self-preservation perhaps; I don't pretend to know. See what you think, and let me know."

"Is she deliberately holding back?"

"I don't think it's deliberate so much as it is some sort of psychological safety valve; I think she's feeling guilty about the death of her friend, and now, learning that her death is a certainty, well . . . she's closed some doors."

"How long have you had her in interrogation?"

"Three hours. Had trouble finding her earlier. She was shopping but she didn't buy anything. No one with her. She's either a bad liar or very lonely."

"She give the composite guys anything?"

"She's been so wishy-washy and iffy that the session was a washout."

Jessica located a small snack room whose tables and hard chairs looked familiar and comforting. She sat down and consumed half her fast-food salad while Eriq paced.

"All right, I'll talk to her, but there's nothing says I'll get any more from her than you were able to."

She was up and tossing the remainder of her salad into a trash container, walking out the entry and into the corridor, going for the police precinct upstairs. Santiva hurried alongside her, asking, "Anything new or helpful come of the autopsies?"

"Just what we suspected. Same MO, same guy."

"On all three . . . astonishing. God, this mother makes me mad."

"Maybe that's his intention—and dive below that a moment, Eriq and ask yourself what that says about us."

"Hey, don't go soft on me now, Jessica. We're doing our jobs, and that's all we're doing. There's a storm sliding across the sea out there that we didn't create. We can only monitor it, locate it, warn others of it and somehow work to diffuse it."

"Warn others of it? Just how have we warned anyone outside police circles, Eriq? Just when do we get these storm warnings out to the public?"

"In due time. That's not your concern."

"Not my concern? Hell, Eriq, it should be our number one concern. You saw how young those girls in Coudriet's Crime Lab were. It's time we got some information out."

"That's just what he wants us to do, write him up big in all our papers, talk about him on our TV and radio programs. Hell, he probably wants a spot on *Oprah*!"

"Then give it to the bastard, and give it to the public. It's past time everyone knew."

"You get this kid upstairs to open up about the killer's identity, and we'll go public—hell, we'll go national. Deal?"

She stopped before the elevator as it opened, depositing a handful of medical staff. She then stepped inside and turned to face Eriq, who remained in the corridor. "Deal," she said as she laid on the close button, the doors responding immediately, closing on Eriq, who shouted, "She's in interrogation six."

Jessica saw Mark Samernow at the water cooler and Quincey on the phone at his desk. Samernow gave Jessica a half smile and asked her how she was doing, surprising her.

"Why can't anyone get any information from this girl inside interrogation room six?" she asked him.

"Ask me, I'd say she's blocked it out. Not a bad kid, really, just scared and feeling badly."

"That's what Santiva tells me."

"We could get a shrink in to talk with her, but our guy's a Freudian and not much with situations like this."

She nodded. "How're you doing, Detective?"

"Me? Hell, I'm fine since the chewing-out I got from Quince and then my captain. He sure put my butt back on track. Tells me I'm being transferred out of Homicide to Vice detail if I don't clean up my act. Guess I'll survive one way or another."

She wondered about the man's sudden transformation. He seemed to have experienced more than just a dressing-down by the boss. She followed his lead to the door of interrogation six. He was pleasant when he said, "Santiva told us you'd be talking to the girl."

"I have carte blanche with this kid?"

"All right by us."

"She's not being charged for obstruction or anything stupid like that?"

"Only if you say so, Dr. Coran."

"No, I don't think so."

She opened the door on the interrogation room where Judy Templar had patiently and sadly waited; the place was bare, cold and unfriendly to say the least, and although it had recently been refurbished with new carpeting and furniture, not even the fresh coat of paint could conceal the years-old accumulation of cigar and cigarette smoke. New or old, cigarette butts were cigarette butts, and they lay in cheap Wal-Mart crockery ashtrays instead of cheap tin ashtrays now, and something like battery acid leaked from Styrofoam cups, the litter of long nights. Add to this picture one frightened young woman who had come in of her own accord—a second time—to repeat her story, and Jessica knew a change of venue was in order.

She introduced herself to Judy Templar and they shook hands, Jessica immediately aware of the trembling within the other woman. "You've been here a long time, I understand. Your parents know you're here?"

"Why? They've got nothing to do with this." She looked a bit like the actress Molly Ringwald minus the freckles, Jessica thought, with pretty red tresses for hair; but she'd given no attention to eye shadow or other makeup.

From the young woman's tone, Jessica guessed aloud, "Your folks . . . they tell you to keep your mouth shut, to keep away from the police?"

"No . . . not exactly."

"They fear your getting involved in any way could make you a target for the killer?"

"They fear it, I fear it . . . and why not? You people haven't been able to stop him, and now they find Tammy and those other two girls, and . . . and—" Her words were cut short by her inability to breathe, gasp and speak at the same time.

"You hungry?" Jessica asked Judy.

"I'm too upset to eat anything."

"Have you lost a lot of weight since Tammy was taken?"

"It's just fallen off. Can't eat . . . can't sleep."

Jessica stood, saying, "Whataya say we get the hell out of here. You like cappuccino or Irish coffee or espresso? You know a place where we can get some?"

"Sure, the Café Promenade, just down the street."

"Take me, will you?"

"Just like that, I can leave with you?"

"No one here's going to hold you against your will, Judy; no one."

She seemed suddenly to relax. "Nobody knows how it feels, how I feel, the problem . . . the sheer size of the problem . . . of it all."

"You want to talk about it?"

"It's like a book I read in school once, a book called *The Pearl*. This man finds a pearl and he thinks it's going to bring him happiness and riches for his whole family, but all it brings down is misery. I feel kinda like that guy in the book, except I didn't find any pearl or riches; but I came that close to this bastard who killed Tammy, so close that I sat across from him like I'm sitting across from you, but it's information—that's the pearl everybody wants to get from me, but I . . . I can't bring it back, and I can't go back and do things differently . . .''

"I understand the feeling, believe me."

She sniffled and held back a tear. "It's like my memory on that one point is . . . well, gone dead. But everybody wants this pearl from me and I don't have it to give, you know?''

"Sure . . . sure . . . I understand. I shut down on a lot of bad memories myself over the years." Jessica gave a thought to her psychiatrist, Dr. Donna LeMonte, whose therapy had helped her to deal with her most frightful memories, guilts and ghosts and demons from within and without. She wondered if she might persuade Donna to come to Miami to help Judy Templar and thereby help her and Santiva's case.

"Not to worry, Judy. I won't lie to you. I'm interested in that pearl of information you're harboring, too, but my first concern is your well-being.''

"Oh, sure . . .'' This was said in the cynical voice of youth pitted against authority.

"Judy, you haven't been able to talk to *anyone* about this, have you?''

She shook her head to indicate no, her eyes swelling now with tears.

Jessica handed her tissues. "The first time you were asked to come in, you told police you couldn't remember anything. Was that a lie or were you just as confused as you are now?''

"I couldn't bring it back."

"You try talking to your family, friends about it?"

"I tried, but no one wanted to hear it, and I . . . I was in bad shape, and everybody just wanted to console me, you know, so like Mom says, 'Put it out of your mind,' and so I did . . . I did . . .''

"Judy, I'm not here to upset you, but I just spent seven hours with what is left of your friend Tammy."

The young woman grimaced and looked away.

Jessica cautiously continued, "My concerns are your concerns now; we're in this together. I'm not a cop, I'm—"

"You're FBI, I know."

"I'm an M.E. first, and I'm a woman before that, Judy. I have also been the target of stalkers, of madmen, and I have felt fear like a cold rod of steel in my bone marrow, so I think I do have some empathy with you, dear."

Tearfully, expectantly, her eyes wide, Judy asked Jessica, "Can you . . . do you think you can help me? I think I'm going crazy."

Jessica stood, came around the interrogation table and reached out for Judy Templar, who got to her feet and accepted Jessica's warm embrace. Jessica felt like a mother as she took the younger woman in her arms and hugged her firmly. The human contact felt good and right for herself too, Jessica instantly realized.

Judy's immediate family had somehow hindered her, encouraged her to hide away from the reality of what had happened, and whatever part she had played in it had been unsuccessfully buried. Jessica felt the eyes of the others on them, penetrating through the mirrored wall at her back. Behind the one-way mirror, the MPD detectives and Eriq Santiva no doubt watched and monitored the words coming out of interrogation six.

"Come on, let's get out of here. Get that cup of cappuccino. Whataya say, Judy?"

The young woman passively agreed to leave with Jessica. They gathered up Judy's things and stepped from the cold room that had made her feel only more guilty than she already did, and together they marched past Santiva and the detectives for the door.

Eriq Santiva called out, "We're not done with Ms. Templar just yet, Dr. Coran." He then took Jessica aside, leaving Judy looking alone and vulnerable again, and whispered, "Just where do you think you are going?"

The hard edge Eriq was showing had a dramatic flair that

instantly told Jessica he was playing bad cop to her good cop to reinforce her bond with Judy Templar. Good move, she silently thought as she snubbed her nose at Santiva and replied, ''None of your goddamned business, Agent Santiva! You've bullied this poor girl enough for one day!''

And with that she whisked Judy out the front door as Judy thanked her for being so kind and so brave.

''I never liked that guy,'' she conspiratorially confessed to Judy. ''Thinks he's Einstein and Mel Gibson rolled into one.''

Judy managed a laugh at this, a good sign in the sparkling Florida evening, where the shadows heralded the last rays of the sun in the west. But they were staring due east, toward Washington Avenue between Eleventh and Twelfth Streets, just down from Española Way and two blocks from Ocean Avenue and the white-sand beaches of Miami.

''Which way to this Promenade place?'' Jessica asked, feeling the light touch of the warm evening breeze kiss her cheek.

Judy Templar filled her lungs with the salt air, and Jessica did the same as if on impulse; but it was conscious mimicry. Judy said of the café, ''It looks out over the promenade walkway and the ocean, just a block or so east. I'll show you.''

They started down the alabaster stone steps of the old City Hall—now the Miami Beach Police and Courthouse Building. It was a beautiful old white structure, the courthouse, done in Spanish hacienda style with red-brick-tiled roofs all around. A newer complex and parking garage had been attached, the add-on forming the new Crime Lab. The entire municipal complex took up a good city block.

The walk to the café was pleasant and passed in silence between them for most of the way. ''It's okay to talk about Tammy, about how you felt about her, about the last night you saw her, Judy.''

''I've tried . . . but it's locked away.''

''If you can give us any information whatsoever, it may save another girl's life.''

"I know all that . . . I know . . ."

They reached the café, a delightful place with outdoor tables and chairs where the waiters outnumbered the patrons for a change, two to a table, each taking turns at improving the comfort of their customers. The view of the sea, with a waning sun reflecting off thunderheads just offshore, was spectacular, and along the walkway between them and the ocean, passersby kept the view from ever becoming static.

They each ordered cappuccino, and after a moment Jessica asked, "Would you see a friend of mine who might help you to remember that night?"

"Whataya mean, a shrink?"

"A dear, trusted friend and my own psychiatrist, who can regress you back to—"

"I'm not sure I can go back to that night."

"If you don't go back now, you will be going back forever," Jessica told the younger woman. "I know . . . I've been where you are now, and believe me, Judy—"

"You're sure it's for the best?"

"I am."

"It'll be going against my parents . . ."

"How old are you, Judy?"

"But who's going to pay for a shrink? I don't have the—"

"The FBI'll pay for it; all you have to do is want help."

"Sign off on some sorta waiver, you mean?" Judy asked. "So there's no lawsuits later, right?"

Two steaming-hot cups of dark liquid were set before them, the waiter asking if he might get them anything else. "Anything at all," he said with a hint of flirtation in his voice that Judy was in no condition to receive.

After Jessica had assured the waiter he could help them no more, noticing how his eyes roved over Judy and then her, and the man had retreated, she spoke again to Judy. "Let me tell you about Dr. Donna LeMonte . . ."

Onshore, the Miami lights were just blinking on, and in the western skies, the heavens lived up to the word *firma-*

ment. In blood-orange hues that radiated from the horizon, the sun had painted the whole area an extraordinary red-orange, save for the soft, reflected underbelly of scudding clouds which melted into muted lavenders and purples. From his sailboat, a powerful schooner-class vessel capable of great speed and endurance, Warren Tauman skillfully raised his sails to catch the new wind.

The evening before, he had plotted a course that would take him in a south-by-southeasterly direction toward the Keys, and to make time, he'd gone out beyond sight of land, to catch the strongest ocean currents.

A balmy wind had come up, and forecasters had predicted that it would grow in intensity. It was a sign: It was time for him to move on. Besides, moving over the ocean at a fast clip helped reduce his anxiety and depression.

He had a great deal to be depressed about. His plans had gone well only up to a point. His ability to ensnare his victims as Patric Allain had gone wonderfully well, but what of his master plan? The one which would please him to no end, and please his faithful god, Tauto? This plan had not materialized; in fact, there had been another major setback.

Now, even as he worked hemp into tightly twisted knots and brought the ship about to take full advantage of the tropical winds, his mind went over and over his failure, which was down below in the cabin, pinned to a wall there with judicious care so as to have no pierced parts showing, so as to have her appear as lifelike as possible: a Madonna—Mother in her prime . . .

He now set the wheel, turning the ship for sea and watching Miami slowly, imperceptibly disappear behind his tack.

He screamed at the wind that blasted his face and body. "To hell with the games here! To hell with the FBI and the MPD and all the fools who thought they could catch me or ever understand me."

They hadn't come close; they had disappointed him as well. Now, they didn't deserve his time or energy. Perhaps, elsewhere, he'd be given more attention by the press, be given the respect and awe rightly owed him. He was, after all, death incarnate.

The ship was well away now, the wind doing its work. It was a beautiful clear night in the Devil's Triangle, where he felt at home. He set the wheel and went below to stare at his last victim once more.

She hung from the wall where the hook he'd placed through her backbone held her in place. From the frontal view, she was perfect in every way, but there was the stench he could not get rid of, and there was the seeping from every orifice, despite the huge amount of absorbent packing material he'd used in the mouth, ears and other openings. He'd discovered only too late that there was seepage out the back, where he'd so meticulously placed the hook and packed the preservative material and plaster of paris about the wound. True, this had been his first attempt at whole-body preservation. But like all the others, this one was hell-bent to refuse preservation. She'd have to be chucked overboard like those before her.

"You disappoint me, Madeleine." He spoke to her, holding up a photo of a young beauty in a wide-brimmed, theatrical hat who looked like the young woman hanging before him. "And you look so much the part . . . more like Mother than any of the others ever had; in fact, the resemblance to the pictures of young Mother are uncanny. But something in the mixture, perhaps the measurements, perhaps the pervasive moisture, continues to frustrate my every attempt."

He lifted a mirror from the opposite cabin wall and placed it before the dead girl, whose form was given a lifelike pose by her outstretched and rigid arms, her feet helping to support her via the steel rods he'd fixed from the deck to the soles of her feet. He'd seen it done with the weight of tigers, so why not with her small frame?

Her body was nude. "Look at yourself; you are beautiful, Mother dear, so why do you not come to me now? Do you fear me so much?"

Warren, alias Patric Allain, looked away from the dead girl once known as Madeleine and into the mirror. In the mirror, he saw her eyes blink open and quickly close, teasing him; her fingers twitched, struggling toward life, but again only in the mirror.

Mother wanted so much to come back to him. She was trying, desperately, but now in the mirror, all was still life again, all was solidly, stolidly dead.

"Damn you!" He slammed the mirror down onto a countertop, and although it cracked, it did not break. "Damn you for taunting me and playing these bloody games, Mother!"

His anger rose, a torrential sea swell, and caught up in it, he grabbed hold of the dead girl and ripped her from her hook and the super-strength glue that held her shoulders and backside to the wall. He dragged the stiff body up the stairs to the staccato beat of its stiff limbs against the ladder.

"It isn't as if I were asking for the moon; it seems a bloody simple enough desire, a plain enough wish to preserve a human body without completely gutting it!"

He'd tried the mortician's way, to no avail; it was good for only so long. He had then tried the taxidermist's method, plying the body with the chemicals of the fish trophy people. He had apprenticed with them, had learned all their secrets—so why wasn't it working now? Because humans aren't fish, common sense told him. Each organ decayed at its own pace and in its own time. Maybe it would be necessary to gut the body—but then it wouldn't be ready for Mother to inhabit and reanimate when she finally arrived. It would be a mere shell. Could all his work, all his earlier attempts, all his experimenting truly have come to this dead end?

He had done all that his god had asked of him; he had caught his mother's spirit again and again, had made her suffer in ways even he had not dreamed possible. He had made her beg and plead for her life countless times; he had repeatedly and pleasingly humiliated her. He had raped her again and again, and still she resisted coming to him and remaining as his permanent trophy.

As he struggled to get the body above deck, he cursed, "If you had any character, any character at all, you'd have come to me long ago to end the suffering I must continue to bring down upon the innocent. Mother, you putrid bitch!''

He had released the three bodies at once, sacrifices to his demon god, so he had truly expected better; he'd expected *Her* to come to him. But this was only followed by another day and night of being unable to fill the need that drove him. And now another day had passed in which he'd had no opportunity to kill, not anyone. His god counseled patience, that the right time and opportunity would present itself, and soon, but the frustration of doing nothing—*of accomplishing nothing*—was overwhelming, boxing him up, making him feel small and useless and helpless and irritable and memory-ridden, so much so that he'd begun to wonder if he had been foolish to cut loose three of the dead at once—one of which he hadn't had the use of for very long at all. A deepening depression continued to enshroud Warren.

Still, there was meaning and reason to his rash act, since he was assured by the voice of the deity driving him—a twofold purpose, in fact. He would taunt authorities for proof of the sheer fact that he could, yes, but in addition, by releasing the rotting corpses of those he'd kept in limbo, he'd be *forced* to go after more, to harvest others, replace those lost . . . to seek a higher plane, a better union with the one power capable of returning Mother to him so that he might hurt Her for all eternity.

Substitutes were no longer enough.

It hadn't been a completely conscious path he had followed to come to this plateau of understanding, no more so than had been the decision to release three victims of his insatiable need at once. In fact, he hardly recalled cutting the ropes, and he certainly didn't recall *deciding* to leave the ropes dangling from the bodies, although he did recall *leaving* the rope attached to their hands and throats. Was it purposeful? Was it to give authorities a taste of the fox, so to speak? He knew the authorities wanted him so badly that they might do anything to stop him, but he did not believe them capable of learning about him, locating him or stopping him. In fact, releasing three bodies at once was a slap in their collective faces, the bloody bastards. Give them not one body to ponder but three at once. It was a stroke of irrepressible genius, if he could take credit for it; but no doubt the idea had been deposited by Tauto.

Now that the collective *they* had the FBI working the case, Warren—or some part of him, perhaps his Tauto, his god—had decided to be more playful, to exact a higher price from those who virtually allowed his ravagings to go on, to give them more to chew on and nightmare over. Three killings were better than one. The newspapers couldn't ignore it. The TV cameras couldn't ignore it. The world couldn't ignore it.

But it seemed they *had* pretty much ignored it. They gave it a minute and twenty-nine seconds of airtime on Channel 3; the *Herald* positioned it on page two while turning page one over to the President's arms embargo of a third-world country, a big trade agreement with Japan and the death of a local politician by suicide.

"Well, screw the whole lot of them," he told the empty expanse of ocean where he stood, Madeleine's body fighting him, the gravity pull on it so powerful it felt like lead. For a moment, he wondered if the pull wasn't from the hand of Mother, ever-teasing bitch that she was.

He looked out over the side, saw the rushing wake and realized his ship was moving at quite a clip and that he must return his attention to the helm. Earlier he had set sail for the south to see where the winds of fortune and fate might take him. And now what had begun as a mild tropical wind had become a strong southeast tack that had tagged his T-cross, filling out her sails, the breath of his god speaking to him, telling him it was time to return to more southerly regions, cast his fate in another direction, see what might come of it. He was, after all, a free soul now.

"Free of the past?" he asked himself as he struggled with the body, working it up and over the lip of the ship's starboard side. "Not hardly . . . not until Mother comes for Hers," he reminded himself, talking to the stiff body he continued to struggle to bring to the rail.

He'd readied to send the body over when it spoke to him. "You'll never be free of me, Warren dear . . ." The weight and gravity pulled the body from his grasp, but Warren held on to it by a thread, by the single hook in its back. It dangled over the side precariously, trying to pull him into the depths with it.

"Mother, you dirty, filthy, whoring bitch!" he shouted at the corpse, feeling the sting of a psychological imprisonment he'd endured all his life.

She just purred up at him from the well of the dead carcass, speaking in her cockney English brogue, "Not bloody likely you'll ever be free of me, dearie . . . not yet, anyway . . ." The dead lips mouthed the words as Warren blinked back saltwater spray and tears and the ship bounced wildly against the increasing waves.

Perhaps, he thought, *I won't ever be free . . . can't be free . . .*

"Not until you're dead, dear," the corpse said in his head.

"Mother, it isssss you! It is you! Finally come . . ." He held insanely to the body with all his strength as it fought to find the water. He struggled as the ship lurched now against the sea, threatening to claim his mother, his hard-won prize. He held on to the corpse, cursing it. "Damn you, I've finally got you, and I'm holding on!"

He almost fell into the ocean with the corpse, but suddenly the hook around the spinal column held, despite the yielding, no-longer-devoted flesh, and Warren Tauman and Madeleine careened against the deck, flailing like two fish there beneath the rain that had begun to fall.

He screamed up at the heavens, cursing Mother over and over again, saying, "Ugly hag bitch! I've got you now! I've finally got you now!"

He lay on the deck, his forehead split open from the impact of the hard shell that had crashed into him. When he realized that he had won the battle, he began an uncontrollable laughing.

The sea had turned against him, churning the ship now like a corkscrew in a whirlwind. He'd entered a storm, and rain continued to pelt him where he lay on the deck with Mother.

He went instantly to the controls below and corrected his course, set the ship on auto again and returned to the corpse on deck, where it was washing from side to side. He had to secure Mother. ''You won't get away from me so easily this time, Mother,'' he told the body. He then lifted it and carried it back down into the cabin.

· TEN ·

Thou has betrayed thy secret as a bird
betrays her nest, by striving to conceal it.
——HENRY WADSWORTH LONGFELLOW

"Clever of you to get Dr. LeMonte here in so timely a fashion, Jess," said Santiva. "How'd you manage it?"

Jessica Coran and Eriq Santiva sat opposite one another in a small and unhealthy little room which the MPD called their task force ready room. Surrounding Jessica, on every wall, were blowup photos of the Night Crawler's victims and a gallery of other, up till now, only missing young women. Some, Jessica had mentally ruled out as simply missing persons, since they were obviously not of the type that he preferred. Blondes, raven-haired women and ordinary brunettes were not targeted, and this was likely why Judy Templar—more brunette than auburn or redheaded—was spared while her more auburn-haired friend Tammy was taken. In fact, the young victims seemed to bear a haunting similarity to Jessica as a younger woman; it was a disturbing similarity, one she'd kept to herself, one which no one else, apparently, had noticed.

"I had to bribe Dr. LeMonte to get her here," she told Eriq.

"Bribe? How?"

"The FBI's picking up her tab."

He cleared his throat. "A considerable one, I'm sure."

"You can bank on it."

"What else did you promise her?"

"A week in Miami."

"Jesus, at our expense?"

Jessica nodded.

"I thought you and Dr. LeMonte were friends." Between them a VCR remote lay waiting for Quincey and Samernow to arrive for a viewing of the taped session between Dr. LeMonte and Judy Templar.

"We are friends," she told Eriq.

He laughed heartily at this.

"After all, she had to put all her regular patients on hold to fly down to meet with Judy Templar."

Quincey burst through the door with his usual aplomb and sat heavily in one of the chairs, which hadn't given an inch for anyone else but made an exception in Quincey's case. Samernow slowly followed, eyes averted, head bowed, again looking despondent. Jessica wondered at his mood swings.

She got right to business, telling the others why she had called them all in to view the tape. "I think Judy Templar saw the Night Crawler and that inside her head, she has a physical description. Dr. LeMonte and a police sketch artist are working on that as we speak. For now, I would just like you to listen and learn what you can about Patric—"

"Patric?" asked Quincey, his brows arching.

"It's what he calls himself; at least, it's what Judy Templar knows him as."

"No last name?" asked Samernow, alert now.

" 'Fraid not."

"Didn't we have another so-called witness to ID some guy named Patric, Mark?" Quincey asked, searching his memory and his partner's bloodshot eyes.

"I don't know . . . maybe . . . Yeah, one of our hundreds of so-called eyewitnesses," he sarcastically replied.

"I'm talking about the one you've expended so much energy in trying to locate again, Mark."

Samernow glowered at his partner, then slowly began to talk about the circumstances. "Said she'd been abducted by this beautiful man, taken to a boat and tied up for several days while he repeatedly raped, sodomized and choked her. Said she survived only by faking unconsciousness and escaping and swimming a hundred yards to shore.''

"When did this happen? Why haven't you told us about this witness?''

"She disappeared on us. Left the state, but we have notes.''

"Get them—after you listen to this.'' Jessica clicked on the VCR and TV screen. On the screen were the distressed teen and the exquisitely dressed, very chic psychiatrist, Donna's hair still with its salon patina and curl.

Jessica then got up and left the men to view the tape alone. She had already been through it three times. She went for a cup of coffee, running the entire scene described by Judy Templar in her mind's eye. Hearing Judy Templar's hypnotized drawl in her ear.

Donna had drawn on Judy's considerable memory of that evening when her best friend, Tammy Sue Sheppard, disappeared down a wharf and to her death.

Judy's hypnotic trance had her speaking in the third person, a technique Donna LeMonte had used on Jessica on frequent occasions, as it supposedly helped patients separate themselves from the moment.

Coffee in hand, fatigue setting in already at 3 P.M., Jessica was listening to the taped session unfold for the fourth time, without benefit of high technology, merely by using her own internal Internet:

They were all at the Magic Wand, a bar and grill built out over the river where it met the ocean at the tip of the South Miami Beach strip.

Judy frowned in a pretense of anger, repeating the name *Patric*, mocking Tammy in a half-kidding, half-angry manner, "Patric without the K, Patric without the K,'' until it became a boozy chant.

Cynthia dug back into her chair and consoled herself with her third Bloody Mary, looking and feeling grumpy. Judy remained standing for a time to watch her exuberant friend Tammy rush after her pickup, literally skipping out to the harbor boats along the planked dock, where she disappeared among the enormous floating city, her form lost to the angles and edges, the rigging and white sails and tall masts which comfortably bobbed in a lullaby of noise created by ocean breeze and swells, turning the poles and ropes into giant chimes there where the Intracoastal Waterway met the incoming ocean tide.

Judy then breathed a great sigh of resignation, turned to Cynthia and asked, ''What's the name of the boat?''

''What boat?''

''Cynthia! The one Tammy's going on. What did she say the name of the boat was?''

''Oh, I dunno . . . and I don't care,'' Cynthia said, lounging unladylike in her deck chair.

Judy suddenly called out after Tammy, both curious and a little unsure of her friend's wisdom at going off with the stranger this second time, however handsome, virile or loaded he might be. Earlier, he had taken Tammy Sue to a nearby restaurant, plying her with wine and shellfish.

''Forget it,'' said Cynthia. ''She's long gone. I thought when he came back here, that he was going to . . . that he might . . . that maybe they were . . . you know . . .''

''No, I *don't* know,'' Judy replied, staring across at her boozed-up friend. ''Know what?''

''Ask us to join 'em.''

''Join 'em for what?''

''Judy, you're so mired in your middle-class mind.''

''God, no . . . not even drunk, Cyn—''

''He's such a hunk, though . . .''

''You're serious. You were going to suggest that we all three do him, weren't you?''

''No! Yes! No, maybe . . . I didn't suggest it. His eyes suggested it. Did you see the way he was undressing me and you while he had Tammy on his arm?''

''God, you, Cyn . . . You would do it, wouldn't you?''

''Well, I didn't say I would, no.''

''A three-way! God, Cyn, you're awful.''

Cynthia flailed her drunken hands in the air. ''I just thought that maybe Tammy'd have the decency to invite us to join them, so we could get to, you know, know him, too.''

''Hell, I've taught Tammy better'n that, Cyn.''

Cynthia only frowned and waved her now-empty glass.

Judy suggested, ''Let's go have a look at the boat while they're pulling away. Get the call numbers, you know, just in case.''

''Call numbers? Planes have call numbers, not boats.''

''Boats have identifying numbers, too. It's the law.''

''I didn't know that.''

''Well, you grew up in Indiana. I wouldn't expect you to know.''

''But we can't go traipsing after them.''

''Just out to the end of the dock is all. Tammy told me the guy wants to take her to the Caribbean.''

''Tonight?''

''Well, no . . . I don't think tonight, but sometime.''

''Damn, he gets better and better all the time. Where in the Caribbean?''

''I think she said the Caribbean . . . isn't the Cayman Islands in the Caribbean Sea?''

''Geography's not my best subject; never was,'' replied Cynthia.

''So suppose she says yes and they just, you know, disappear for two weeks on that gorgeous sailing ship? What're we going to tell Tammy's parents when they call?''

''God, they'd flip, wouldn't they? I'd pay to see that.''

''So, come on. Let's at least go see the boat off.''

''But it won't look right. She'll think we're jealous.''

''Goddamnit, Cynthia, we *are* jealous.''

''Yeah, but she doesn't have to know it.''

''Cynthia, Cynthia . . . she already knows that much.''

''But to give her the satisfaction? No way!''

''Well, I'm going to watch them shove off.''

''Not before you dig deep into your pockets.''

''What?''

''This's your round of drinks, remember?'' Cynthia waved the empty again, this time like a flag.

"Oh, yeah . . . sure . . ."

Judy Templar located the necessary cash and tip, dropped it on the table and started away. She returned, however, for one last-ditch effort to get Cynthia to tag along. "You coming?"

"Naw . . . Think I'll just sit here."

"Come on, Cyn . . . We'll just pretend to be looking at the boats. She won't know any different. She's too preoccupied with Paaaaatric-without-the-K anyway. Come on, Cyn . . . Cyn . . ."

"Oh, all right, all right. Stop your whining. God . . ." They'd gotten up to go toward the dock when two young men not quite their ages intercepted them, asking if they'd care to dance. Judy whispered a bit of feminine philosophy in Cyn's ear, saying, "What is it about a place like this? It never fails that in a place like this, the losers always find us. Are we wearing signs on our backs or what?"

One of the band members hit a bad note and it brought Judy's attention full circle to the musicians and the fact that some people were dancing.

Cynthia wondered what her friend had just said even as she whispered back, "What is it about places like this that attract boys too young to drink and too cash-poor to buy *me* a drink?"

Both of them giggled, trying to mask their amusement with their hands and failing miserably to do so. Then they each grew more serious and stared at the other for the right answer to their would-be suitors.

Finally, Judy Templar said, "I'm sorry. I'm just going for a walk."

Cynthia said, "I'll dance."

That left one of the boys tagging along in Judy's footsteps toward the boats. He introduced himself as Todd Simon, said his father ran the local True Value hardware, said he went to nearby Sea Breeze High School, said he was graduating come June, enrolling at Florida State in Tallahassee in the fall, and said he thought she was "about" the prettiest girl he'd ever met.

But Judy only half listened, searching as she was for the

boat that Tammy had gotten aboard. She scanned left and right, and when she finally zeroed in on it, she found that it had already been expertly maneuvered beyond the docks, and that it was now far out into the river—so far, in fact, that she couldn't make out the name at the stern or the numbers below the bow.

A wicked thought flitted through her brain now: how she might disrupt Tammy's romantic evening so easily by reporting the boat to the harbor patrol or even the Coast Guard, telling them she thought Patric was drunk when he pulled out of port and that maybe they should just have a look. If she had the name and numbers off the boat, it would be a simple enough joke to pull off, but she would have a tough time describing the boat without the details. Still, it was a stunning sailing vessel; not too many like her in the harbor, and if Judy worked fast . . .

As she stared out at the boat, lit now with lights that made it appear enchanted, she felt another wave of distrust of the man who'd whisked Tammy off, and she felt an uncomfortable, indescribable and grim sense of concern for Tammy's well-being. She even thought about a line in a poem Mrs. Hargrave had kept shoving down their throats in high school, something by Coleridge or Keats or somebody like that which said: *A savage place! as holy and enchanted/As e'er beneath a waning moon was haunted/ By woman wailing for her demon-lover!*

Maybe she was just jealous of Tammy; maybe she felt more vindictive about how the evening had gone than she wanted to admit. Maybe she was worse off than Cynthia in that way.

"Bullshit," she said aloud, alerting her "date" to her disquiet.

Her fears were unfounded, she told herself. They didn't compute. Tammy, like herself, had gone off with strangers met at bars before, so what was the big deal? Was it something her mother always said? That if it looks or sounds too good to be true, then it *is* too good to be true?

Judy continued to stare out at the boat as it slipped further into the distance. There was something about the boat which triggered her concern, but she wasn't sure what it was. Earlier, when Tammy, Cynthia and she were idly playing with the swizzle sticks in their drinks, they'd seen the boat approach, and the sun's final, shimmering rays had made it appear something out of a fairy tale. None of them had expected the man who got off that boat to come near them, but he had. He'd honed right in on them, on Tammy in particular, catching her up with his eyes, asking if he could buy them all a drink. But soon he had somehow maneuvered Tammy away from the other two.

Judy had watched the boat approach, had seen the name of the boat and had wondered about it, but she couldn't recall it now. It had seemed odd to her, but then people named boats with words that spoke of very personal moments in their lives all the time, so the names of boats were often colorful, filled with innuendo or double entendre, like *Money Pit* or *Reckless Nerve*. Still, this one was just strange.

And there was something else nagging at Judy as she stood staring out at the boat in the twilight of the harbor lamps. Those thick black nylon ropes hanging over the bowsprit and at the stern seemed out of place, unnecessary bindings. Everyone nowadays used thick nylon ropes, but there was something odd about these lines.

"How damned many lines do you need to secure a boat?" she asked herself aloud now while the boy beside her scrunched up his nose and raised his shoulders.

Todd Simon finally replied with a question, reminding her of his presence beside her. "What're you talking about?" He continued to stand there, staring out at the distant lights of the boat with her, not knowing why.

It did seem odd to her. She knew a little about sailing, had taken a class years before, and these lines were in excess of what was normally used on a sailing vessel, although there were always innumerable lines. There was something else strange about the boat, too, something odd. Still, it was the several catch lines or ropes, thick

nylon things dangling in the water, that stayed with Judy.
Each line curled over the edge like a waiting serpent.

They couldn't be anchor lines—not that many—and yet
the ropes didn't float or waft atop the water as one might
expect rope to do if it'd simply been forgotten and left to
dangle overboard. Even now, in the dark and in the distance, she could see the reflection of light off three dis-
tinctly different slick nylon ropes. *Maybe it's just where he
stashes his beer,* she thought; *but he's got an entire galley
below for that,* she reminded herself, careful now not to ask
Todd anything more.

Each of the three lines she focused in on had some
weight at the other end. Her curiosity remained unsatisfied.

Foolish, she thought, being something of a sailor herself
since she'd taken it up in college. Why intentionally create
drag at the back of the boat that way?

Also below the reflecting light out over the bay, she
could just make out Tammy's silhouette pressed up
against his. They were kissing, dancing, making out on
the boat—so far just harmless petting. And since the boat
was sitting still now out in the middle of the harbor, it
didn't appear that Patric was going to take Tammy too
far off.

Tammy's a big girl, she finally told herself. *She can take
care of herself.*

"I sure would like to dance," said Todd Simon in her
ear. "But a walk around the pier's nice, too . . . I guess."

"You wanna dance?" she asked loudly, almost frightening her young suitor. "Then come on, we'll dance." She
had to get her mind off Tammy and Patric, one way or
another; her little fixation was only hurting herself. She
hated Tammy more than just a little for having stolen her
place beside Patric without the K. *Forget it . . . forget her . . .
forget him*, she firmly admonished herself.

Still, the entire time she danced with the heir to the True
Value in South Miami Beach, Judy thought about Tammy's
turn of luck with the accented Patric, who had deftly moved
his huge sailing vessel from port within minutes. It was so
beautiful, the kind of sailing vessel you dreamed of owning.

It was trimmed with durable East Indian teakwood, that lovely golden-brown sheen all around, always looking as if just varnished.

And Patric's eyes were so beautiful and alluring, and his voice so scrumptiously foreign, Australian perhaps, but more likely British, with a little cockney turn to it . . .

God, Tammy, she thought as she twirled about the pier to the sounds of Bob Marley's inept imitators, *you're so freaking lucky, girl . . .*

"She actually saw the guy?" asked Quincey, amazed. "She and her friend both saw him and the boat he used?"

"And spoke to him!" said Santiva.

Jessica was just reentering the room when Mark Samernow griped, "Why didn't the dumb bitch report this information when it happened?"

"She did," said Jessica.

"What? When?"

"Why haven't we heard about it sooner?"

The two detectives were clearly upset.

"She filed a missing persons report," Santiva informed them.

"In Miami?"

"Precinct 15 took her report over two weeks ago, but it somehow, through human error, did not get into the computer."

Jessica paced the room, adding, "She came back to check on progress about Tammy Sue's disappearance. When Missing Persons realized what they had, they sent her over to us."

Eriq exasperatedly added, "So even our attempt to compile and network with all existing information on the Night Crawler hasn't been a hundred percent, gentlemen. Can we get some corroboration, on what Judy Templar says, out of this Cynthia? And how do we find her? And who's this other eyewitness you spoke of?"

"I've got all the notes on her, an Aeriel Monroe. I'm still putting a lot of my notes on-line myself," confessed

Samernow. "She may also go under the name of Lovette."

"Goddamn you, Mark!" shouted Quincey, losing control, kicking over his chair and smashing both his massive fists onto the table, causing the remote to hop twice. "You've fucked up once too often on this case."

"I'll get the information to you, Agent Santiva. You'll have it within the hour, on-line," Samernow promised.

"Meanwhile, see what you can do to relocate the girl who gave it to you."

Quincey assured him that they would find her, then left the room ahead of his partner, the steam of rage still rising from his head. Before the door closed on the partners, Jessica heard Quincey say to Samernow, "You drop the ball on this one more time and we're through, Mark. I find myself a new partner."

Santiva heaved a sigh and frowned. "Let's go down to see how Judy Templar's doing with the sketch artist. What about this Cynthia, the girlfriend of the girlfriend? You think LeMonte might shake something additional from her?"

"From what Judy tells me, no. Cynthia's in worse shape over this thing than Judy, and she's been unable even to speak to Judy about it."

"Sounds like her level of intoxication that night may've been way over the limit. Just the same . . ."

"If Quince and Samernow can come up with the other witness—and near victim as he tells it—she could be a much more reliable source. If their stories match, then they're both credible. Let's give it time."

Santiva nodded and made for the door while Jessica retrieved the taped session which had come to mean so much to them all. On the way downstairs in the elevator, Eriq asked Jessica, "How much store do you think we can put in Templar's testimony?"

"My gut reaction?"

He nodded.

"A great deal. I think she's sincere and very observant."

"What she said about the ropes hanging over the

bow . . ." he mused, letting the words linger in the air between them.

"If those damned reporters had been kept back, nobody'd have learned about the black nylon rope we took off the bodies today. As it is . . . well, she told me that what got her to return to us—to authorities—in the first place was the report of the black nylon ropes used in the murders. It's not as if she's trying to put one over. I think the news about the ropes triggered a lot of pent-up guilt in her."

"And Dr. LeMonte? She believes the girl is telling the truth?"

"She says she hasn't a doubt."

They stepped off the elevator and located the Police Sketch Artist sector of the MPD, where Judy Templar sat before a man who kept asking her question after question about noses, eyes, ears, chins, cheeks, temples, foreheads, facial hair, hairlines and hair in general. Donna LeMonte stood nearby, offering encouragement.

Jessica took Donna's hand in hers; they'd become the closest of friends over the years, Jessica respecting the hard-edged, tough-talking Dr. LeMonte not only for her professional acumen but for her personal triumphs. She had herself weathered many horrid hardships to overcome problems in life, the most awful being the loss of her child to leukemia and the subsequent divorce from her husband, stemming from the dissolution of her family due to the dreadful disease. She started over late in life, returned to college, finished and went on to graduate study in medicine and psychiatry to become the best head doctor Jessica had ever known.

They exchanged warm regards now, Santiva noticing the warmth and closeness in the firm hand-holding they shared. Jessica next introduced Eriq to Dr. LeMonte, whom he had heard of but whom he had never met. Dr. LeMonte didn't work for the FBI, but she had counseled many of its agents over the years. She appeared ten, maybe twelve years Jessica's senior, but she was a strikingly handsome woman.

"You may've worked a minor miracle here, Doctor," Eriq confided. "It may be the first break we've had in this case."

"And hopefully, it will lead us to this demon," agreed Jessica.

"I'm happy that it has worked out so well, happy to've done what I can," she whispered back, "but I don't think I'm finished just yet. Judy here"—she intentionally raised her voice so that Judy could hear—"she's not doing so well on the specifics, but I think she's agreed to another round of hypnosis, with an eye to details, facial and otherwise, of our mysterious Patric without the K. Haven't you, dear?"

Judy bit her lip and reached out to take Jessica's hand now, saying, "I'm trying my best, but it's just no good."

"Do you feel up to another hypnosis session with Dr. LeMonte, Judy?"

"I'm tired, but . . . okay, I guess."

"Good . . . then we'll set it up."

"We'll do it right here, right now," countered Donna LeMonte, "while we've got this young man here to draw from your words, Judy."

Judy and the young officer with the sketch pad exchanged a long, meaningful look that ended in smiles. Jessica realized that a flirtation was in full swing. Maybe something good could come of this nightmare Judy was reliving time and again.

Donna had Judy under in a matter of seconds. She asked her to revisit the night of Tammy's disappearance, to go back to the wharf where she stood beside Todd Simon (who had already been interrogated, found lacking in information and released) and to stare out across the water at the boat and the man holding Tammy in his arms. She next asked her to return to her table when Patric was sitting across from her and whispering in Tammy's ear.

"Tell me now, Judy," began Donna. "What does his hair look like?"

"Raven-black, near blue; he may've used a gel. It was slicked back, wavy."

The artist began sketching on a new pad, listening intently now.

"His forehead, it was like . . . like . . . ," Donna encouraged.

"Covered with a shock of hair on the right, but large on the left."

"Clear-skinned or blemished?"

"Blemished a bit, like a large freckle or maybe a birthmark where the hair lay over the forehead. It was the only imperfect thing about him."

"Anything special about his eyes?"

"Oh, was there! They were so blue, I wondered if they were real or contacts."

"Eyebrows?"

"Thick but not bushy, perfectly arched."

"Anything else?"

"Set deep in, below the brow."

"And his ears?"

"His hair lay over them, but what I could see of them . . . well, they were well-proportioned, not too large, but not small either."

The sketch artist worked furiously now to keep up with Judy and Dr. LeMonte, working next on cheeks, nose and lips, in that order, Dr. LeMonte asking if he smiled a lot or remained aloof. Whether he spoke often or only when spoken to.

"He spoke mostly to Tammy, in whispers, licking at her ear, the bastard."

"How tall was he, Judy? Judy?"

"Not terribly, maybe five-eleven, six foot."

"Weight?"

"I don't know."

"Estimate it; your best guess, Judy."

"One seventy or seventy-five, maybe."

Soon the team had a sketch, which held Jessica's rapt attention as she stared into deepening, glinting eyes that seemed to be alive on the paper. After a moment, the sketch was placed on the table and turned away until Judy was brought from her trance and asked if she was ready to look at what Brent Conway, the artist, had created.

"I . . . I think so," she confided, steeling herself as Officer Conway reached out to lift up the picture.

The effect made her nearly jump from her seat. "Ahhh, God, it's—it's him," she swore. "My God, it's him."

"Excellent," said Eriq, raising a fist in a show of victory. "Excellent work."

"I wouldn't have believed it if I hadn't seen it with my own eyes," confessed Conway.

"Me neither," said Samernow from behind them. He'd obviously stepped into the room earlier. His hands were full with a file folder, some loose envelopes and a cigarette. "I've got the information on the other possible witness. She said in her interview the guy had an accent, possibly British, and that he used the name Patric Allain. Says his boat had a name on it with a T figuring prominently, but she wasn't sure of the complete name."

"Startling cross-references, Detective," said Jessica, taking the paperwork from him.

"Was Quincey able to locate the girl?" asked Eriq.

"We've got relatives we're checking. We'll locate her. Meanwhile, you've got everything we have on her." He indicated the file now in Jessica's possession.

"I'll see to it the information gets keyed into the computer; see what other kinds of matchups and cross-references we get, if any," Jessica replied to this. She then turned to Judy Templar and asked, "Does that name, *Allain*, ring any bells with you, Judy?"

Judy shook her head. "All that Tammy told us was that his name was Patric, spelled without the K," she repeated, dropping her eyes.

"What about the boat name having a T in it?" Jessica pursued.

"No, I told you, we didn't pay any attention to the name, and I couldn't make it out when I decided maybe I should, you know, pay attention."

Jessica squeezed her hand. "You've got to stop blaming yourself for this awful thing he did, Judy . . . Judy . . ."

Donna LeMonte stared intently upon the scene, and when

Jessica looked up into her clear green eyes Donna realized that the pupil—Jessica—had now become the teacher, the healer. Her words were exactly those spoken by Donna to her many years ago, when Jessica had first come to Donna seeking absolution in the death of Otto Boutine, a wonderful man who'd died because Jessica had made a fatal mistake in judgment while tracking down Mad Matthew Matisak. Boutine, Jessica's first true love, had given his life to preserve hers.

"It's not my fault, huh?" asked Judy, pulling away and going for the door. "Tell that to Tammy's parents, her sister and brother. And while you're at it, tell them it wasn't Cynthia's fault, either. Go ahead! Tell them!"

"Judy . . . Judy!" Jessica started to go after the young woman, but Donna stopped her. "Give her time, Jess."

Officer Conway quickly handed over the sketch to a female assistant, telling her to run it through the usual process and to get copies out to every precinct. He then pushed past them, in search of Judy, saying, "I'll see that Miss Templar gets home all right."

"We'll need to keep those copies in-house for now," Santiva told the assistant. "Send them out to the precincts, like your boss said, but with a word of caution. Nothing on this goes to the press as yet. We have a deal with the *Herald*, remember?"

"Yes, sir." She was off and running.

"Ahhhh, I know I'm kinda new here and all," said Donna LeMonte, "but am I to understand that you're going to willfully withhold information vital to the safety of every woman in this city, because you've struck a deal with the local press? Excuse me, but—"

"We don't release anything to the press on a case without a powwow, Dr. LeMonte, and you . . . well, you're not involved in policy, so I wouldn't lose any sleep over it tonight."

"And you're part of this policy-making, Jessica?" she asked, turning to her friend with an accusing eye.

"We've had to make certain concessions to the *Herald*. It has to do with the fact that the killer has been sending them exclusives, like I've told you, Donna.''

"Well, just how long do you intend to withhold information like this from the public so that you can play games with this madman?''

"As I said, that is none of your concern,'' replied Santiva.

She glowered at him. "None of my concern. I beg to differ, Agent Santiva.''

"Look, you're on retainer; we're paying your bill, and I understand that you're intending on a weeklong stay, to catch some sun and surf. Why don't you get at it?''

"That young lady who just left here is likely going to need months, if not years, of psychiatric support, and I've got to sift the countryside here for someone capable of helping her. I won't be able to long distance. In the meantime, she thinks she just possibly helped to save another Tammy or maybe even herself from harm by this fiend you're after. Now what in hell do I tell her?''

Santiva's Cuban ire was up. "You don't tell her a thing.''

"We'll release the sketch to the public when we as a team feel that it is right to do so,'' interjected Jessica, trying to mediate between her boss and her best friend while wondering how things had blown up so quickly.

"And not before,'' Santiva added.

"Donna,'' Jessica tried to soothe her friend, "it's policy.''

"Fine nonsense to hide behind: *policy.* Jess, I never thought you'd stoop to this.''

Donna stormed out, leaving Jessica feeling drained and deflated. She and Eriq exchanged a shaky glance and then she asked, "Why not release the sketch now, immediately? Give it to the *Herald* and everybody else.''

"You know's well as I do: It could send our man fleeing into oblivion faster than a freak wave.''

"Yeah, I know that.''

"It happened in Hawaii when you got close to Kowona, didn't it? You know that the consequences can be devastating.''

"I also know that maybe, just maybe, if we'd gotten Kowona's picture out twenty-four hours before we did, a young woman I saw tied to a wall and mutilated with swords from head to toe might be alive today."

"There's no room for argument on this one, Jess. This one's my call, and I say law enforcement and need-to-know only until we know more about this Patric Allain. We're armed now with a name and a full description. We're getting close; let's don't blow it now out of some notion about serving the public good when we know that the public doesn't heed a damn thing we say in the first place."

"How long?"

"Whatever it takes."

"How long do we withhold this from the *Herald* then?" He bit back on his lower lip. "I don't know."

"We made a deal with Merrick."

"I want to take this carefully and by the book."

"There are no books to go by here, only one's instincts, and mine tell me that—"

"I want to get a sculptor in here to do a 3-D bust from the sketch before we go anywhere else with it. Then, maybe we take it to the next level."

She slowly repeated, "We had a deal with Merrick."

"There're others to consider in this besides Merrick and Judy Templar and Dr. LeMonte, Jess."

Jessica relented, backing away. "Oh, I see . . . others." Her tone mocked him.

He pursued. "Don't give me that, Jess. You knew going in that this was as politically red hot as coals from hell; that every bloody politician and hack in this city is trying to make hay one way or another with these killings. The mayor and the city council are concerned about—"

"—about the downturn in revenues from a distrustful tourist population, I'm sure. As if all these money matters matter!"

"We don't work in a fucking vacuum, Doctor. We never did, and you of all people should know that. Wasn't it that way when you were head of pathology at Washington Memorial?''

She clenched her teeth and fists and turned away from him. She thought of the political ramifications of the case in New Orleans the year before, of the dirty politics in Hawaii that had gotten an innocent young man killed, of Chicago and New York, L.A. and D.C., where politics also ruled, holding sway over the lives of individuals who couldn't fathom what hit them until it was too late.

''Nothing's changed on that front, Jessica. It never will.''

''You told Donna that releasing the police sketch of the killer would be a team decision. Well, I'm part of this team, and I say we release it immediately to the *Herald* for tonight's late edition, and soon after to the rest of the media.''

''Sorry, but this half of the team disagrees with you, and I've got a little more experience in dealing with personalities like this Patric guy than you do, so I'll ask you to bow to my judgment in this instance.''

''But, Eriq—''

''No more discussion, Jess. For now, we leave it alone. We forward what we have only to law enforcement officials with the disclaimer that it's not to be released to the press. Meantime, I'll take what we have to the mayor's office, and from there it'll be filtered through the governor's mansion in Tallahassee.''

Her stare forced a cold, steel lance through his chest now. ''You're going to withhold this even from other law enforcement agencies until you get the nod from the governor, aren't you?''

''It goes a little higher than that, Jess. There are several former presidents and White House execs and senators who live in this state, and—''

''Christ, I don't want to hear it, Eriq.''

''And there's something in the wind about a spot on *America's Most Wanted* if we can fit into their programming schedule, which—''

''Are you nuts, Eriq, or just ambitious? I know you think you're Errol Flynn but—''

"Goddamnit, Jess, you haven't got a clue. This isn't about me or you or Tammy Sue Sheppard. This is about Allison Norris, the senator's daughter, and by God, we've got—I've got—orders, Jessica . . . orders I can't just disobey. Paul Zanek is no longer in Washington because he ignored orders once too often. You know where he is now?"

A part of her was curious about Zanek; obviously Paul was not in cushy Puerto Rico after all. She exploded, "Donna was right: Policy stinks, Eriq." She marched from the room.

· ELEVEN ·

*If the devil doesn't exist, but man has created him,
he has created him in his own image and likeness.*
— FYODOR DOSTOYEVSKY

*Somewhere on the Atlantic off the Florida Coast
The Next Morning*

Far out to sea, under clouds which painted the sky a cold, gunmetal gray, Warren Tauman thought about his current circumstances. He felt safe, secure in the knowledge that no one knew him or his deeds, and yet he wanted notoriety; he wanted the world to know what he'd done and why, for the why of it was important, and it was for this reason that he kept a diary of his activities and travels. He wrote haltingly, awkwardly and badly, however, never quite able to smooth out the words the way his mind wanted. Maybe he would never be a real writer, as he had always dreamed of becoming. Perhaps he wasn't good enough, and maybe he wasn't interesting enough, and maybe what he wrote about no one but the most bookish police science types would find the least bit interesting. Maybe the exact words of the killer would all become as arcane as some lost alchemist's recipes.

"Another reason to leave the Miami area," he spoke aloud to the dead Madeleine. "I was beginning to get bloody morbid and negative there. Not to mention the fact that women were becoming more distrustful, wary and cautious of strangers, and I was, after all, a stranger to everyone there."

He was already well below Islamorada Key, according

to his calculations. He had weathered the storm well. It had turned out to be a simple blow, over quickly and painlessly. He had spent much of his time replacing Mother on the wall, but she had gone stone cold again, not speaking or moving or showing any sign that she remained or planned to reanimate what again seemed a useless corpse.

He had spent the rest of his time at the wheel and writing in his notebook, chronicling the night's experience, the fact that Mother had finally showed herself, that it wasn't madness or a fantasy that drove him but a real quest, and a winnable one at that.

He lamented the fact that Mother's spirit and time here had been so damnably short-lived, that Madeleine's body was found wanting, for Mother had obviously and completely vacated it. He had come close, but not close enough.

In calm seas, with the ship making a steady clip of eleven knots, he pushed southward. Warren once again placed the sleek schooner-class ship on automatic pilot and began removing Madeleine's body from the wall of his cabin. This chore accomplished, he carried it, this time more gently, to the waiting sea.

At the stern, he calmly looked down into the dead features, somehow knowing that Mother wanted better, and said, "Good-bye, sweet slut; go now to our lord and master; make Tauto as pleased with you as I once was . . ."

He now watched the corpse as it slid over the side and out to sea. He watched the stiff form bob over the top of the water, caught in the ship's considerable wake.

The body, so loaded with stiffening agents and preservatives, would float atop the water like a log. "You'll be discovered shortly and they'll give chase, Madeleine. Maybe that's what we need to relieve the boredom, hey, Mother? A good chase? Perhaps that's what Mother wants . . . and we always do what Mother wants, don't we, Warren . . ."

He grimaced up at the blinding sun.

He knew that leaving the Greater Miami area was the wise thing to do. He had been seen now countless times by women, many of whom were in the company of the women he'd sent to Tauto. He anticipated a police sketch of his likeness would come next, and so he had already begun to grow a beard to add to his repertoire of disguises and makeup. Once again thanks be to Mother, who had taught him the proper use of rouge, lipstick and other assorted feminine items. Mother had used Warren in her act from time to time to play, of all things, a little girl, a daughter or niece. Mother had always wanted a little girl to dress up and play dolly with.

Mother had been wonderful when she was on stage, a force to be reckoned with. Patric Allain was just another of his own stage names, taken from his mother, whose stage name was Patricia Allain. He'd picked up the art of makeup from a life in the theatre, with Mother dragging him about from one engagement to the next, from London to the nether reaches of Scotland and Ireland and beyond, all the while giving him what she called the "best education she knew how." The knowledge of second rate theatre in Britain, makeup, how to play a part—it was all the best, most practical gift that had been left him, aside from the estate.

Mother had married well near the end of her life; fortunately, too, for she was beginning to lose both her looks and all hope of ever becoming the actress she had set out to become—slowed by a kid, she had so often reminded her bastard son, Warren.

He never knew his father; he rather doubted that his mother knew his father. She wised up later in life, accepting a proposal from a dazzled old country squire, upon whom she worked her considerable feminine wiles. The old man had not for a moment stood a chance, not since the moment he saw her on stage and showed up at her dressing room door, annoyed from the first to discover Warren there in a corner.

The old man, William Anthony Kirlian, had soon turned over everything he owned to the ravishing Patricia Allain, stage star—shortly before his death of "natural causes," or so the coroner's inquest had put it. Everyone suspected poisoning at the hand of the new wife, but no one except Mother had suspected suffocation at Warren's hand.

It was then that she had shipped Warren off to a boarding school, where he did indeed acquire a fine education, but where he also remained lonely, depressed and sullen. When he would visit Mother at her palatial estate outside London, he was made to feel like a guest, an outsider, even an intruder, for Mother always had a man around, and she liked her privacy up until the day she died, in an apparent accidental fall from a cliff near her seaside estate.

He had inherited everything, which after taxes did not amount to near so much as it had appeared it would. The estate had to be sold, and with it went most of the prestige and privilege of class that Warren had for the first time in his life enjoyed, and despite the occasional remorse at having killed his mother, over the years his only constant and tangible remorse had congealed in a desire to have killed her with more aplomb and alacrity, to have drawn out her suffering for long days and nights—and why not? Hadn't she made his life a living hell? Hadn't she made him suffer like a pet collie at her hands all his miserable life?

So he had had to sell off the gaudy estate and pocket what he could of the proceeds, and he was left with a sailing ship which he knew not a whit about. The ship, however, became his home and his one true source of pride and excitement. That had been four years ago, and since then he had killed many, many women. He didn't at first know why he was driven to do so, knowing only that he must, and that he could not control the urge.

When he had killed his mother that day on the precipice, it had come about in a moment of passion born of sheer rage when she told him that he must earn his own way, that she could not in clear conscience provide for his needs a moment longer after having financed his education at Southwark and having learned of the indelicate indiscretion he had committed with another boy there. Southwark wanted no part of Warren, so she had nowhere to send him, and this angered her.

"After I die, Warren, then all this will be yours, Warren, but until that time, Warren, I would like to see you strike

out on your own, Warren, make a go of it, Warren, make
Mummy proud, Warren, make as much of yourself as
humanly possible, Warren . . . show me some backbone,
Warren . . . After all, you have an education now, Warren,
far more than when I started out in life. Then . . . well,
then . . . we will see . . . don't you see that it's for your best,
Warren?''

They were the last words she ever uttered to him, the
last sounds aside from the scream that echoed all the way
back up to him.

Since that day, he found himself inextricably drawn to
kill others, women in particular. He had killed things before, small birds and animals, and there was the incident at
Southwark in which he had tortured the homosexual boy
who had made advances. He had lured the boy to a desolate
place and kept him trapped there for forty-eight hours before anyone suspected him of having a hand in the disappearance. The nude boy's body was covered in welts and
bite marks. He hadn't killed the boy, but he might well
have, if given more time.

And nowadays he continued to torture and kill, but it all
had a purpose, a reason. He targeted only women who reminded him of his mother when she was a young, stupid
little tramp. His kill spree had begun with whores and prostitutes along the Thames River in the White Chapel District,
women who were closer in age to Mother when she'd died,
but he had slowly worked his phantasm of murdering the
old sot over and over again so often that he grew tired of
the game; he wanted more, especially now. Nowadays, his
greatest dream was to kill Mother's spirit, the soul spirit
which visited and tormented his mind whenever he slept,
and he had to destroy it before Tauto, in His eyes.

Warren had not known Tauto when he had killed out of
rage. Now he wanted to introduce Mother to Tauto, in the
only way that such an introduction could occur. He also
wanted to destroy her at an early age, before she turned
twenty, before she had an opportunity to turn his life into
a shambles. He wanted her when she was not much more
than a child. He wanted most to kill her at a time in her

life *before* she had given birth to him.

The corpse he'd just thrown overboard was now out of sight, flushed from the wake of his ship like so much refuse. He wondered what authorities would make of this last one, all those chemicals pumped into her . . . the hook in her back . . .

It would be such a deviation from the others. He had experimented on some of the others' limbs, a hand here, a leg there, but this was the first time he had left one whole, preserved body. It would serve only to confuse and anger the faceless people who pursued him. The recent papers carried a photograph of a pair of FBI investigators, one a man, the other a woman, who were in dogged pursuit of clues leading to his whereabouts, or so the reporter said. A total exaggeration, so far as Warren could make out. Still, he knew that when his skin told him to get, he should get, and so he had instinctively decided to flee.

He returned now to the wheel and steered his ship, the ocean pleased with his work, in harmony with him. He was one of two beings in the universe which the ocean smiled upon. The other was his god.

He returned in his mind to those first killings in London. He had enjoyed each better than the one before, his ritual of humiliating and creating suffering in his victims becoming more and more elaborate as he went, more exciting and satisfying as he continued building onto the ritual labyrinth of inducing pain and horror in his prey. They were all so easy to kill; but it took some imagination to torture them, and so his imagination grew.

After his thirteenth victim, he began to keep a record of his activities—''perversions,'' the press called them. His diary chronicled his methods of torture, but also his work in attempting to perfectly preserve one of his victims—a thing which if accomplished, he could stop killing, he was sure. If he could find a way to capture Mother's soul and keep it captive inside a perfectly preserved double of her, then he wouldn't have to go on killing; there would be no point, and he would be at peace with Tauto.

When he'd first started killing, most of the women, at

first, little resembled his mother except in age and habit—
they were all whores. The *London Times* and other newspapers in England had called him a modern-day Jack the
Ripper because he worked the infamous White Chapel District where the Ripper had done his work. But he was no
ripper. He took no delight in mutilating the beautiful female
form, and he detested the odor and the sight of blood. He
didn't cut the bodies open. In fact, other than suffocating
and drowning them, he barely touched his victims during
his first forays into murder. At first, he was rather shy about
it, actually, rushing it and running quickly from the deed.

The elaborate scheme to somehow fetch his mother from
the nether regions into which he himself had sent her, to
return her to himself so that he might inflict eternal suffering on her, only evolved over long time and experience
with murder.

Those first fledgling attempts at feeling something, of
making contact with his own soul, with which he had become unfamiliar, were important bridges. They were
bridges leading to the soul of his dead mother as well, although he had been awkward, crude and blind in his murdering meanderings. Only when he found the teachings of
Tauto and read them, understanding that all things in life
carried a spiritual double, did he realize that it might be
possible to recapture the moment of murdering his mother
through the soul of a stand-in. Rudimentary as they were,
those first killings became the cornerstone upon which he
had built a relationship with his god and his deceased
mother.

Tauto, in his great wisdom, told Warren to leave London
and to seek his mother's image in younger women, women
who in every way mirrored her as she was the year of
Warren's birth. He calculated that she was between sixteen and eighteen when she gave birth to him, so he
had sailed from England to America in search of a fresh
start and a fresh approach to his problem. Now, in the land
of milk and honey, along the sun-drenched coasts of Florida, he had found what he had come in search of many
times over . . .

Still, he remained unfulfilled, his need insatiable, so long as Mother remained aloof and out of reach, capable of tormenting him at will.

He brought his pleasure craft into the wind and looked forward to his return trip to the Keys and beyond, perhaps a little trip to the Gulf of Mexico and the east coast of Florida. He'd heard that Tampa Bay and the Naples area were both beautiful this time of year . . .

Jessica yawned even as she worked over her microscope at the crime lab this morning. She hadn't gotten much in the way of sleep the night before, tossing and turning due to her earlier argument with Eriq and a late-night phone call from Dr. Kim Desinor which only solidified the fact that their killer was a sailor, and an elusive one at that. The psychic's take on the killer told Jessica she was looking for a man with a frightful multiple personality disorder, possibly schizophrenic, with a brain full of voices, certainly delusional and possibly hallucinating.

"This man convinces people to go off with him, Kim," she'd challenged Desinor. "How can he be hallucinating and in control at the same time?"

"I get the picture of a complex personality—complex."

"Say that again."

"I mean, he plots out his actions against his victims, Jess, but he's also quite mad, not unlike your old friend Matisak."

"I get the picture."

"And he's a man of many disguises who has seawater for blood."

Jessica pictured the pretty psychic at the other end of the line. She was sharp and intelligent and quick, and most of the time, in one fashion or another, she was right, her instincts dead-on. However, Jessica had learned to take what Kim said with caution. She saw signposts and symbols as often as she saw actualities, so every word had to be weighed in the context of its possibly being a reflection of some other meaning.

"Your killer has many ties, but he has no ties."

Enough with the riddles, Jessica thought, but kept silent.

"He is tied to his past. He is filled with venomous anger, a fiery rage, and he is on some sort of bizarre quest to locate something he lost as a child—some great object he must regain."

"He's murdering young women to regain something he's lost. Now that's a bulletin, Kim," Jessica replied, unable to hold back on her sarcasm any longer. "That hardly narrows my search."

"There is one other thing."

It sounded as if Kim was about to give out with the good stuff. "Go on."

"The letter T which he signs with . . ."

"Yes, well, we've come to expect tea with this crumpet."

Kim paused before saying, "Cute, Jess. I read about the accent, and that maybe the guy is British. You're thinking there may be some validity to it, but be cautious. He's a player, a thespian if you get my drift, so the accent could well be part of his act."

"Are you saying he's a pro?"

"If not, very close to it, yes. Now, back to the cross-T signature."

"What can you tell me about it?"

"It's actually the sign of the Tau Cross; a cross in the shape of a T. I had a friend in the department, Peter Ames, an expert on ancient markings, look it over."

"And?"

"He says it has an ancient and rather mysterious history. It has a history as a Christian marking, but there's also an offshoot religion called the Tau which keeps coming up in the literature."

"And? What about it?"

"Well, very little is known about it, but he says one thing is sure."

"What's that, Kim?"

"Human sacrifice was part of the deal."

"Why am I not surprised?"

"One other thing, Jess."

"Yes?"

"He's like a confused or wounded animal—he's extremely dangerous."

"We know that much."

"He makes love to the dead; he's a necrophile."

"There's no way to know that scientifically since all evidence of such . . . such perversion was washed away by the sea. We know the women were raped, but how can you be sure he . . . he does their bodies?"

"I saw it."

Over the course of the rest of that night, any pleasant dream Jessica conjured churned itself into a convoluted nightmare, her rest shattered by the screams of modern human sacrifices.

Now bleary-eyed, Jessica sat in the lab, contemplating microscopic trace evidence taken from the victims and at the same time recalling Dr. Kim Desinor's psychic and psychological profile of the killer. They seemed no closer to catching this cretin than the day they'd arrived in Florida, and this frustrated her to no end.

A lab technician called to Jessica, bringing her out of the scope and her reverie. "There's a phone call for you. Press three," said the Oriental technician, a small woman with a sweet smile and smiling eyes.

She lifted the phone beside her to hear the warm hello of Dr. John T. Thorpe. J.T., her lab director and friend back at Quantico, had been put onto something which he had kept secret from Jessica up till now.

"Your timing is impeccable, J.T."

"As always," he joked.

"I'm right this moment staring into my microscope, looking at the slide which you FedExed me yesterday." With the phone in one hand, her microscope at the other, she and J.T. talked about the strange new findings in the Night Crawler case.

"What does this mean, J.T.?" she asked even though she knew.

"You tell me," he replied. "I'm really in no position to say, Jess."

"Well, is it a case of accidental contamination somewhere along the journey of the evidence chain? Did the botching come as a result of those people in Islamorada Key, maybe?"

"Well, they're researchers; what do they know about handling forensic evidence?"

"We've got to know if this was intentional—committed by the killer—or accidental, committed by Wainwright or someone in Coudriet's lab, here in Miami."

J.T.'s voice was suddenly thick with disbelief. "Jess, if it's intentional, then the chemical agents were introduced by the monster behind the killings . . ."

"And what does that tell you?"

"He's into some sort of preserve-the-flesh fetish?"

"On top of everything else. We have reason to suspect he's a necrophile, and if so, attempting to preserve the body for as long as he can fits."

"So an icebox isn't good enough for this guy."

"Cold bruises the skin tone, discolors the product." She continued to stare through the dual ocular eyepiece of the electron comparison microscope, to assure herself that what she was looking at made sense in light of the information J.T. had found back at Quantico, where he'd put their best chemists to work on tissue samples she'd taken from some of the body parts found that day in Islamorada. There had been something peculiar about the isolated chemicals; they didn't belong.

Now she had confirmation; the bizarre turn of events unearthed at the microchemical level brought about a shower of new and disturbing images of the killer. This new information showed trace amounts of chemicals routinely used in the mortician's trade. Perhaps their killer had worked for a time in a mortuary. Such a fact would tie in with a fetish for preserving the tissue. "Listen, J.T., this is to be kept between us, understand?"

"No problem whatsoever, Jess."

"We've got precious little to convict on if we ever do connect anyone with these killings. If a true confession is ever taken, and the killer opens up about this aspect of his fantasy, then we'll know we've got the right man. At the moment, we have thirty-four confessed Night Crawlers undergoing various stages of arrest, booking, psychiatric testing, scrutiny and release.''

''Damn, that's amazing.''

''What's amazing?'' she asked.

''That anyone would confess to such heinous crimes.''

''Maybe we'll get lucky. Maybe the real Night Crawler will crawl up the MPD stairs and turn himself in today or tomorrow. But I rather doubt it.''

''Yeah, don't hold your breath.''

She involuntarily nodded. ''He's having too much fun to stop.''

''But what about the letters? Isn't that a subconscious cry for someone to stop him, a sign that he wants to confess?''

''Like you said, J.T., don't hold your breath. No, this guy's letters are strictly to please himself, to taunt us and to vent more of his venom.''

''Talk about confessions . . . Had a call the other day from a guy in Hawaii,'' J.T. abruptly changed the direction of the subject.

Jessica felt her heart skip a beat. ''What? Really?'' She wondered if she'd successfully kept her excitement out of her voice.

''He was looking to talk to you, Jess. Maybe you should give him a call. Sounds like he really misses you.''

''Good . . . he should.''

''Hope you don't mind, but I told him where you were staying. So be warned: He may call.''

She imagined Jim Parry, a hemisphere away, and she longed to be with him. ''J.T., don't go playing Cupid now. The role doesn't suit you.''

He laughed lightly and said good-bye and they hung up, Jessica left with this extraordinary new twist in the case, wondering if she should rush to share it with Eriq Santiva or hold the information in abeyance, at least until after the episode of *America's Most Wanted* was aired, so that they might keep it under wraps for future use against the Night Crawler.

She could go to him, argue the point. And if she didn't share with Eriq, her chief? She could get into a hell of a lot of trouble with him over failing to bring the news to his attention through the lie of omission. He'd be wanting soon to know also if she'd had contact with Kim Desinor.

Jessica rubbed her tired eyes, lifted her head and leaned back on the stool. She stared out through the glass partitions all around her. The partitions ran the length of the lab offices like a house of mirrors, each reflecting light from the other to create an illusion of endless corridors within corridors, an everlastingness reflecting science—man's need to know the truth at all costs. The Miami-Dade authorities certainly had spared no cost in building the new facility here.

Now, through the various partitions, Jessica saw Dr. Andrew Coudriet approaching. He seemed to be looking for her, so she waved. He came now directly to her and in a near whisper, he said, "I heard about your blowout with your partner."

She frowned up at him. "The walls hear everything?"

"Is there more? I heard you disagreed over whether to release the artist sketch and description."

Jessica's hands seemed to work independently of her at the lab table. She'd been made aware that all of Allison Norris's parts were to be interred today, per order of the family despite what Coudriet or anyone in the FBI had to say about it, and personally, she didn't have the strength or desire to fight the politically powerful family—not at this late point in time.

Finally, she looked into Coudriet's eyes and replied, "It's a sad day when the M.E.'s office can't control the evidence it oversees."

"If you mean the Norris body, well . . . that's out of our hands. If you FBI people wanted to contest it, then you have my blessings, but it sounds as if Santiva has already caved, as they say."

She shook her head. "There really isn't much more that Allison can tell us now, is there?"

He nodded. "Pretty sure she's given up her last secret."

Jessica withheld even from her colleague the fact that the girl's hand had actually been severed *before* she died and used in an unholy fashion, in the killer's attempt to permanently preserve it. Little wonder that body and body part had become so separated in their quest for final burial. The killer had held on to the hand for a long time, along with the bracelet, before he gave up on it, tossing it overboard as shark fodder. And Jessica had no doubt that the killer had given up this trophy with the name bracelet intact—superglued, in fact, to the wrist—with thoughtful intent, for his reasons; most likely, he wanted to tell Jessica—or someone like her—the truth. The monster wanted a voice, wanted to speak, wanted to communicate its plans.

The terrible truth told at the molecular level was that the hand had been severed while the girl remained alive and that very soon after the severed hand had been injected with embalming fluids.

"So what are the juicy details surrounding this big problem that has arisen between you and your chief?" Coudriet asked.

Pretending busyness, Jessica returned to the microscope.

"Don't pretend you don't hear me, Doctor, or that you don't know what I'm talking about," Coudriet said, placing a meaty hand over her microscope lens.

"Precisely how did you hear about our disagreement?" She had told no one of her and Eriq's argument.

"As you said, walls in a police precinct have ears." He noticed only now, by their labels, that the series of slides she was working on had come from the severed hand of Allison Norris. The attention she showed the slides created in him even more interest in what she was about. "What more do you hope to accomplish with that material?"

Jessica needed an ally, needed someone she could talk the scientific facts out with. Andrew Coudriet would have to be it; he would soon have access to the information anyway. "I'm not sure, but I noticed some odd anomalies with respect to the chemical makeup."

"Really? Now you're a forensic chemist as well?"

"I had our chemists at Quantico check it out."

"I see."

"Something didn't quite jive, but now I'm sure."

"Sure of what?"

"I noticed an odor when I first had this specimen in Islamorada, but I chalked it up to the embalming fluids used on the shark carcasses there. Early on, I sent tissue samples up to Quantico, to chemists there. Quantico confirmed a hunch I had, so now that I've got corroboration, I thought you might care to have a look." She got up from her stool to allow him access to the microscope. "Go ahead. Tell me what you see."

He looked from her to the scope and back again before settling his eyes over the dual eyepiece. "What am I looking for?"

"Just keep looking."

Coudriet settled in, removed his glasses and stared hard down into the microscope. After a moment, he thoughtfully said, "This came from the severed hand?"

"Yes."

"What is it, precisely?"

"I just got off the phone with an expert chemist with my outfit in D.C. He FedExed these slides overnight."

Coudriet's eyes squinted, the red brows looking like bird feathers. "And . . . and?"

"And from the chemicals they were able to isolate, J.T. says it's clearly a preservative or fixative of some sort . . . not unlike the kind we use to keep our own specimens in limbo." Jessica rubbed the sleepiness from her eyes.

"Good God, are you saying this madman is or was a . . . a medical man?"

"Not necessarily. The chemicals could be had at most any drugstore. He might also have a link with a mortician's office, or for that matter any number of places in the business of preserving flesh," Jessica speculated.

"From Jell-O to WonderPlus Glow 19? But why is he using preservatives on the hand alone? We saw nothing of the kind in the autopsy, and a thing like that, you don't miss."

"No, there was no evidence of it in the body proper, no."

"Islamorada then. They somehow stuck the hand full of it. It's the only logical explanation," Coudriet said.

"Yeah, maybe . . . I thought the same."

"*Thought*? As in the past tense?"

"Well, Doctor, one of my jobs is to think the unthinkable."

"And precisely what unthinkable are you thinking?"

She considered her answer carefully. She knew she ought actually to be talking to Eriq about this, and she planned to, but he had so infuriated her the night before that she meant to steer clear of him today. "If I were relentlessly killing people, Dr. Coudriet, in cold and brutal fashion, I'd need some sort of construct or scaffolding built around me, as a safety measure for my own sanity. You follow me so far?"

"I . . . I think I do."

"So, I kill and kill and kill again, enjoying the delight I take in robbing others of the most potent and powerful force on the planet—life itself. I feed myself on that loss of life and suffering others must pay me. However, I need a reason, a rationalization for my cruelty and perversion which will in effect wash my hands of guilt."

"What has this to do with preserving the girl's hand?"

"As a trophy, as a prize, to keep forever or to give in offering to my master and god."

"To God?"

"Not just any god, but the god who talks to me, the god I've created who buttresses and shores up the scaffold of my perverse rationale. It becomes an offering, the hand, but it must be as perfect as I can make it."

"But it's perishable, impossible to preserve."

"Up to a point, yes . . . So over the side it goes. It was not released at the same time as the body."

"So the shark that swallowed it—"

"Did not attack Allison's body to come away with it. It had already been severed."

"But the bracelet? He would have removed it, wouldn't he?"

"He's playing at god himself; he's neither sane nor afraid of us, Doctor. There's resin—epoxy—residue from Super Glue where he attached the bracelet."

"Heartless sonofabitch . . . But the arm was hacked off by what appeared to be a shark's bite; you said so yourself."

"I wanted to believe the parts matched, and they did. Self-fulfilling prophecy. We go back for another look, a more critical look, we'll find differently. We do it all the time in our business, Doctor."

Coudriet remained recalcitrant, unconvinced, shaking his head. "We can't possibly hold the body any longer. They want the body released yesterday . . ."

Jessica said nothing.

"But why? Why would this madman sever the hand and embalm it? What possible purpose could it serve?"

"We've got to stop looking for purpose; this bastard's purpose is totally a construct of his own making, having no validity outside his brain."

"No validity save that which his fevered mind has concocted . . ."

"Precisely, no reason in our world, only his; but if you want my opinion, the hand is just the beginning of an escalation."

"An escalation of what?"

"His attempt to preserve flesh, to preserve a victim whole . . . It's in keeping with how long he has held them in the water."

Coudreit didn't want to believe it, but it shook him nonetheless. "Such madness allowed to move about freely out there."

"We're going to catch this monster."

"Sometimes . . . sometimes it makes me wonder where God is in all this. And what about this madness *in here*, too . . . The way this investigation is being run, it's all insane."

"What do you suggest we do about it?" She was touched by his sudden show of concern, the depth of his feeling.

"Look, I have a fax machine in my office and direct E-mail on my computer, should you care to avail yourself." He dropped a stark photocopy likeness of the killer onto the lab table beside her. "But of course if policy prevents you, I'll understand."

"You don't know what you're asking."

"The hell I don't. Frankly speaking, Dr. Coran, I never much cared for the politicizing of this office or any murder investigation, and I'm sure, if you are your father's daughter, you don't either."

It was a challenge to her, the gauntlet thrown at her feet. She looked from the eyes of the killer in the artist's composite to the soft, even and determined eyes of Dr. Coudriet. There seemed to be a fresh, new glow about the man today, and he smelled different, like a man who'd discovered some new delight in life. "What do you know of my father?" she asked.

"Are you serious? I learned a great deal from him; read every word he ever wrote on forensic medicine, twice over. I once heard him speak—brilliant man—and once I met him at a gathering in Oregon."

"We . . . the family was stationed there for some time in the late fifties," Jessica offered. She noticed that Coudriet smelled of musk oil. Or was it a natural musk odor? That was it. The good M.E. had just come from having had sex with someone. He was aglow in the wash of it, and could no better hide it than he might his red hair.

"Tell me how you learned about the disagreement between Eriq and me."

"News travels fast around here," he commented, stepping a little away. "When people learn that this fiend is embalming his victims atop everything else . . ."

"That news stays within these walls, between you and me, Doctor."

With a solemn bow of the head, he nodded his agreement. "Will you then at least do the right thing, Jessica Coran?"

Damn, she thought, *he sounds like my father.* "And exactly what is that?"

"I'm in utter and complete agreement with you, Dr. Coran. What little information we have on the killer's identity and the threat he poses to certain victim types, that all this information be released to our still largely unsuspecting public, many of whom—*many* of whom—could fall victim to the killer before daybreak tomorrow. My God, he released three bodies to us yesterday. That clearly tells us that he means to *replenish* his supply."

Coudriet was right; the killer meant to start over, she thought but did not say. "I'm not in a position to authorize—"

"Damnit, Jessica, someone's got to authorize it; we can't wait for the governor or the mayor or the fucking Boy Scouts!"

"That's enough!" Jessica weighed the decision for a long moment. She lifted the computer-enhanced image of the killer before her eyes and stared at the dreaded and hated creature, the Night Crawler, known now also as Patric Allain. He was, as Judy Templar had attested, a handsome and alluring creature of dark, mysterious features. The shock of boyish hair over the forehead, the telltale birthmark peeking from beneath, the thin jaw and even teeth, the somewhat weak upper lip and sensual lower lip. But it was in the eyes that she saw the allure. These eyes of a madman, filled with mystery.

"You have E-mail," she stated.

"I do."

"I'd like to get in touch with Scotland Yard, an Inspector Moyler there, about the case. Tell him our man speaks with a British accent and uses the name Patric Allain. See if it turns up anything there."

"And what about here, closer to home?"

She breathed in a long breath of air, weighing her friendship with Eriq and her loyalty to him as a superior. The whole thing felt like a cracked mirror, a wingless bird, a blind owl, a dolphin without sonar. If she pushed Eriq far enough, he might send her packing; she'd be off the case, possibly up on disciplinary charges. But then, maybe that would give her reason to walk away from Quantico altogether, to rejoin Jim Parry in Hawaii . . .

"You get me through to this fellow in London, and I'll release the damned police sketch. But it goes first to the *Herald*."

"Other law enforcement agencies throughout the state, up and down the coast, first," he countered.

"That's been done already."

"No . . . no, it hasn't, I'm afraid."

"What? Damn . . ." Jessica now saw with certainty that Eriq Santiva would continue in his conservative approach to catching the killer. "The *Herald* first." She stood firm.

Coudriet read her face. He realized that she was stepping out onto a shaky limb. "All right; done."

"Let's get to work then."

·TWELVE·

The pure and simple truth is rarely pure and never simple.
—OSCAR WILDE

An hour later, all was accomplished—or demolished; it all depended on how one looked at it, Jessica thought. While Eriq was busy appeasing the big boys, she had taken the dangerous step of crossing him and whatever superiors he was presently kowtowing to.

To hell with it, she recklessly told herself, a part of her secretly hoping to get into enough trouble to stir the pot. If she was blackballed, if her reputation was besmirched by a healthy bit of insubordination, then perhaps she could trade in her "celebrity" status in FBI circles for a commonplace job in the agency where she might work in a lab twenty-four hours a day, to never come out to hunt another human monster again. She'd be perfectly happy to do so. Who needed the kind of stress she'd been working under for the past five years? And perhaps a move to Hawaii then would not be out of the question . . . Now she said aloud, "To hell with it."

"What's that?" asked Coudriet, still in an unusually up-beat mood, like a kid pulling a high school prank and enjoying the exquisite moment in which his plan comes together.

"Nothing . . . never mind," she replied.

"You know you've made the right choice; you're doing the right thing here," he told her. He was about to shut down his E-mail when a message for Jessica came over.

"Something for you here . . . from London . . . that fellow Moyler."

Nigel Moyler said that he was sending a fax over, a description and police sketch of the man who had terrorized the White Chapel District for four years only to suddenly cease, desist and disappear last year.

"It should be coming over your fax there any moment now. Sorry it took so long to get back to you there. Took some time to locate the file. It had gone to our dead file office. But now here it comes, and I daresay you will find it of peculiar interest." He signed off as Insp. Moy., Scotyd.

The fax machine began a staccato chorus of cranks, churns and beeps, the paper crawling ahead like an inchworm, too slow for Jessica's patience. "Come on . . . come on," she nursed it along before ripping it out.

The likeness was remarkable, stunning and stark.

"Send Moyler a message. Tell him we are ninety-nine percent sure that his man is here. Ask him to find out what he can about a Patric Allain over there. Anything on file— police record, prints, anything at all."

"Where are you going?"

"Going to find Santiva, tell him what I've done and inform him that this bloody case has greater jurisdictional boundaries than he imagined."

"Yeah, right." Coudrient chuckled lightly.

"What's so funny?"

"Santiva . . . He may just want to get the Queen of England's fucking views on the case before he steps on her bleeding toes."

"Hey, just a minute, Dr. Coudriet," she brought him up short. "It's not Santiva's fault that your local politicians are more concerned about the blight on their tourist trade than the lives of the victims. Or that only Allison Norris, of all the victims, counts!"

"What are you saying, Dr. Coran? That it's hardly so simple as all that?" Coudriet was being facetious now, still on a high.

"If Eriq hadn't had his hands tied by others, that electronic wanted poster we just sent would've gone out twenty-four hours ago.''

''You think for a moment that he's going to place the safety of prospective victims of this madman ahead of his own ambitions? Think again. I used to be him. I know. It comes with the territory.''

''That's not Eriq.''

''Power seeks out power, corrupts the soul and—''

''You don't know what you're talking about, Doctor, so please be silent!'' She stormed from the laboratory offices and took the elevator to the top floor, where she got out, located a stairwell and climbed to the roof. There she breathed in the night air and stared into the blinking eyes of the black firmament overhead. She felt tears welling up—tears for the victims, their families, Judy Templar, herself—and she wondered little why she'd so easily and readily sided with first Donna LeMonte and now Coudriet against Eriq Santiva. Still, she felt a wave of remorse flow over her, and she silently wondered, *Why am I being so self-destructive?* But neither the stars nor the land or sea or sky gave her reply.

Early the Next Day in Coudriet's Office

Women all over Miami and the state of Florida were now being more cautious, for the *Miami Herald* and the six o'clock news had carried Patric Allain's likeness into the homes of anyone whose newspaper subscription hadn't lapsed or who owned a TV set. Armed with the knowledge that Allison Norris, Tammy Sue Sheppard, the more recently identified Kathy Harmon and others like them were abducted through chicanery and charm at local seaside restaurants along the Intracoastal Waterway, police officials had stepped up their surveillance of the area and had gone in with a vengeance, questioning bartenders, employees and frequent patrons of such establishments.

Jessica Coran had contacted Inspector Nigel Moyler again, only to learn that there was no record of a Patric

Allain, and that the closest match was an arrest record of a *Patricia* Allain, an alias for a prostitute whose real name was Madeleine Tauman.

She electronically asked Moyler if his killer had used a boat for his deviant operations.

Moyler's response came up on the computer screen as "Never any killing ground located; however, it was theorized killer used a boat of some sort, yes."

Jessica sent a reply immediately: "It's almost a foregone conclusion here that our killer is using a boat as his killing ground. Please, see what you can learn about Patricia Allain. Long shot, but we haven't much else to go on here."

"Right, and good luck. End transmission."

The moment she ended the E-mail transmission with Moyler, Eriq Santiva entered Coudriet's office. Livid, Eriq repeatedly slapped a copy of the *Miami Herald* into the palm of his hand. "Just who the hell gave you the authority to release this information, Dr. Coran? It's all over the wire services, on every damned network in the nation now. Are you crazy or just an egoistic—"

"So shoot me, Eriq."

"Don't tempt me! What were you thinking? I gave you a direct order to stand down on this information until you heard otherwise from me. You know this is going to hurt us both, and you in particular, in Washington."

"So I'll bleed some, but maybe in the interim, we've saved a life?"

"Don't count on it. Damnit, you might've at least consulted with me first."

"We did *consult*!"

"Again then! This going over my head, looks . . . looks . . ."

"I'm sorry if it makes you look bad, Eriq. If it hurts your male ego. That wasn't my intention."

"It makes it appear that we're at cross-purposes, Doctor."

"Well, maybe we are."

He stared hard at her, fighting to control his emotions, gripping at the back of a chair, his knuckles white against his Latin skin. "Appearances are important, Jessica. You know that, I know that. I asked for a day, a lousy day, and you stab me in the back?"

"Damnit, Eriq, it isn't about you; it isn't about me. It's about the truth and the *out there*"—she pointed to the windows—"remember? Remember our obligation to the truth, and to people outside these walls?"

"Nice sentiments, Jess, but—"

"—And it's about saving lives," she continued without a blink, her hands raised to him. "Besides, you led me to believe that the composite would at the very least go out to authorities up and down the coast."

"Save your crusading, Doctor. We both know this will likely send our man into hiding, possibly never to be seen again."

"We don't know that, and I don't believe it—not this guy. He's too interested in communicating with us, and he's out of control."

"You don't know what's going on in this madman's brain; you can't know it. You're not psychic and you're not inside his head, Jess."

"I know he's still got two more verses to write."

"What?" Santiva was incredulous.

"The e. j. hellering poem; he'll have to complete it. He'll contact us again, and he'll go on killing."

"So, now you do believe you're capable of reading his mind?"

"Maybe . . . maybe . . ."

Santiva's pride had obviously been badly bruised, but he was fighting to keep his calm and rational exterior intact. To this end, he now paced like a caged lion back and forth, holding his grinding teeth tightly together. Jessica appreciated this great effort.

To keep him focused, she began telling him what was in *her* mind. "I've struggled to hold up a mirror to this maniacal killer, to see him at close range, to understand him, as I've understood other monsters I've had to cope with over the years, and believe me, doing so is no simple or easy task. In fact, it costs me a great deal of sleep. Makes a person no longer at ease with herself to think like this creature, but it's the only damned way I know to catch such a monster. You've got to go through the looking glass.''

''And so . . . what does your mirror tell you?''

''It's cracked, spiderwebbed, difficult to see through, but if you want proof we're on to the right man, take a look at this.'' She held up the faxed copy of the sketch that Moyler had forwarded. ''I faxed what we have to Scotland Yard. You'll want to see what their response has been.''

She now laid out all that Inspector Nigel Moyler had shared with her.

''Coincidence, maybe? Most likely?'' he wondered aloud as his eyes played over the information.

''A big coincidence, if you're asking me. Look, Eriq, if it's the same killer—''

''Big if. To go along with your big coincidence. Crap like this happens in the movies, on TV, in novels, Jess, but like this, laying it all right in our laps? Hardly likely.''

''Who says anything's been laid in our laps? Look, just suppose for a moment that our killer and Moyler's is the same guy. He starts with prostitutes in London, and he's since decided that we're all whores, especially those of us of a type he fancies. I just believe that in this instance, women of the victim type, in particular in this city, have a right to know that they—as a group—have been targeted by this madman and are being stalked by him as we speak, Eriq.''

He stared long and hard at her. Jessica matched his intensity in her hard glowering eyes. ''Do you have any idea the trouble you've caused?''

''I have a notion, yes.''

''You've placed me in a difficult position with a lot of people, Jessica. And you didn't factor in the political ramifications of your actions.''

''Oh, please! Don't talk politics to me when life and

death are at stake!'' she exploded, but he held up a restraining hand to her and pushed on.

''In my office, I've got to consider all the ripples in the pond every bloody waking moment, and sometimes in my damned sleep, so pardon me if I seem a bit upset, okay?''

''My intention didn't factor in your comfort, Eriq.''

''Damnit, it's not just my comfort I'm talking about. We're talking about power, government contracts, defense spending.''

''You're talking about the new U.S. payroll centers which may be slated to be built here if government bigwigs are sold on the area.'' The local newscasts and the papers were full of the story of how Miami was vying with other major American cities to build three U.S. payroll centers in the Miami-Dade area, which meant lucrative government jobs.

''It means seven thousand federal jobs with salaries and benefits averaging out at thirty-five thousand dollars. That's one hell of an economic boost, Jess. It means a better way of life for a lot of people here. Nothing this big has come along for Miami in a decade. Depending on its size, a single payroll center could pump between sixty and two hundred million a year in direct earnings into the local economy. And in an economy that's supported almost solely on tourism, such an infusion of dollars means a gilded future for our friends in high places here. But, bottom line, it also means one hell of a payroll for the city.''

''And Miami stands to lose it all because of the Night Crawler.''

''Exactly. A city's image is everything.''

''Yeah, more important than its life's blood, obviously.''

''Damnit, Agent, you're not listening to me!'' Her coolness to his upper-echelon problems didn't sit well. ''The goddamn Economic Development Council, the Metro Vision for the Year 2000, the 1050 Beach Street Business Coalition, the Downtown Development District Council, the Miami Chamber of Commerce—you name it—they're all on the mayor's back, so the mayor's naturally on the police commissioner's back, and the lot of them are on my back!''

A thick, palpable hush fell over the room as the two FBI agents breathed in the political and economical realities of their situation. Eriq found a chair and sat, raised his hands apologetically and added, ''Jess, the average Miami salary is in the neighborhood of twenty thousand dollars. Now the United Miami Coalition and some professors out at UM have figured it all out, and I tell you, an average pay of thirty-five thousand . . . Well, that's big-time bucks to these people. They have very, very few industries in and around the city that can generate that kind of money.''

''Money talks.''

''It always has, and we're both adult enough to understand its impact, even here on our case, Jess. Now perhaps you better understand where I'm coming from? In a few weeks the government steering committee to decide if Miami gets those centers will be back in the city. We . . . I . . . had hoped to nail this Crawler bastard before then.''

''We can still clean house within three weeks, if we work together. Dr. Desinor forwarded this to me this morning. It's from additional psychic readings she's done on the case.'' Jessica handed Santiva the list of physical characteristics which Kim Desinor had created. They matched the description given them by Judy Templar.

''Something you want to share?'' Eriq asked as he took the fax from her, a razor edge to his voice. He still hadn't had time to forgive her qualified allegiance to him. Like most men, he'd expected and wanted total and blind fidelity, without having to offer the same.

''Kim only called very late last night. Don't get spooky on me, Eriq.''

Eriq read the fax aloud in a near whisper. ''Taurus . . . astrological sign of the bull, but actions are more like recluse spider . . .''

''She's got that right.''

Eriq continued to read, pacing as he did so. ''Comes out only to feed. Safe only in his own surroundings. Light, sandy-brown hair, dark, mystical eyes, possibly aquamarine, handsome, pleasant, even-tempered, manners impeccable in public. May wear a T-cross around his neck, an emblem of his obsession. Stargazer.''

''That was Kim's first read, which she called me about last night. This morning, she conducted a second reading. Her results on the second go-round came over right after she faxed the first. Here it is.''

She handed him a second fax, which Eriq now stared at. It read:

> height: 6'1 or 2
> weight: 160–80 lbs
> broad-shouldered, large-face, big forehead
> neck and shoulders all one
> large, oval, dark and piercing eyes, possibly blue, dark green
> either birthmark or bad tattoo of a star on right shoulder
> wears loose-fitting clothes, sneakers, boat shoes size 10–11
> lives in isolation, yet within close proximity of many
> has fascination for stars and water
> deep-seated hatred for his mother
> has generalized hatred for all women

Eriq read aloud the psychic's final words. ''Sorry, nothing more. Caution you to think symbolically and not literally regarding my findings.''

''She is full of disclaimers,'' Jessica muttered, digging her palms now into her eyes, trying to will the fatigue off.

''Obviously general enough to fit most of the male population of the planet,'' he replied, not overly impressed.

They again stared at one another; then first she and next he began to laugh until their laughter filled the room. ''Damnit, Jessica, we've got to be together on this thing,'' Santiva finally said. ''That's all I'm going to say about your *rank* insubordination at this time—''

Jessica started to protest, but thought better of it and kept still.

"—except to say that in the future, we decide things of major consequence together. For now, we drop it and move on from here. We still have a killer to catch."

She nodded. "I couldn't agree with you more."

"I've got a tight net around every boat dock and riverside establishment for fifty miles either direction of Miami," he informed her.

"Are you talking Port Authority, Coast Guard, Florida Marine Patrol or your buddies in the Cuban underworld?"

"All of the above. Somewhere along the line, this bastard's going to slip up, and when he does, we'll be there, Jess," he assured her.

"You'd better extend your net to every conceivable slip, including boat repair shops, dry docks, and maybe any shops where they preserve fish as trophies."

"How's that?"

"A strange new development. Let me tell you about it."

Eriq felt his flesh crawl. "All right, fill me in."

In the midst of making Eriq's stomach turn, Jessica was told she had a long-distance call. She grabbed the nearest phone and identified herself and was suddenly surprised and elated to hear James Parry's voice on the other end, asking, "Are you taking care of the woman I love?"

"Oh, James . . . Where—where are you?" She pictured James Parry at the other end of the line, pleased beyond comprehension that he'd located her.

"I'm calling from the islands, which have lost a great deal of their luster since you left. I've dearly missed you, darling."

"God, I've missed you." Out of the side of her eye, she noticed Eriq impatiently waiting. She turned her back on him and continued her conversation.

They had a long talk in which they exchanged vows of love. It was enough to send Santiva from the room. She asked Jim to call her later before bedtime, to tuck her in. He promised that he would. She was happy for the first time since arriving in Miami.

"What was that all about?" asked Eriq when he returned to finish with her.

"Personal."

"Oh, I see . . ."

"Let's get back to work."

"Long distance?" Santiva was smiling for her. "Hawaii maybe?"

"Maybe . . ."

Ten Days Later

When *America's Most Wanted* did its segment on the killings in Florida, it appeared the trail of the killer had gone stone cold. No more notes coming in from the killer and, thankfully, no more bodies either. It was as if the creature had simply vanished while camera crews had replaced police and medics, film barricades had replaced police tape and Jessica had been replaced by an actor, Santiva by a director.

The images on the TV screen of women floating in the sea, although simulations, were emotionally stirring—but not when Jessica considered the fact that those young women would, off camera, lift their heads from the surf, stand, wade back to shore and go home to dinner. And as for truly simulating a bloated drowning victim, prime-time TV simply wasn't ready.

There was both relief and anger in the Miami area when, a week and a half after the discovery of three victims of the Night Crawler in the space of hours, there were no further developments and no new leads in the case, so far as the public knew. Meanwhile, the national attention given the case, the TV exposure and the fact that it remained open had helped persuade the government steering committee on payroll centers to steer elsewhere.

Theories regarding the whereabouts of the killer abounded: He'd killed himself; he had been arrested on some other charge, been convicted and put away, and from behind bars he could only contemplate murder at some fu-

ture date. Others theorized that he had left the country for
more fertile ground—virgin turf, as it were. Missing Persons departments all over the state continued as always to
file reports on young women disappearing or running away
from their homes, but not all of these fit the victim profile.
There was a growing, sinking feeling among law enforcement officials that the Night Crawler had simply been
frightened off by the news accounts and the police sketch,
which had gone out across the state and the nation, and that
despite his flirtation with the news media, he had turned
out to be extremely camera-shy after all.

Jessica had begun to believe she'd blundered badly, that
Eriq and his superiors had been right in wanting to withhold
information on the killer until some future date. But upon
her voicing this concern to Eriq, he shook his head and told
her that what had upset local politicos most was that they
had made certain promises to America's Most Wanted: that
the poster would be shown there first and that other vital
clues in the case would be revealed only on the show. He
ended with an apology that he hadn't confided all this nonsense to her earlier, but said that he'd been unable to.

Still, Jessica wondered if Patric Allain had not fled as a
direct result of her actions. She believed now that Allain,
or whoever he was, had simply decided to vanish, and that
to do so he had been forced to control his killing urge. To
control such primitive, overwhelming compulsions, she felt,
he had to demonstrate a willpower few men, good or bad,
possessed, and she wasn't buying it; and neither would the
monster for long, she figured. She recalled with chilling
detail the case of the Claw in New York, who could not
control his need to cannibalize. It was a need which had
compelled the monster to follow her for several hundred
miles in an attempt to make a meal of her.

Knowing what she did of the criminal mind, including
its need for a familiar landscape upon which to operate,
Jessica had contacted Moyler in England to warn him that
the killer could be returning there. On the other hand, she
noted this particular killer seemed at home on the oceans

and seas of the world. He might be anywhere on the globe.

In the meantime, Moyler had found additional information on the female named Madeleine Tauman whose alias had been Patricia Allain. She had grown up amidst what Moyler termed "difficult situations in a difficult area of London," and she'd become a prostitute at a young age. Soon she had gone from prostitution to the small-time stage, using the same alias, Allain, as her stage name. Late in life, she had married a well-to-do landowner named William Anthony Kirlian who owned an estate in Grimsby on what the ancients called the *Nordsee*—the North Sea—far to the north of London. Not surprisingly, the old baron died a year after the marriage, but a coroner's inquest turned up nothing beyond a massive heart attack. The kicker came when Lady Kirlian, the former Patricia Allain, herself died soon after in what was ruled a fatal accident involving a cliff near the estate. Lady Kirlian's tumble from a precipice near the estate, Moyler told Jessica, was witnessed only by her devoted son, Warren Tauman.

Moyler had located some people who had worked for Kirlian and Lady Kirlian before their deaths, and as to the young man, Warren, they had little to say except that he was sullen, brooding and always staring out over the horizon to the North Sea, commiserating with nature on the very precipice where his mother had slipped and fallen to her death on the jagged rocks below.

Moyler now believed that Patric Allain might possibly be an alias for Warren Tauman, who'd disappeared after dissolving the estate and keeping what monies he could, along with a sailboat valued in the hundreds of thousands, which he diligently learned to work.

It seemed that while the trail in England had finally heated up, the trail in America had dried up, and when another week slipped by and still nothing remarkable occurred, FBI operations in Florida seemed at an end.

Santiva was talking about packing up and returning to Quantico, where more pressing matters awaited. In the meantime, Jessica had kept in touch with Judy Templar, whose therapy had done wonders for her, according to Donna LeMonte.

Meanwhile, Quincey and Samernow had finally persuaded Monroe and Lovette family members to give up the location of the other supposed eyewitness by making certain they saw the *America's Most Wanted* segment which requested information on Aeriel Marilee Lovette Monroe, who was wanted for questioning in relation to the killings. Something in the notoriety of being mentioned on national TV, or of being close to someone named on national TV, got a lot of people to talk to authorities.

Samernow and Quince had first found Marilee's trail when they were pointed toward relatives in Georgia, where the girl had gone to recuperate, heal and forget after her alleged attack by the Night Crawler. But in the interim, she had returned to Florida, moving in with other relatives in Lower Matecumbe Key, where friends and relatives had urged her to get in contact with authorities, which she had done through the 800 number flashed across America. She was now reportedly working as a maid in a motel called Nomad's Pillow in Lower Matecumbe Key.

Eriq had only come by to inform Jessica that he was returning to FBI Headquarters in Quantico and shutting down the operation here in Florida, and that he expected her to follow in a day or so. They once again were in Coudriet's lab when she informed him that they had nailed the whereabouts of Marilee, the other witness. "But Jess, what can we possibly learn from this woman that we don't already know?" asked Eriq, frustrated as they all were by the dead ends.

Still Jessica argued, "I think we need to follow up on this one, Eriq."

But Santiva was not listening. "Besides, I've already told Coudriet and the MPD thanks for the use of the space, and that we're moving out."

"I think we owe it to Allison Norris, Tammy Sheppard, Kathy Harmon and all the others to at least—"

"Jess—Jess—Jess!"

"—meet with the Monroe girl, learn what we can from her," Jessica said over Eriq's objections while Santiva paced the very laboratory he had moments before suggested they begin to vacate, so as to turn back over to the Miami authorities and Coudriet that which was theirs, with the heartfelt thanks of the FBI.

Santiva replied, "Some cases don't get solved, Jessica."

"Not my cases," she countered.

"Although, by God, it's never happened to me before, it's . . . well, it's time we accepted the facts of the matter."

She relented a moment, going to him, forcing him to stop pacing, positioning him eye to eye with her. She knew that, in his mind, he had already closed the file on the case. "Give me one more week here, Eriq. Just one more week."

"Too much time and money's already gone down the tubes here, Jess."

"Then I'll move out of the Fontainebleau, damnit."

"Too much time has elapsed since the last killings and communication from the killer."

Jessica stood in his face, daring his next move.

He blinked first. "All right, you want to drive or fly down to the Keys again, talk to this girl, be my guest. You do that. I'm on the next flight north. You can follow after you learn no more than we already know. It's finished here, Jess, over . . ."

She breathed in a long, shaky breath of air and pushed her hair from her eyes. "I take full responsibility for what's happened here, Eriq. I think you're going to need a fall guy when you get back to D.C., so here I am."

"Oh, no you don't. You don't get out of this so easy; no martyr or dumb-shit stuff, okay, my medical friend?"

From the tenor of his voice, she realized that he had already taken the full brunt of the heat over the matter, and that he hadn't sold her out or short.

"I've got a plane waiting, and as much as I hate to fly, adios, amiga. And for what it's worth, good luck with the Monroe girl, although—"

"Don't say it, Eriq. Let's part friends, shall we?"

"Now that's something I'll agree to."

They exchanged a warm smile and a hug. He said in her ear, "That Parry guy is one lucky SOB, you know it?"

"I think so."

Eriq was on his way down the corridor and eventually to the airport when she saw from the lab window that he had been stopped in his tracks by Samernow, who was displaying more emotion than she'd ever seen from the man before. No doubt he wanted Eriq to stay long enough to talk with Aeriel M. L. Monroe. After all, he had put in a lot of investigative hours pursuing her at Eriq's specific request, and now Eriq was walking out on the investigation. She saw Eriq mouth the words *It's over* several times. But then suddenly Eriq glanced up from a slip of paper Samernow had pushed into his hands and his eyes fixed on Jessica's. Jessica could see from the intensity of his stare that he was going to miss that plane.

Quincey had joined the group, and all three men came barreling toward the lab and Jessica like a small squad, each intent on her.

Jessica stripped away her gloves and lab coat and met them in the office which had been provided for her adjacent to Coudriet's. Lately, Coudriet had been absent from the place. He had fallen in love, she was given to understand. More power to him, she thought with a pang of remorse about the absence of love in her life, despite Jim's having called her now repeatedly to profess his love for her.

"What's going on?" she asked of the men who piled into her temporary office, making the little cubicle feel like a telephone booth.

"This was received by the *Naples Constitution* early this morning," said Samernow, handing Jessica a flimsy fax machine copy of a handwritten note. She gasped uncontrollably, repeating, "It's him," while staring at the note, which appeared to be in the killer's hand. It read:

t tenderly floats
all the little girls
in the sea
as opportunity...
Opportunity to be
if only for one
inclusive moment
the daughter of t
and to breathe as he

"He couldn't help himself. He had to show himself," she said after reading the ugly words.

Samernow said to the floor, "A Sanibel Island girl matching the victim description has disappeared and remains unaccounted for. He's on the west coast now!"

"He's definitely back," Quincey immediately agreed.

Eriq vehemently shook his head. "We don't know that, not for certain."

"It's the third installment of the e. j. hellering poem," Jessica countered. "It's got to be him. Who else?"

"You forget, the damned *Miami Herald* printed the first two installments, not to mention a background story by that Eddings guy on hellering. Don't you see, any number of nutcases out there might've decided to reinvent the killer, and so this shows up clear across the state. I'm sorry, but I'm going to have to reserve judgment."

"But you're the expert on handwriting!" Samernow exploded. "And you said the handwriting appeared the same."

"The key word is *appears*, Samernow. With the killer's handwriting out there for any and everyone to see, hell, anybody could forge it now."

Quincey quietly reminded Eriq of the missing Sanibel Island teen.

The *Herald* had disappointed Santiva. The FBI and Santiva had disappointed the *Herald.* As for the newspaper, who could blame it? The FBI hadn't kept its bargain, after all, and was pulling up stakes, now, so Merrick hadn't seen any need to withhold on the whole story once it was given to *America's Most Wanted,* especially now that it appeared the Night Crawler had disappeared from the vicinity. The entire fiasco seemed a catch-22.

"We don't know that it's the killer's handwriting, not for a fact," repeated Santiva. "We really need to get the original, put our documents experts to work on it."

Samernow was instantly in Eriq's face. "You said it was the same handwriting!" Jessica wondered what had fired Mark Samernow up so.

"I said on first appearance, it *might* be the same, but it

will take much closer scrutiny than I can give it in a hallway.''

Quincey raised his considerable hands to quell the two
other men and said, ''Mark's got a daughter about the age
of the victims—''

''Shut up, Quince!''

''—and the divorce took her to *Naples*.''

''Is that why you're so interested in establishing the authenticity of this letter?'' asked Eriq.

Samernow stammered, ''I've been torn up over this
whole damnable business from day one, the way this creep
does them. My little girl . . . I haven't seen her in six
months, but she could pass for Allison Norris. And here I
thought with her in Naples, at least she was out of harm's
way, but now . . . now this . . .''

''We need to get somebody over to Naples,'' said Quincey, ''but we also need to get somebody down south of
here to Matecumbe Key to hear the testimony of the Monroe girl. We want . . . we're asking you both to stay on long
enough to talk to her and to look into the Naples connection
a little more closely.''

''Someone's got to go to Key Largo,'' said Courdriet,
materializing from nowhere at the doorway.

''Why's that, Dr. Coudriet?'' asked Jessica, wondering
what the ME was getting at.

''Friend of mine is a pathologist at the local hospital
there. They have a body washed up on shore bearing all
the marks of the Night Crawler's handiwork *and then
some*.''

''Show me on the map?'' asked Santiva. They moved
into the laboratory, where a map of south Florida and the
Keys had been pinned on a bulletin board, each colored
stickpin marking another of the Night Crawler's victims.
This southernmost tip of Florida resembled a slovenly J,
the islands like ink spatters at the bottom. Coudriet did the
dubious honors of tacking in this most recent kill.

''What do you mean *and then some*?'' asked Jessica.

''Washed up between the Key Largo Hammocks State
Botanical Site and the Carysfort Yacht Club, right here,''

Coudriet said as he jabbed the tack into the corkboard. "Came in on the Gulf Stream."

"Well damn, then that's got to place our killer well south of Key Largo, as the stream would ripple the body in a northerly direction at that point," said Quincey. "I know—I've fished those waters."

"And then some?" Jessica repeated, tugging at Coudriet's billowy shirt. The man had dispensed with ties and jackets, it appeared. "What did you mean when you said 'bearing all the normal marks of the killer *and then some*?' "

He looked directly at Jessica when he replied, "Seems this time he embalmed the girl, and not just a piece of her . . . the entire body. You were right. Prophetic, in fact, Doctor."

She didn't enjoy being right like this, and such power of prophesy was more a curse than a wonder. "It's him, Eriq. Now one of us has to go to Naples and the other to Key Largo," said Jessica.

"What's this about, Jess? What haven't you told me?"

"I told you about the embalming agents found in some of the body parts. This just confirms it," she said, sighing heavily. "The killer's trying to preserve a victim. He's been experimenting with embalming methods."

"Naples is straight across the state by way of Alligator Alley," said Quincey. "Mark could drive you," he told Eriq. "And me, I'll take Dr. Coran to Key Largo. From there, we can go down to Matecumbe Key, interview the Monroe girl in person."

"Yeah," agreed Samernow, "sure, I can take Agent Santiva to Naples."

"Not before I authenticate this letter," Eriq said. "It could be a hoax."

"Who would put together such a hoax?" asked Coudriet, a bit facetiously.

"I wouldn't put it past that creepy bald guy Eddings at the *Herald*, for one," replied Santiva.

Jessica's eyebrows shot up. "Eddings? I rather doubt that, Eriq. I know he was a bit strange, but—"

" 'A bit strange?' " Eriq laughed. "Try *X-Files* weirdo supernerd paranoid fringe dittohead."

"I thought he was kinda cute and sweet," she said with a laugh.

"Just the same, I'm going nowhere until we authenticate the letter."

She countered with her own challenge. "Well, I'm going to Key Largo. Detective Quincey, I just have to get my bag and a change of clothes. Can you pick me up at my hotel?"

Eriq only shook his head and found a chair to plop into, seemingly beaten.

"I'll swing by in, say, half an hour?" Quincey asked Jessica.

"Agreed."

"Jess," said Eriq, climbing again to his feet and now taking her away from the others. "I thought we agreed to discuss any major moves we take in relation to this case. Now you're rushing off to the Keys, and you want me to race to Naples without our having had a chance to authenticate the letter or discuss it."

"I thought we just did authenticate and discuss."

"We did what?"

"We discussed how Eddings would not've plotted such a hoax and the fact that there is a missing girl meeting the victim profile the other side of the state. We have to move on this, Eriq." She briskly walked back to her temporary office, grabbed her black ME's bag and rushed out with Quincey.

Eriq stared across at Mark Samernow. "All right, Detective, let's go to Naples . . . Maybe pay a visit to your girl and your ex. I can make the comparison points on the letters along the way."

"I'll get you there in two and a half hours without leaving the ground," Samernow promised. "And thanks, Agent."

· THIRTEEN ·

Pursue like a shadow . . .
—ANONYMOUS

•

In the Gulf of Mexico, Somewhere off Naples, Florida

Warren Tauman hadn't thrown everything overboard. He still had shanks of hair and fingernails he'd clipped from several of his victims, some jewelry and underclothes he had clung to—all of which he could bring to the nostrils, for these items opened up an entire vista of memories.

He recalled each of his victims in turn, and what he'd done to each one in his years-long attempt to reach out for the soul of his departed mother, to lure her back to him. He wanted to reincarnate her in the image of one of his victims, and once done, he wanted to make her suffer as all his victims had suffered. As he had suffered. Was that asking so much?

After all, his god Tauto had promised that there was a way. That he need merely to find his way. The poetry of e. j. hellering promised a way. Through sacrifice, a path would open.

Something in the warm Gulf air told Warren Tauman that he had been right to come here to Naples. Sanibel and Captiva Islands had been beautiful and filled with tourists, but they were small and insular, filled with a xenophobia, despite the tourists, and the loss of one of their own had sent ripples throughout the communities, ripples he cared not to feel.

The warm, balmy wind and the stolen items from his

victims brought back moving, exciting images in his mind. He recalled the one called Tammy Sue. He had placed her in the water and, while she was still alive, had dragged her at great speed. She didn't last long, and she'd not put up much of a fight from the beginning. Annoying and disappointing, really, because he knew that Mother would not seek to inhabit such a body, that she'd require a strong-willed fighter, like the one who'd gotten away so early in the game, the one who called herself Aeriel.

He recalled his excitement in having her scratch and tear, spit and kick out at him as he'd choked the life from her. Then how he had to do it again. He had not found any victim so motivated to live as Aeriel—certainly not the bitch strapped to the rear of the boat now whom he had wooed aboard at Sanibel Island.

Now he prayed that Naples would be kinder to him than Sanibel had been, or Miami or London or Grand Cayman Island, for that matter. When would he ever find the one acceptable ''bride'' for Mother?

His thoughts wandered back to those early attempts at reaching out to Mother through the filthy crones and tramps of London streets, derelicts one and all. Even then, he knew he must alter the way he did things. From the first, he instinctively knew this. Tauto had only reinforced what his own soul was trying to convey to him when he'd intentionally changed his ways, seeking out for the first time a younger body.

Her name had been Pauline Charlotte Warmellby, and what a fine, warm name it was, too, he'd told her before he had taken her life. He knew then, after killing her, that he must start over, and that this meant going elsewhere. The police, Scotland Yard, everyone in England was on the lookout for him by then, yet he was so far from attaining his final and prime objective. He knew he had to relocate, start over, and this time with younger women. Mother was vain and always had been vain; why should that change just because she was dead, an inhabitant of another world? She'd been vain till the bitter end, and she'd remain vain in the afterlife.

She would never come back to reincarnate the body of an older woman with wrinkles and a chicken neck. It stood to reason.

Besides, the police had thrown a scare into him. Two bobbies had come to his flat, soliciting information about Pauline, who'd lived a few flats down. She was reported as missing at the time, her body as yet unfound. No one knew that she was tied and weighted down at the back of his boat, a small craft with a barnacled bottom, hardly capable of floating; no one knew that Pauline was below the surface of the water, awaiting the time when he could experiment on rejuvenating her in the form of his mother.

When all his experiments failed, and when finally he relented, releasing the body into the Thames, he decided it was indeed time to leave London and England altogether, to seek out new hope and opportunity in America.

Warren had made the trip over the vast ocean in solitude, testing both himself and his knowledge as a sailor. It was a rigorous crossing, a marathon, and the sea almost engulfed him during one storm, but he had prevailed, and during the long, lonely lull days when the wind had abandoned him, he had read again the *Book of Tau* and the teachings of Tauto, especially the teaching that all life was reincarnated, that all life-forms sought out their doubles and bonded with their double spirit in an effort to grow. His spirit could only grow if he could fetch back his mother's, then destroy it completely so that it could not return to this life ever again.

He recalled his earliest childhood memories of life at the back of a brothel, of being chained for days to a bedpost. "For your own safety," she'd lie. He recalled beatings, both physical and mental, which he endured in stoic silence for so long that Mother thought him unfeeling, unreachable. But he had felt plenty.

The trip over had taught him that Tauto was on his side; that Mother's spirit deserved capture and punishment. The trip over had also taught him that there was no predicting the future.

"Hell, look how far I've come," he told himself now,

folding his arms over his chest, allowing the wheel to turn the ship inward toward landfall as he maneuvered his craft toward shore.

He was keen-eyed now, intelligent, cunning, self-taught. "One must not allow the constraints of time, place, kinship or birth to confine, curtail or otherwise handcuff the superior self," he instructed himself in the words of Tauto. "Otherwise, one is robbed of character." He saw the warming lights of the shops, hotels and restaurants ahead, and this made him smile.

"One must instead actually invent one's future," he told the sky and himself. "And so I have, and so I have . . ."

And so he had changed who he was, he thought. He had escaped the mold, the construct, the working definition everyone had held true of him, beginning with Mother.

Women had held sway over him his entire life; first Mother, the other whores she consorted with and the chorus line in the various theatres and then the matrons at the school. Everywhere he turned, women were there with their rules and order, constantly pecking at him. Women had held so much power over him for so long that he had, for a time, begun to think that this was the way of the world. But no more. No longer could others imprison him; he disallowed any constraints. He could flex his mind, he had become a flexible fellow.

He had begun to take the power from them; he *was* taking the power from them. He truly hated them, each and every one, but Mother in particular.

Without realizing that he was falling back into his old habit of dwelling on the past, he now flashed memories of himself as a weak and ineffectual child, tormented and abused by his mother. She would tie him naked to the bed and burn him in unspeakable places with her cigarette in order to keep him in line, to maintain control and power. Sometimes she'd use a hot lightbulb, and sometimes she'd use electrical shocks. She did it when he wet the bed; she did it when he spoke back; she did it when he cried over broken things.

Mother would use ropes, garter belts, guitar strings—

anything at hand. She'd use multicolored scarves, the sort used by clowns in the theatrical troupe they traveled with. She'd twist one scarf about his hands and another about his feet, and shove a third deep into his mouth, gagging him to the point of suffocation and unconsciousness. He often awoke in a black closet, locked from the outside. She let him know every day who was in control, and she let him know that she detested him—that he was the cause of her failed career and her failed life. That he was a miserable wretch. That he was exactly like his miserable father whom he had never known.

Then she changed. She mellowed and became the charming lady of the stage persona, all an act. Yes, quite certainly, she had matured, but by then, so had he; he gave her no more trouble and seldom exchanged words with her, or anyone else for that matter. Warren went hiding in books instead, searching for the meaning of life, for a clue as to why he was ever born . . .

She became settled, and when she met the man from Grimsby who promised to take her away from the theater and settle her life once and for all, Warren was sent to the best finishing school money could buy, Southwark.

Warren didn't flourish at Southwark, nor did he "finish" well.

In fact, he remained a loner, absolute in his noncommunication, a stone. But Southwark pointed the way, not only because he learned there how delectable it was to make another human being suffer the kinds of torment and pain he had endured at Mother's hands, but because it was there, one day in the dusty stacks while researching a paper on comparative ancient religions, that Warren came across the doctrines of the Tau.

It was a magnificent book, one he had to have, so he stole it from the library. Within its pages, the book revealed a whole new life for Warren in the teachings of Tauto, a twelfth-century monk whose life was significantly influenced by Eradinus, one of the eighty constellations of Taurus, the "bull in the sky."

The ancient monk Tauto meditated and prayed and after

a lifetime of diligent study finally became one with his god, Eradinus. Young Warren Tauman was immediately taken by Tauto's plight—both a solitary and a deformed figure, having by some accounts a hunched back and a club foot, he was banned by his order for "occult practices" and "perverse sacrifices" to his god.

Tauto shared himself with his god, becoming his instrument on Earth. Warren was at peace and oneness with his god, as was Tauto so many years before; together, they shared so much. They shared the same symbols and icons such as the Tau cross, and even the same name: Tau(man) ... Tau(to) ... Tau(rus). Now, in the twentieth century and nearing the twenty-first century, the name *Tauman*, Warren decided, was but an extension of Taurus and Tauto, for he had so much in common with the historical Tauto and the god Taurus.

He had read of how Tauto's victims were repeatedly strangled at the altar erected for his god; he had learned that Tauto believed that anyone willing to make the ultimate sacrifice, as he had, of becoming the living instrument of his god on Earth, would one day become a significant part of that god's being in the next life.

Warren had read also about how Tauto himself had died, at the hands of commoners who stoned him to death out of fear and ignorance and revenge, for he had sacrificed a large number of lives to his god by then. Warren fully expected to die at the hands of the ignorant masses who were currently provoked by what they termed a killing spree and what he called necessary sacrifices, offerings to his god on high.

One of the few luxuries Warren managed to get from his mother's newfound wealth upon marrying Sir William Anthony Kirlian of Grimsby was a telescope. She said she wished to "encourage the boy's interest in the stars." Many a night, he had used the telescope at the precipice over which he had thrown Mother, there in search of the constellations of Taurus and Tauto in particular. Warren believed himself a reincarnation of the self-taught monk of the twelfth century.

With his telescope, he had discovered the light of Eradinus as if all over again. That light—Eradinus himself—began talking to Warren. First it was in a low, unintelligible voice in the tongue of a forgotten language, but soon, after Warren learned to open his mind, the gibberish became clear, the words concise, the voice in his head now a comforting lull, a welcomed visitor from afar, from the stars. Warren easily, blissfully opened his mind, soul and heart to the godly voice that now spiraled about the convoluted corridors of his sometimes fevered brain.

Once the voice of Tauto breached Warren's inner mind, there was no question but that he had to seek out all the power denied him all the years of his life, and not surprisingly, he began his concerted effort at regaining power and control over his life within his new family. First old Kirlian must go, the voice told him, and then his mother.

Laughter now wafted across the bay and into Warren's mind, making him look toward the wharves, the harbor lights closer now, reflecting wild colors off the mirroring water of Naples, warming the darkness like some ancient campfire, and him just outside the light, beyond the human pall. These impressions and thoughts reached Warren's mind now, making him blink and return to the present moment. He had almost overshot the wharf where he wished to ease the *Tau Cross* into a slip owned by a restaurant, one that went unpatrolled by Coast Guard or city dock inspectors. He worried little about someone with a clipboard asking for his port of origin, his background or the call numbers of the boat. It was one of the little things he loved about America, her many freedoms so taken for granted by people here. Besides, the boat had multiple papers made out on her, and he changed both her numbers and her names routinely to throw such agencies as the Florida Marine Patrol off his wake.

As his boat neared, he heard more clearly the tinkle of glass and the sound of women's voices amid the clatter and chatter of this place. How cunning they were, the female of the species, always hiding their satanic nature in garlands of sweet words, toothy smiles and lilting laughter. Few people knew just how much pure evil resided in their so-called purity and virtues. Women were snakes to be beheaded, so far as he and Tauto believed.

There was little he detested more than false piety and false purity in women; these two qualities reminded him more of Mother than anything else, and it was with an eye to these qualities in a woman, along with their physical appearance—which must suit Mother's—that he went hunting. Mother would wish to inhabit the vilest creature, the one with the most makeup and guile, the lewdest of them all, but she must also be beautiful, with trailing, auburn hair like Mother's own had always been.

He moved the *Tau Cross* in closer, closer, inching it forward. The lights from the wharf reflected wildly, hauntingly off his masts and rigging, showing off the luxurious teakwood molding all round his ship. How could he help but attract Mother's new body? His constant, perhaps obsessive polishing of the boat's wood would pay off here.

He had given fair warning by way of the newspaper, and if they hadn't seen fit to print it, then by Eradinus, that wasn't his deceit or his problem. He had warned that he was coming, and so he washed his hands of guilt in the coming and in the actions he contemplated on behalf of Tauto. Anyone accepting his invitation tonight could only have deceit for a heart, and that was precisely what he was looking for.

No one here had seen him or his ship before. This was, as the Americans were fond of saying, "virgin turf." He'd have to be careful, but given the level of intelligence of those in pursuit of him, he decided that he hadn't that much to fear.

Another reason Tauto had chosen the Naples area was because here Warren could and had indeed located Gordon Buckner, the most knowledgeable of men regarding trophy fish taxidermy. Warren had ingratiated himself with Buckner by telling him of his apprenticeship with Works of Art Taxidermy in Key West. Buckner respected the work that went on at Works of Art and had in fact founded it along with the current owner, the man who'd trained Warren before he'd caught him stealing supplies. But Buckner didn't know about that.

Warren had asked Buckner about doing a number on a game fish so that the internal organs might stay intact.

Buckner had looked him over queerly and said, "It can't be done without embalming the entire fish the way you would a . . . a corpse." When Buckner wanted to know why Warren wanted to do such a thing, he quickly told the old man that it was to be a gag gift for a friend.

"I get it," Buckner had dubiously said. "When the guy goes to mount the thing, it'd be heavier'n hell, and it would begin to stink." Buckner had laughed at the notion and wondered aloud why he hadn't ever thought of it himself, and had then slapped Warren on the back and repeated, "I get it. You wanna present a pal with the thing and then gut and scale it, with a chain saw maybe?" Buckner's laugh had become raucous by then, his laughter filling the trophy-making warehouse he oversaw in Naples.

Now Warren knew he must embalm the entire body in the manner of the mortician, as he'd done with his last victim, but that he'd have to use chemicals beyond what the normal wake called for, to make the effect last not weeks or even months but years. He had been diligently studying the matter and had come to the conclusion that the most successfully preserved bodies had come about as a result of men who were obsessed with women, usually their wives; when the wife died, the husband would preserve her in the manner of mummies. This involved chemicals of a highly potent variety, but it would mean that the corpse's internal organs, along with the shell, could remain indefinitely, or at least until Mother was reincarnated.

He began by gathering up the chemicals he would need. Ordinary formaldehyde would not be enough. He already had an IV drip, which he'd used on his last victim. What he hadn't used was the new formula. Now all he needed was someone like Mother to try it on. The Sanibel girl might have to do if he could not find someone more suitable, someone with a lot more fight in her . . .

So now Warren and the *Tau Cross* cruised the Naples

area shoreline for nightspots suitable for and frequented by such tramps as his mother might appreciate. Gulls called out; the sunset sent up a shower of colors that ran the gamut from yellow-gold to bloodred; smatterings of lavender coated the underbelly of scattered clouds over the Gulf. Naples looked like an inviting community. The welcoming committee was a gaggle of pelicans soaring straight over the boat in a half-V formation.

He'd cleaned himself up, making himself presentable, and was sporting a beard now, giving him a more dashing and distinguished appearance, he believed. He was hoping his prey would be in abundance here when he killed the engine completely and steered the now-floating *Tau Cross* tightly and neatly below the lights of a place called Bay-front Charlie's. The *Cross* fit snugly into a wide slip on the end, begging him to take it. Warren was just in time for happy hour, the two-for-one drink deal ending at sunset at Bayfront Charlie's. There was much to be grateful for; America had been good to Warren.

Jessica had been to Key Largo once before, during a vacation. She'd flown into Miami with friends and they'd driven to Key Largo, where they'd dived the famous John Penneykamp underwater preserve and coral reef park. They'd taken two dives the first day, one beyond the barrier reef in rough, wild waters which were dangerous even for seasoned divers. She believed the sea captain who guzzled beer from the moment they boarded to the moment they returned to shore was not only a derelict but was derelict in his duties and responsibilities to the divers, most of whom had become too ill to dive in the waters beyond the barrier reef and did not enjoy themselves in the slightest. Jessica had ushered her party into the wild waters before seasickness could reach out and grab hold of her, and once in the water, everyone felt a hundred percent better, but diving was treacherous, the current a good thirty-plus miles an hour as seaweed and even sea life caught up in it went racing by Jessica's mask, and the coral reefs were a hundred feet down.

Returning to the boat had been an exercise in frustration. It was near impossible to get back aboard, the boat's ladder shifting like a wild schoolyard swing. Each diver had to time his jump onto the ladder exactly right, and most were thrown clear of it repeatedly before they could get a foothold, especially with their ungainly flippers in the way. The first mate stood at the back of the boat, coaxing the divers back on, doling out advice and warning them to keep their fins on lest they drop them and lose them for good. Meanwhile, the two-ton, bare-chested captain was on his ass at the bow, drinking more suds.

When Jessica had boarded, she'd decided to throw a scare into the fat-assed captain. She went forward, flashed her badge and said, "Take us to where we can all enjoy our dive, Captain."

The bulging-eyed response had said it all. He tossed his beer into the big wastebasket and went straight to work. The second dive had been in calm, glass-clear waters, and everyone had a good time in a picture-perfect, thirty-foot-deep, magnificent coral reef. Reboarding, Jessica found that the captain had even donned a shirt for her. Looking back now on her last visit to Key Largo, Jessica had nothing but exciting memories of her earlier time here, but this afternoon, she was here for anything but a holiday.

She and Quincey found the body dredged ashore in Key Largo at the local hospital morgue, where the pathologist friend of Dr. Coudriet's, a colorful, stomach-protruding little man named Maury Oliver, led Jessica and Quincey past a handful of other corpses, old men and women from the look of them, people who'd lived a long life, retired to Florida and were now awaiting shipment "home"—wherever that destination might be. The pathologist joked, saying, "Here we have Florida's largest export. You probably thought it was oranges and grapefruit, but no . . . it's dead bodies. Ask any airport in the state."

Jessica spent only a couple of hours with the more bizarre, more morbid case of the girl who'd washed ashore here, her body stiff as though rigor mortis had clutched her and would not relax its grip—as is normal after a few hours. But this body was stiff due to preservatives, and they had preserved the floater's facial features and body far better than those of her sisters in death farther to the north.

The pathologist, a little man who resembled a gnome in a children's storybook, smiled as he watched Jessica examine the body, saying, "There're a few more surprises on the other side."

"Roll her," Jessica asked of two attendants who stood nearby.

The men did so, each swallowing hard, still capable of some empathy with the hardened corpse.

"Hell of a strange wound, wouldn't you say?" asked Dr. Oliver, in his best Sherlock imitation, his hands rubbing, scrubbing over one another in teasing fashion. "Care to make any guesses?"

She thought she saw slaver drip from the little man's mouth, as if he found the wound a turn-on.

Oliver continued, "It looks like some sort of hook, piercing here and returning here. Maybe wrapped around the spinal cord? We could tell in a jiffy, if you'd like a look inside at the bones?"

She conceded the ugly truth. "Right along the spine; just like he racked her to a wall."

"So, do you want a peek inside, at the spinal cord, or no?"

"I don't think that'll be necessary," she bluntly replied.

"Coudriet said you were thorough, so I want to be sure we're—"

"I don't think it's necessary," she repeated, losing her temper.

The sight of the wound at the back, where obviously she'd been "hooked," as it were, made Jessica think of Lopaka Kowona, the Hawaii serial killer she had run down and helped put an end to two years before. He had had a rack on the wall in his black hole of a bungalow overlooking Honolulu from the mountain foothills—his deadly killing ground. Kowona's rack was made of bamboo, and his victims were tied by rope fashioned from hair taken off previous victims. Kowona had been a fetishist and a cutter, using blades of various sizes and shapes to carve his victims slowly, methodically and ritualistically while they helplessly dangled from his rack. The similarity was in the trophy-making. Kowona always held on to something belonging to his victim, and Jessica believed the same was true of Patric. His was the work of another trophy maker, and if what Dr. Oliver was surmising was true, then the body itself had become for Patric the ultimate trophy, so that now he sought to preserve his victim in her entirety. Obviously, he'd given up when the stench had become too overpowering and he'd realized he'd failed in the preservation attempt.

"It reminded me of a mark I saw once made on a sailfish, one of those giants. It was done on the side turned to the wall, to create a hook to fasten it to the wall," said the pathologist. "'Course, it was a botched job, and 'course this ain't no fish . . . or is it?"

"Have you taken photos of this wound?"

"Of course."

"I'd like a full set, the wounds along with the woman's features."

"Sure thing, Dr. Coran."

Something about the man reminded her of C. David Eddings; she wanted to get away from him as soon as possible.

"Will you be doing a complete post-autopsy? I understand you do a lot of that."

"And how long have you and Dr. Coudriet been friends?" Jessica countered.

"We go on the occasional fishing trip when he blows through on his way to Key West or some such glamorous point. Key West . . . now that's some place. You mustn't miss it. Most expensive place in the nation to lay your head. Did you know that? On average, cost of a bed is a hundred fifty dollars a night if you figure year-round, so just imagine how astronomical it is during the height of tourist season."

"I don't think we'll be going to Key West," she replied, thinking their next stop would be Lower Metacumbe Key.

"That's too bad. You'll miss the Hemingway Festival, the Hemingway home, his cats!"

God, this guy's as annoying as Gilbert Gottfried, she thought.

He pressed onward. "And the sunset street festival, performed every night as a kind of semipagan, almost tongue-in-cheek tribute to the sun god. And the place has such charm, if you can overlook the tackiness, the human misery and filth, and if you can stay focused on the cute trolley cars and the boutiques and street vendors and perform—"

"Where on this island might we locate the electronic capability to get photographs of this new Jane Doe's face, along with a detailed description, sent to authorities all along the coast, north and south?" she asked, ignoring his Key West chamber of anti-commerce prattle.

"We've got a state-of-the-art scanner, fax and modem setup right here, just upstairs, Dr. Coran," he countered with a rakish grin. "We're not Miami or D.C., but we aren't without our electronic gizmos and—"

"That's perfect."

"The pictures are in my files. I'll get them for you."

Soon Jessica was sending a detailed photographic depiction of their latest Jane Doe to every law enforcement official in the state, asking Missing Persons departments across the state to seek a match. Given the condition of the body, Jessica had little doubt that this one would soon be identified.

"Sad business," said Quincey, sounding as if someone had let the air out of him.

"You've been a rock throughout the investigation, Quince," she volunteered.

He managed a smile. "I've watched you, Dr. Coran. You . . . now you're a rock."

"Hardly. How far's Matecumbe from here? Can we reach it tonight?" It was already dark out.

"Sure, no problem."

"Then let's push on."

• • •

When they arrived in Lower Matecumbe Key, it was pitch-black out, so dark in fact that the sheen of the waters all around the enormous Florida Bay to their west and the Atlantic on their east were brighter than the night sky. The darkness of the heavens was due to low-lying clouds, and not a star could be seen in the heavens. Water surrounded them on all sides as they made their way along U.S. 1, the Overseas Highway, spanning what seemed one interminable bridge after another.

The sand-laden land mass they drove across narrowed to a strip of ribbon fronted by an occasional gas station, a boat rental and sales office, a wharf surrounded by patient vessels of every size and type, a surprising number of beer joints and hidden homes, huddled amongst saw grass and giant palm fronds. Only the reflection from glowing orange vapor lights lining the bridges gave any respite to the bleakness, the building fog and the general feeling that they'd come to the end of the continent.

The watery landscape, dotted by uninhabited keys off in the distance, each with its own strange-sounding name, looked as if it might at any moment erupt and engulf and swallow whole the puny land mass here. The place was not very different in appearance from Islamorada Key at night, although she hadn't seen very much of Islamorada by night on her earlier visit to the Keys.

Detective Charles Quincey became lost only once in trying to locate Aeriel Marilee Lovette Monroe's residence, and this with a guide from the local police station. On the trip down, Quincey explained that Aeriel actually went by two names, depending on where she was and with whom she stayed. Aeriel Monroe was her legally changed name, but when she was home with family, she went by her given name, Marilee Lovette. This was one of the many causes for confusion in her case, and one reason why she'd been so hard to relocate.

Side streets here were paved only so far, turning into dirt roads—sand, actually—and pinching down to paths. Sandy, tree-lined, overgrown paths down which men in cars and trucks ventured at their own risk even by day was the rule and not the exception in Matecumbe. Surprisingly, a large population was hidden within the sanctuary of this world, which rejected middle-class America and all her values for life on the edge of poverty and beauty, meanness and abundance existing side by side here. A whole village of boat people—Quincey called them squatters—lived along the interior bays here, most living on their houseboats, some just off the water in the kind of "sugar shack" Linda Ronstadt's song had glamorized in popular music. But there appeared little or no glamour in the hovel where Marilee lived here in the backcountry of Matecumbe Key. In fact, it looked like a rough, grueling life where existence was eked out with each passing moment.

One major storm—and not necessarily one of a hurricane force—could wipe out the entire island, every house of straw easily coming down and its floating counterpart quickly engulfed by a patient, hungry wolf at each door—the Atlantic on one side, the Gulf of Mexico on the other. Not unlike living near a dormant volcano biding its time, awaiting its moment of supremacy. These were Jessica's thoughts as they pulled into the dark shadows of this isolated world.

Their car and that of the local deputy did not seem to disturb the solitude here in the least, and no one came out to greet their headlights. They climbed from their vehicle and followed the silent deputy to the door.

No one met them at the door, but on the inside, TV voices fought for preeminence with children in various stages of yelling, laughter and complaining; the household seemed bent on sending its industrious noise out into the world, but when the deputy knocked, the house fell as silent as a tomb, and when the man of the house cracked the door, he did so with a sleek-barreled twelve-gauge shotgun firmly in hand.

"Whataya want? Oh, it's you, Carl. What the devil brings you out here after dark?"

"Got a couple people here from Miami to see Marilee."

"Miami?"

"Detective Quincey's with the metro police up there, and

Dr. Coran—she's from the FBI, Mr. Lovette. They want to talk to your niece Marilee 'bout—''

"Reckon I know what it's 'bout, Carl.''

"It's official business, Mr. Lovette. They need to interview her about what she knows . . . you know, all that business on *America's Most Wanted*?''

A glance around the grounds showed Jessica that these people hadn't completely ignored the American Dream. They were wired for cable via a satellite dish, and a broken-down, used '67 Cadillac sat alongside a pickup under trees beside the house.

"They got the reward money with them?'' he asked.

The deputy dropped his gaze. "It don't work that way, Carl. They talk to Marilee, and if it leads to this pervert, then you'll see some reward come of it.''

Jessica and Quincey had been told by Carl the Deputy that Marilee had refused any interview outside her home with anyone but *America's Most Wanted* or *Unsolved Mysteries*, both TV programs having been contacted with her story. Jessica immediately understood the situation. Her uncle, a man in his fifties, was trying to sell her story to the highest bidder, the American path to riches.

"You can't withhold information from these folks, Mr. Lovette. You do and it's called obstruction of justice, interference with an ongoing investigation, Jake.''

The door remained closed, a chain still between them and Marilee. The deputy warned the man, "Jake, you really don't wanna climb into that hole . . . Trust me, Jake.''

"Don't worry,'' added Quincey, "whatever the girl tells us stays confidential.''

"You can still work out whatever deal you like with any of them TV producers you like, Mr. Lovette,'' added Deputy Carl Wotten.

Jake Lovette sized Quincey up, paying no attention to Jessica at the moment. He then unlatched the door, slowly stepped back, and lowered the shotgun to its resting place beside the door, telling them they were welcome to enter.

When Jessica stepped into the ramshackle little house, she immediately noticed the number of babies and children littering the floor, which was plenty littered enough already. Marilee was the eldest child and the woman of the house, it appeared. She was shy, hardly capable of looking at the intruders, fearful of them, keeping her eyes pinned on Quincey as if he were the enemy. Jessica only now felt the lascivious leer of Jake Lovette pass over her. She tried to ignore the man, who smelled of stale beer and perspiration. The air inside was thick with smoke and the odors that come with dirty linen and dirty children.

"You're Marilee?" Jessica asked the tall, thin and emaciated young woman who was desperately trying to clean up the place and losing the battle.

She turned, faced Jessica and replied, "Yes." Her voice was raspy.

"Also known as Aeriel, Aeriel Monroe? You resided for a time in Miami?"

"When I run off from home, in Screven, Georgia, I did, yes." She spoke in a thick Georgia accent which was further hindered by her constricted vocal cords, scars left from her encounter with a man bent on her destruction, if her story could be believed. She hoarsely chastised the children to remove themselves to a back room and to play quietly. It appeared she was not so much being taken care of by concerned relatives here as she'd become, by some mutual consent or contract, her uncle Jake's live-in maidservant, bottle washer and cook. Jessica momentarily wondered where the children's mother had run off to.

Marilee/Aeriel had been expecting them, for she wore a flower in her hair, and she'd donned her best, perhaps her only dress which wasn't a uniform from Nomad's Pillow Motor Inn, where she worked by day. She wore a cloth choker about her neck in an effort to conceal both the visible and the invisible scars left there after so long a time, and her voice was smoker-thick hoarse, hardly above a whisper. Jessica didn't need to ask why; it was painfully obvious that she'd lost partial use of her vocal cords due to the murder attempt, which had left her partially obstructed physically and perhaps permanently scarred psychologically.

Whether it was due to Patric Allain or some other monster she'd encountered in the world to which she had run away, this much of her story appeared painfully obvious. Marilee was in a hell of a lot worse shape than Judy Templar had been, Jessica told herself as she dug out a tape recorder from her bag and held it up to everyone's eyes. "I need your permission, Marilee, to tape our session, for the record."

She looked to Uncle Jake before responding. "I ghat no pro-lem wif that." Her voice was grating to the ear.

Jessica placed the tape recorder on the water-ringed, wobbly wood table between them, introducing herself and Quincey by their titles and for the record. "You are willingly giving your consent to being taped, Ms. Lovette?"

"I . . . I do," she replied like a nervous bride.

Jessica added, "And we would like to thank you for your cooperation."

Again Marilee glanced up at Uncle Jake, who hovered about like a second conscience. She asked, "There be henny ra-ra-ward money in dis?"

"Perhaps . . . if it leads to an arrest," Jessica assured both Marilee and her uncle, who winked and smiled back when Jessica looked up at him.

"Lady, we could sure use it," Uncle Jake replied, his face and arms tanned so darkly that the skin had become a leather sheath with wrinkles and worry lines as deep and long as wagon ruts. Uncle Jake had been chewing on tobacco the entire time, and now he coughed up a wad of disgusting brown bile and spat out a nearby window. Through the window, Jessica could see the requisite rowboat bobbing, tied to the shack. "Guddem Florida Lottery ain't worth spit," Jake added.

"Marilee, would you tell us now, in your own words, what happened the night of the fourteenth of May when you said you encountered a man who abducted, raped and choked you?"

"He was the Night Crawler. One I've read 'bout, but

atta time, no one . . . give him a name. He near't kilt me; it's a miracle I'm still alive.''

Her lines sounded practiced, Jessica thought, and her voice was sounding more normal as the interview progressed. With Jake hovering nearby, Jessica didn't doubt Marilee had had plenty of practice. Maybe this was a wild-goose chase. Jessica next asked, ''He picked you up at a bar in South Miami?''

''Tollee's . . . I was working nearby.''

Jessica had information that she was hooking nearby and had sat down at the riverside bar to rest her feet and have a beer. ''You went to the bar and had a beer, and then what happened?''

''He seemed nice; real polite.'' She had to speak at an excruciatingly slow pace, each word painful. ''Thought he must have money; he was well-dressed, you know, so when he offered to take me river-riding, why, hell . . . I said, why not? So I went with him.''

''Did you ever tell the police this?''

''Sure I did, but they didn't any of them want to hear it, not from me . . . not at the time.''

Jessica realized why. The girl had been found naked, swimming in from the sea. Police at the time quickly determined that she was new to the area, an ''out-of-town prostitute'' with an arrest record. Detective Mark Samernow took her ''story'' of innocence and filed it away and forgot about it. It explained Samernow's sourness from day one. He'd had information relative to the case but hadn't recognized it at the time. He knew later, long after losing Marilee's trail, that he'd had an eyewitness and that he'd let her go. But Marilee was among the first whom the killer had taken in Samernow's jurisdiction. Samernow, having a daughter of like age and appearance, was likely sickened and disgusted by Marilee and wanted to be shed of her as quickly and efficiently as the system allowed, and so it went.

''Go on, tell us what happened,'' encouraged Quincey, whose size made the walls here bulge.

She got up, paced to the door leading to the bedroom;

she closed it on the children. "Don't want them to hear this. Told it all to Uncle Jake."

The man was her senior by perhaps twenty-five or thirty years, and Jessica realized that Marilee had literally turned herself over to him for a roof over her head, and food to eat. "Go on," Jessica gently repeated.

She told of her seduction in broad strokes, embarrased still before Uncle Jake. Jessica kept interrupting, asking questions, searching for specifics. "What exactly did he say to you? What promises did he make?"

"Promised to take me all around in his boat."

"All around where?"

"Everyplace."

A bit exasperated with the girl, Jessica again asked, "Around the harbor, around Miami, the state?"

"Said he'd take me to places I never heard of before."

"What places? Do you remember any of the names?"

"Carmen islands, I think he said, or maybe Caramel or Caravel?"

"Cozumel, maybe?"

"No . . . not that. Someplace in the Caribbean, he said."

Jessica didn't want to lead her, but she wanted the girl to corroborate what their other witness, Judy Templar, had said about the Cayman Islands, but Marilee simply could not recall the exact name on her own.

"Go on," Jessica gently nudged her on.

Marilee described how the romantic moment turned sour in a sudden blink; she told of his brutality toward her, his repeatedly choking her and how ferociously she had fought back. She told of waking up in the cabin of his boat and pretending she was not yet conscious, and how she could not swallow. She knew instantly that he was dangerous, and that she had been choked near to death more than once by him. A clock on the wall told her that hours had passed.

"Where did this happen?"

"On the river."

"Just offshore?"

"Yeah, he never lef' sight-a land. Houses, beautiful hotels not two hunerd yards from the boat." Her hoarse voice caught, snarled on every syllable in the river of her speech. She sounded like a stuttering computer.

"What else did you see in his cabin?"

"Nothin' much . . . the usual stuff. A bed, a dinin' area, but I was flat on my back on the floor, without . . . without no clothes on. He'd torn off my clothes, had raped me and beat me and choked me. I thought he was through with me then, that he thought I were dead, you know? I thought he was sittin' there wondering what to do with my body by then, but I was wrong."

"What do you mean?"

"He . . . he had me come to; poured water—damned cold water, salty water from the river—down on me to bring me round."

Jessica and Quince both knew that the Intracoastal river fronting Miami, as in most areas of the Intracoastal, linked as it was with the sea, was, during high tide in particular, a salty environ.

Jessica put her hand on Marilee's and gently pressed. "And then?"

She was crying softly now. "I . . . I . . ." The stammer, the tears and her now naturally hoarse voice conspired to outwit the tape. "I was choked."

"Choked by hand?"

"Again, yes. He brought me around so he could do it again—even said so. Said I pleased him; said it—killing me over slowlike—it pleased him. Said he liked how I fought."

"Then you held a conversation with him?"

"I pleaded with him, but it only made him wilder."

"What kind of voice did he have?" Jessica asked.

"Mild, pleasant . . . never above a whisper . . . as pleasant as pie. All in a pretty accent. English, I think."

"How did you escape?" asked Quincey.

"Second time I came around; it was nearly dawn then, but he was up on deck, tending to something or other there. I . . . I got up all my nerve and slipped up on deck. My hands were tied with rope, and he had a noose around my neck—a hangman's noose! I knew if he found me alive again, this time he'd kill me sure. So, I just got out of there. I got up to the top and . . . and . . . I ran like a banshee, screaming, and hit the water.''

"With your hands tied?" asked Jessica.

"No, no . . . I found a knife . . . on the counter, cut the rope 'n' got outta there soon as I . . . I snatched off the noose. But I didn't have no clothes. Swum ashore stark naked . . . run up to a house and begged help. Thank God they didn't turn me away. They give me a blanket and called 911.''

"He didn't pursue you?"

"Sure he did, but by time he'd turned the boat, I was long gone.''

"Marilee's as strong a swimmer as ever I seen in a woman," added Uncle Jake.

"Then when you awoke, the motor was chugging?" asked Quincey. "He was taking the boat out of the Intracoastal? What kind of boat was it? Was there anything special you recall about the boat?"

"Big is all I know . . . and no, I don't know where he was taking it, but we were moving, yes.''

"Tell me, Marilee, and think hard now," began Jessica, "when you were in the man's cabin, did you see anything—anything—the slightest bit out of the ordinary?"

"What do you mean?"

Jessica tried another tack, asking, "Can you tell me if you saw anything that might tell us something about this monster or his habits? What did you see lying around that cabin, on the bed, on the countertops?"

"Place was full of instruments.''

"Instruments?"

"Computer stuff. A lot of blippin' and mechanical stuff.''

"State of the art, would you say?"

"It was . . . seemed so, yes.''

"Anything else catch your eye?" pressed Jessica.

"Besides the knife? I thoughta using it on him. But jumpin' for shore seemed the wisest choice I had.''

"Did you notice anything else unusual before leaving the cabin?"

"Well, there were some sewing things."

"Sewing things?"

"Like they use making nets, I think."

"Anything else?"

"Some papers; you know, magazines and stuff like that."

"What kind of magazines and papers?"

"I couldn't tell you, but they all had to do with fishing and boating, I think."

Uncle Jake prompted with, "Just try to remember, sugar."

"I was half crazed with wantin' to get out of there. I didn't look at no damn papers, so how'm I 'spose to recall . . . something 'bout . . ." She suddenly stopped, as if a flashbulb had just exploded on the horizon of her brain.

"What is it, Marilee?" asked her uncle Jake.

"Oh . . . oh, Lordy, God, yeah, he kept sayin' I'm goin' to mount you . . . goin' to mount you . . . I took it he meant he was goin' to rape me again, but . . . but . . ."

"Try to remember," Jessica encouraged. "It could save lives."

"Bastard . . . bastard . . . said he was going to stuff and prepare me for mountin' on his wall, like I was some god-damned billfish or marlin. One of those papers was on how to prepare game fish for . . . for mounting. I . . . I guess I forgot 'bout that part. Maybe, maybe I wanted to forget."

"Are you sure that's what he said?" pressed Jessica, excited by this unsolicited corroboration.

"I'm more than sure. He . . . he even said he had experience 'cause he worked at a place once where trophy fish were done up."

"Are you sure he said that?"

"Said they were turned into works of art, and asked me if I didn't want to be a forever work of art as a sacrifice for his god, something like Thou or . . . Thor or something."

"Did he say where this place was, where he learned to

mount trophy fish? Did he give you a name, anything?'' Quincey pleaded.

''No, nothin'.'' Marilee had become too distraught over the memory to go on now, and Jessica felt they had gotten all they might from the young woman who—although far from robust *since* her encounter with the killer—fit the victim profile preferred by the Night Crawler. Jessica imagined her as having had natural good looks before all this had happened, but the debilitating aftermath of her encounter with this fiend had worked dramatic effects upon her appearance, as well as her self-esteem and confidence as a woman. Of this, Jessica had no doubt.

They said their good-byes to Marilee and her uncle. Just outside the cabin, they said good-bye to Carl Wotten, the deputy, who wished them success. His final epitaph: ''I hope you catch this sonofabitch and fry him several times over in the chair.''

The night sky was impenetrable, the ocean breeze a purring, sniffing cat, and Jessica, on first hearing the unmistakable sound of soaring tobacco spit thudding into dry leaves, now saw that Uncle Jake was leering out a window at her. She shivered and thought only of getting back to the blacktop safety of U.S. 1.

''Let's get to a motel, get some rest,'' Quince suggested, his eye resting on Uncle Jake for a moment as well.

''I'm with you.''

''You-all don't forget us now when it comes time to divvy up the money,'' Jake called out after them.

Climbing into the car, Jessica said to Quincey, ''We've got a long way to go to Naples, catch up with Eriq and your partner on the other coast.''

''To hell with driving,'' countered Quincey. ''I've got a friend on the key who's a charter captain.''

''Really?''

''Old war buddies. Toured in Nam together. He'd do anything for me, drop whatever he's doing, if we meet his usual fees.''

''What're you suggesting, Quince?''

''Why don't we see if we can't get into this creep's

wake, and then maybe his face.''

"What have you got in mind, Quince?"

"Elliot Anderson knows these waters. Since the last body washed up at Key Largo, and now our guy is in Naples, the bastard had to've taken to one of the channels. Teatable Key Channel is just north of here. Elliot could take us along that tack. It's got to parallel the path the Night Crawler took in getting to Naples. Along the way, we can flash his picture. See what comes of it . . .''

She looked out at the darkness and the water lapping at the land. "All this water out here . . . Guess it is a waste not to use it. All right, you're on, Quince.''

Quincey's smile was wide and endearing. "Great choice. You won't regret it. But tell me: Did you believe every word of our Junior Miss Clueless back there?''

"She couldn't have known about the mounting, the trophy fish business.''

"I don't know. These people have their own telegraph system, and Key Largo's on the wire.''

Jessica bit her lip and asked, "You think that news is out already?''

"If some of the doctors or cops up there at Largo are talking about the hook in that Jane Doe's back—and I can't see that Dr. Oliver being shy about talking it over with every Tom, Dick and Harry—well . . . it could've filtered down this way.''

"But what would the girl gain by lying?" Stupid question, she told herself even as she spoke it.

"Reward money and a moment on prime-time TV's enough incentive for most.''

"I don't know . . . I didn't get the impression Marilee was acting," countered Jessica as Quince pulled away from the house, sending a sand and pebble cloud in their wake.

"Maybe not . . .''

"I tell you this much: I'm beginning to get a hell of a picture of our Night Crawler, Quince.''

"Know what you mean.''

"A picture of a guy who wants to create the perfect trophy for his wall.''

"But why?" he asked as he located a broken-down sign for U.S. 1.

She didn't skip a beat. "So that he will no longer have to go on killing."

"Really?"

"Once he has the perfect prize, then there's no use in continuing; at least that's what he's telling himself now."

"So, he thinks he's getting closer with each new victim?"

"That's what I think he thinks. Remember, there is no new victim to him, because they're all the same. That is, he thinks they're all the same. Treats them all the same, as if they are the same object. They've all become objects of his obsession."

"How can a human mind get so freakin' warped? And how can such a beautiful lady such as yourself think like such an animal?"

She slapped him on his considerable shoulder and said, "Quince, really . . . and you've known a few crazed and obsessed sportfishermen? And you can, if need be, think like them?"

Quincey laughed a full, hearty laugh in response. "Damn, you're something, Dr. Coran."

"Listen, Quince, do you think your charter captain friend'll know any of these fish-trophy taxidermists working the area?"

"There's quite a few freelancers and little shops all up and down, but Elliot, he'll know the majors, sure."

"Excellent." She flipped now through the pictures she'd taken with her from Key Largo, pictures of the latest victim. "We'll see what your friend makes of the marks on the Key Largo Jane Doe's back."

Jessica leaned her head out the window, realizing only now how awfully warm and red-faced she'd become while in Uncle Jake's presence. "That Jake Lovette made me feel like a piece of meat," she confided in Quincey.

"Yeah, I got that impression. The man even made me feel like a piece of raw meat. His eyes actually seemed to be asking the question, 'Ever 'et raw meat afore?' " He laughed at his own summation, and Jessica joined him.

"I got another impression about Uncle Jake as well—one not so funny," she added after the last guffaw.

"I asked the deputy about the arrangement."

"What'd he say?"

"He said they're building a case against Jake on a drug charge, but that without Marilee's testimony or some of the other, older children, that child abuse charges aren't going to stick. But after tonight, Marilee asserting herself a bit, who knows?"

Jessica winced up at the night sky, so filled with thickening clouds and with not a star in sight. "Damn but this world gets ugly and uncaring at times, doesn't it, Quince?"

He nodded, understanding.

"Wish we could save all the children and right all the wrongs," she mused. "I guess there's really no Catcher in the Rye, save God."

Quince didn't understand the allusion to J. D. Salinger's novel, but he didn't let on. "Appears we've got larger fish to fry than a child abuser, so to speak."

"Yeah, and meanwhile the bottom feeders carry on." Her fatigue and frustration with the case was showing through. She sank deep into her seat, resting her head against the headrest and closing her eyes.

"That about sums Lovette up." Quincey was going five miles over the posted limit in search of his friend's boat. "We find Elliot home, he'll put us up on the boat tonight and we can both catch some Zs, Doc."

But Jessica was already asleep.

· FOURTEEN ·

Nothing binds so fast as souls in pawn, and mortgage past.
—SAMUEL BUTLER

The Following Dawn

Jessica didn't recall boarding the boat or how she'd gotten into the berth upon which she had slept, but she woke to the pleasant beat of waves lapping at the sides of the big sportfisherman's boat, a beautiful forty-five-footer. She smelled coffee and stretched, located a change of clothes, as she'd slept in her blouse and skirt, and found Quincey and his friend on deck. They were well on their way westward through the channel, heading toward Naples, Florida.

Captain Elliot Anderson took Jessica and Quincey on a west-by-northwesterly trek toward the other coast, where Florida met the Gulf of Mexico. They passed luscious, vivid and untamed areas, as wild as anything in the Amazon, she thought. They passed the Thousand Islands area at Florida's southernmost tip, an area teeming with wildlife and fowl. Here the waters were strewn with vegetation, dotted and peppered by islands of every size and shape, their deep green and emerald colors meshing with the sea, looking for all the world like a meteor shower of land masses on Captain Anderson's maps and radar. However, on the horizon, the scattered islands looked more like sentinels, their silent byways witness to long-ago pirates.

Captain Anderson explained that most of the area was a national wildlife preserve, "good for little else except maybe oil drilling, and God help us all if it ever comes to that.''

Only when they neared the eastern coast of Florida did they begin to see some homes deep in the density of the island world, most being houseboats, more squatters. Houseboats gave way to the occasional Texaco sign, and here and there a welcoming wharf, at the end of which would be a watering hole where a person could get a beer and a sandwich. These establishments were soon replaced by the occasional resort, nightclub and full-fledged restaurant fronting the water.

The intense sun beat down, creating a brightness so radiant as to be nearly unbearable as it surrounded Jessica from all sides and reflected up from the water. Feeling strong and a bit daring, she was the first off the boat and onto the dock when Captain Anderson brought them ashore for a quick bite and a rest. She busied herself playing the sailor, snatching at one of two lines which needed securing to the dock and going about this in good fashion while Quince and Elliot exchanged a word about her, whispering so that she couldn't hear. She smiled across at them and felt the touch of her skin against the thick, black nylon rope the skipper used. It suddenly reminded her of what she'd left behind in Miami and Key Largo and of darker moments in the lab when she'd cut away the exact same brand of nylon rope from the victims of the Night Crawler several weeks before.

She composed herself and glanced around from behind her dark glasses. Quincey joined her on the dock.

''You know Elliot finds you very attractive, Doctor,'' Quince said. ''Wants you to consider coming down permanently to live on his boat with him.''

Jessica went along with what she imagined a joke between friends. ''Can he keep me in all the piña coladas and macadamia nuts I require?''

''On what he makes?'' Quince bellowed aloud for his friend's ear. ''Not hardly.''

•   •   •

Naples, Florida, That Night

Eriq Santiva and Mark Samernow looked across at one another as they sat in Samernow's squad car, the lights of a Naples street playing over their features.

"Hell of a gas voucher you're going to have to put in," Eriq said to hear himself talk. They'd traversed what the maps referred to as Alligator Alley, the entire strip of sunbleached concrete slicing through the Everglades, the wild beauty after many miles becoming monotonous and awe-inspiring at once. Now, here in Naples, they had every wharfside, dockside beer joint and restaurant on the Gulf Coast under surveillance. It had taken a massive effort to coordinate, but Santiva had called for assistance and more manpower from surrounding counties, sheriffs' offices, the Florida Marine Patrol, the Coast Guard, and the local FBI field office.

According to the local authorities, every conceivable hunting ground for the Night Crawler was covered, and now the killer's description, alias and sketch were all in the hands of law enforcement everywhere. The summer breeze wafting off the Gulf of Mexico felt like a woman's scarf being pulled lightly across Santiva's face. It was a night to excite the senses.

"Whataya think, Samernow? Do we have a chance in hell of catching this turkey in Naples?" Eriq asked, trying to get up a conversation with the stoic Miami detective and wanting a release from his thoughts, which kept returning to Jessica Coran. He wondered how she was doing in the Keys, and why she had not contacted them yet.

Samernow raised his shoulders in response to Eriq's question and said, "The bastard moves fast when he moves. He could well be up the coast by now, on to Tampa, Cedar Key, points north . . . the panhandle, who knows?"

"Ahh, I don't know," countered Eriq. "Maybe we'll get lucky. Our luck's gotta change, right? Who knows, maybe he thinks he can settle in here like he did in Miami."

"You mean, maybe he's a fool?"

The stakeout had been on for twelve hours, having begun

at five in the afternoon, happy hour for most upscale restaurants fronting the Gulf of Mexico. The fatigue was beginning to show in Samernow's features, but the man was a much happier camper than he had been in days past, Eriq thought. Samernow had seen his ex-wife and his daughter, and apparently, the reunion had been quite successful and there was the hint that they might reunite permanently. Santiva had wished him the best when he'd heard.

"Let's go look around, talk to this guy Ford who's got the most men posted. See what's going on."

Captain Richard Ford of the Naples Police Department was inside the Blue Whale, doing his part, working undercover at one of the tables. His best undercover guys and some uniforms who had volunteered to do undercover were doing it in shifts all over the city. It was a fairly small force, but they'd called in all off-duty and temporary-duty cops to fill in elsewhere.

"Better take the remote with us then, just in case," suggested Samernow.

"Right." Santiva lifted the heavy remote radio and jammed it into his coat pocket. Together, they casually walked across the street and were preparing to enter the Blue Whale when suddenly the radio crackled to life inside Eriq's pocket.

He found an alcove and responded to the call. A Detective Bear of the Naples undercover squad had a suspect in hand, "apprehended at a place called Bayfront Charlie's, next door to Captain Jack's," he said, "Decker and Riverside Drive."

Neither Eriq nor Samernow knew Naples well enough to fly straight for the scene, so they waited for Ford to appear at the door. Wired, he'd have gotten the same message where he waited undercover in the Blue Whale.

When Ford came racing out, he saw the men from Miami, and he immediately told them to follow him out toward the northern section of Naples along the waterfront.

They sped toward the scene of the apprehension, each man silently praying this was it: a final end to their shared nightmare and vigil.

Over the radio, another call came through from Bear. He was shouting for medical assistance. "Suspect down! Apparent heart attack! Captain Ford, if you can hear me, bring medics with you! I repeat, we need medical assistance at the scene!"

The other restaurant was within twelve city blocks of where they'd come from. When they entered Bayfront Charlie's, a waiter whisked them through the place and out the back and onto the dockside dining area, where Detective Steve Bear was alternately pounding on the suspect's chest and administering mouth-to-mouth, but the man lying on the weathered deck flooring looked as stone-still and unresponsive as a mannequin.

"Damnit, we've lost him before we had him!" Eriq cursed, rushing ahead of the others, going to his knees over the suspect.

A young girl stood nearby, simpering and blowing her nose; her eyes wide with fear; she kept repeating, "Is he . . . is he . . . is he . . ."

Santiva looked down at the blue-faced man below the dim light, knowing that he was dead, sensing it, and also sensing that he was not the Night Crawler. He put a hand on Bear and told him to back off, a bit more harshly than he'd meant to.

"There's no more you can do, Steve," Ford assured his man.

Eriq then took a pulse and found none. Medics rushed in and confirmed Eriq's quick diagnosis while Eriq and Mark Samernow tried to match the face with the sketch of the Night Crawler. It was close, very close, but there were significant differences. This man was older, for one, more wrinkled; heavily tanned, yes, but it appeared a cosmetic tan, the sort one purchased in a bottle or a salon. His hair was streaked with silver, blue under the lights here, and it was wavier than Patric Allain's.

"He . . . he just keeled over when we moved in to make the bust; just freaked," said Bear, a burly man doubling as a waiter in a black-and-white penguin-style tux tonight.

Santiva went to the girl. "How well did you know him?"

"I didn't . . . I just met him."

"How did you meet him?"

"He offered to . . . bought me drinks and dinner, and he . . . he propositioned me."

"Propositioned you?"

"Said we could do it on his boat. It's in the harbor. He offered me money. Nobody never did that before . . ."

Stupid child, he thought. "So you met him here, at the restaurant?"

"I was at the bar . . ."

"Do you know which boat is his?"

"No . . . we didn't get that . . . far . . ."

"Anybody here know which boat is . . . *was* his?" asked Samernow of the lingering crowd and other police officers.

"He said it was the two-masted schooner at the other end," said the girl. "Said it was his baby. Said he named it the *Southern Cross,* after the diamond, not the star. He laughed about it. Said he was a retired real estate broker and former naval officer. He seemed like a real nice gentleman, and then all of a sudden he's being arrested, and then he grabbed his chest, and . . . well, now he's dead . . ."

"Checks out from his wallet," said Samernow, rummaging through the dead man's cards and photos.

"Doesn't quite appear to jive with our information on the Night Crawler—" began Eriq.

"Night Crawler? This guy's the Night Crawler?" begged the young lady.

"We don't know that," Mark Samernow assured her, gesturing for her to keep her voice down. "Very likely no." But it was already too late; by now everyone in the place was buzzing with two words: Night Crawler.

"Our information on this creep is that he's capable of disguise and sleight of hand as well as charm, so . . ." continued Eriq as he once again kneeled over the man, whom the wallet proclaimed to be a retired American naval officer named George V. Slaughter. Eriq placed his hands over the forehead and right cheek, checking for cosmetics, and finding none he yanked at the man's mustache and hair. "Nothing false about this guy, except maybe his line." Eriq had noticed a photo of a woman and three children as Mark had rifled through Slaughter's wallet.

"What next?" asked Ford.

"We have a look at his boat. We have to be sure, one way or another."

"That might take a court order. Could take a while."

Santiva pointed down at Slaughter. "He's got no place to go. Get the search warrant. Meantime, we'll see if we can't locate next of kin."

The young detective who made the collar had turned white by now. He shakily said, "You think . . . you think my nabbing him, you know, caused his heart attack?"

"Most likely he has a history," Ford assured his man. "Don't go punishing yourself, son. Wait here for IAD and—"

"IAD?"

"Internal Affairs's is going to want to talk to you briefly. Just state the facts as you know them, Bear."

"Yes, sir."

Naples wasn't exactly a small town, but Eriq found that the police captain and his men had a small-town cohesiveness which was charming and rare.

"What about the girl?" Samernow asked Eriq.

"Send her home for now, but get all her vitals."

"Gotcha."

"Meanwhile, I'm going to get a bite to eat here and sit on this boat while Captain Ford or one of our local guys gets us that warrant. Federal warrant might carry more weight . . ."

"But you don't think this guy's our man, do you?"

Santiva shook his head. "No, no, I don't. Not even in the ballpark."

"Then why're we bothering?"

"Protocol dictates. We've come this far. People here know we're after the Night Crawler. This is going to be all over the news in an hour. We have to see if we can pluck some phoenix from these ashes, even if it's a speeding ticket or boating violation. Hell, in a sense we have to cover our asses; this could blow up in our faces, like the police counterpart of a medical malpractice suit. A guy may've died as a direct result of our stakeout."

Samernow nodded, understanding. "You think the guy's family might sue the city or the FBI, or both?"

"Nowadays? Who knows—all of the above, including you and me, Mark."

"Yeah, right. People've tried to sue for a hell of a lot less."

Santiva went to the bar and ordered a whiskey sour, wanting to see what Jessica Coran liked about them. He wondered how she had fared in Key Largo and Metacumbe, wondered why she hadn't been in contact, wondered where she was at this moment. When the bartender returned with his drink, he ordered a ham and swiss on rye with fries.

He found himself missing Jessica, missing her company, their partnership and camaraderie. Being apart from her now these several days, he realized just how important to him their friendship was, how much he valued her trust and respect. He admired the way she had barged in with regard to the investigation, and even her attitude toward the release of information which she believed vital to the well-being of others. It showed she had courage and heart, a brave heart. She had shown such backbone, that one . . .

Around him people buzzed; Ford was trying desperately to keep a lid on things, guiding IAD officers through the maze of what had happened here, and how it had happened, finally leading them to a still shaken Detective Bear. Ford seemed a good man, a solid cop.

Once more Eriq's thoughts floated away to where Jessica might be. He might easily have taken a hard-nosed approach with her for having released information to the press without his express consent, but he hadn't, for the simple reason that he had secretly agreed with her move. If the damned agency and the damned politicians would let him do his job, if they'd stop roping his hands behind his back, he most assuredly would have released everything they had on the Night Crawler himself the night Jessica had done so. Maybe then she'd see him in a better light, maybe. It had become extremely important that she not view him as the enemy, and that she continue to hold a positive opinion of him.

Once the proverbial shit had hit the proverbial fan—when Jess had chosen to release the artist sketch and APB on the killer—Eriq had simply told himself to hell with it, but that attitude hadn't lessened in the least the amount of flak which he'd had to endure from above. He had taken a great deal of crap for Jessica's actions; half or more of it she would never know.

Now however, here in Naples, removed from the situation and from Dr. Jessica Coran's presence, he wondered if there weren't more to it—the admiration and respect he held for this fine woman of science and integrity. Despite the fact that they actually had not accomplished a great deal here in Florida, Eriq found himself admiring her at every turn, and he'd come to realize that he didn't want ever to lose her trust and friendship to bureaucratic bullshit, neither now nor in the future. Still, something else had been nagging at him all day, and sitting about with Samernow hour after dour hour had given him a great deal of time to think. So he had begun to wonder . . . If it were any other agent than Dr. Jessica Coran, would he have behaved in the same calm, polite, accepting manner that he had? Anyone else and he most likely would have lobbed off the head and sent the body to Siberia, or at least to Pocatello, Idaho.

He wasn't sure what his feelings meant or precisely how to deal with them, but one thing he was increasingly sure of: This chief agent in Hawaii, James Parry, was a fool to have lost Jessica.

The radio on Captain Elliot Anderson's charter boat crackled with stories about arrests taking place overnight in and around the Naples area; apparently authorities everywhere were on a full-scale effort, or so reported WKIK—*Kick Radio*—in Naples. Jessica learned of the heart attack victim, "who," the reporter said, "was arrested after he expired, police taking no chances . . . and every precaution . . ."

The joke wasn't lost on either Quincey or Anderson, who

shook their heads over the announcer's words and tone.

Other outlandish arrest stories followed: One female-male impersonator, one African-American, one man with an Austrian—not an Australian—accent. This fellow was a man named Neubaurer who was on holiday, just come from Mickey Mouse Land in Orlando only to be accosted by police in Naples. "The moment he was released," the radio announcer said, "Neubaurer rushed directly to the nearest law office to file a complaint in the hope of winning the great American dream, a fortune through litigation."

Along their watery route to Naples, Captain Elliot Anderson had been studying all manner of charts and maps, but now he had snatched down a gazetteer-styled map of the entire state of Florida and its waterways. He spread the map across the top of the cabin of his charter vessel and asked Jessica and Quincey to give him the exact locations where each of the Night Crawler's victims had washed ashore.

This done, Anderson placed an overlay onto the map which showed precise ocean currents and drift factors. From a small black journal, he factored in wind coefficients and velocities on or about the day of each gruesome discovery. He then began a startlingly intelligent geography of the crimes using educated guesses as to the location of the killer's boat at each instance a body was, as he put it, "launched" from Patric Allain's craft.

Given the degree of wind and water current in from the sea, Anderson's projections were startlingly on target.

Even as an approximation, the map of killings revealed a great deal about the movements of the killer—a great deal more than the large map on the wall back in Miami had ever revealed. Anderson's quick hand and expert eye had created a clear picture of a ship that'd sailed from the Keys north to Miami and back again along a certain time line. Given the northward drift of the eastern coastal waters, a body that had been discovered as far north as Pompano Beach, north of Fort Lauderdale, which police had not put together with the Night Crawler's heinous collection could, according to Anderson, be among the victims if the killer had toured at all toward Fort Lauderdale.

Jessica looked out over the emerald-green waters of the peaceful Gulf of Mexico and away from the white buildings and red-tiled roofs of Naples on the port side of the bow now.

"As to your earlier question," said Anderson, "there is a taxidermist of considerable reputation here, name of Buckner—rather famous, actually. Does all kinds of animals, even does this thing where he puts the head of a gator onto the body of a blue- or yellowfin, or the head of a possum on a fish, names the things and sells 'em to the highest bidder."

"There you have it," said Quincey. "Maybe our guy's come to see Buckner's special creations."

"We haven't had any sort of uncanny luck before in this case, so why should we now?" Jessica asked. She momentarily wondered if Santiva wouldn't soon be throwing it in her face, that it had all been a wild-goose chase coming here. She wondered if Eriq had determined with any degree of certainty if the handwritten note from the killer postmarked Naples was indeed the same handwriting as earlier notes.

Anderson tried to soothe Jessica's fear that perhaps the killer had taken another direction altogether and that they were now pursuing a copycat killer. Anderson said, "If the SOB did come this way, he took one of the channels up, just as we did, and we're in his wake now."

Jessica remained cynical, crossing from one side of the boat to the other, pacing as she spoke. "Even if we were sure that we were in his wake, as we came along the southern tip of Florida there were literally thousands of islands amid which he might have hidden. We're working blind here, gentlemen, and I can honestly tell you that I don't believe I've ever worked a case with so little to go on but frustrated efforts . . ."

"But if his ship is a seventy-footer and as beautiful as you say it is . . ." Anderson rejoined.

"No," she corrected him, "we only know what witnesses have said about the boat, and Quince, we both know how unreliable witnesses are. We can't even be sure if our sketch of the *man* is accurate, much less his boat.''

"On the other hand," Anderson continued as if speaking to himself now, "we've passed some of the most gorgeous sailing vessels ever to frequent these waters—there are so *many* here fitting your description."

Quincey pushed Anderson in a good-natured way, saying, "That's right, side with her."

"Well, she's a damn sight prettier than you!"

Jessica, Quince and Captain Anderson now eased into a harbor and boat slip in downtown Naples, a sign proclaiming the slip for the express use of the harbor patrol only. Captain Anderson had warned they might have problems docking here and that he was concerned, as fines were measured out in the hundreds of dollars at a city-owned harbor, telling Jessica and Quince that the harbormaster would rent out as much space as possible to make a buck under the table, cutting corners when it came to holding open slips for Coast Guard and police vehicles.

"At the moment, this is a police vehicle—undercover," Quince assured his friend. "Commandeered, as they say."

"That mean I don't get paid, pal?"

"Not to worry. Your check'll come from Miami-Dade as soon as I get back and make out the voucher."

"Six to nine months after the voucher, you mean."

Jessica piped up with, "Maybe with the FBI putting a little juice on it, we can do better this time, Captain."

Elliot Anderson grimly looked in Jessica's direction but only found her raising a disparaging shrug and saying, "We'll see you're reimbursed for your time and effort here, Captain, my promise."

As they entered an empty slip—which appeared to be the only one open, just as Anderson had warned—a stubby little man with a clipboard came racing out to them, waving them off and shouting, "Can't you damned fools read?" The little mustached man reminded Jessica of the gate-keeper in the Wizard of Oz, and he didn't look above a bribe.

• • •

Captain Anderson chose the Naples municipal harbor as perfectly suited to their needs, for City Hall and the main branch of the Naples Police Department were within view and walking distance. After securing the boat, Jessica said to Anderson as he was about to alight from the boat, "Captain, please bring your navigational chart, the one you used to get us here, and the map and overlay you created which shows the movements of the killer since discovery of the first body by Coudriet in—"

"You can take them," he replied, "but I'll need replacements."

"Replace them while you're in port here. I'll reimburse you on the receipts."

"Fine."

"But I want you to come with Quince and me to show our associates your chart. It's of great importance."

"You want me inside a police station? Don't know if I'd feel comfortable, Doctor, much as I'd like to help . . ."

"Damnit, Elliot," bawled Quincey. "It's not like we're asking you to step into a war camp. It's just a big office, and you're not under arrest."

"Just a big office, huh? With rooms in the basement with lots of bars—and not the kind of bars I like to frequent." The man reminded Jessica of Jimmy Buffet as he scrunched up his face and nose, considering his options a moment until he saw Jessica's pleading eyes.

"Just long enough to explain the maps to my partner," she asked.

"All right . . . anyone ever say no to you, Dr. Coran?"

"Sometimes, sure."

"Stronger men than I . . ."

Jessica now took note of the beautiful setting and lush greenery here. The city was alabaster-white, almost all the buildings bright pastels or whitewash with exotic-looking orange- and red-tiled roofs in old Spanish style. Moss hung like strange garlands around ancient trees, giving them the appearance of alien Christmas trees. These ancient oaks and poplars lined wide streets, and palm-lined avenues—corridors to the city—were clean and inviting. From here she could see that the business, historical and government districts all shared the stage along the same spacious avenues. There were no skyscrapers here, the tallest of buildings perhaps ten stories, and these were rare—hospitals and banks. Like many or most Florida towns, Naples maintained a small-town atmosphere where parks along the waterways were filled to capacity with boaters and picnicking families, the children flying kites, chasing dogs and Frisbees and climbing up and down the town gazebo.

All in all, it was an elegant little city, the kind of place found only in dreams, the kind of place where evil died of loneliness, the kind of place where fear, ignorance, rage, prejudice, pestilence and poverty never entered—or rather hid very well amid the scarcity of shadow; still, it appeared the kind of place where only gentleness, kindness and light-heartedness could thrive, the kind of place lost in America's past and found now only in imagination, the kind of place where people were lulled into believing that peace and safety and brotherhood and sisterhood and tranquillity and an unlocked door could actually exist on the planet. The little city by the emerald Gulf seemed quite out of keeping with the Night Crawler's usual teeming haunts.

On their walk toward the expensively laid-out grounds of the police station here—a sure sign that all was not well in this little jeweled city—Jessica thought of the allusions in the Night Crawler's poetry to stage and theater. She now voiced her thoughts to Quincey. "This doesn't exactly look the perfect stage for the Night Crawler to crawl out on to strut his stuff."

Quincey cleared his throat and thoughtfully replied, "Well, there're areas, especially along the outer islands and north of here, that are teeming with nightclubs and night-life."

Elliot Anderson added, "If your guy's here, the bastard's most likely just casually trawling these waters while on his way to a larger arena . . ."

Jessica's step slowed. "A larger arena?"

"A major metropolis, like Miami," Quincey filled in.

"Tampa-St. Pete, I believe," said Anderson.

Quincey agreed instantly.

Jessica sadly agreed as well. ''I guess you're both right on one score.''

''He needs a big kettle,'' Anderson finished for her.

She nodded. ''He feeds on the anonymity afforded by a large city.''

Quincey quickly added, ''Every predator needs a jungle.''

She added. ''And every predator's jungle must conceal him.''

· FIFTEEN ·

To go and find out and be damned ...
—RUDYARD KIPLING

At police headquarters, Jessica had no trouble locating Eriq once she and Quincey found Mark Samernow nursing a cup of coffee and a gone-cold gyro. Although it was not quite 11 A.M., Samernow explained that he and Chief Santiva had been up all night with a character who might or might not have a line on the Night Crawler, a fellow who may've harbored the killer for a time. They'd just finished up with a lie detector test on him.

Jessica followed Samernow and Quince to the interrogation room, along the way locating the ready room where Elliot Anderson could set up his maps.

Quincey joked with Samernow, ribbing him about the news accounts they'd been hearing out on the Gulf. "So, I hear you collared a dead guy, Mark?"

Samernow's ears reddened and Jessica could only imagine the scowl on his face, unable as she was to actually see the gaunt man's features as he kept walking.

Quince dug the knife in deeper and twisted it by repeating what he'd said as if Mark hadn't heard. "Heard you collared a dead guy?" He just couldn't resist.

Samernow didn't miss a beat this round. "You try it sometime. Hardest collar I ever got. Bitchin' paperwork, and when we tried to stand him before the judge, well, all hell broke loose," recounted Samernow, in rare form. Seeing his daughter had obviously helped his disposition.

"Yeah," Jessica teased Mark now, her smile growing.

"Heard you brought in an Austrian?"

"Cops here are gung-ho to bring in the Crawler. Can you blame them? They've never had a chance to make *Top Cops* or *Unsolved*, so they're working overtime at it. Can't say that's the worst attitude they might've taken. So, how'd you guys do down south? How'd it go in Key Largo and Matecumbe, and why'd it take so damned long to get here?"

Quince answered with his own question. "So, Mark, what gives with Aileen and your kid?"

"They're great, really . . ."

"That good, huh?"

Samernow marched on toward the interrogation room, and they trailed after, the corridors here being extremely narrow, all the government outlay of funds having obviously been for exterior show. "Oh, by the way, the rechecks and double checks of the Miami harbors turned up zip on our guy, so we can kiss any leads coming out of that trail good-bye. Got word over the fax this morning from Noonan back at headquarters."

There was a full-fledged interrogation going on, Captain Ford and Eriq Santiva doing the grilling on the inside while Jessica and Quince were shown to the one-way mirror where they might watch, but it didn't sound promising. "Who've they got in there?"

"Looking less and less like a suspect," replied Mark. "Some guy who claims to've seen the killer. Claims he knows who the killer is, that he held a conversation with Allain."

"What does he have?"

"The name Patric Allain, which everybody has by now, remember?" He didn't mean for it to come out an indictment of her having released the information, but it did and it stung.

"So what makes him special?" asked Quince.

"Two things. He claims he knew something of Allain earlier, and that Allain showed up a few days ago at his shop."

"His shop?" asked Quince.

Jessica added, "What kind of shop?"

"Taxidermy shop."

Quincey and Jessica momentarily gawked at one another, unable to believe their ears, and then back at the man under interrogation, a man who looked as if he'd fallen off a seventeenth-century ship and washed ashore in rags, a Robinson Crusoe appearance about him, even down to his earrings, shorts and open shirt. He wore a long, scraggly beard that looked both dirty and uncombed. As thin as a dime, he looked like part of the growing homeless population.

"Rode his bike into headquarters just to tell us his story," said Mark Samernow with a little shake of his head.

Quince asked, "What's he ride, a Harley?"

"Not hardly. Try a Schwinn, a bicycle. Old one at that."

Jessica frowned and asked, "This guy is a businessman? He owns his own shop but rides a bicycle?"

"What's this guy's name?" asked Quince. "Wouldn't be Gordon Buckner by any chance, would it?"

Samernow glared at his partner. "What're you psychic now? Or did you overhear the name while we were approaching?"

"Mark," replied Jessica, "you never mentioned his name, not once. Captain Anderson told us about Buckner before we landed."

"Anderson? The guy you came in with?"

"Buckner's got some sort of reputation among sportfishermen for what he can do with dead fish."

Samernow looked at the old man with rekindled interest. "So?"

"He makes trophy fish for walls. If the girl in Matecumbe can be believed, and if the dead body in Key Largo can be believed, it all begins to make warped sense why the Crawler pulled up stakes and chose to come here, in search of the master—Buckner."

"Let's listen up, see what Mr. Buckner has to say," suggested Quince, finding a hard seat and trying to make himself comfortable.

Jessica remained standing, her arms folded, her eyes

studying the man under interrogation, her ears filling with the questions he posed and the answers he provided.

Gordon Luis Buckner was certain of his information. He was approached by a man who wanted to know everything that "Buck" Buckner knew about preserving fish flesh, down to the chemicals he used. However, the man, while a stranger to Buckner and sporting a British accent and a beard, was no novice himself. He had a working knowledge of taxidermy, albeit limited, and claimed to have worked in a place in Key West that specialized in the "art form," Works of Art Taxidermy, a place Buck himself had started and sold out to a partner when, in his words, "Key West had became too fulla fags and too damned commercialized even for Jimmy Buffet."

Buckner was a weather-beaten, scrawny and aged man, late sixties, perhaps even early seventies. And he looked like something that had gone out with the tide and the trash through a portal on a sea scow. Unwashed and unkempt, his devilishly sporty gray beard, a multicolored scarf over his nearly bald white head and an earring dangling from both right and left ears marked him as a modern-day Florida pirate—no doubt an image he relished, especially when he grinned to show broken teeth and some gold. The man had pirate written all over him, in every sense of the word. He was a roguish man, and he liked using colorful and off-color words as he spoke. Every one of the cops present wondered if they dared believe half what he was saying.

"Blasted bastard foreigner, he was . . ." Buckner was going on at length now, describing his incident. "Spoke just as sweet as Mom's apple pie, like a lily-livered, be-damned limey if you was to ask me." He stopped to chuckle through those awful broken teeth. "Claimed he was going to open his own shop, like mine, made a lotta noise about how he admired my work, all that crapola. Said he'd seen my work in *Sport Fishing Today*—"

Jessica had stepped into the interrogation room moments before, making Buckner perk up and say, "Well, *now* you boys are talking. This I can deal with."

Captain Ford slapped a magazine into Jessica's hand, a marker at the pages where Buckner's creations were given several pages of space in photos depicting what Jessica could term only as hideous monstrosities, mounted fish bodies with the heads of badgers, opossums, alligators as well as whole, intact yellowfin and marlin. The article indicated an international market for what Buckner and a few other Florida trophy taxidermists had discovered in the way of a new "art form." There was some mention also of litigation as to who owned patent rights on this dubiously creative invention in fish mounting.

"He had a copy of the article with him," said Buckner. "Said he'd heard about me all up and down the Eastern seaboard and all the way here."

"And it was afterwards, when you saw the wanted sketch on *America's Most Wanted*?" asked Eriq, who was leaning against one wall now, showing signs of extreme fatigue.

" 'Zactly. My wife watches the program. I don't care a whit 'bout it or anything else on the boob tube, 'cept maybe a fishin' show now and again, but for some reason, she says look at that guy, talking 'bout how that dirty killer looked so normal and handsome, yet he was wanted for strangling and drowning so many young girls, so I look up and damned if it ain't the same man who was in my shop just the day before."

Jessica realized that the episode had obviously aired on a local network as a rerun. She had already heard enough, and was convinced that the old man spoke the truth. She moved in further to tip her badge in Buckner's direction and introduce herself to him. Then, with Eriq staring a hole through her, she asked, "Did Aliain, did he actually use the name Patric Allain, sir?"

"He did."

"You're sure of that?" she pressed, and Buckner shifted in his seat.

"Well, either he did or my partner Scrapheap Jones down in Key West did when I telephoned him, you know, to verify this young'un's story, that he'd worked for a time down there with Scrapheap. But that was 'fore I realized he was that killer, the Night Crawler, and Scrapheap, he didn't have no clue about that, no more'n I did, don't you see?''

Captain Ford nodded as he tried to follow the convoluted trail of information spewing forth from Gordon Buckner, an obviously heavy drinker whose bloodshot eyes and broken teeth only added to his image and the incredulity in which he was being held by the police.

"Did he say anything about returning to your shop?" pressed Santiva.

"Sure, sure he did, or I did rather."

"Well, which is it, man?" Eriq was being extremely short now.

Captain Ford asked more calmly, "When, Gordon? When'll he be returning?"

"He's 'sposed to be back today, to start in on his training."

Eriq breathed a deep sigh, and Jessica on the other side of the table followed suit as the two of them exchanged eye contact. It seemed hardly likely that the killer meant to spend any time in such a port as this, certainly not long enough to train at anything. Jessica also saw that Eriq was dead on his feet, and she felt a little guilty. She had slept like a baby on board Anderson's charter boat, *The Misfit*.

"He told you he was coming back?" Jessica was both astounded and pleased to hear this.

"That's what I told your friends here, but they haven't the sense to believe me."

"Coming back for . . . for more lessons in taxidermy?"

"Mostly understands the process. He wanted to know about my most potent chemicals. Wanted to know if I gut a gator before I preserve it, and if there was a way to do it and leave the internal organs intact." He looked up at them, around the room. "By God, it's what he said. I told him it'd be foolish to leave the innards; they'd spoil, and the stench would be overwhelming after a time."

"What did he say to that?" she asked.

"I offered to do him some lessons in trophy setting, since he was being so generous with his money."

"To show him how to do what he wanted?"

"He said he'd pay double my usual salary for the job. Couldn't turn it down, but now . . . hell, I don't never want to be alone with that motherfucker ever again, ever. That's why I come to you boys; figure you can do one of them whataya-callits?"

"A stakeout," supplied Chief Ford. "You bet we will."

"What else do you know about this Patric Allain?" asked Jessica of Gordon Buckner as she began to pace the room, taking Eriq's eyes with her. Was he upset that she'd stepped into his interrogation? Perhaps, but she had questions for Buckner that couldn't wait. "Had you ever seen him before?"

"No, never. Friends of mine in Key West told him about me, or so he said. Showed me a note scrawled in Scrapheap's handwriting."

"A note?"

"Yes, ma'am."

"Do you have it with you?"

"Naw, pitched it back at the shop. Prob'ly out at the dump by now. Why? Is that important?"

Santiva shook his head. "Could be . . . might've been. If he wrote anything on it, anything at all, we could match it to handwriting samples we already have on this guy."

"Matching his handwriting ain't gonna fetch him, though, is it?"

"It could help convict him, should he fail to confess, Mr. Buckner," Jessica explained. "It would also tie him to the crimes if we can place him in shops like yours. You see, he's been using chemicals such as those you use for preserving for . . . in an attempt to preserve human flesh."

Buckner cringed. "He musta been the one who broke into my shop last night, made off with some chemical compounds . . . Disgusting, despicable SOB."

"Did the note he carried have a date affixed to it, sir?" she asked.

"Yeah, he'd just come from Key West. It had a date on it for Saturday last."

"Thank you, that's very important, Mr. Buckner."

"Buck, honey . . . you can call me Buck."

Buck continued where he'd left off before Jessica had interrupted him. "I did some calling, checked up right after this fella left, and sure 'nough he was down Key West way, making a nuisance of himself just 'bout ever'day, according to my former partner at Works of Art. So, they put him on for a time. That'd been last fall, almost a year now."

"They hired him on?"

"Right, 'cept it was more like they apprenticed him."

"In other words, he paid your friend?"

"They don't have many jobs to come open, so he worked for nothing. Said he wanted to learn the business, so—" Bruckner gasped to a stop, looked around to Eriq and asked, "You Feds aren't going to get after ol' Scrapheap Jones in Key West, now are you?"

Jessica assured him they weren't IRS agents.

"What time did you tell Allain to return to your shop?"

"Two this afternoon."

Jessica and Eriq exchanged a look of satisfaction. Finally, they knew they were on the right track, although each wondered if putting the arrest moves on the Night Crawler could be this simple. After all, if there had been a break-in and the killer was behind it, he might well not return. It would take some arrogance to do so. Then again, they knew this character had plenty of that commodity to spare.

"Can you get us a surveillance van, something with a logo on it, something inconspicuous?" asked Eriq of Ford.

"We can get an FPL van from Florida Power and Light."

"Perfect."

"Let's move on it," agreed Jessica. "Mr. Buckner . . . Buck, I'm your granddaughter for the time being. Is that acceptable to you?"

"You a good shot?"

"She's the best," assured Santiva.

"Welcome to the family." Buckner's face broke into a wide grin and his leathery hand took hers and held it until the sweat made her uncomfortable.

"You go back to your shop for now, Gordon," Chief

Ford told the man. "Try to carry on as if it were a normal day."

Eriq interjected, saying, "And don't let on that you suspect this guy in the least. If he comes in, treat him courteously, like you would any customer."

"The hell I will—"

"Mr. Buckner!" shouted Ford.

"I have to yell and shout at the bastard if he's to be treated like any of the fools I've taught my trade to over the years. 'Sides, if I don't treat 'im just as goddamned rude as I done before, then he *will* suspect something's up."

Jessica joined Ford when he broke into a smile and laughed. "That's just fine," agreed Ford. "You do that. That'll be just the way to play it then, old-timer."

" 'Old-timer,' is it?"

They wrangled with one another through the doorway and down the corridor. Alone with Eriq now, Jessica turned to him. "He's here—the Night Crawler's here—and we're going to snare him this time."

Eriq had found one of the chairs and collapsed into it. "Careful, our batting average in Naples—hell, in the whole state—hasn't exactly been sterling. For all we know this old coot could've entertained a perfectly harmless guy who wants to take up a weird hobby and doesn't in the least resemble our killer."

"But the British accent, and the fact that he wants to know more about trophy setting, preservatives . . . Eriq, it's got to be Allain. The old man said he used the name Patric Allain."

"So did *America's Most Wanted.* Do you think the killer would continue to use the name, knowing we're hot on it?"

She frowned and tried to look everywhere but into Eriq's eyes. He seemed intense, almost distraught, "I know you're still upset with me about releasing as much as I did on the Night Crawler, and you have every right to be, Eriq, but—"

He shot to his feet, waved her down with his hands and, hissing, said, "That's water under the bridge. We're partners here, and we're going to end this thing together."

"Today, today at two P.M.," she insisted, wanting very much to believe it possible.

"So, yeah . . . let's keep that happy positive thought lodged firmly in our minds, okay? You're probably right. Ol' Buck seems to be very knowledgeable about our man, and he's most likely telling the truth."

"So far as he knows it, you mean? You sound skeptical, Eriq."

"So far as he knows it . . . so, right . . . right . . . and I'm pretty sure . . . there's one thing seems certain enough."

"What's that?"

"This creep wants to take the next highest step in his evolving fantasy, like you said, Jess. His is not a fixed fantasy like most killers, but one that is growing larger and more deadly each day."

Jessica hesitated a moment before answering, choosing her words with great care. "The Night Crawler most likely had to have used his Patric Allain alias with Buckner, don't you see? It would've been on the recommendation from Buckner's partner in Key West. His partner may well have Allain's handwriting on some agreement they made. I'll contact him, see if anything shakes loose there."

"If it's as Buckner remembers, yes . . . But he's a bit strange," Eriq again cautioned, "and so he may have just picked up the name from another source, like his TV set. He may be a *Most Wanted* junkie who's decided to seize upon an opportunity to get his face on the boob tube."

Again the *Most Wanted* episode, with details about Allain, had come back to haunt them; and yet without it, Buckner might not have come forward.

"So, how did everything go in Key Largo and Matecumbe? Gain any new insights? Any new evidence?" he wanted to know as he worked up a smile for her. She read into his unspoken words: *Was the trip worth the taxpayers' money?*

"You prepared to be astonished?" she replied.

"I would love to be astonished."

"Then come with me."

She led him from the cold, institutional interrogation room and down the corridor.

"Where we going?"

God, he sounds weary, she thought before replying, "The ready room. Someone there I want you to meet." Along the way, Jessica explained what they'd found in the Keys, what vital new information they had learned about their prey, and why they had come to Naples by boat. She finished up as they relocated the task force room where Captain Anderson's maps had been pinned to a wall. She found Anderson pacing with a Styrofoam cup of coffee in one hand, a packet of photos of the victims in the other. He flipped through the photos with growing anger.

Eriq, ever alert even if he did look like hell, went directly to the new maps, asking, "What's this all about?"

Jessica brought Anderson over to meet Eriq and introduced them as they shook hands.

The room was alive with buzzing computers, in stark contrast to the silence of the interrogation room. Men and women moved from desk to desk, checking readouts, swapping information and the occasional joke; the place had the feel of an army being mobilized. A large blackboard and podium at one end gave the impression of a classroom, and a huge corkboard at the other end only added to the effect. Ford had somehow gotten photos of all the victims, and they'd been spread across a discovery time line and displayed at eye level.

"Chief, these maps represent Captain Anderson's depiction of the moving crime scene, the—"

"The Crawler's boat?" Eriq was instantly curious, studying the maps.

"Against a map of currents and drifts, showing Patric Allain's possible movements."

Eriq was both impressed and incredulous. "Why the hell didn't our experts create something like this for us from the beginning?"

"Maybe it took a seaman's point of view," suggested Anderson.

"This is like . . . like a damned psychic thing. How did

you come up with this?'' he asked Anderson.

"Eriq," began Jessica, "Quincey and I watched Elliot put this together. He did it after we answered his questions, during the boat trip here.''

"My ship is registered out of the Bahamas," volunteered Anderson, "and she's called *The Misfit*." Anderson again offered his hand and firmly shook Eriq's.

"Yeah, okay, I see, and you're telling me you arrived here by . . . by boat?'' Eriq's expression was pinched, as if he weren't understanding, as if one of his burners remained unlit.

"Yes, Captain Anderson's boat.''

Eriq gave her a look of stunned curiosity, but he said nothing more.

Anderson picked up the slack moment, saying, "When the first body drifted away from the killer's boat, he was south of the discovery site by at least ten and possibly fifty miles, given the northward drift of the current along Florida's eastern seaboard so far south.''

Eriq looked again at the suntanned, handsome sea captain and said, "Hell, maybe we ought to have you conducting this investigation, Captain . . . ahh . . .''

"Anderson," Elliot repeated, trying on a nervous laugh, but he wasn't sure if Eriq was kidding or being sarcastic, and neither was Jessica, who now glared at Eriq. She realized that Eriq had been up all night and was fatigued, but he was being rude now to a man who only wanted to help, and she didn't understand why.

"From the sound of things, I'd say there're already too many chiefs in your army, Chief Santiva," continued Anderson, taking a new course and tossing his used cup into a nearby container, "so I'll not add to your problems. I'm out of here, Dr. Coran. See you back at the boat?''

She nodded, knowing she'd have to return there to retrieve her belongings. "Yeah . . . yeah, later.''

She wheeled on Eriq and through grinding teeth asked, "Do you want to explain to me what that was all about?''

"What? What? Did I offend the guy? Well, pardon me.''

"Eriq, you're beyond fatigue, you're out of it, and you're hardly making all the right . . . connections.''

"I think I know a connection when I see one, and the way that guy was looking at you, well . . . two nights on a boat with you, I guess that might get to any guy."

"There's nothing going on between Elliot and me! Quincey was with us the whole time."

"Yeah, that'd put a damper on any budding romance." He tried a laugh, which failed. Then he groggily and foolishly added, "And if Quincey hadn't been aboard? What then, Jess?"

Jessica inwardly admitted a certain attraction for Anderson, who was the quintessential freedom-loving, sun-worshiping sportfisherman. But she hadn't acted on what little she admired about the man, who in essence remained a stranger to her; nor had she encouraged Anderson to make any moves on her. "This is ridiculous, and worse, what business is it of Eriq Santiva's in the first bloody place?"

He dropped his gaze to the floor and nodded. "Yes, of course, I'm . . . I'm sorry, Jess. I haven't the right to . . . to have . . . to say . . ."

"Listen, you'd better get some sleep before two rolls around, if you expect to be in on the net, Eriq. You look awful, you're dead on your feet and your mind is in the gutter."

"There're a hundred things to orchestrate."

"I'm a fine maestro; let me orchestrate. Go find your bed and set your alarm."

Eriq ambled away—like a dejected puppy, Jessica thought, feeling somewhat sympathetic about his condition, and still a bit stunned by what he had said. Where the hell was his mind? Quincey and Samernow joined her now, along with Captain Ford, interrupting her musings.

"Let's see what the Naples PD has in the way of undercover wear, people," suggested Ford.

"And just how would the granddaughter of the famous and infamous Gordon Buckner dress?" asked Jessica with a rakish smile.

"I think she's definitely a jeans and plaid shirt girl, so you're halfway there," Quincey replied with a chuckle.

"Ragged cuticles and open-toed shoes," added Samernow.

Eriq was suddenly back, and he pulled her to the side and walked her into an empty stairwell, wanting a private word with her. "Whatever happens out there today, Jess, you don't take any chances."

"Not a chance . . ."

"I mean it—no stunts or foolish hotdogging. Got it?"

She looked again into Eriq's handsome face and penetrating eyes, which were glazed over at the moment like those of a druggie. Probing, wondering what he'd been on all night, she asked, "Where's this coming from, Chief? Eriq?"

"Just be careful. No one wants you hurt."

"Someone been telling you stories out of school about me? Or have you been reading my jacket again? I'm not a risk, not for myself and not for others, and certainly not for you."

"Not a risk, huh?"

"No." Then she saw it in his eyes: a glimmer of lust, a flourish of desire, a bird spreading wings to take flight in that moment that his eyes lingered over hers, and she realized for the first time since seeing him that between Naples and Miami he had somehow concocted some sort of love interest in her. "No, no . . . this isn't going to happen, Eriq, not between us. It would just get in the way and serve no purpose because—"

"I can't help the way I feel, Jess." He reached out, took her shoulders in his hands and was about to pull her to him when she pulled away.

"No, Eriq . . . I'm sorry, but this . . . it's just not what I want or need at the moment. It's nothing against you, nothing like that at all. It's just that—"

"It's Anderson, isn't it?"

"Damnit, Eriq! Blink once for *hello*, Eriq, and twice for *no, I'm no longer on this planet*! There is nothing going on between Anderson and me. Got it?"

"Then it's Parry, isn't it?"

He knew she found him attractive, so she needed a good

excuse to stiff-arm Eriq with, and Jim Parry certainly presented a larger-than-life explanation which Eriq could both grasp and find solace for his male ego.

"Yeah, yeah . . . that's it. I'm still very much in love with Jim."

He nodded appreciatively. "I've been there. I just want you to know that if you ever need someone, Jess . . . if you ever need anything from me, day or night . . . well, I'm not just your superior, I'm your friend."

It was a genuine remark, despite the "superior" crap. She smiled, nodded and thanked him.

"I mean that one hundred percent, Jess. You okay with that?"

She nodded. "Now, you go get that rest, and for God's sake, Eriq, don't ever change."

"And what're you going to do in the meantime?"

"Meantime, we're going to see what Ford has for us in the way of a van and some decoy clothes. What size shoe do you wear?"

He couldn't recall.

"Shirt size?"

He couldn't recall.

She escorted him back to the others and called Ford over to ask him to have Eriq escorted to a place where he could lie down and sleep, all to a chorus of Eriq's protests. But finally he was persuaded to locate some rest in a room upstairs where there was a couch.

"What's up with him?" asked Quincey.

"Too many pills and too little sleep," suggested Samernow.

Jessica gave assurances. "He's okay . . . He'll be okay by two."

· SIXTEEN ·

Disappear like a tale that is told.
—SIMEON FORD

The stakeout had gone way past two P.M. and no one remotely resembling Patric Allain had shown up, but still Jessica and the others held out a desperate hope, she from inside the trophy shop and the rest from outside. Santiva and Mark held forth in the Florida Power and Light-turned-surveillance van at a remote point across and down from the trophy shop, Quincey from a nearby doorstep, where he played the role of a homeless man.

The trophy shop and its adjacent warehouse, in which fish of every size and shape and color hung in suspended animation from rafters, each in its own crucial stage of preservation, was quite unusual.

Jessica found Buckner's shop reminiscent of the fictional *Little Shop of Horrors*. It was a graveyard for fish, large and small, but more than a graveyard, it resembled a cross between a biophysics lab—with its many chemicals and hydroponics agricultural experiment, with fish instead of vegetation hanging from a ceiling—and a dirty, noisy warehouse that might as easily have housed men shearing sheep as men mixing great vats of papier-mâché, creating plaster casts and molds and gutting and skinning fish.

The warehouse section was stacked full with supplies in various corners and rooms--a labyrinth of rooms, actually—each given over to a certain stage in the reverent process of trophy mounting. The army of workmen committed to the process wore T-shirts, jeans and rubber boots.

The shop out front was just that, a front for displays of blue and yellowfin, jack, marlin, grouper, shark and some of Buckner's monstrosities, coming out of what he called his "pure creative side," the cross-bred taxidermy of trophy creatures he'd termed Twisted Evolution. He proudly displayed the obnoxious results—a "gator-fish"—under a large sign of the same name: Twisted Evolution. Other items of every conceivable sort necessary to both his main trade and fishing—both big game and small—was sold in his shop, including bait and tackle of every size, shape and suggestion. It was all crowded in with Snickers bars, Lay's potato chips, and Pepsi-Cola, which lay in the same cooler as the big-game bait.

In his attempt to impress Jessica, Buckner proudly announced that he owned stock in Pepsi-Cola, told her that it had risen recently to forty-six dollars a share and asked if she wouldn't like a piece of that.

Since Jessica had to be on the inside and pretend familiarity with her "uncle" and her surroundings, she was more than happy to take Buck's ear-grinning tour of his place which, as he put it, he'd "built up from scratch."

"The premises was once a used-boat dealership, long since defunct. Took the place off the Realtor's hands for a song," he boasted to Jessica now, as if meaning to propose marriage as soon as he demonstrated how he could get rid of his old lady and keep her.

Jessica, in jeans and plaid shirt, her hair pulled back severely, a ponytail bobbing behind her head, was quickly getting a feel for, and a smell for, Buck's Trophy Shop, as it was called.

Buckner had a number of men working for him, some obviously for day wages, and they had a routine which they never veered from, which Jessica assured them and Buck they should continue to the letter. But Buckner and the others were fascinated with her, acting as if they had never seen a woman in the place before, and perhaps they hadn't, so she finally gave in, allowing them to show her every detail of the process of mounting the game fish, of which they were solemnly and worshipfully proud.

Buck talked the whole time as each of his men in turn demonstrated one or more facets of the process. "You won't find no damned plastic marlins here, darlin'," he informed her. "We do it the old-fashioned way, but with state-of-the-art preservation techniques, mind you."

"Did a marlin for Paul Newman a ways back," said Buck's first assistant. "That was a gas."

Buck raised his shoulders, "We got some of the world's most famous big-game anglers coming to us, 'cause they know we're the best, and Stu here wants to tell you about Paul Newman! Anyhow, you see, here we do game fish trophies by the hollow-sculpture method."

"Meaning?" Jessica stared into one of the papier-mâché vats, where an assistant mixed the materials with large wooden ladles, finally plunging his hands and forearms in up to the elbows and mixing the sticky white glue.

"We use the actual skin of the actual fish. Most places nowadays use fiberglass or Teflon or goddamn graphite! 'Magine that? Damn thing's no longer a fish, no more fish than you or me."

No more a fish than you or I, she thought, wanting to correct his grammar but realizing that to do so would be the grammatical equivalent of spitting into a hurricane wind—useless and messy.

"Using the actual fish skin means we get the most authentic reproduction of size and shape," added Stu, a thin, angular man with dark skin and an eagerness to please.

"It costs more the right way," explained Buck, "so most times we're asked to create a reasonable facsimile. Hate to do it, but if you're gonna use plastic—"

Stu, hearing this so often, finished for Buck, adding, "—at least get a trained skinner who can provide exact specifications!"

"When we get a fish in, it's first measured and weighed," continued Buck. "Then we pose it—you know, in a lifelike position, say leaping or lunging."

"Next, plaster of paris is poured over it, to create the spit mold," contributed Stu. "And after the material sets, it's removed and the skinning process follows."

"We use as delicate surgical instruments as you, Dr. Coran," Buck assured her. "It has to be done that way, if it's to be done right."

"You use a scalpel, then?"

"To assure no damage to the specimen, yes."

"Were any scalpels stolen from your place along with the chemicals the other night?"

"Some instruments were taken, yes."

Stu wanted to get back to the subject at hand, so he deftly stepped between them and continued, saying, "This point's where I come in." Stu was obviously proud of his handiwork. "The skin is next given several chemical baths, you know, to remove excess oils, organic matter, microbes."

"High-tech insect repellent," muttered Buck as if to disparage Stu's expertise.

Stu pretended no offense. "Once cured, the skin is fitted inside the mold, to return it to its original shape, you see." He demonstrated with a blue marlin.

"That's when several layers of paper, glue and papier-mâché are applied through an opening. Here, I'll show you." Buck lifted one of the molds at this crucial stage to show her the hole on the side that would be against the wall, not showing. "This forms the core, replaces the innards so that there's no collapse after time. At this stage," he added, "we say the fish is truly *mounted*. We don't use the term *stuffed*. Stupid to refer to trophy mounting as stuffing, like you'd stuff a bear or a circus animal. As you see, we don't stuff the damn things."

"The mount is then ready for the dehydration process, which can take up to three months, depending on size, of course," Stu explained. "We'll pass by the curing and drying room next."

Jessica saw that the marine taxidermists kept a large inventory of molds on hand to provide a base for, as Buck explained it, "fish received only in the skin. It's a great deal less expensive to forward a previously gutted fish on ice than one of full dead weight."

Stu piped in, "But Buck won't never guarantee perfection unless we can begin with the whole fish when it comes through the door.''

Having been in the business all his life, Buck had amassed so many molds that he could reproduce any fish size or species within a fraction of an inch of its life dimension.

They peeked into what Stu had called the curing and drying room, where bright heat lamps were turned on and focused toward the ceiling. Every available inch of ceiling space was occupied by the enormous trophy fish, many of which were swordfish, their proud swords spiked downward now from their carcasses, lifeless and hard and eyeless, their eyes having been removed at some earlier stage in the process.

The men working in the back of the factory, in white aprons pulled over sleeveless T-shirts and jeans, walked about in rubber boots or sneakers completely covered in globs of papier-mâché like so much pizza flour and dough. They worked with great intensity and concentration and smiled at Jessica as she toured the place.

"We boast a record of forms fitted to within a thirty-second of an inch of the original fish," said Stu with pride.

They moved on to another room. Here Jessica saw the finished work, she thought; but Buck cautioned her otherwise. "This is our primping room. Here's where I come into play—not doing any of the heavy stuff no more."

"They look alive," she said, staring. Here the fish had remarkably lifelike eyes that stared out at her.

"I check for any final flaws here. Call it quality control. I correct any skin flaws and reinforce the fins. With the one exception of the glass eyes, everything you see here is from the original fish, 'cept the mold over which his skin is stretched, of course . . . but the skin is the animals and basically that's what we preserve here, the skin."

"Except for the billfish," cautioned Stu.

Frowning, Buck explained, "A bill's dorsal fin has to be prefabricated. No amount of processing can preserve some of the more delicate membranes."

"Any rate, now the science part is over," said Stu. "In

here it's time for the art. To restore these babies to their original hues and lifelike appearance, it takes a master like Buck here. It takes talent—''

"Bullshit, *talent*," interrupted the spike-bearded Buckner. "*Talent*'s a dangerous word. More like skill born of experience and know-how. That's more like it."

"Whatever you wanna call it, Buck here's got more natural talent or skill born of experience and know-how than anybody on the damned planet."

Buckner was blushing red below his gray beard, but he pretended nonchalance and went on with his explanation. "First we spray them with a white base coat; then we layer on several color shadings, some done by hand to gain the exact texture required for authenticity."

"A decent photo of the catch at the time it's brought aboard a boat, or at least the moment it's brought ashore, becomes invaluable here," interjected Stu.

"Tropical fish begin to lose their color the moment they're snagged," added Buck. "Anyway, a final clear coat is splashed on for protection and the wet look."

"How does what you do differ from the work done by other taxidermists?" asked Jessica.

Buck laughed a horse laugh, slapping Stu on the shoulder before replying, "A guy like me, specializing in marine work, is a whole 'nuther animal from some bozo who stuffs birds and reptiles and bears and bobcats and squirrels, believe you me. We don't have hide, fur or feathers to cover our mistakes."

"There's no room here for error," added Stu.

"All we got to work with is a thin layer of skin which stubbornly resists preservatives."

Jessica smiled and replied, "You mean, it's no job for amateurs?"

"That's why Scrapheap didn't care for that punk hanging around down in Key West. Said he always wanted to take shortcuts . . . was careless. Hell, you can see that from the yellowfin he brought in with him."

Jessica gave Buckner a stunned look while Stu continued to fill her ear, saying, "Most of our customers are individuals, but Buck's done work for corporations and museums, haven't you, Buck?''

Buck nodded with grace, a faint, prideful smile parting his lips. ''I've done work for Mickey Mantle, Hank Aaron, Charlton Heston . . . you name it.''

''King Hussein and former Presidents Jimmy Carter and George Bush.'' Stu beamed with pride, too.

''Pardon me, Buck, but did you say this Patric Allain brought something in with him and left it here?''

''Yeah, a yellowfin . . . kinda like a calling card. He'd already skinned it, so he wanted us to do the mounting, but after I looked at it and found a hole large enough to drive a golf ball through, I told him we couldn't guarantee anything approximating perfection.''

''Did anyone other than you handle the skin? Would you know, if anyone else had done work on it?'' she asked.

''Oh, sure.''

''So, had anyone other than Allain handled the skin?''

''I had no reason to think so, no.''

''Show it to me. I want that skin.''

''It's in the next room.''

''Anyone else touch it?'' she pressed as she followed Buck.

''Stu? Anyone in or outta here this morning?''

''Not a soul.''

''Did you paw the fella's prize?''

''Naw, too busy to take any notice of it,'' Stu assured them.

''There it is, right on the peg where I hung it,'' said Buck.

''I'll need to have someone come in and take your prints, Mr. Buckner, so we can rule them out. Any others we find, hopefully, will be those of the killer.''

''You can peel off fingerprints from that?'' He pointed to the lifeless scales of the yellowfin with which Patric Allain had allegedly walked through the door.

''I can with the right tools . . . We have the technology, but it'll destroy the skin.''

''Take the damned thing. It's old and brittle now anyway; said he had it packed in ice the whole time, but obviously that was a lie. Said he caught it in the Cayman Islands, but that was a lie, too.''

''He said Cayman Islands specifically?''

''Yeah, I recall he did.''

''Hmmmm. How could you tell that he was lying about the condition and age of the skin?''

Stu jumped in, saying, ''Hell, one look at it . . .''

Buck offered, ''I don't figure it'd be in such good shape as it was if he'd hauled it so far as the Caymans. My guess, he snatched it or bought it at some other shop along his way to here from Key West.''

''Why lie about the Cayman Islands? Why not simply say he caught the fish in the Gulf out there?''

''I don't know, pathological? Or maybe he knew the quality was bad, so he made up a cockamamie story.''

The tour had ended with something tangible, a possible clue that could specifically identify the killer. Moyler in England had a print, and if they could match his print with what they found on the fish skin, they could be surer of their prey. She asked Buckner for the use of his phone and contacted Santiva in the nearby van with this news. It took some, although not all, of the sting out of the Crawler's having not shown up.

''I'll pack it and send it off to J.T. at Quantico; see what the lab can find for us in the way of useful prints. J.T.'ll put our best fingerprint tech on the job. It may be the first real gift that Allain has given us. If J.T. finds something, we can put it under an electron microscope and photograph it, maybe match it to what Moyler has in London.''

''May's well pack it in,'' he suggested. ''Not doing any good here.''

''Let's give it a little more time,'' she suggested. ''Maybe he got unavoidably held up.''

''Yeah, don't we wish the Coast Guard or the Florida Marine Patrol has picked him up for questioning?''

''Could we get so lucky?''

''I'll get Ford's best men down here to relieve us, let

them watch over this place tonight, and we'll get some R and R,'' said Santiva.

After calling J.T. to tell him what he might expect in the overnight mail, so as to not entirely shock him, Jessica found herself with time on her hands, so she asked Buckner for the phone number of his old partner in Key West, and she then telephoned Scrapheap Jones and plied him full of questions relevant to his encounter with the Night Crawler.

Jones simply refused to believe that the Patric whom he had taught the rudiments of fish-trophy mounting was the Crawler. His mind could not wrap around the concept; he claimed the kid he trained was a wimp, fearful at the sight of blood even in a dead fish. Scrapheap told Jessica that she was on a fool's chase if she were after that sullen, quiet one-joke boy he had known.

But even as Scrapheap Jones denied her, she read between the lines of what the man said. Allain was sullen, quiet, fearful of the sight of blood and apparently humorless. In point of fact, this profile sounded a great deal more like her prey than Jones realized.

"What do you mean by one-joke boy?"

"He'd say the fishing in the shark aquarium museum here in Key West was the easiest place to fish. Damned fool. Thought it was funny; thought it irritated me when he'd suggest taking a charter to the museum, let 'em all dip their bait into one of the tanks there. Silly stuff like that, like it was real funny, but it wasn't. Joke was lame, like the kid.''

"Did he ever steal from you?"

"Some . . . some chemicals, maybe, I ain't a hunerd percent sure.''

"Do you have anything in writing about your agreement with him? Did you have him sign a contract or agreement? It's important.''

"I did . . . at the time . . .''

"Do you still have it?"

"It may be in my files.''

"If you find it, fax it to me at the Naples Police Department.'' She gave him the number.

"I'll see what I can do. By the way, is Buck there? Can I speak to him?"

She told him that he could speak with his friend.

"Oh, just a minute . . . another thing he always kidded me about . . ." Scrapheap suddenly said.

"What's that, sir?"

"Ahh, always said he'd like to go somewhere cooler, complained of the Florida heat, so he was always talking about going to the Caymans."

"The Caymans?" Jessica wondered at the coincidence.

"That was the joke, get it?"

She didn't get it.

"The Caymans are hotter'n Florida and all hell the time o' year he was talking."

"I see. Had he ever been to the Cayman Islands?"

"Said he had been there, yes. Not much with trophy mounting, but he sure knew how to sail."

She told Buck that Jones wanted to speak with him. Relinquishing the phone, she looked up at the clock to see that it was now nearing 3:05 P.M. and still no show.

They waited past three-thirty. Ford and Santiva had by now earnestly discussed pulling up stakes. Jessica could hardly blame them, but she said over the remote that she would give it another hour, till four. Meanwhile Ford arranged for a man in civilian clothes to enter with a fingerprinting kit and both Buck's and Stu's fingerprints were taken for the record. What remained of Patric Allain's trophy fish, the yellowfin he'd walked in off the wharf with, was placed in a large paper sack and carried out for laboratory analysis and fingerprint detection. Jessica would later properly box it in absorbent material and FedEx it off to Quantico, Virginia.

By now Ford had seen enough; he quickly pulled his men—acting as backup—from the area. He and Santiva had gotten into a tiff, and Ford flatly refused to have his men watch over the shop all night. So, for a bit longer, Santiva, Quincey and Samernow remained nearby.

Mark and Eriq were in FPL uniforms at the van while Quincey sat at a bus stop now, his makeup—that of a feeble old man down on his luck—beginning to thin.

Four o'clock came around and still no show. Somehow, the killer knew; perhaps he sensed that it was too dangerous to return, especially after having robbed the place of materials the night before. Perhaps he realized that he'd been foolish to use the same alias, even with a man like Buckner, and doubly foolish to have left something of his in the other man's possession, something with his prints on it. Or perhaps he had simply smelled trouble about the shop, even before coming near it. Like a tiger or a cougar, the Night Crawler obviously had good instincts.

Now he could be anywhere.

Tired and disgruntled and disappointed, the four remaining law enforcement officials found themselves trying to comfort Gordon Buckner, to assure him that he would be safe and to tell him to be in touch the moment he was contacted again by Patric Allain.

"Then you do think he will contact me again?"

"No way of knowing, but not likely at this point." Jessica tried to put the old man's mind at ease.

"He could've just got the days turned around. If he's as crazy as they say, why not?"

"We'll send some undercover men tomorrow for a possible two P.M. meet. They'll pretend to work out back for you," suggested Jessica. "And who knows, maybe I'll be back with them."

"All right, good. Damn this man . . . damn this whole bloody business," moaned Buckner, his head in his hands. "I sometimes wonder what God was thinkin' of when he created the human animal and the perverse human brain. Damn this monster!"

"Our sentiments exactly, Mr. Buckner."

They left in the van, which had to be returned to Ford. At the precinct, each promised to meet for drinks and dinner after changing and cleaning up. Jessica, in particular, pleaded that she had to get the fish smell out of her hair and off her body.

When they arrived back at police headquarters, Jessica climbed down from the van and Eriq met her at the rear, helping her out. They stood staring out toward the park, the boat marina, the great Gulf of Mexico beyond and the setting sun. "Where do you think this malfeasant creature is tonight, Jess?" asked Eriq. "What part of the coast is he haunting?"

She stared out at the waning sun in the west where it flared bloodred, a giant fire in the sky that spread dark shadows now along the clean, well-kept streets and park of the picturesque city. "I don't know what shadow he's hiding in, but I fear the worst, and I think we have to persuade Ford to keep his men on guard at the riverfront bars and restaurants. All we know for sure is that the bastard will strike again. I haven't had time to do a full autopsy, but I had a look at the body that washed ashore here . . ."

"And?"

"It's as if he let her go by mistake, as if she were unfinished," Jessica said. "None of the staging of the others; no quarter-inch nylon rope, no sign of any attempt to preserve or mount this one. You ever catch a fish only to lose it over the side?"

"Whataya mean?"

"She got loose from him somehow; he hadn't tied the knot correctly or quickly enough when a wave took her, probably in the dark. Everything else is to the letter—double, possible triple strangulation, the whole nine yards. But her lungs were not as full of water as the others."

"About earlier, Jess . . . I want to apologize."

She didn't want to deal with *earlier* now. "'Fraid it's textbook Night Crawler," she continued on about the most recent dead girl's body. "He is definitely in the vicinity, and like Quincey surmised, the bastard may be making his way toward the Tampa Bay–St. Pete area."

"I've sent word to our field offices there. They're on the alert. They know the drill."

They had walked from the van to the park, exercising their legs and lungs while Quince and Samernow saw to the van and the equipment inside. "You look trim and handsome in your FPL uniform, Chief," she teased.

"You, you look like the cutest thing in rags I've ever

seen," he fired back. "But you're right about the fish and formaldehyde odor. That's gotta go."

From behind them, Jessica heard Quince's distinct voice carry on the evening trade wind. "Bastard has just raked the whole state from one side to the next . . ."

"Promise me one thing," she asked Eriq.

"Anything . . . within reason."

"No more quaaludes or uppers or whatever you've been on."

Santiva took in a great breath of air. "I needed it to keep pace. It was just a one-time-only."

"Careful, my friend, because one-time-onlies have a way of becoming one-time-*eternities*."

"I appreciate both your concern and your advice, Jess. It means a lot to me, but rest assured, I don't have a drug problem."

She looked from the deep wells of his dark, kind eyes back out to sea and the setting sun, a fiery orange orb threatening to engulf the world even as it was being engulfed by the horizon. So much depended on one's limited perspective, she quietly told herself, wondering anew where the Night Crawler was at this moment.

· SEVENTEEN ·

Through the looking glass and into the abyss angels must spy.
            —from the notebooks of Jessica Coran

On a hunch, Jessica Coran made a long-distance call to now Chief Constable Ja Okinleye of the Official Police of the Cayman Islands. Ja had become a good friend since the time some years ago when Jessica had assisted him on a murder case on his island of Grand Cayman. At the time he was a lieutenant in the Investigatory Division there. The case had involved a wealthy and highly regarded man who had been involved in the import business and was the owner of the largest clothing and jewelry store on the islands. Ja thought the man had gotten involved with some sort of smuggling operation, a common practice at all levels of society there. The man's throat had been slashed and there were repeated stab wounds to the body. Ja wondered if it were not the work of an angry co-conspirator in the smuggling operation or the botched work of a burglar, but Jessica merely had to look at the body to tell him otherwise. It was neither business nor mistake that had dispatched the elderly gentleman. She explained that the wound to the throat, while similar to a Colombian necktie—a throat slit from ear to ear—would have been enough to kill the man and that the other repeated stab wounds had been unnecessary save for one need—rage and vengeance of a sort. "So," she had surmised, "it is the work of some person who knew the deceased well enough to hate him."

On further investigation at what passed for a crime lab on Grand Cayman, Jessica revealed other, even more startling facts: that the body had been moved from another location and posed; that the stab wounds had come first; that the wound to the throat had been a last-minute addition to the staging of the event; and that in fact the man had died of a broken neck. Someone had simply snapped his neck in a quick, brutal and efficient manner, someone both strong and possibly well-trained in the martial arts.

"Then, in a fit of rage, he or she did the butchering, quite possibly after spending several hours with the body hatching out what to do with it."

Ja knew instantly whom he must interrogate further, and it quickly came to light that the man's nephew was in extreme debt to island loan sharks, that he'd pleaded with his uncle for money and that the old man had stood adamant against lending him another cent. The younger man, it was soon revealed, had lost control and attacked his uncle; in the scuffle, he'd made short work of his uncle's vertebrae and neck bone. Death had come about as a result of the trauma suffered when the nervous system was severed.

Ja Okinleye had done most of the work that cornered the nephew, but he had been aided immeasurably by Jessica's display of scientific knowledge, beginning with the fact of lividity, indicating that the man's body had lain on its side for at least three hours after death before it was lifted up a flight of stairs and thrown across his bed, where the butchering ensued. The body had been left facedown where the throat was cut. The amount of blood soaking into the bedcover, or rather the lack of it, was Jessica's first indication that things were not as they seemed on the surface; the absence of blood from such an enormous gash had clearly indicated that the old man was dead long before his throat was slashed, another relatively easy surmise.

These facts, thrown in the face of the suspect in Ja's interrogation room, had brought him to confession and the entire case took a mere three days to solve—all while Jessica was on vacation on the islands. How Ja learned of her and of the fact that she was on his island, she never knew. At any rate, Ja Okinleye estimated Jessica Coran a wizard and a magician and was able to close the baffling case with head-spinning speed. He remained to this day, as he put it, "a great believer and friend." And if ever she needed a favor . . .

Ja had since moved up the ranks on Grand Cayman. He had used his new authority to send some of his officers to the United States for training at the FBI Academy, and had been pleased with the results.

Jessica recognized his voice immediately when she was finally put through to Ja.

"Okinleye here!" Ja was always loud and clear, having had a British education and a military upbringing. He was stiff and formal even at a party, but his formality had become so much a part of his personality, it seemed pleasantly integrated, charming even.

"Ja, it's me, Jessica Coran. I'm calling on a matter of some urgency."

"Aha! To congratulate me, no doubt."

She laughed into the phone. "Yes, that of course, but I sent a card when I learned of your promotion. Just the same, congratulations."

"And your card and well-wishing is much appreciated. Dr. Coran, it is always a pleasure to hear from you! Where are you calling from? Are you on the island?" He sounded surprised.

"I'm in Florida—Naples, Florida, to be exact. I'm working a case here; one you may've heard about?"

"*Hoooo*, yes, an evil business that one in Florida I hear of."

"That's my case."

"I have word of your string of children, all dead at the hand of this fiend they are calling the Night Crawler, but I didn't know you were handling the case. If there is anything—*anything whatever*—I can do, please never hesitate one moment to ask, my dear Doctor."

She pictured Okinleye's Sidney Poitier appearance, his wide forehead and piercing, nearly black eyes as she replied, "Ja, have you had any like Missing Persons cases—disappearances—turn into murder victims? These would be young women, American or British, my basic appearance—

height, weight, color of hair.''

"Teens, tourists?''

"Or early twenties, yes.''

"In point of fact . . . yes, but are you suggesting a connection?''

"I'm not sure . . .''

"I will have my best man scour our records for . . . for how long past?''

"A year . . . no, two years ago?''

"That far back may take some time. I of course recall several instances of bodies washing ashore, all clustering about a year ago, yes.''

"Were they bound, gagged?''

"No, nothing like that.''

"Nude?''

"Yes.''

"Cause of death?''

"First it was suggested as drowning, but one of our men who is academy-trained by your fine FBI realized it was strangulation.''

"And the killer was never apprehended, I take it.''

"No, never . . . to our shame.''

"We may be trailing the same man here. Can you send all you have on the protocols there?''

"Absolutely, as soon as it is amassed.''

She gave him the NPD's address in Naples. ''Make sure it's marked for me personally.''

"It will be done. I wish you all good luck there, Dr. Coran.''

"Thank you, Chief Okinleye. It does appear that we'll need all the luck we can find.''

"I apologize for my surprise when you first called,'' he said.

She unnecessarily shrugged. ''What for?''

"I mean, I thought you were in Hawaii, that you had relocated and had married some fellow there?''

"Well . . . not quite . . .''

"Not quite? Or not quite yet?''

"I'm not quite sure yet. Does that answer your question?"

"I am sorry to pry; your happiness is all that I wish."

She smiled at this genuine, simple desire, so sincerely stated. "Thank you, Ja, and I'll look forward to hearing from you."

"When will you come to dive The Wall in Cayman again? When will you come to see us? You will not believe how big my children have become. They were busting the house, so in keeping with my new duties, we have purchased a suitable abode far above the city, overlooking the city and the harbor."

"It sounds lovely, and I'll visit as soon as I can, promise."

"Remember to take time to play; that life is not made for work alone, that work alone is not life."

"Thank you, Ja. I'll remember that island wisdom."

Ja hung up and she played over his final words inside her head and heart. She knew he was right, that once again she'd become so entangled in her work that it had become her life. For that kind of advice from her shrink, she paid through the nose; getting it through Ja's simple wisdom was cheaper, but no less painful.

Quincey and Samernow knew the so-called best barbecue place in Naples, so the foursome wound up at Brace's for drinks and dinner. They tried to talk about anything and everything besides their great disappointment in not having had the chance to pounce on the Night Crawler this day. They talked of sports and weather and the Eddie Perlman trial, which had started in earnest in Seattle. Perlman was accused of the brutal murder of his six children, his wife and his mother-in-law. The case had been in the headlines for almost a year now as prosecution and defense jockeyed for position. It was a classic example of a defenseless defense resorting to blowing smoke, burning unrelated incense in the courtroom, fanning the flame of confusion and creating doubt where no doubt existed by playing one mirror off another, all in a superfluous effort to deflect and ultimately derail the truth while boring the jury to death.

"When we do finally catch this bastard Allain, or whoever the hell he is, the damned legal system will drag it out, ass-over-backwards, for ten years," complained Quincey, "and it'll take some prison-cell justice to see the SOB gets what he deserves." Jessica and the others drank to the sad truth.

Jessica reminded them how, after capture, Mad Matthew Matisak had been placed in a federal prison for the criminally insane, and how he had played the system for years, and how the moment his doctor's defenses went down, he'd struck like a waiting cobra. He'd escaped, wreaked havoc and murder from Philadelphia to Louisiana, where he began stalking her, until finally she had cornered and killed him in a New Orleans warehouse. Final justice three long years after he was found guilty of the slow-torture deaths of the countless victims he had drained blood from to feed an insatiable appetite for the red fluid.

And so the conversation worked its way back around to what was eating away at them all tonight, the whereabouts of the Night Crawler.

"Where the hell can he be?"

"He's like a damned crayfish, hiding in the mud out there—invisible but there."

"How'd he know we'd staked out Buck's Trophy Shop?"

"Was he maybe using Buck to decoy us away?"

"What do you mean?"

"Keep us here, while he goes north to Tampa?"

"Is he just playing more cat-and-mouse games with us?"

The questions spiraled and threaded through their conversation, and Jessica sadly and resignedly began to believe that they were no closer to apprehending the monster than when they'd begun their effort so long ago in Islamorada Key. She voiced this feeling and the others stopped their drinking and eating to stare.

"How can you say that, Jess?" asked Eriq. "We know a lot more about this creep now than when we began."

"But that's not enough. Knowing about him hasn't stopped him."

"Fact is, he gets off on letting us know bits and pieces, seems to me," said Quincey. "Isn't that why he cut loose three bodies in one day and left the nylon rope behind?"

Samernow agreed. "Isn't that why he keeps writing the damned papers with his damnable poetry?"

"Yeah, he feeds us . . . we feed him," grumbled Santiva, who'd had more to drink than the others and was now completely despondent.

"Anybody here by the name of Coran or Santiva?" shouted the bartender, waving a phone in one hand, hefting a stein of beer in the other.

"Yeah, over here," replied Jessica, going for the phone.

Quincey asked, "Who knows we're here?"

"Ford," explained Santiva. "Told him to keep us informed of anything from his side."

Jessica held firmly to the phone, as if its hard density might keep her from reeling; she felt a little light-headed, and too much beer, not enough pretzels and the news she was receiving wasn't helping any. She gritted her teeth and stared back at the men she'd just left at the table. She met Santiva's eyes, and he proved sober enough to read her body language. He could tell the call was serious, so he got up and joined her, asking, "What is it?"

"*Tampa Tribune* got a love note from the Crawler. Looks like he's in the Bay Area all right. Postmark is St. Petersburg."

"Damn, the bastard's got us hopping to his tune."

"All part of his game. Only good news is that there haven't been any other bodies to wash ashore from the Gulf."

"As yet, you mean . . ."

"Let's get up the coast. Think you can get us a helicopter?"

"We'll get some local help on that score. Be ready to leave"—he looked at his watch—"at midnight. What about a facsimile of the letter? Has Ford received one?"

"He has."

"Tell him to send a copy to my hotel room, and tell him we're on our way to Tampa–St. Pete."

Jessica did as instructed, thanking Ford for his cooperation and the help of his men, asking him to be on the lookout for a package arriving there for her postmarked the Cayman Islands and instructing him to forward it to FBI Headquarters in Tampa. She again thanked Ford before hanging up, then rushed out of the restaurant with Eriq, who'd left instructions with Samernow and Quincey. The two detectives would follow them by way of car or boat—depending on Anderson's mood—the following day.

"Tampa, Jess," Eriq said to her in firm conviction.

"What about Tampa?"

"That's where we're going to corner this bastard."

"Yeah, well, for a time we thought the same of Naples, but it didn't happen."

"The noose is tightening. We just have to pull on the rope."

She realized he was just doing a bit of cheerleading, attempting to bolster her sagging spirits. It was Eriq's way of trying to comfort her and bring her along emotionally.

"I hope you're right, Eriq," she relented somewhat as they got into the car that would take them to the airport, where a chopper was holding for them.

"I am right. I have to be right," he assured her.

"He's led us on one hell of a chase."

"It comes to an end in Tampa."

"Promise?"

"Promise."

· EIGHTEEN ·

I advance to attack; I climb to assault,
Like a choir of young worms at a corpse in a vault.
—CHARLES BAUDELAIRE

Tampa Bay, Florida

Another jet bringing more tourists and money into the Tampa–St. Pete area careened overhead, perfectly aligned with the lights at Tampa International. Being on the bay, out on the water like this, watching the planes come and go, was akin to watching a fireworks and laser display, thought Florida Marine Patrol Officer Ken Stallings. When he mentioned it to his partner, big Rob Manley, the other man grunted in his usual fashion and said, "Give me a boat any day."

Viewed from the water, Tampa Bay on a Saturday night was surreal, the canals and waterways like a broad boulevard where riverfront restaurants and harbor lamps reflected multicolored lights off the inky surface of the bay. The waterways were lined with mega-yachts, utterly fantastic in size and scale in relation to the little Boston Whaler police boat patrolling here.

On the FMP boat, Officer Stallings shouted from behind the wheel down to his partner in the flatbed, "Problem with these yuk-yuk yacht guys . . . the bigger the damned boat, the longer they think their dicks extend, so the worse the attitude they give you."

Rob Manley raised his black hand and waved knowingly, agreeing. "Big pricks and bad-ass attitudes is right; that's what this place is full of, bad attitude."

"Can't totally fault 'em, though."

"The boaters? The weekend water warriors? The yachtsmen? And just why not?"

"We board their boats out here, they see it as home invasion, which—"

"You talkin' invasion of privacy?"

"—which it is, kind of."

"That's crap, Ken, and you know it," Manley shot back. "They give up any right to privacy when they put another person's life in jeopardy or run the lanes at full speed. They get boarded when they break the law; if they want to keep their boats sacro . . . sacro—"

"Sacrosanct?"

"Yeah, that. If they want to keep that, then they should observe the law. Simple as that. You do the crime, you pay the fine or the time as the case may be, and you lose that saccharine thing."

Stallings laughed in response. "That's why I like having you around, Rob. You intimidate these suckers out here, and you understand them at the same time."

"Don't take much to understand stupidity and arrogance. Had a lifetime of that with my drunk-ass daddy."

Manley had been on the job for seven years against Stallings's eleven. They joked about that, calling themselves the 7-11 Team—unbeatable and unstoppable. Manley had once been a bouncer, and he still looked the part; Stallings had once been a prizefighter, lightweight division, and he still worked out and entered amateur contests. Each man was in top physical condition. They had to be for this job.

They waved as the blue strobes of another police boat passed by in the lane. There was a lot of police traffic here tonight, maybe too much. Every available officer was on alert that the creep they called the Night Crawler was possibly visiting all the way from Miami. Everyone had heard how this mooncalf demon freak who'd done all those girls could now be in the Tampa Bay area. Everybody was looking to score big.

Stallings and Manley were no exception.

They held the record for most stops on a normal night,

and they could rack up more OUIs and registration violations than any of their counterparts out here, but Stallings and Manley had made a pact earlier: They were going hunting for larger fish tonight, and no OUIs or regs. violations were going to stand in the way of that covenant.

Any other midnight Manley was flashing his light at every damned boat that dared go by, pulling them over for safety inspections—life jackets, flotation devices, dinghies intact; liquor cans at a minimum—all in Manley's constant crusade to "make a damned strong impression: Wherever there's water, there's *muthafuckin'* watercops!"

Tonight, however, Manley was flashing registration numbers using his power light, and Ken was checking every single one against the FMP computer net for previous violations. "July-Oscar-Niner-Six-Delta," Stallings called off another "suspect" registration number. They were hoping to win the lottery, the prize being the Night Crawler. They were hoping to be like the now-famous cop who'd stopped Timothy McVeigh for a traffic violation after the bombing in Oklahoma City.

Their blue lights bounced around each marina, reflected off decks and shoreline establishments as they passed, a menacing warning to heavy drinkers and an annoyance to diners and dancers. The air here in the boat lane was crackling with electricity. The squeal of the Mako radio, emitting a nonstop barrage of police calls, mingled with the palpable rancor of boaters who just wanted all signs of law and order gone, out of their liquor-hairy faces.

Stallings and Manley were used to angry customers thinking FMP vehicles an interference in their holiday cruising. People on boats didn't want to observe any rule that applied to land; they seemed to feel that open water meant open-ended morality, that familiar Mardi Gras attitude that said, "Anything goes." Boaters didn't want signs to mark their way, to tell them about slow wakes or manatee crossings or fish hatcheries. And they generally regarded watercops as arrogant, reckless nuisances with 225-hp motors, badges and guns. Still, whatever the public thought, the FMP units were equipped to outmaneuver and outrun the public at every turn.

"Maybe we shouldn't stray too far," Stallings suggested to Manley, "seeing that we've got plenty o' trouble brewing right here in the lanes."

"Hell, any overflow problems, the other guys can just send 'em to the county sheriff's patrol boat at the city marina. They can just line up there and wait their turn," Manley replied, anxious to follow through with their earlier plans.

A huge yacht with horsepower to spare opened up in the slow wake area, whose limits were posted in plain view. "We gotta take that one," Ken told Rob.

"Damn fool bastard," replied Manley, exasperated at the obvious speed violation. Stallings revved up their speedboat and hailed the yacht with siren blaring and lights flashing, followed by the bullhorn.

Cursing the yacht pilot under his breath the whole time, Manley targeted the bridge with his light, and lifting his bullhorn he ordered the yacht, a boat with the dubious name of *Hellfire*, to dock for a safety inspection now.

Once the yacht was secured to a nearby wharf, the inspection went in routine fashion, by the book, no problems on board except for the single lush sitting in a deck chair who kept saying, "You can't be serious."

"Yes, sir . . . we're quite serious," Manley repeated each time the little guy opened his mouth. Stallings stifled a laugh.

"You weren't OUI here, were you, sir?" Manley finally asked the small man in the chair.

"No, no, no! You saw me operating the boat, officer," bellowed the pilot.

"OUI?" asked the drunk. "Don't you mean IOU?"

"Operating under the influence, Tom," explained the pilot, "and no, no no," he pleadingly added for Manley's sake, "no one here's operating while intoxicated."

Ken suggested into Rob Manley's ear, "Send 'em on their way."

"Watch your speeds through here, sir," Manley tutored

as he and Stallings returned to their patrol boat.

"Damn nigger watercop . . . " muttered someone from behind them as they shoved off.

"Any other night, I'd've found sixteen violations for those turkeys," Manley assured his partner.

"But this ain't just any night," Stallings agreed. "There'll be eight, nine, maybe ten other units on the water tonight—our guys, the Coast Guard, Hillsborough County Sheriff's Office, Pinellas and Manatee County Sheriff's Offices, and the Tampa Police—they all wanna see action. Let them keep an eye on ol' *Hellfire*."

Tampa Bay, with adjoining Hillsborough Bay and the wide channel, skirted three counties, their boundaries clear only on the maps, smack in the water. There were also islands to the south and the Gulf side of St. Petersburg to consider, where the "Pete" Police would have a couple of units in the water. If what the FBI was saying had any validity to it at all, the damned ugly Crawler would be a fool to come into these waters. And from what Stallings had gathered, this creep would be most attracted by the St. Petersburg strip along Reddington Beach. So he now quietly suggested they cruise out into the Gulf and northward to have a look.

The watercops of the well-trained Florida Marine Patrol had been efficiently scouring Florida's coasts from Jacksonville on the Eastern seaboard to Tampa Bay and Pensacola on the Gulf, checking every boat that resembled anything like that belonging to the alleged killer—but then, given the general nature of the description of the boat, they knew it might match literally thousands in these waters.

Stallings revved up his engine to the max and gave her full throttle, then laughed when Manley grabbed on to the railing of the now speeding Boston Whaler. The siren blared out across the enormous waters of Tampa Bay. It was exhilarating to open her up.

Both men knew all there was to know about the Night Crawler, and from the descriptions put out on the killer's boat, they had created a guessing game, naming boats that might suit the killer's liking and perverse needs. Manley had decided it was a fully equipped Davis 71 Sailsprinter, but Ken Stallings disagreed, saying it was more likely to be a faster, sleeker fifty-five- or sixty-foot Alden Motorsailor like the one he'd seen win a race from Florida to Tennessee with a crew of one! Everything aboard the boat was fully motorized and easily worked by this one man, who knew what he was doing at all times. Stallings believed there was no more seaworthy a vessel than the Alden Motorsailor, and if inner police circles could be believed, this creep had come sailing into Florida waters from as far away as New Zealand or Australia. Such a boat for loners would be to the killer's perverted liking.

The water was choppy tonight, the waves growing in intensity due to a storm sitting out in the immense Gulf beyond, one which forecasters warned could become a serious threat to coastal towns and cities, depending upon shifting winds and that lottery called fate. Thus far, it was a tropical depression, but everyone hereabouts knew how soon a TD could be upgraded to a full-blown hurricane, so while at the moment no one outside of law enforcement and other service groups had given much of a damn, the unofficial watch was on. If Stallings had learned one thing during his tenure as an FMP officer, it was that the sea was a very unforgiving ''mother of nature,'' that she simply did not condone, excuse or absolve stupidity or arrogance or any of their relative combinations; nor did the sea care if the people floating across her surface knew her intentions or not. It looked now as if the Bay Area would, in a few hours, be shrouded in fog. A light mist had come up, thickening as they got farther and farther from Tampa Bay proper and moved northwest along the coast, the Boston Whaler skimming now over the Gulf of Mexico under controlled speed.

They moved along more slowly as they passed areas where yachts and sailing vessels were moored. In the distance, Stallings spotted a boat with teakwood markings all along her sides, and from the look of her, if she wasn't an Alden, she was damned close enough to stand in for one.

They had the right to routinely pull alongside any boat

to make a spot check for licenses and booze containers; if they found captain and crew smashed, they had the right to arrest people and tow their boats into shore. If this proved another false alarm—as had so many since they'd been put on the alert for the Crawler—they'd simply feign a routine call on the boat.

The fast little Whaler was high up on plane now, her blue-to-red strobe light flashing, siren wailing as they approached the sleek, beautiful ship whose markings were obscured—perhaps deliberately, Stallings thought aloud, calling out his misgivings to Manley and asking, "Whataya think, Rob?"

Manley replied by jotting down what he could of her numbers, and he attempted to locate a name, but because of the angle of their approach and the seemingly mystical, evolving fog that'd rolled in to engulf them, this was impossible. "You may wanna send in the numbers we have as a precaution," suggested Manley, handing the figures to Stallings, who had the radio at his fingertips.

County cops in Florida who filled in during peak seasons and watercops in other states might have little or no training, or even boat experience, before they were given the keys and told to cast off, but that wasn't the case with the Florida Marine Patrol. Admittedly, they were spread thin— their duties covering eight thousand miles of coastline. Still, Stallings and Manley had put in their training time in the most rigorous marine law enforcement program in the country. They'd done an additional stint together at the Federal Law Enforcement Training Center outside Brunswick, Georgia, in a three-week advanced marine law program, and a weeklong course in protocol on seizures and boarding on the high seas.

Stallings momentarily thought of the financial crunch which had recently halved the Florida Coast Guard's budget, handcuffing those guys. FMP was up for cuts, too. He and Manley had studied under the Coast Guard for a time, but the Guard's training program had since dried up due to those same budget constraints. Now the entire course consisted of classroom theory only—*no practical experience on the water!* Kind of nuts, Stallings felt. Then, taking advantage of the sudden scarcity of watercop training facilities, the Florida Marine Patrol repackaged its academy training into a one-week intensive course offered to state and local jurisdictions. So far, some sixty Florida police departments and departments from eleven other states had availed themselves of the FMP training. Now Stallings was considering an offer to become a training officer himself and lead a more stable life as a result.

His wife and children were all for the change, but he knew he'd miss the excitement out here on the water with Manley. They'd been through hell and high water many times together, from making drug busts on the water to fighting with drunken baseball players on holiday to wrestling with alligators wandering into people's backyards. One damned fool had even captured a gator and dragged it aboard his boat, then called them in when the animal refused to die from the clubbing it was given. Damned fools. They didn't like the fines or the time doled out by the judges, but somehow water recreation bred stupidity.

Stallings knew that a standard national training program in maritime law enforcement was absolutely necessary and remained a long time in coming, and he'd have liked very much to be a part of formulating the standard. Certainly, he had seen enough in his nine years out here. For a place like Tampa Bay, or Miami, guys could train for months every year and it still wouldn't be enough, he thought.

Looking to Washington for money was futile . . . Funds would only come from a constituency committed to and in need of better-trained marine cops, and unfortunately, the boating public made it quite clear that they didn't have any urgent desire for watercops, trained or otherwise.

Manley had the bullhorn now, and as they came alongside the suspect ship—*and she was a beauty*—Manley announced who they were and told the parties aboard the three-masted, schooner-class sailing vessel that they should prepare to be boarded.

There was no immediate response from the ship, and no one could be seen at the helm or on deck.

In his hand, Manley, like Stallings, held a gun. This was no routine check. This looked suspicious as hell; this could be the Night Crawler, or it could be nothing. Either way, there was nothing routine about boarding another man's boat, another man's property line in effect. Unlike a road cop, Manley couldn't ask the suspect to get out of the vehicle and kneel on stone-hard pavement so as to gain control of the situation; rather, the FMP officer had to follow an even stricter code of conduct for an effective, safe arrest.

Stallings and Manley stared at what they had. It appeared an empty, anchored vessel. Unless they found probable cause, they could not board the ship.

The wind was picking up, buffeting them about. Stallings had to work to keep the patrol boat steady and pointed in the right direction. Manley showered the other boat with light from the Megalite 300 spotlight attached to their stern while Stallings called in the few numbers they had on the boat, saying into the radio, "Alpha-poppa-thirty, this is Stallings, Delta-four, 7-11, come in."

This was met with the friendly banter of the night dispatch officer, who replied, "Gotcha, Ken. What's up?"

"We got a suspicious-looking boat out on the water with obscured markings. We think the numbers are Oreo-Two-Charlie, Niner-Eight-Niner, something, something, Niner, but can't make out. Going in for a closer look."

"What's your position, Delta-four?"

Stallings offered up their position, even though they were somewhat far afield of their assigned area. As he did so, he also worked the Boston Whaler in an effort to counteract the oncoming wind and the swollen waves, which had become hungry mouths feeding on the bow and spilling over the gunwale. Now they were idling just off the side of the suspect boat, in textbook fashion.

Manley instructed through the horn, "Marine Patrol! Anyone aboard the schooner, come above deck, show yourselves, please, with hands raised behind the neck."

If anyone showed, Manley would continue to instruct them in the proper and safe steps to take next, telling them to tug at their collars to raise their shirttails and to do a full

360-degree spin to show they had no concealed weapons. Only after protracted contact with the suspect through the bullhorn would Stallings pull in tight against the other boat, and only then would he and Manley board the other vehicle.

Handcuffing suspects on a bobbing boat posed other problems, but before one removed a suspect from a boat and placed him on an FMP boat, he had to be cuffed, hands behind the back.

Manley continued to hail the dimly lit cabin across from them, still getting no response; then he suddenly claimed to have seen a shadow against a window. But the windows were tinted, so Stallings wondered how his partner could see a thing. Stallings had seen nothing, but he trusted Rob's eyes and instincts as if they were his own, so he gave a blast on the foghorn, the sea tossing them in an increasingly unfriendly manner toward the other boat now, the two boats kissing, buttressing one another at this point, each protected only by the big foam bumper guards Manley had quickly tossed over the side.

"Everything calm there, Delta-four?" asked the voice over the radio.

Manley shouted over his shoulder, "Back us off a little ways, Ken."

"She's not holding out here, partner," Stallings told Manley, and then said to dispatch, "No problem. It appears no one's aboard." But he wondered even as he reported this to dispatch if it weren't in error.

So far as Manley was concerned, whoever was on the sleek schooner was either ignoring them or in a drunken stupor. The suspect boat was anchored well in waters off Madeira Beach, where lights from shoreline restaurants twinkled back at them only to fade amid the catlike, encroaching fog. The ship sat out alone, by itself, apart from the hundreds of others anchored here, all as if by design, Stallings thought, a loner . . .

"Let's go easy, Rob," he cautioned, feeling Manley's impatience to board the other boat. Stallings could see the black man's skin itching to move. "We got no probable cause, and we can't go nosing around on board without something," Ken reminded his friend of the restraining law.

They were out some distance from most of the anchored ships, most people preferring to sink anchor in a bit shallower depth. This time of year the locals knew that these waters—even the more protected bays—could never be completely trusted. This guy looked like a newcomer to the area. He had all the markings of a visitor save the one the law required: His port of origin was clearly missing—having been painted over perhaps? Or was it below the waterline, as the waves were cresting higher and higher.

"Marine Patrol!" Manley bellowed again, but still there was no response from anyone aboard. "Maybe they've taken a launch in?" he suggested, but the lone dinghy was lashed to the deck.

"Let's try that registration number."

Manley began the chant. "Oreo-Two-Charlie-Niner, Niner—no damnit, that's an eight—no, hell! Can't make it out. Damned if it doesn't look's'if it's been intentionally obscured with paint or something."

Marine law prohibited their going aboard without knowledge of the owner unless there was probable cause, provocation or impending need. If anyone were aboard, the siren ought to've blown out his hearing, and certainly he had to feel the bump and grind of the boats. If a guy were looking out a porthole—and there were several on this starboard side—he'd have to know they were cops, Stallings told himself. From their Stetsons to their 9mm Glock pistols, they were dressed identically to their state trooper counterparts. Besides, their boat was clearly marked.

Stallings brought the Boston Whaler around to the rear of the mystery ship, where they read her name, the *Tau Cross*. Hadn't there been talk that authorities in Miami were looking for a boat in which the letter T and a cross might figure prominently in the name of the boat? Didn't the killer sign his bloody notes with a T-cross?

Manley almost whispered, "You see what I see, Ken?"

"Yeah, I see . . ."

"You take that and the obscured numbers and missing

port of origin for probable cause in a murder investigation?''

''Could be . . . could be . . .'' Stallings knew they had plenty of reason to board the other boat, but a foreboding had overtaken him, a sense not of fear but of a palpable and distressing evil, a darkness, a force not unlike the now encroaching, engulfing fog, and he wondered if they ought not call in backup right this moment, surround the godforsaken suspect boat with numbers. ''Maybe we'd best call it in, tell 'em what we've got before we go any further. Get some backup out here, Rob.''

''Something sure smells here, Ken.''

''Agreed.''

''No, I mean something really smells over here, just over the surface of the water.''

Stallings had worked with dogs on boats to search out drowning victims. Dogs could smell decay out over the surface of the water and when they sent up a howl, the divers knew where to search. Had Manley's nose picked up something similar? Ken could smell nothing but the salt air, and a touch of metallic copper was filling his nostrils, a sure sign of an impending rain, possibly a squall. But he knew, too, that Manley's instincts and senses were razor-sharp, like those of a hound.

Stallings was about to call it in when he heard his partner say, ''Damn, damn . . . whata we got here?'' Stallings looked over to see Manley tugging on a sleek black snake, a quarter-inch nylon rope hanging off the rear of the mystery ship. The rope was obviously weighted down with something.

Manley tugged hand over fist, and suddenly an eyeless, bloated, dead face rushed up at him, making him slip and fall on his elbows and butt, causing him to explode in a litany of curses as the unholy package he'd lifted from the water dropped back into the depths with an easy splash. ''*Mother-J-fuckin'-Christ-a-minny-damn!* Call it in, damn you, Stallings! Call it in now! Get us backup out here. We've got a crime scene here! Damnit if it ain't him; Jesus if it ain't the freakin' Night Crawler!''

Stallings began making the call, saying "Urgent, urgent" to clear the airways as much as possible.

Manley had regained his feet, but not his composure. "Call it in, damnit! Call it in and take us round to the side," he demanded.

"All at the same time? I'm doing my damned best." Only a static-filled radio replied to Stallings's call. Dispatch had obviously gotten busy with other calls.

Manley announced, "I'm climbing aboard."

A Florida summer fog continued rolling in as if from nowhere, as if the clouds from heaven had come upon them to mask their doings. It seemed the work of a devil's lieutenant, Stallings thought. The fog only lightly covered them at the moment, but it was thickening as it moved across their bow and creepily veiled the mysterious death ship, the *Tau Cross*.

"Hold off on that, Rob." Stallings worked the marine radio even as he maneuvered the Whaler into position alongside the port side of the seventy-foot schooner. His eyes took in the teakwood beauty presented them by the ship. It was a ship of foreign manufacture. Stallings called in their location once again, this time being more precise, drawing on his twelve-week training at the FMP academy, doing it by the book. Into the radio, he gave their unit number—Delta-4—followed again by their exact quadrants, the partial number and name of the boat they were about to board, and the fact that they had a body dangling over the side, and the fact that they believed the boat belonged to the suspect Patric Allain, otherwise known as the Night Crawler. "And if it ain't him," Stallings wryly added, "it's his first cousin Beevo! We've fished out a body lashed at the rear of the boat. I repeat, these quadrants, just west of Madeira Beach, a crime has been committed, a body located at this site."

There had been word in police circles that the killer had entered Gulf waters, that he'd spent time in Naples and was expected to move northward, and now here he was. "Go careful, Manley," Stallings cautioned, but Rob was already over the side, standing flat-footed on the deck of the *Cross* and tying their smaller craft to a stanchion.

Night operations were always more difficult than day, Stallings was thinking when he heard a strange little *pa-plunk* noise. At first he thought it some odd sound floating across the bay from shore, maybe a backfiring car or the bad note from one of the many ocean deck bands, but then he saw Manley stumble backward and fall over the side and back onto the Boston Whaler with a crack-thud, and now Manley was flat on his back, looking just as he had when the corpse had so frightened him, except this time he wasn't cursing, not a sound was coming out of him, only a long spear protruding from his chest. Stallings whipped up his 9mm Glock, but he found nothing to target, nothing to focus his anger on, no one in the fog shroud.

He then shouted, "Manley!" tearing to get to his partner.

He momentarily crouched over Manley, realizing the finality of the moment, that the other man wasn't breathing. His best friend's eyes were wide open but unseeing. A noise to his right sent Stallings into a sprawl on the deck of his boat, his gun poised, ready. Still, he could see nothing to target his weapon on.

The damnable fog and the lights mirroring off it had created a surreal pocket here on the water. Stallings realized suddenly that their own lights had blinded them to the killer's whereabouts.

He inched along the deck, trying to stay down, to get to the high-powered spotlight, to click it off, knowing that it'd created a large and easily targeted silhouette of big Rob Manley. And now the damned light was doing the same to him, sending up a clear picture of him for the killer to focus on.

He got to the light, crouched on his knees to reach for the off switch, then slammed it home. At the same instant, he heard another *pa-plunk* sound, followed by something hitting the water the other side of the boat. Was it the noise of a tightly strung speargun, followed by a miss—the arrow striking the water?

Alone now, unable to do anything for Rob, Stallings des-

perately tried to keep his head. He kept his eyes trained on
the killer's boat, every inch of it. Then he saw a shadow
flicker into his peripheral vision, making him wheel and
fire, the explosion of his Glock sending shock waves across
the water, but hitting no one. It was as if he'd fired on a
ghost, completely ineffectual.

He then saw another slight movement, this one at the
rear of the seventy-foot schooner. Were there two Night
Crawlers? He'd wheeled and fired off several more rounds,
when at once the ear-splitting noise which he'd created was
silenced, *when* in a moment something hard and cold
grazed his forehead, *when* he felt his leg turn into a raging
fire, *when* he went suddenly blind and cold and weak and
hurt from slamming so hard on his back. Unable to move
now, paralyzed, he smelled blood—his own; he felt the
heavy weight of the shaft that'd torn through his leg muscle, and he could sense the terrible gash to his left temple
where the earlier spear had tagged him, sending him
sprawling to the deck alongside Rob's body.

All went silent for a time, but then he could hear his
crackling radio, Bob Fisher at dispatch trying to hail him
and Manley; he also heard a birdlike, choking, devilish
laugh, footfalls, curses, but he could not see, and something
in his psyche told him that if he so much as groaned, he
was a dead man.

He heard the Crawler's guttural curses from the other
boat as he worked to separate the two boats, casting off the
line which Manley had tied to the *Cross*. Again, he heard
his radio, hailing him by name now. "Ken, Ken . . . come
in! Stallings? You out there?''

He heard the motorized lift on the *Cross*'s anchor as it
began to mechanically tug the chain from the water. He
heard a voice from deep within himself, calling him a cow-
ard, telling him that he should someway, somehow find his
sight, find his feet, find his lost weapon and blow this
freak's head off. He also heard a voice of reason, a child's
voice, his child's voice telling him to survive this night.

Another voice, a cold, clinical voice, told him that a powerful spear had creased his temple, turning the world into

inky blackness. If he got to his feet, even if he could locate his weapon, he'd stumble, feel for a handhold and clumsily alert the killer to the fact that a third spear needed to be put into Ken Stallings. His leg had now gone completely numb. His mind raced for a way to beat this, a way to counter this, a way to find vengeance before he blacked out. His last thought was a running question: *What about Jenny, the kids, tomorrow? Will I die here like this, never see them again, never open my eyes again, never feel again, never live to stop this bastard who's killed me and Manley? Never . . . ever . . . ev . . . er . . .*

The dispatcher's voice from Stallings's radio wafted across the water as the *Tau Cross*, with Warren Tauman aboard, made its way out into the Gulf and into the stormy sea.

· NINETEEN ·

The blank page; difficult mirror,
gives back only what you were.
— GIORGOS SEFERIADES

Other FMP officers, Coast Guard and county marine cops
arrived at the quadrants called in by the 7-11 Team, and
they were at first confused by the onslaught of pea soup
that they had motored into, a wall of rain and darkness.
Somewhere in here their comrades were in trouble, unable
to respond to repeated radio calls. Fear for Manley and
Stallings ran high. The officers now searching for them
were both friends and admirers of the two men.

Patty Lawrence was the first to spot the listless, bobbing
little Boston Whaler, all instincts telling her there was
something terribly wrong. She had been listening in when
Stallings and Manley had made their last radio call to dispatch, advising of their position and intent. She and partner
Bill Mullins hadn't hesitated, but had raced toward the unfolding incident just off Madeira, hoping to be first backup,
and then when dispatch lost contact, she'd become terribly
worried. It wasn't like Stallings to leave his radio for so
long a time.

She advised Bob Fisher at dispatch to continue hailing
the Delta-4, the 7-11 club, as loudly as he could, and that
she and her partner would use his hail as a buoy, since a
blinding fog had overrun the waters off Madeira.

"How bad is the fog?" Fisher at dispatch wanted to
know.

"Like a goddamn blanket of misdirection, like a star
nebula."

"Star what?" asked Fisher from his safe haven ashore.

"Like in those *Star Trek* movies when the ship goes into a cloud of gases created by an ancient exploding star, so you don't know what's up, what's down, what's right or left."

Bill Mullins agreed, saying, "You got that right."

Lights from onshore and from boats all around bounced off the low-lying cloud that'd rolled in. "They're out there!" She pointed, adding, "I got a glimpse of the boat. Move it, Mullins! Eleven o'clock."

"They're out there and so's the Crawler," countered Mullins. "Did Fisher let the rest of the world know what's going on out here?"

"Says he reported it to the guard, the mainland police and the sheriff's office. We'll have company in a matter of—there it comes."

They heard sirens blaring as other Marine Patrol boats began to encircle the area.

It was then that Patty caught a second glimpse of the appearing, disappearing, directionless little Boston Whaler. The turbulence was unusual, threatening, so her partner called for a weather report. The boat they searched for was identical to her own, save for the markings. "It's them! There! See?" She pointed ahead, her partner now putting on some speed.

"If you see any sign of a sailing ship moving off in any direction," Mullins advised all the other patrol boats joining them now, "go at it cautiously, but contain it."

"Roger that," replied another nearby patrol boat.

"Any sign of your men?" asked a county sheriff's boat.

"We have the boat in sight. Going in for a look." Mullins gave their coordinates so that the others might readily converge on the area.

Patty Lawrence felt the scene as if it were a floating graveyard. She didn't smell death here on the water with the ocean odors and the light drizzle falling from the cloud they stood in; she didn't taste death here—all was too sodden for that, the now steady downpour and lapping waves like a warning bell—but she sensed death here nonetheless.

It felt like a palpable visitor, a dark figure shrouded and standing on the water between them and Stallings's boat as they approached. Patty had once enjoyed a wonderful, carefree affair with Ken, long since over, and now all her fears for his safety seemed realized.

Patty and Mullins's boat had to slice through this Mr. Death, and it did so, dispelling for a moment the Grim Reaper's hold on her imagination. Only it wasn't imagination staring back at her as they came alongside the 7-11. The boat fairly cried of crisis. It wasn't anchored and was without mooring of any kind; it bobbed and waved and threatened to hit them as they approached. There was no one aboard, at least no one who could be seen. The lights reflected crazily around them, hitting and shoving and pushing one another for the right to penetrate the fog, when nothing could penetrate it now. Patty's own spotlight was more trouble now than it was worth, reflecting back at them like a ghostly mirror. She thought for all the world she saw a kind of airy spirit in the lights and the fog, rising up from the unhappy scene, like the spirit of a departed friend.

Mullins pulled their boat in tight and Patty worked a grappling hook on a ten-foot rod into position over the errant gunwale, snatching the 7-11, the noise creating a din. She tugged and hauled with all her strength, pulling the lonely FMP boat into them.

Patty fairly well jumped onto the 7-11 when the two Whalers bumped, and she quickly tied off the two boats, feeling her way in the darkness but quite aware that what appeared to be two dead men with long spears sticking from their bodies lay at her feet.

"Christ, Bill, it's bad . . . really bad!" she called back to Mullins, who steadied the boat and cast off the anchor line.

Patty felt Manley's carotid artery for a pulse but found none. His skin felt like wood. His eyes looked up at her like large question marks. She'd always liked Rob Manley—his swagger, his humor, his kindness to her over the years—and she gave a thought to Louisa and his four kids, the oldest just finishing high school at George Washington in St. Pete.

"Is he . . . is he dead?" asked Mullins as he leaned in over the death boat.

" 'Fraid so, Bill."

"And Stallings?"

Fearfully, she looked across Manley's wide chest, saw the bloody tissue about Ken Stallings's head and the spear shaft in his leg and shook her head, afraid to touch him, afraid to move, terrified that if she tried, she'd faint at the smell of blood and the sights around her, which threatened to overwhelm her anyway. She'd handled bodies before, but none where the faces were familiar, the ties so strong.

Suddenly breaking the silence, Stallings himself answered Mullins from within the confining darkness of his useless eyes, "Bill? Patty? Is . . . is zat . . . you?"

"Good God, he's alive!" Patty shouted. "Ken, Ken, it's us. We've got you. Hang in . . . hang in there."

"We've got to get him to a hospital, now!" Mullins shouted. "Take the wheel and follow my lights!"

Bill cast off and raised anchor, turning his boat directly for shore. Patty situated herself at the helm of Delta-4 and did precisely as Bill had instructed, following in his wake, her tear-filled eyes ever on his lights rather than on the bodies of her two friends in her peripheral vision, rushing her precious cargo to shore.

Bill radioed dispatch as to what was going on, and Bob Fisher promised that an ambulance would be waiting at Madeira Beach.

Meanwhile, the other Marine Patrol boats continued a frantic circling about the fog in an ever-widening arc from the original quadrants that'd pinpointed what Ken Stallings had called in as the *Tau Cross*, the suspect ship. They intended to search all night for it if need be. But somehow, Patty Lawrence feared, the Night Crawler had already escaped the net.

When Jessica and Eriq arrived in Tampa Bay, the TV newscasters and the radios were aflutter with news that two Florida Marine Patrol officers had been struck down by what officials suspected to be the infamous Night

Crawler, who had been approached by the FMP officers on a routine check which had turned out to be not so routine when one officer saw the body of a Night Crawler victim. Both men were fired upon, the suspect boat owner using a speargun. One of the officers was dead, shot through the heart, while the other was fighting to regain consciousness from a coma induced by a nasty blow to the head by another spear which, fortunately, had not penetrated his skull.

Both Eriq and Jessica knew how valuable Ken Stallings had suddenly become to their case; what he saw out there on the water was the ship which everyone in America wanted to see hauled ashore with its evil captain in chains. He had information no one else had.

They raced to Grant Memorial Presbyterian Hospital in Madeira Beach, where Stallings was hanging on to life. When they arrived, they found an army of family, friends and newshounds, gathered in an enormous vigil which the hospital personnel were perturbed about and trying desperately to force into a small waiting room. A spokesperson, a Dr. Cameron Daniels, told the waiting crowd, "Mr. Stallings appears stable in every respect; we don't expect to lose him. At this point, we can only give time the opportunity to do its magic and heal this man. We are hopeful, but as yet, he remains in a deep coma."

"When do you expect he'll be out of the coma?" asked one foolish reporter.

"If I knew that, I could tell you all to come back fifteen minutes before, now couldn't I? I could also make book on the next Buccaneers game and make some real money. I'm sorry, people, but I can't make such predictions at this point."

"Doctor! Doctor!" the press called out after Daniels, but the spry little man was through a pair of double doors marked Hospital Personnel Only before anyone could cut him off.

"Let's get out of here before someone spots us," Jessica warned Eriq.

"Right you are."

Outside in a drizzle, they decided to locate Bob Fisher, the dispatcher who had been in contact with Manley and Stallings during the crisis. "I want to hear that tape," Eriq told Jessica.

"That makes two of us."

They made their way back to the rental car and were soon motoring toward the local headquarters of the Florida Marine Patrol. Local FBI field operatives, having expected them, guided them about the unfamiliar territory and informed them of all that had transpired out on the waters fronting Madeira Beach.

Fisher was not hard to find. He was, in fact, still manning the board when Jessica and Eriq were introduced to him. "I've got two boats out there still, along with two county patrol boats and a fifth from the sheriff's office. Coast Guard is out there, too. They've searched high and low for that damned bastard you people've chased clear up here, but they haven't so much as a whiff of diesel oil to track him by, and that fog out there's playing havoc with our guys. We're ready to call 'em all in."

Fisher was a bony, gaunt man with piercing gray-green eyes, a mustache and thinning hair dyed an awful shade of red-brown.

"That's your decision, of course," replied Eriq.

"You don't want to risk any more lives, and that's quite understandable," agreed Jessica.

"That's all well and good, but these men and women out there now, they're out for revenge. They're not out there for the FMP or the county or the state; they're out there for Manley and for Ken Stallings. Ours is a small community. All these watercops know one another. Don't know if they'd come in off the Gulf if we ordered them, and if we do, and they refuse, then we'll have sanctions against men who've worked all night at risk to life and limb to end this thing. So, I've given 'em rope . . . let them take the tether for the time being, and I've got my boss on the wake-up line. He's been checking in every few minutes and's on his way."

"We'd like to hear whatever you have of Stallings and Manley on tape," Jessica told Fisher.

He nodded. "Sure. There's a soundproof room there," he said, pointing. "I'll run it through to you. You just go on in there."

They listened to the moments leading up to death for Manley and coma for Stallings. They listened a second and a third time, and they told Fisher that they'd like a copy of the tape, and that it wasn't to be given out to the press or TV. He readily agreed and obliged, dubbing them a copy and listening for any new excitement out on the water all at the same time, but he also warned that TV types were going to be offering big sums of money for the tape, and that the FMP was in dire need of funding, and that it wouldn't be up to him to make the final decision on that one.

"Certainly sounds like our guy," Eriq whispered in Jessica's ear.

"Ninety-nine percent sure. A body trailing off the back end of the boat, the boat has the words *Tau Cross* painted at its rear, registration numbers blurred, teakwood all around. Possibly of foreign manufacture." These were all statements which Stallings had made at one point or another during the course of the night to Fisher's dispatch office.

Eriq began thinking aloud, saying, "So now that someone's reached out and touched his boat, he's got to know we know; he'll be painting it, changing her look, renaming it. We've got to canvass every dry dock along the coast from here to Louisiana and back again to the Keys and the Eastern seaboard to be on the lookout for anyone anxious to maul teakwood with paint and anyone with a boat that bears a name with the word *Cross* in it. And now this—the *Tau Cross*. I'd count ourselves lucky: This creep is no longer quite so completely invisible."

"The kind of scare those watercops must've put in him, I agree. This guy I know. He's afraid of capture and exposure; he'd probably prefer death. So now he's running scared."

"That's what I mean," agreed Santiva. "He'll run to the

nearest boat works, try to sell the boat or overhaul it. If we put out an APB on the boat, he's dead in the water, so to speak.''

''He's scared, but he's not stupid, Eriq.''

''What does that mean?''

''He's running; he's going to open that schooner up, take her out of these waters altogether, sail for another location entirely, if he's as scared as I think he is.''

''How can you know how frightened he is?''

''Somebody's got to think like the bastard.''

''And you think he's going to run?''

''As far and as fast as that schooner and his will will take him, yes.''

''Back to England?''

''Maybe.''

Fisher ceremoniously handed over the tape to them, adding, ''I hope you people catch this bastard, so I can be on hand to watch him fry in the electric chair.''

''We're going to do our damnedest,'' Eriq assured the man before they left.

In the parking lot, the drizzle now a silver-toothed annoyance, Jessica leaned across the hood of the car and called out to Eriq, ''What's our damnedest, Eriq? You mean our best? Well, damned if so far we've not done our best; so far, we've let this bastard run us around the entire coastline of this state and we've been unable to spot him even once.''

She left him standing in the rain, his mouth open, while she climbed into the passenger side of the car.

He climbed in after her. ''Just what do you propose we do, Jessica?''

''I say we get a plane or a helicopter out of here.''

''What? We just got here.''

''And we fly it out over the Gulf, and we take it on a course due southeast of here.''

''Southeast of here? For what destination?''

''The Cayman Islands, I believe.''

''What? You told me about the Caymans . . . that he was there, and that possibly he had left a body or two there.

But you don't know that for sure, now do you?"

"Instinct tells me that he got away with murder in the Caymans, and that he never felt the least threatened there, because no one came close to IDing him there, *unlike* here. Fact is, they never knew what they had on the islands, and that's got to sweeten the allure of a return for him. Here, we have an artist sketch, an a.k.a., a possible fix on his real name, and now a good idea of what his boat looks like. He's got to know those two watercops were on the radio, that they gave a description of the boat—"

"Precisely why he'll try to unload it."

"Or he'll take it out of American waters and unload it in a place like the Caymans."

"Even if you're right, and he *is* running from American waters, why do you suppose he's returning to the Cayman Islands? Why not Mexico, Guatemala, Puerto Rico, any number of places?"

"He likes the Caymans. He's familiar with the islands. He'll go there first."

"You're sure of this?"

"I am," she firmly replied, trying to quell all her secret uncertainties.

He thought about her notion a moment. "I may be crazy to go along with this, but okay. We go to the Caymans at first light. No point in going in this darkness with a storm approaching, is there?"

"We must beat him to the islands, before he has a chance to sell the boat there."

"Do you think he'll sell it or recondition it?"

"Either way, he can't get there ahead of us."

"So when do you propose leaving?"

"As soon as possible."

"Do you think we can get a flight out on such short notice?"

"I'm not interested in taking a jetliner, and I don't want to use a marked police vehicle—I don't want to spook this SOB into a suicide. I want him captured and brought to justice."

"For crimes against Florida, he'll fry in the chair."

"My sentiments are with his victims."

"Let's do it. Set it up."

"I want to fly low along the most direct path to the Caymans in search of the boat."

"And Captain Anderson can plot the course you are assuming this creep is taking?"

"Anderson's still in Naples. We asked him to stay put in case we needed his services again. We can contact him through Ford, and he can send us word if there's time, but we'll talk to experts here, too."

"All right . . . do it, but are you really sure about what's going on in this monster's mind?"

"It's my best guess right now. Do you have any other suggestions?"

Santiva passed a hand along the stubble of a twenty-four-hour growth of beard, and gnashing his teeth, he finally muttered, "Another helicopter ride?"

"It's got to be private, or an unmarked police chopper. Either that or a cub plane."

"Either way, I'm a sick man."

"We'll get you more Dramamine."

"I'll double the dosage."

"And be asleep in my lap?"

He laughed. "I've been in much worse spots . . ."

Patty Lawrence felt she had to do something, and sitting in a hospital waiting room, crowded full with Manley's people and Ken Stallings's family and friends, wasn't good enough. She had yanked her partner from the hospital and they'd agreed to return to the search out there off Madeira Beach for whatever sign they could find of the bastard who'd done this to Ken.

The search front had gone in carefully squared-off areas, the search boats squeezing the playing field, hoping to catch up to a killer who was likely as lost in the fog as they themselves felt. Their instruments, they hoped, were better than his, as they hoped their instincts were.

But several hours of searching had turned up nothing. Perhaps this maniac killer did know what he was doing when it came to maneuvering a sailing vessel.

Bill was now in the flat of the boat, scanning the waters with a pair of night-vision binoculars while Patty inched the Boston Whaler through the soup. A running joke had given their boat its private name, *The Pantry*—named for all the food Bill brought aboard, from potato chips and cold cuts to Pepsi-Cola and cranberry jam. Bill was a big man, as big as Rob Manley had been, and he had seen all manner of problems on this job. *Patty's Pantry*, as some of the guys called their boat, was a misnomer; it ought more rightly to have been *Bill's Pantry*. She ate three regulars a day and never strayed from her regimen, never snacking in between, however tempting Bill made it at times, however much he goaded.

They were in near-constant contact with the other search ships. People were getting short with one another; personnel were beginning to feel the emotional and physical strain, the stress growing minute by painful minute as the obvious began to sink in: They'd somehow let the Night Crawler crawl right past them all. The bastard was aptly named.

Tempers flared, ignited by frustration and anger and unresolved feelings. Patty certainly felt her share of the latter. She and Ken Stallings had left so many feelings unresolved. Bill knew about the special bond between them and had always been a gentleman and friend and never once made her feel guilty. But now Bill hadn't spoken a word in the past fifteen minutes, and she couldn't help but wonder what was going through his mind. Perhaps it was the same simple thought plaguing her: All appeared helpless, useless effort now.

Their radio crackled anew with the voice of a county sheriff's guy she hardly knew, a man named Trilling, announcing something in the water at their location. He quickly gave the exact coordinates, repeating his message: "Something in the water! Something floating on top of the water! Something out of place . . ."

Patty had to fight through the radio traffic to ask, "What've you got? Describe it."

"Looks . . . looks like . . . yeah, Jesus . . . it's a body."

All the search vehicles were close now, so close they could see each other's searchlights even in the fog. Patty Lawrence silently wondered at the new find. Had the killer left his own brand of calling card?

The find was called in to various dispatches on land, including Bob Fisher, Patty's own dispatch. The news that they had someone in the water spread like wildfire. Moments later, it was confirmed by Trilling's partner, and some details filtered over the radio waves: *female, five-nine to six foot, thin, well-proportioned, nude and DOA. Apparent late teens, a black nylon rope twisted in a noose around her neck, strangled and drowned.*

Each additional bit of information was like another blow to them all. Everyone had heard of the recent disappearance of the young woman from Naples Island, south of Tampa. Everyone wondered if this could be her. There seemed little doubt that whoever she was, she'd been victimized by the Night Crawler, and that he'd brutally used her. The word buzzing over the airways indicated that the girl's body was as stiff as a long-preserved medical cadaver's might appear.

Bob Fisher, at the FMP dispatch office in Tampa, promised to get word to the FBI so that they might have someone on hand to examine the body. He started with the local FBI office, telling them what his people and the county had come across off Madeira Beach, adding that it appeared related to the earlier incident involving his people, Officers Manley and Stallings.

The FBI was interested, and said they'd locate Chief Santiva and Dr. Jessica Coran to have their best people on the scene when the body came ashore.

An hour later, when the body was brought ashore, a county coroner from Pinellas was the only medical man found readily available to take charge of the body. Jessica Coran could not be located.

Jessica found local aircraft vehicles useless for her needs; neither Tampa nor St. Pete had any to spare, and those that were in repair and might be ready in twenty-four hours were all marked clearly as police vehicles. Officials here in Tampa weren't in any mood to cooperate in any case; they blamed FBI bungling for the death of the FMP officer named Manley and the maiming of Ken Stallings, a notion fueled by recent newspaper accounts, radio and TV broadcasts and political speeches, some with an extremely irrational, fringe-element twist reminiscent of the kind of talk that had been coming out of militia companies across America since the Waco, Texas, "massacre" and the two-years-in-the-making plot against the federal building in downtown Oklahoma City. All Jessica knew for certain was that there had to be one hell of a paranoia at work in the heartland to convince people with brains in their skulls that the U.S. government was interested in creating mass murder of innocent children just to get control of the NRA lobby in Congress.

The killer can't have gone far, Jessica told herself in keeping with her prediction that he'd gone southeast over the waters, passing back along his track like a cougar, marking his territory well. His going farther westward toward Louisiana and Texas, after a scare like the one the watercops had thrown into him, seemed unlikely. However, to be certain, another search team made up of Samernow and Quincey would go in that direction, hovering over the Gulf waters in a second helicopter. At least, that'd been the plan; but the plan was coming apart at the seams.

First, fellow law enforcement officials were being uncooperative, and now private small-plane and helicopter companies were doing the same. And now Jessica found herself in a lonely, dank helicopter hangar on a fogbound airfield just south of Tampa with no way to pursue the killer. The helicopter owner here simply looked at her badge and said stonily, "We're not endangering any of our pilots for the FBI, not in this foul weather."

The man left her, returning to his office, which was dwarfed here in the massive hangar. She wanted to shove something like a court order down his throat but she had none, and getting one could take more time than she had.

Although only small aircraft flew in and out here, the

airfield was large, and there were a number of other companies she could turn to, so she looked out at the blinking lights in the fog that signaled men at work somewhere out there. She looked around for someone to perhaps guide her to another location. The usual heat of a Florida morning had been wiped away by the sodden wet blanket of air hovering over them.

While Jessica worked to get airborne, Eriq Santiva had gone back to the hospital to wait in the hope that Ken Stallings would find a voice in his search for consciousness and reality. Everyone was hoping against hope that he might come around, not only for the man's sake but because inside his silence lay the key to locating the Night Crawler.

In the meantime, a copy of Patric Allain's signature on an agreement made between him and a Mr. Scrapheap Jones in Key West, Florida, had come in at Tampa Bay's main headquarters, Police Precinct One. Eriq was unequivocal when he declared it to be the same handwriting as that on the letters to the press.

To quell the rancor of local politicians and the media, who were doing camera interviews, this new bit of information was carefully spooned out in terms that made it sound as if the Night Crawler might as well already be in custody, since they were now certain that the man named Patric Allain was one and the same as the Night Crawler. The impression Eriq left with the press was that the FBI was closing in on the demon.

Still, local loudmouths claimed that police had failed to protect and serve "even their own" in this instance, and that in fact, authorities had used the Tampa Bay area as a kind of watery "box canyon" into which they flushed the killer—yet had still managed to let him slip free! The implication was that the FBI had completely mishandled the case, as if politicians and reporters could have done law enforcement's job for them in much better fashion. The Florida press set up a hue and cry like so many armchair detectives.

The other implication was that the FBI had placed all of

the Tampa–St. Pete area in danger by chasing this perverted monster into their midst in the first place; why had Miami's problem become Tampa's problem? So that now two good, solid citizens, FMP officers, had been brutally assaulted by the man FBI agents couldn't seem to catch in a months-long, intensive pursuit. Furthermore, the Night Crawler remained in this region, and he might be anywhere, and he might take anyone's daughter.

Some were demanding that the FBI give a full accounting of its activities in the matter, along with a detailed explanation for what steps it next planned to pursue. Florida politicians around the state were outraged at the duration of this case, as well as what appeared to them to be a lack of efficiency and professionalism.

The word apparently had gone out from the governor's mansion that it was open season on the FBI in general and on Jessica Coran and Eriq Santiva in particular, the mainstays of the investigation who perhaps ought to be removed and replaced. The groundswell of anger was further fueled by Tammy Sue Sheppard's family, who were making daily statements to the press, especially the *National Enquirer*.

The *Enquirer* did an entire page on how Jessica dressed, how she wore her hair, what kind of lipstick she used and who manufactured her eye shadow, and the kind of extravagance she and Santiva had displayed in staying at the Fontainebleau in Miami. Its headline read, *Tall & Beautiful Scavenger for Scientific Fact Short on Results in Night Crawler Case*. The story summarized the case, beginning with facsimiles of the killer's sweetheart notes to the press. It listed the victims and where each body had been found, giving ample space to the time three bodies washed ashore in one day in Miami. Eddings of the *Herald* in Miami was quoted throughout the article and claimed to be writing a book on the Night Crawler which would blow the case wide open. The article went on to tell of how painstakingly every port, dock and wharfside restaurant along the Eastern seaboard had been meticulously papered with wanted posters once a witness had come forward with an account and a police sketch artist had created a likeness. The story showed the likeness and a picture of the plaster-cast bust made from the artist's sketch.

Jessica wondered where they had gotten such details, but it mattered little now. Let the politicians and the press kick all they wanted. She sensed that she was, for the first time, on the trail of the killer, in his direct wake. All they need do now was locate the miserable excuse for a human being out there on the vast ocean, close in on the putrid SOB and finally put an end to the bastard's killing spree. Men like him and those who'd bombed the federal building in Oklahoma City, she mused, must know that there was nowhere for their souls to go, that not even Satan held a place for their kind.

Due to reasons beyond her control—both the meteorological and the political climate—Jessica found that the local small-aircraft people weren't cooperating either; no one was willing to take a helicopter up in the soup of this morning's fog, or brave the winds that were reportedly coming in behind the dense fog, winds that were howling about the airfield. It was the same damned fog that'd gotten one watercop killed and put another close to death in a coma, the same fog that had masked the killer's movements. And now this damnable wet haze hung, an enormous blur suspended, rooted, as if controlled by Allain, as if there were some supernatural purpose in fog, so that when old-timers at the airport said, "Never seen a Florida fog stay on so damned long before," Jessica didn't take it as idle talk.

"Damnit, we'll be heading east, away from the Gulf storm," she said to one chopper pilot who she thought might break down and say yes. She had always believed helicopter pilots fearless, a bit crazy, willing to do just about anything. That had been her experience with chopper pilots in the past.

"Sorry . . . I've got too much invested in my bird, and I'm told by air traffic control to keep her on the ground for at least five hours."

Tropical Storm Karl, as it was now being called, didn't care about Jessica's problems.

She replied, "To hell with it—I'll fly myself. Where can I charter a cub plane?" She'd gotten her pilot's license six months before, soloing with ease after the intensive training she'd received from one of the best pilots she'd ever known, a man who flew jets of all sorts as well as small planes. Kenneth Massey had given her all the confidence she needed to fly through the perimeter of the storm edge. All she needed was a plane, but time and nature appeared to be conspiring against her.

She found a mechanic at the airfield who was sitting idle, glancing over a copy of the special-edition *Enquirer* which Quincey had earlier pointed out to her, and the man easily recognized her from a picture taken when she was walking out to the beach to inspect one of the three bodies washed ashore on that awful day back in Miami, the day Allain threw his power in their faces.

The burly, pigeon-toed mechanic almost dropped his teeth when she spoke to him, looking from her to the newspaper photo and back again.

"I need to charter a plane or a helicopter, now. Can you help me?"

"I, ahhh . . . I can take you to somebody who maybe can, ma'am."

"That would be wonderful, if you don't mind . . ."

He didn't mind in the least taking time away from his duties to drive her across the taxiing strip. "I like driving the golf cart," he confided as they skirted the runways in search of a plane she might charter. The airfield was so covered in fog that only the lights of the tower were visible, and these were shrouded. They pulled from the darkness to within inches of a white cub plane which had been painted with tiger stripes below a sign that read White Tiger Aviation.

"It's a cargo operation with tourist flights as a sideline," explained the mechanic. She thought it more likely a front for smuggling of some sort. She imagined the little plane going back and forth to Cartagena, Mexico, perhaps even Cuba. And if so, they'd be antsy about knowing that an FBI woman was on the premises.

She tried slipping a twenty to the mechanic, but he flatly refused any payment for his troubles. "You kidding? This was my pleasure, Dr. Coran. Meeting someone like you. Ain't nobody at the house going to believe it, though. Hey, maybe you could maybe autograph this for me?" He lifted out his copy of the *Enquirer* and turned to the page where a glaring picture of her without makeup and on her way to the scene of a killing stood opposite a shot of her dressed to kill, taken the night she was out with Eriq in Miami's Little Cuba area. She had not seen any reporters that night, but obviously, someone had seen her, and cameras being everywhere and anywhere these days, now the entire world had.

She scrawled her signature across the article for Lyle, the mechanic, and again thanked him. He replied, "If anybody can get you airborne in this soup, it'll be Pete Geiger. He flew in Nam, you know."

"Thanks . . . thanks, Lyle."

"Didja hear the news 'bout that girl missing from Naples?"

She hadn't heard anything recent. "No, no, I haven't."

"Saw it on the tube just an hour ago. She's been missing a couple of days now. Some say the Crawler got her. Anyways, poor thing . . . They fished out a body at Madeira Beach where—"

"Isn't that where—"

"Yeah, the two Florida watercops were brought ashore; anyways, some are saying the body's the Naples girl, that they're the same."

"I pray not."

"Sorry about the way the boss treated you, back there at the hangar, I mean. He can be an ass," Lyle confided as he turned his cart and headed back the way he'd come, disappearing into the shroud and whistling "Misty."

She'd had extremely bad luck with the helicopter guys across the field. She hadn't been wrong in feeling some hostility from Lyle's boss, which even the less than alert mechanic had taken note of. No doubt the guy had eaten heartily of all the negative press about the FBI's handling of the Night Crawler case.

Now, telling the White Tiger guys the truth might easily alienate them, she feared. She needed a plan, one that didn't include stories in the press and photos in the *National Enquirer*. She sauntered into White Tiger, knowing she would tell them nothing about her true identity or mission.

Inside she found a man with his feet propped on a desk amid stacks of paper, books and charts, his office a mold and mildew pit below the Quonset hut shell. Dust mites teemed here, it was a place where cheese mold would feel quite at home. A half-eaten sandwich and a Pepsi can indicated a quasi-meal had been only partially consumed some days before.

The moment he saw her come in, he dropped his feet to the floor and began tossing wrappers and empty cans and grossly neglected items such as bread crumbs into a wastepaper basket. He clearly hadn't expected anyone to step in from the fog outside. All the while, she saw his mind racing with questions: *Who is she? How'd she get way out here? Is she alone?* Jessica guessed that he also wondered about her marital status, and perhaps how much effort it might take to get her into bed with him. Knowing the male mind as she did, she suspected the truth of it, and it had nothing whatever to do with her opinion of herself. In fact, the weaker her opinions, she knew, the more likely he'd be attracted to her. Perhaps, she told herself, she could use this typical male attitude against the guy to get what she wanted.

Despite all of her patently biased thoughts, all the man said was a polite, "May I help you, ma'am?"

He was a tall, gaunt young man with rugged Clint Eastwood features. In fact, the fellow most certainly didn't look old enough to have been in the Vietnam War; neither did he look as if he'd be comfortable in the cockpit of a small plane, given the length of his legs. Still, his flak jacket hung on a coat rack behind him, and pictures of him and other men standing around Air Force fighter jets signaled that he was a wartime flier at one time, perhaps during Desert Storm.

"I need a plane out of here, Mr., ahhh . . ."

"Lansing, ma'am. Don Lansing."

"I thought your name was Pete Geiger."

"I'm Pete's, ahhh . . . partner. We've been told to stand down till this weather's over, though, ma'am, so I'm—"

"Don't say it! I've heard 'sorry' up and down this damned airport. You've flown in worse, I'm told."

His smile was wide, charmed and charming. "I have, but going against the tower, ma'am, miss . . . well . . . it rubs those boys the wrong way, and I've got to live with them after . . ."

She read into his words that he'd also have to answer to Pete.

"I'll make it worth your while."

He was instantly interested. "How much?"

She drew on her best Lauren Bacall voice now. "Double your usual rate." She saw his eyebrows twitch.

"*Phewww* . . . wish I could. I hate turning down green, and being grounded all in the same day, now that's a bitch. Pardon, ma'am."

"Then let me take it up; I'll fly it out, return it in a few days."

His hands shot up in a defensive gesture as if she'd pulled a gun on him. "*Whoa* . . . you're going to take it up in this fog?"

"I've flown in fog before," she lied. "Besides, once I'm above the soup, there should be no trouble."

" 'Cept from Pete or Harvey up there in the tower. You hear those winds revving up to eighty, ninety miles an hour? You know what that does to a little bird like that modified Sandpiper out there?"

"I'm heading due east," she lied again.

"Straight for where?"

"The other coast."

"Must be awful important, Miss, ahhh . . ."

"Little, Pamela Little, and yes, it is important, extremely."

"What's your exact destination?"

"The . . . the Cayman Islands."

"Really? That's not exactly due east. Damn, you'd be

lost in a blink up there alone. Love the Caymans myself. Haven't been there in some time.''

"Maybe now's a good time? We go sharp east first, avoid the storm, get south of it and continue in southeast over Cuba.'' She purposefully, rapidly blinked her lashes at him as she spoke. "That ought to get us to the Caymans sometime late today.''

Jessica could tell that he was giving it serious thought as his eyes played over her; he imagined she was propositioning him. *She really wants a pilot, badly . . . maybe some sort of pilot groupie,* he no doubt was thinking. She really didn't have any notion whatsoever of flying out of here for the Caymans on her own.

"Whataya say?'' she prodded. She really didn't want to have to fly out of here herself, especially not with Santiva screaming in her ear that she was a madwoman to attempt it.

"Twice my usual rate?'' asked Lansing, biting his inner right cheek.

"That's what I said.''

"You must be in an awful hurry. You runnin' from the law or something?''

"Will you do it?'' *Let his imagination fill in the blanks,* she told herself.

He looked out at the fogged-in airfield. "Well, I can't let *you* do it.''

"All right, then you take me out of here.''

"No, I can't do it neither, much as I'd like, Miss . . . Little, did you say? I could lose my license; I could lose my business.''

"Triple your usual rate.''

"Damn . . .'' He started to pick up the phone. Then he thought better of it, replacing it in its cradle. "How soon can you be ready?''

"I have to make a call; you'll have two passengers.''

"Two?''

"Is that a problem?''

"Well, it means more drag . . . the weight, you know.''

"Is it a problem?'' she repeated.

"No . . . no . . . guess not. How soon do you want to depart?" he asked again.

"As soon as my . . . my friend can get here."

Jessica, already armed with the water route that Anderson had outlined for her, thanks to Quincey's being in contact with him, needed now only to get Eriq out here to the airfield. She telephoned the hospital, waited on hold, finally reached him and asked in a conspiratorial voice for Mr. Santivas, intentionally adding a final letter for Don Lansing's benefit. *Santivas* sounded even more exotic and intriguing than *Santiva*.

Lansing, while remaining the other side of the desk, cocked an ear in her direction as she spoke to Eriq, hearing only Jessica's voice.

"Has the situation there changed?" she breathily questioned Eriq.

"Yes, it has," he surprised her.

"What's happened?"

"Stallings is out of critical danger, and he's fully conscious; it appears he's going to make it, and with some rehab, he'll be fine. They're not so sure his eyesight will ever return, however."

"That's good news; has he been able to tell you anything, anything at all? About the boat, perhaps?"

"He's still weak, and his eyesight is zero like I said, and his emotional state isn't so good; he's blaming himself for Manley's death."

"So he's not talking?"

"Well, I managed to make him see the light, so to speak. He gave me enough to recognize the schooner when I see it."

"Schooner?"

"World class. He said it had three masts and state-of-the-art equipment, that it was fully automated so that one knowledgeable seaman alone could sail her. That even the sails could be brought down and put up by a single man. Said it was of British manufacture, made for racing, had excellent teakwood moldings all around, and that while the name and call numbers were obscured, it appeared to be the *Tau Cross*."

"Excellent. Then we're on our way to the Caymans."

"Not so fast. Something else has surfaced."

"I heard something about a body in Madeira Bay?" Jessica was acutely aware that her words were causing quite a stir in Don Lansing; she was either going to frighten him away or excite him into following through on the flight out of here. It all depended on what kind of man he was.

"Well, it's not a bay, actually." Eriq was giving her a geography lesson. "It's oceanfront, and yes, a body has been left in the bastard's wake, a kind of present for us. She's already been IDed as a Naples Missing Persons case."

Jessica audibly groaned. "We've got to end this freak show, Eriq."

"You've got to get back here, locate the Pinellas County Coroner's Office and do your thing. See if the body can tell you—"

"Tell me what, Eriq? Tell me what I already know? No, I'm not coming back there. I'm flying to the Caymans within the hour."

"Jess, it's not good protocol to just let the body—"

"It's exactly what he wants, Eriq. Don't you see that? The body was left for us to find in order to slow us down."

Santiva was silent for a moment at the other end. She jumped on his silence, adding, "He's yanking our chain. That dead body is his way of trying to control our movements and to cut down on his own damned drag!" Jessica realized only now that Lansing, on hearing additional snippets of her conversation, had carefully armed himself, placing a gun in his belt. She feared that perhaps she'd gone too far with her masquerade and that Lansing had only heard the most provocative words, most out of context.

"You've secured transportation?" asked Eriq.

"I have, and I want you here ASAP. Otherwise, I do this alone."

"No . . . no, you don't. Give me your location."

She gave him directions and the name of the place from which they were booking the flight. "You're in a hospital. Pick up what you need in the way of Dramamine there, and then get right over here, Eriq."

"Jess, this latest victim deserves our best, as much as any of the others."

"Then send our best field M.E. or pathologist over there. Tampa's got to have someone who can take over."

"This young woman, Jess, lived her entire life in Naples and was some sort of a queen at her high school there; she wasn't a tourist but a resident, a towny. She loved Naples and they loved her."

"Eriq, trust me. If I don't see you here in forty minutes, I'm gone, so like I said, get right over here."

"And you'd do it, too, wouldn't you?" he said, but she'd already hung up, wondering if the killer had any other bodies aboard the ship which Stallings had called the *Tau Cross*; did the bastard plan to drag the body of yet another victim the entire distance to the Cayman Islands with him?

Now Jessica stood looking across the room at Lansing, who was nervously pacing, wishing he hadn't said yes, anxious to find out more about her—or just anxious to get out of the deal? He kept looking across at her, sizing her up, curious about her and her story—and her friend on the other end of the line. The situation seemed more shady with each passing moment. The questions were pinging about his brain like a pinball, so palpable she could almost hear them ringing, and she realized she had him exactly where she needed him to be.

"How long'll it take for your friend to get here?" he asked now.

"An hour, maybe."

"Maybe by then some of this stuff'll blow over. Maybe . . . if things don't take a turn for the worse . . ."

He tuned in the weather report, but the news only made both of them more nervous and fidgety, filled as it was with the latest happenings and the strange disappearance and possible literal "surfacing" of the girl from Naples, followed with reports that her body may have "washed ashore in a state of preservation, as if lost by a mortuary," in the reporter's words.

"Damn, Madeira Beach's not too far from here," mused Lansing.

Jessica tried to recall if she'd said anything about Madeira Beach which Don Lansing might've taken the wrong way. At the same time, a picture flashed on the TV for a few moments, a photo of the dead girl in happier times, telling Jessica that the victim had the same general appearance as all the others before her. Finally, Lansing clicked the TV off.

"I just brewed some coffee. Would you like some?" he asked her.

"Sure . . . that'd be great . . . might warm my insides a bit." She was very aware of the small-caliber but quite deadly .22 he'd holstered in his belt.

There was no clean place in the hut to sit. She remained standing, pacing, looking from time to time out the window as if any moment the strobe lights of a police car might be out there, giving chase to the fleeing suspect in Don Lansing's florid mystery as it played out in his brain.

When he came to stand beside her at the window, the coffee extended, he, too, peeked out at the fog as if expecting someone.

"Triple my usual's going to come to a hell of a lot of money, lady. You do understand that?" He jotted down a figure on a pad and handed it to her. His twenty-four-hour day rate was $575 plus fuel, so the mysterious "Maltese Falcon" lady who'd just stepped into Don's life was looking at over $1,700 just for starters. That'd buy him and Pete some time on those bloodsucking creditors; Pete would thank him for this later, Don assured himself, tell him that if he hadn't taken this job, Pete would've killed him, and if Pete were here, he'd do exactly what Don was doing right this moment, up the ante.

He went to the phone, asked if it was all right if he called his partner, to let Pete know what was going on and where they'd be taking Pete's plane.

"Pete owns the plane?"

"Yeah, it's Pete's plane . . ."

"Sure, do what you have to do."

Lansing got only an answering machine, into which he spoke a cryptic message for his partner.

"You're doing the right thing," she assured him. A long look into her eyes confirmed this for Don, she was sure. The clock on the wall seemed frozen in time at 5:09 A.M. She wished Eriq would get here before Don changed his mind and backed out.

"Triple my usual," repeated Lansing, "almost enough to go to hell for."

She looked up at him. "Paradise, remember," she replied.

He moved in a little too closely, and she stepped away. She wondered how far the Night Crawler might've gotten in the six hours that had elapsed since he'd eluded Stallings and Manley. She wondered how long it might take to catch the killer's ship, imagining that moment when it would come into view; she imagined going on to Grand Cayman Island and simply waiting for Patric Allain to ease into port there and how simple it would be to apprehend the bastard beast when he stepped off the boat. They could then secure the boat as a crime scene, and she'd nail him six ways to Sunday and beyond for multiple murder. Next stop the Florida electric chair, the same as toasted the likes of Ted Bundy; see how Patric liked sailing that mother.

She imagined that Okinleye would want to hold Allain for questioning in the murders that had occurred in his jurisdiction, but knowing Ja and the problems of the islands, she also believed that the Cayman government would not stand in the way of an expedient order, so that Allain would stand trial in Florida, where he'd face the death penalty. She was only sorry that he could not be electrocuted separately for each victim he'd so tortured.

Eriq finally arrived in an unmarked police car, in the company of Samernow and Quincey, the small crowd making Don Lansing even more nervous about his decision than before, Jessica realizing how like Mafia types the two burly Miami cops and the tall, stolid Santiva appeared. Jessica caught the others outside, out of Don's earshot, explaining that the only way she could get a flight out was to con this guy into thinking they were running

from the law, so she told Quincey and Samernow to get a
chopper from the police hangars as soon as the fog lifted
and the storm had passed and to take it on a course west
along the coast as insurance. She asked Eriq to go
along with her, follow her lead, and to pretend that he was
a Cuban nationalist trying desperately to get out of the
country.

"You play Bogey?" she asked, the wind now whipping
her jacket about her.

His tie flagged across his forehead and eyes. "I'll do my
best, shh-weet-heart."

"Do you have Captain Anderson's notes and map?"

"I do, but I don't know how helpful it's going to be."

She took hold of the route the killer might take if he
were to leave Tampa straight for the Caymans. "Okay, let's
get airborne."

Lansing was already on the radio to the tower, explaining
that there was an emergency need to take off. They weren't
buying it, from the sound of things.

Jessica laid Captain Anderson's projected route before
Lansing. Lansing told the tower he'd be back in touch with
them, then stared at the proposed flight plan.

"You said you wanted to go due east. This is south."

"Southeast," she split hairs.

"That's a lot of miles in storm conditions."

"Don, it's important we follow this path as closely as
possible."

"No way we're going through the Straits of Mexico, not
in the given weather pattern. It'd be safer and simpler to
go direct for the east coast and south from there, and maybe
even a layover in Miami to refuel . . ."

Lansing desperately attempted to ignore Eriq Santiva,
and he did well, save for the out-the-corner-of-his-eye suspicious looks. Jessica took Don aside to reason with him
while Eriq continued the silent, stony role he'd fallen into,
his inscrutable Cuban features befitting the situation.

"It's important we get out over international waters as
soon as possible," she told Don.

He nodded as if he actually understood. "All right . . .

all right. Get your friend out to the airplane, and we'll be on our way.''

She went to Eriq and when she turned around, Don was already out the door and on the airfield. When they stepped out, they saw that Don was doing a preflight check of the plane, and he shouted over the wind for them to get aboard. Obviously, Don had made up his mind.

The wind pummeled the airfield and the people on it. Eriq was pushed into the plane. Jessica's coat did a wild flap dance about her body as the wind lashed out at her and the small plane, creating a shiver in the aircraft. The skies were just lightening up but remained a gunmetal gray all the same, painted and smeared with the ominous hues of storm clouds preparing to burst. But at the moment there seemed a fortuitous lull in the precipitation.

Looking out over the grass, the taxi strip and the small runway now, Jessica saw how slick everything was. But she was determined to go ahead with her plans, climbing into the cockpit after Eriq, who'd opted for the backseat.

Once inside the plane, Don asked, ''What am I going to tell the tower? I take off without talking to them, my butt's in a sling when I get back here.''

''But you did talk to them, inside, earlier . . . '' shouted Jessica over the wind.

''And they didn't like it; told us to stay put,'' he countered.

''Radio them it's a police emergency,'' Jessica countered his counter.

''They're going to want to know more than that.''

''Tell 'em it's got to do wid dat, ahh, ahh, whataya-callit case. Dat, uhhhh . . . '' began Eriq, in rare form.

''The Night Crawler thing?''

''Right . . . dat's it, kid. Tell 'em dat.''

''Suppose they want to talk to one of the policemen?''

''Tell them we're FBI,'' said Jessica. ''And if they want to talk to me, tell them I'm Agent Coran and this is Agent John Thorpe . . .''

''Thorpe; FBI?'' He looked Eriq over as if he hadn't

seen him before. "You think they're going to believe that?"

"We'll give them badge numbers if they ask," she replied. "Let's get out of here, now."

"Roger that . . ."

Don had gone sullen on her, and his new somberness had begun the moment Santiva had entered the picture, Jessica believed. He no doubt had originally accepted her offer in the comfortable male fantasy that a woman alone, a woman like her—vulnerable and in need—could prove to be fun and "rewarding" in every sense of the word to take on as his lone passenger to a Caribbean paradise; that they'd fly off and into a romantic adventure together, à la *Romancing the Stone* or some such thing.

The tower, on hearing their FBI numbers read, had no trouble allowing Lansing to take off, but the dispatcher did so with caution heaped upon caution. And the takeoff itself proved to be like rushing into a blinding wall. Unable to see ahead of them, Lansing did a marvelous job of getting airborne in the dense fog.

Jessica, in the copilot's position gasped when the plane smashed against the mountain of cloud they were under. With Jessica clutching at her copilot seat and Eriq tucked into the rear, the little plane was buffeted about like a toy in a wind tunnel once lift was reached. With the rush of noise and the engine so near, Jessica saw—rather than heard—Don muttering to himself, likely kicking himself for taking on this job. Only when she placed on the headphone set could she hear him cursing himself.

The sky was lighter now, but this was of little comfort. They were still flying blind into an unpredictable wind shear. Still, they rose higher, trying to escape the thermals and the fog, the bumps, grinds and whips, when suddenly they were above the enormous pillow of clouds—popping free like a bird escaping a cage, flying directly into the brilliant sun, a welcome sign even if it, too, was blinding.

Lansing leveled the plane out, its roar like a cat's purr in the infinity of sky, and in a moment the compass indicated their heading as due south. They would follow along the western coast of the Sunshine State; only today, there was neither sunshine nor view below them, only above.

Jessica wondered at the killer's luck. With this kind of cloud cover, how were they going to go in low over suspicious boats? How could they possibly ID the suspect sailing ship even now, armed with Ken Stallings's description? Furthermore, the winds would have given the sailing vessel full power to skim over the water. And Allain had six hours on them.

Eriq seemed settled for the moment in the rear seat, having steadied his nerves after the bumpy takeoff. He appeared beat, so dead tired in fact that when Jessica glanced again at him, his eyes were closed. She prayed he hadn't overdosed on Dramamine.

With Lansing beside her, they filled the little cockpit from top to bottom. He seemed a capable pilot. She had given little thought to his skills or possible lack thereof before now, but he'd handled the thermals and the wind well, appearing a capable master of the air. She felt somewhat guilty at having duped the young man. Now that they were airborne, she wondered how much of the lies had been absolutely necessary to get them here. It now seemed foolish to have run such a charade on Lansing to get what she wanted, but telling him the truth now could mean a 180-degree turnaround and a return to the ground—*and to hell with that*, Jessica quietly told herself, keeping silent counsel as the plane soared southward toward the emerald Caribbean Sea.

· TWENTY ·

I have eaten your bread and salt.
I have drunk your water and wine.
The deaths ye died I have watched beside
And the lives ye led were mine.
                              —RUDYARD KIPLING

The wind itself—sometimes called Satan's leash dog—
seemed now to Warren Tauman his ally in escape, for it
had risen with the saving fog that masked his escape to
now send him at twice and thrice the speed he would have
been making without its help. He needed to conserve on
fuel. It was a long trip to where he was going, and he knew
his route was at best a circuitous one, no beelines since
Cuba lay in his path. Although he felt certain that he had
all the time in the world to get to where he was going,
since no one knew his plans or his destination, he wished
to be out of American waters, and he wished to start over
elsewhere, even as he meant to convince the authorities
anxious to see him dead that he remained in Florida. He
had a plan for that, too. He had paid well to have a final
letter delivered to the press. This one would be sent to
Florida's panhandle to throw police and FBI off his trail.
When news that the *Pensacola Democrat* had received another letter from the Night Crawler, everyone would scurry
to that location, thinking he was headed west along the
coast of the Gulf of Mexico.

   Still, the incident in Tampa had frightened him, and it
had put his mind to work. He must do what was necessary,
if he were ever to get Mother back, to control her. He
probably needed to cut his losses for a while, and he'd done
just that. To keep the Tampa area cops on hold, he'd cut
loose the dead girl who had been dangling off the aft side.

With a body bobbing about in the water during their search, the cops would focus more on it and less on him.

They could send out all the radar equipment in the world against him in that fog, and with his ship's built-in radar scrambler, he could just bounce signals right back at them. The authorities had only proven once again how inept and inadequate they truly were.

He'd heard news reports of how an FBI forensics expert had been put on his trail, how she was supposedly the best in the land; he'd seen the tabloids in supermarkets which claimed that in their frustration, authorities had turned to such nonsense as psychics and handwriting analysis to track him. If that was the best they could do . . .

The wind continued at his back even as he neared the northwest tip of Cuba off in the distance. Southward, a hundred miles south of Cuba to be exact, he would come into sight of the Caymans. He'd come through the roughest of the storm, which had moved northward as he had maneuvered along the backlash at its southeastern edge to turn into his now southwest course.

And with the storm winds around him having abated, Warren switched on the two-diesel engines which powered the boat onward. He turned on the autopilot and finally had a moment's time to relax. The odor of diesel wafted across the water, but due to a state-of-the-art air filtration system in the cabin below, the odor did not linger as in most sailing vessels.

He went below, relieved himself in the head, located a beer in the fridge, and although he wanted to lie down, rest, there was too much yet to do. He wished now that he'd kept the body he had forfeited during those first moments of decision after killing those two nosy FMP officers. It would have given him pleasure to pass the time with her body now. Still, he knew it had been wise to cut all his losses.

The speargun killings had been a *rush*. He hadn't expected it, but it was true—a real rush. Maybe killing people in any way whatsoever was exciting, stimulating, fulfilling for someone like him, he now thought. The sight of the FMP officer's blood on deck the entire day recalled to his mind the geyser spray of it at the moment the spear had opened a hole in the big man's chest. Most of the blood had been washed off by rain, but the original blood loss had been tremendous; it had come spurting out across the *Tau Cross*. He had never cared for the sight of blood, especially his own; it had always made him nauseous, even a little finger cut, but the speargun killing had changed his mind in an instant. There was something extraordinary about punching a hole in a balloon and seeing the air explode, and so too with the human heart.

He was no fool; after a brief moment of lying on his back, and a bite to eat, he knew, he must scrub down the boat, erase every inch of blood and other evidence that might link him to murder. He seriously doubted that anyone could put him and his destination together, since no one had all the pieces. Still, there was that someone who could place him on the route he had chosen, there was at least one man who knew about his liking for the Cayman Islands—that old fool in Key West. But it seemed highly improbable that authorities would learn of his connection with the taxidermist.

He now planned to take all the materials he had collected to preserve the bodies of his victims for Mother's reappearance and throw them into the sea. It would be difficult to do so, not only because of the physical labor—cleansing the ship of his secret identity, forever altering Tau's haven and thereby the Night Crawler's workplace—but because of the momentousness of the decision as well, asking Tau to wait, asking Mother to wait. But there was no hope for it otherwise. Common sense dictated that he find a new ship and a new killing ground.

He quickly got together a bucket filled with cleaning fluids and ammonia, carried this out on deck and scrubbed away any evidence that the FMP officers had ever stepped foot on his boat. Finishing this, he returned to autopilot check at the controls below. Seeing that his ship was on course, he then returned to the scrubbing, but this time he worked the interior cabin. He scrubbed the floor and the walls where stains from previous kills had remained as memory prompters for his fantasies. It was painful to see all his fondest memories disappear before him, vanish without a trace, but his sense of self-preservation was strong, so he scrubbed until his hands became raw, until every stain was invisible to the naked eye.

He planned, once he reached the Caymans, to purchase some marine paint and paint over all these areas as well. As it was, all he had was a partially used, small can of black stenciling paint, and he planned to use it to paint over the name of the boat and rename her, which he'd begun doing last night only moments before hearing the siren and seeing the approaching strobe light of the Florida Marine Patrol boat.

After a brief respite from the intense work, he got a little sun and sea topside, lying out on deck. He seldom partook of the sun, but he wanted to appear darker-skinned, to accentuate the beard he'd begun to grow. Returning to the controls below, Warren next checked his course against the maps he used. He had another job to do which couldn't wait for tomorrow. He set the ship on her own once more, the two diesels pushing the craft over the glassy surface of the Caribbean easily and smoothly now. Then he went about collecting up all the items aboard that could implicate him as the Night Crawler. He tossed trinkets taken from his victims into a single box. He added to the box as he moved about the cabin, collecting all the skinning knives and loose rope and embalming fluids he'd collected over the months and months since he'd left England. Going now up the stairwell deckside, he went directly to starboard, where he dumped boxful after boxful of incriminating evidence, the sea gobbling it all up.

When he reached the Caymans, Warren planned to sell the boat or trade it in, get a new one, something less of an attention-getter. Then he might more easily fade into the background and out of the light. The light was his enemy, and he normally slept during the day, ill at ease with the brutal sun here, his eyes sometimes so swollen as to be shut, so irritated were they by the wind and sea air. But he needed the tan as part of his new disguise, so he worked shirtless in shorts on deck, looking over what needed doing next.

Over the side went the recent additions to his chemical collection, what the taxidermist shop and the funeral home in Naples he'd broken into had profited him, including a huge bottle of what was labeled ''Perma Glow,'' fluid which was pumped into the dead to preserve the body for the wake, organs intact. He had been mixing chemicals, trying to find the exact right solution, like an alchemist in search of gold. His chemical gold would have to wait until better days. There would come a time; there would be other opportunities.

With so much daylight left him, he decided to complete the look of innocence he wanted for his ship and himself when he went to sell her. So he worked under the intense sun behind his dark glasses to repaint the registration number on the ship and to give it a new name, using stencils and paintbrush. All of this he did while the ship continued relentlessly forward, no small feat in itself. He first obliterated the original registration numbers and the name of the boat. He then taped on the stencils with care, changing the registration numbers, the port of origin of the ship and finally the name. The work took well over an hour and a half. He went to check the con panel from time to time, resetting his course as necessary while he worked. Later on, he'd do the necessary paperwork.

Once finished with the painting, he tossed the near-empty bucket of paint over the side, got painfully to his feet and made his way below deck again. There, with a cold beer at his side and using his computer, he worked on creating new documents of ownership of the boat. He had purchased an official-looking seal from a street vendor in Cayman which was in fact a seal of government inspection from Grand Cayman, where ships were built. His ship's registry now was George Town, Grand Cayman Island. He figured he'd have no trouble bartering there.

Once finished with the serial numbers and the boat name, which was now *Smiling Jack*, he began again to maniacally scrub away at Manley's blood, seeing a tint of red, like a twelfth shade of gray, clinging to the deck. Angered by the spot, having to go back for more scrubbing materials, he began to mutter to himself now as he scrubbed anew. "Taught that nigger cop a lesson that he won't forget. Oh, he's dead . . . I guess that he won't forget in the next life?" He laughed at his own crude, little joke.

Now he scrubbed and scrubbed at the blood on deck, but the deck was made of a porous material into which the blood had soaked. Oh well, he told himself; fish blood had stained the boat before, and this pinkish-gray hue looked no different.

He continued to scrub nonetheless, his fingernails breaking, his hand rubbed raw by the force applied to the brush. "Soap, water, ammonia," he kept repeating like a mantra, "soap, water, ammonia . . . best way to a clean the rascal," he added, recalling one of his mother's more favored sayings.

"Soap and water . . . No amount of soap and water can clean out the rotten core of your heart, Warren Tauman, you rascal, you devil, you serpent, you Satan seed . . . " he heard Mother say in his ear.

Santiva got on the headphones, likely to keep busy in his futile attempt to control his airsickness. Conferring with Jessica, he said, "See anything?"

"It's still like soup down there."

"What is it you're looking for?" demanded Don Lansing.

"We're searching for a boat."

"A boat? A particular boat?"

"That's right."

"We've been following the coast in pursuit of some guy on a boat?"

Santiva barked, "Yes, is that so hard to understand?"

"What happened to your accent?" Lansing wanted to know.

"Look, Mr. Lansing . . ." began Jessica, realizing they'd traversed nearly a third of their journey to the Caymans now, "I think it's time you knew the truth."

"Truth? What truth?"

"We're not being chased by anyone, especially not the cops; we . . . Eriq and I—are FBI, cops you might say . . ."

"What?" His look of shock seemed out of proportion to her revelation.

Eriq explained, "We didn't lie back in Tampa to the tower guys."

"Whataya saying?"

"We *are* FBI agents."

"Oh, Christ, you're shitting me. Holy Mother, Pete's going to kill me when he hears about this. I'll be damned. How in hell'd I not see it?"

"We're good at what we do. But really, Don, we are really FBI, and we're really in pursuit of the—"

"—the Night Crawler," he finished, the light coming clear on. "Sure, why not? Story of my life. Always in the wrong place at the wrong time."

"Mr. Lansing . . . Mr. Lansing . . ." Jessica tried to quell his concern, but he kept babbling to himself through the headphones.

"I must not live right. Something I did once to my mother, maybe. God has a way of punishing even the blind and ignorant . . ."

"Sorry to burst your bubble," she weakly apologized.

"Then one of the two stories you made up back at the airport was . . . was the truth?"

" 'Fraid so."

"Damn . . . damn, you must think I'm some kinda fool. Hey, I want both of you to know that I'm nobody's fool."

Jessica realized that Lansing didn't believe them now any more than he had on takeoff.

"Whatever your game, I'm not interested. All's I want is to set down in Miami and we can settle up there. Plenty of guys in Miami'll be happy to take you on to the Caymans. Just don't tell 'em you're the fuzz, all right?"

"Miami? We're not going to Miami," she countered.

"It's on our flight pattern to the Caymans. It's the only safe way. We attempt another way and we could get in trouble over Cuba. Trust me. Besides, like I told you, we need to stop at Miami to refuel and get in the flight path over Cuba to the Caymans, so we log where we're going in case of problems.''

"Do you always follow such rules to the letter?" asked a suspicious Santiva.

"Always," he lied.

"Mr. Lansing, we want you to take us all the way to Grand Cayman," Jessica pleaded.

"I don't know . . ."

"We've offered to pay three times your normal rate," she reminded.

"Three times?" asked Santiva, whistling into the headphones.

"Not if we're dumped in Miami, no," she responded.

Lansing broke down, saying, "All right, but we stop over in Miami to refuel and file a flight report, and once we touch down in Cayman, I collect my dough from you people and wave bye-bye."

"Agreed," she assured him, and the cockpit grew silent now as they soared over scattered cloud cover.

"Can't you get us down a little lower, so we can see better?" she asked.

"Lower means more turbulence right now," he countered, "and your so-called hotshot FBI agent friend is already three shades of green."

They were on a due-south tack now, coming out of the storm clouds, getting beyond the front. There was bright sunshine and gleaming blue waters ahead. "You can start bringing us down now," she ordered.

Perhaps to test just how honest or dishonest she'd been with him, Lansing frowned and let go of the controls. "You take the controls," he said. "Seems to me that's what you like, being in control."

She grabbed on to the controls almost immediately, but the plane was already in a screaming nosedive, everyone but Lansing losing his stomach to the cockpit ceiling, Eriq shouting through his headphones, freaking out while Jessica grabbed and then pulled hard on the controls, bringing the plane back under control, leveling her out, tiger stripes and all.

The plane was a twin-engine Beechcraft Baron, Lansing having chosen to take it over the smaller, modified Sandpiper back in Tampa. The machine was not nearly so old as it was made to appear. Lansing, or more likely his boss, Pete, had painted the Baron to appear older and perhaps more romantic than it actually was. The seats were plush, the controls state of the art. The World War II look of the tiger stripes, the lettering of the call numbers—all a ruse to mirror what? Experienced, vintage fliers? Lansing was too young for vintage, she thought.

"What the hell're you trying to do, Lansing?" Jessica shouted now.

"Wanted to see if you lied about being a pilot, too. Guess not."

She shook her head and gave him a half smile, to which he responded by frowning. He wasn't amused at having literally been taken for a ride. His arms were folded tightly against his chest as he watched her take the bird lower over the water.

Jessica had felt the power of the light plane the moment she'd grabbed the controls. It was a feeling like nothing else she'd ever experienced—flying. She couldn't hold back the sense of wonder, or her smile.

Lansing, looking at her reaction as she soared ever closer to the emerald waters of the Gulf of Mexico below them, suddenly broke into laughter.

"What's so damned funny?" demanded Eriq from the rear.

Then Jessica began to laugh.

"Go ahead, enjoy yourself for a while, and buzz every damned boat you see down there for all I care," said Lansing, "but give a thought to the fuel gauge while you're doing it, all right?" Behind his protestations lay an understandable frustration. He didn't know or trust them; he didn't know what their game was; he didn't know who they were chasing; he didn't believe they were FBI agents in pursuit of the Night Crawler any more than he believed her Alice in Wonderland and Eriq the Wizard of Oz.

But something in his tone told Jessica that he did care,

that he was *worried* about who they were and what they intended. "Look, reach into my bag and pull out my wallet, Mr. Lansing," she told him.

"What for?"

"You'll find my badge there."

He looked from her to the bag that'd been jammed into a space too small for it just beside her ankle. While he went for the bag, he admired the creamy-skinned legs below the skirt she wore. He rummaged about, feeling the cold metal of a gun, which he lifted along with her wallet. "What the hell's this?"

"Be careful with that; it's a Browning automatic, same gun I used to kill Matthew Matisak with in New Orleans last year."

He looked at her as if she were mad. She wished now that she had brought along that stupid *Enquirer* story with her picture for this show-and-tell moment. "I really, truly am Dr. Jessica Coran, and this is Chief Eriq Santiva of the FBI."

"And I'm supposed to believe that?"

"Yes, damnit, it's the truth."

He raised both hands to run through his hair, as if to do so might ease his consternation. But the gesture had little effect. "You now want me to believe that you . . . that you're an M.D. with—"

"An M.E. for the FBI, yes."

"The one who caught that heart-eating, banshee killer in New Orleans last year?"

"One and the same," added Eriq from the rear.

"Same one who also cornered and killed Mad Matthew Matisak there?"

"That would be me, yes."

He reserved judgment as he opened her billfold and closely examined her FBI photo ID and badge. Then the light in his brain finally flickered on. "Damn, hellfire, unbelievable . . . here in Pete's plane, sitting just across from me. Well, here, let me shake your hand, Dr. Coran." He extended a hand and took hers, shaking so vigorously she had trouble holding the plane steady.

"Then you've heard of me?" she unnecessarily asked.

"Are you kidding? I mean, who hasn't heard about you? The Eskimos? But why didn't you just tell me who you were in the first place? I wouldn't've balked a moment taking off at the airport the way I did, had I known it was you . . ."

Eriq grumbled through the static of his headphone upon hearing this and added, "Does that mean you won't charge us triple?"

"No, no . . . didn't say that."

Again they laughed together, now with the plane coming in over the water at seventy feet above the surface. They saw a few scattered boats, but most boaters had wisely chosen to steer clear of these waters for the duration of the storm retreat.

"Look, over there in the distance!" shouted Eriq, blowing out their ears through the phone sets.

"Where?" asked Jessica.

"Over there!" repeated Eriq.

"Give us a direction, Eriq. Ten o'clock, two o'clock, what?"

"Oh, yeah . . . ahh, three o'clock."

Jessica and Lansing looked immediately to their right, Lansing leaning in and over Jessica a bit, catching her perfume as he did so. "Small craft, nothing like what you're looking for," he advised.

"How would you know what we're looking for?" countered Eriq.

"Hey, I listen to the news reports. I read the papers. They say it was a schooner-class ship, and that thing down there's no schooner. A schooner has three masts, for one thing, and it moves over the water differently . . ."

"How can you possibly tell from this distance?" Jessica wondered aloud.

"The way she moves in the water. A schooner slices through the water. She doesn't bounce atop the waves."

"You're sure of that?"

"I am, so don't waste your time or our fuel."

"Looks pretty impressive to me," countered Eriq, still staring at the boat below. They were south of Naples now, out over the water, nearing the straits of Florida. "Jess, what do you think?"

She had to crane her neck to see back over her shoulder now, twisting in her seat, showing some backside to Don. Lansing encouraged her to release the controls and rise out of her seat to lean over for a better view while he took in his own better view of her form, all the while telling her that it wasn't a large enough boat.

"I can't tell from here," she confessed.

"Then take her in for a closer look," Santiva said, his voice grating now, giving way to his stress and fatigue.

Jessica brought the plane around, and they gently glided in over the boat and saw her markings clearly enough. There were several people aboard the large two-masted sloop, all waving in wild abandon at the buzzing, puzzling plane some thirty-five-odd feet above them now.

Don Lansing had been right: They needed to pick and choose better. It wouldn't do to waste fuel on so many red herrings, especially if the killer arrived at Grand Cayman before them and managed to unload his boat for another one while they were uselessly shopping the sea from boat to boat.

"So you're Dr. Jessica Coran; damn . . . " Lansing said as they climbed to a safer altitude.

"Are we back to that?" Eriq irritably asked.

Lansing ignored Eriq, continuing, "Pete's just not going to believe this. But I gotta tell you, even if he cans my ass, it will've all been worth it. Something to tell my kids someday."

"Oh? Do you have children?" Jessica asked.

"No, not at the moment, but someday I suppose I will."

Jessica smiled back at her newfound admirer and tried to simply enjoy flying the craft. But his remark stuck with her, that *someday he supposed he would have children.* Something about him said otherwise. And she thought of her own *someday* plans, the ones she had made with James Parry. They seemed now like clouds that had dissolved and floated off over the cerulean-blue sea and into oblivion. She felt a pang of loss. To combat the feeling, she concentrated on the sense of power and sheer delight in manipulating the aircraft. She was a beauty, this little plane, and Lansing, smiling over at Jessica, understanding her rush of emotions, didn't seem in the least concerned about reclaiming the controls.

"We've got to turn her due east, Dr. Coran," he told her now.

"For Miami?"

"It'd be the safest and best route."

"But it seems so indirect. Why can't we refuel in Key West?"

He hesitated a moment. "You don't want to be with me the next time I touch down in Key West. Trust me on this one."

She looked into his eyes, saw the sincerity there and relinquished, turning the plane's nose toward the sun. "Miami it is. We can check in with the MPD while we're there, Eriq. Let them know of our whereabouts."

"Yeah, I suppose that's a good idea."

"Going over Cuban airspace is a little tricky," confided Lansing. "We'll do much better getting into the established flight lanes."

· TWENTY-ONE ·

*The world is governed more by appearances than by realities,
so that it is fully as necessary to seem to know something
as to know it.*

—DANIEL WEBSTER

The tropical maelstrom, which the *Tau Cross* had carefully
sluiced through by keeping at the outer fringes of the storm,
had been nothing compared with the North Atlantic sea
squall that Warren Tauman had endured coming over from
England. In the earlier storm, the waves were as tall as
houses, and he'd been hurt and had to handle every problem
with a sprained ankle and a snapped mast. He and the *Tau
Cross* had limped over the ocean after that for days, and
he'd feared that he would never see land again; he'd found
no wind for seventy-two hours and had to rely on his diesel
motors and his less than keen sense of direction. Somehow
he'd gotten hopelessly lost, his ship having passed through
the western Caribbean waters and amid any number of
small island ports, none of which he had seen until he'd
come far to the southeast of America and sighted land—
the Dominican Republic. He'd put to port there, but for
only a brief few days, finding it less than hospitable, and
even before all necessary repairs to his ship could be
done—largely due to the fact that he could find no one
capable or quick enough—he left this island world only to
locate another: Cayman Brac Island, as he came to know
it later.

Cayman Brac was like a godsend. He'd been alone for
too long with his thoughts and Mother, who taunted him,
telling him he was a fool and that he would die alone at
sea. But his spirit guide deposited him instead at the Cay-

man Islands. The Caymans were composed of three islands: Grand Cayman, Little Cayman and Cayman Brac. All were at low elevations, but Cayman Brac rose 140 feet into the sky with its limestone bluffs, and it became a beacon for him that morning after leaving the inhospitable Dominican shore. He saw Cayman Brac rise from the water like some sort of Loch Ness Monster, yet it was nonthreatening, beautiful. He stayed on at Cayman Brac for two weeks while true craftsmen worked on his mast and windows and whatever else needed repair, paying in funds still available to him on his mother's life insurance policy. As for the more serious problems with navigational equipment—nav, as the seasoned sailors called it—computer hardware and software damage, he'd have to await his arrival in America. In Cayman Brac he learned just how close he was to America, to Florida waters.

While remaining in the safe port during that time period, Warren had wisely restrained from any hunting and killing until all repairs were finished and paid for. He'd stocked new food, fixed broken equipment, beefed up weak points in the boat and rigging, repaired old sails and got some new ones. After that, he began exploring each of the three islands in the chain, and while doing so, he began to collect a handful of willing victims.

Now he raced for this safe port again, low on food but with his boat intact and sound. He sat at the navigation station, studying weather maps. Sitting in this area of the cabin was a bit like sitting at the center of a teacup; at the center of the cup was the nav station. His chair faced a phalanx of electronic equipment, blipping radar screens, computers, radios and instruments towering to the cabin's ceiling. At the top was a portable CD player strapped in with bungee cords. From here, he could read wind speed true, wind direction and wind speed apparent in the bright red letters of the light-emitting diodes before him.

The chair and the table were gimbaled, so as the boat leaned to one side or the other, Warren could sit perfectly level to work, eat or drink. He studied the weather maps every day, each generated from his own on-board computer weather station. A lean man at six-two, he averaged 170 pounds but burned them like a panther. On a one-man sailboat where speed and progress depended on reading and agilely responding to wind and waves, his incessant activity—trimming and changing sails, tweaking this, modifying that—translated into miles between him and Tampa Bay, the Florida authorities and the FBI.

So now Warren was blasting along on a calm and unhurried West Caribbean wind at about twenty-five knots, allowing the autopilot to steer while he checked the maps again. From what his speed and the maps were telling him, he knew now that he must rig the new sail, his old one having been shredded by the storm at his back after an abrupt wind shift.

Warren went above deck and wrestled with an enormous snake—actually, a giant sock encasing a new sail which he'd purchased in Sanibel Island during his stay there. He knew it would take him two, possibly three hours to get the new sail up, more if the old sail were to get knotted in the rigging. But it was his only chance to hook up with the Caribbean sailboat race called the Jamaica Run that he intended to infiltrate and ride in on. It made perfect sense, if he could time it exactly right, for entering Cayman was like finding a postage stamp out there, and the race would act both as a guide—thanks to more experienced sailors than he—and as a cover. Entering port at Cayman amid such confusion and mayhem would afford the perfect cover. If he could only pull it off. The new sail, too, with its sundial face, would fit right in with the racers.

The sock system made it a great deal easier for one person to handle such a large sail. Still, it took an hour just to hook each eye. But then he was ready to raise one end of the enclosed sail to the top of the mast on a halyard. It took another hour and a half, using a system of lines and pulleys on the sock itself, to raise the sail to its full height. He secured lines to the color-coded lines which fed back into the boat's cockpit and allowed him to raise, lower or reef his sails with assurance. He now tugged on a line, and the sock slowly and by increments rose, heavy as hell, finally to the top of the mast, where it billowed sheetlike in the strong trade wind.

Satisfied, Warren Tauman pounded his chest at his single-handed accomplishment, sweat pouring from his brow, the sun burning into his scalp, his tan lines showing now.

He went below again and checked his course. The autopilot had kept him nearly perfect. He made up for the machine and reset the autopilot before going to his port charts. He had charts for Brazil, South America, Puerto Rico, Mexico and other places, as well as the Cayman and Jamaican Islands. He had to have a chart for any port he might visit. He'd have to check in with the port authorities in any country he visited, and thus far his alias had held and he'd aroused no suspicions in the Cayman Islands, but he planned on creating a new set of papers and a new alias before reaching the islands, just to be sure. It hadn't hurt that he'd greased a few palms there during his last visit. He knew who to see and where to see them.

The *Tau Cross* carried a system that captured satellite photographs around the clock, and Warren analyzed the photos religiously while alone at sea; it only made good sense and was a safety precaution to do so. Still relatively new at being a sailor, he'd learned much during his crossing of the great Atlantic, in a kind of ordeal by fire. He knew that in the southern latitudes, storms rolled out of nowhere without warning, so he must be ever vigilant. On his weather charts, these low-pressure storms appeared to be so many malignant growths, and from these big lows many small tentacles grew, twisted and gnarled to become as treacherous as the mother storm. It was from one of these he was now running.

He had an eighty-five-foot-high mast, enough to cause alarm in any storm. Thank God he had two large inboard motors to fall back on. These motors also charged the batteries that ran the autopilot, computers, radar and other electronics. Losing power was high on Warren's nightmare list, for this meant losing communication, information and the crucial help of the autopilot, which freed him to cook, clean, repair, navigate, sleep and do other extracurricular activities, such as enjoy himself with the ladies whenever one was brazen and stupid enough to choose to step aboard his death ship.

He was mildly worried now. Pushing a boat twenty-four hours a day was a recipe for system failure, as an old sailor in Key West had once warned him. He recalled his trouble coming over, the moment when the boat fell off a wave like a truck from a bridge. He'd felt the sickening jolt in his bones and teeth, as when Mother had once struck him so hard he'd fallen unconscious. The ship, as it had come crashing down off that wave, had shivered and flexed her entire length like a dying horse, and he knew something big was wrong. He prayed to his gods even as he stared out at the one remaining mast that night to see it bowing like a bone about to break. He could see that a metal fitting clasp, holding a crucial support stay halfway up the mast, had snapped, and that it just hung there, a useless ornament blowing in the storm. By then his other two, smaller masts were long gone. And by this time, Warren had done all he could to save the boat from capsizing, so all he was left with was the wheel. It took all his strength to hold the wheel against the storm while he'd continued to pray.

He recalled the nightmare vividly. How that dark night in the Atlantic a huge wave smashed the *Tau Cross* and snapped off the two weaker masts and drove the mid-ship mast down to dip into the water. Water spilled over her decks and into the cabin, the floor and the nav station awash in it. Tools, plastic bags, food, parts, computer paper and a printer and other things were left floating about. Canned goods and equipment manuals had taken flight.

Then the blackness of the storm had somehow grown even darker than Warren imagined possible, a kind of black-green both inside and outside the cabin, and Warren, terrified of dying before completing his mission in life, huddled below. He felt the pressure on his ears, his chest, his heart. He was going to die here, like this, alone, just as his dead mother's voice had told him he would, his life unfulfilled while Mother smiled down on his pitiable situation.

Mother always had the last laugh.

Suddenly a window had exploded, bursting inward with wind and water, which flooded through as if to punctuate his dark, embracing resignation of death.

Even before the window had blown, he had realized that his ship was over in the water farther than any ship had a right to be. But then, she righted like a cork, bobbing upright, as if to curse the powers of the ocean, to defy them. She continued to flounder about all that night, and Warren grew violently ill, but never did the *Tau* dip so low again into the water, and the window only took on rainwater after that.

It was as if he'd been given a sign, that he must go forth, that his own gods would not allow those of the sea—or those devils that drove Mother—to end Warren's career; that he would give offerings and sacrifices in the form of humans to Tau, since Tau in turn protected him.

Last night's storm which had chased Warren down the Gulf and the one chasing in from west of his position now were no match for the *Tau Cross*, Warren assured himself. He would, in a matter of fifteen, maybe sixteen hours, be on the Cayman Islands. Once there, he'd start over.

Mother whispered otherwise, her voice hiding in the trade winds, mewing like a grinning cat, saying, "You'll suffer now, Warren . . . They're after you, and they will catch you, and they will burn and torture you in ways I never burned or tortured you—in ways you never imagined possible . . ."

"Shut up, you dead bitch! Shut up!" Warren screamed at the wind.

Jessica and Eriq's flight to the Cayman Islands, with its detour to Miami, was clear and bright and smooth and without complication. Once they came on radar at Miami International, Don Lansing took the controls and did the honors, impressing Jessica with his nerve at bringing in such a small plane amid such giants as the 747s and wide-bodied jumbos, which looked like modern-day dinosaurs and fire-farting dragons.

While Eriq had been catching some sleep in the rear,

Jessica had asked Don to tell her more about himself. He'd gone directly from high school into the military and had done a stint as a pilot in Desert Storm, he told her. She was once again impressed.

"What kind of planes?"

"Nothing too romantic. ARFs—Aerial Reconnaissance Flights. Photographing—low-level spying, I guess you'd call it. I didn't see any real action, although my plane took a couple of flak hits."

"So, are you sorry you didn't get to drop any bombs?"

"No . . . not really . . . Managed to get back with a fairly clean conscience and a healthy respect for life . . ."

"So, why isn't a good-looking young man like yourself married?" she asked him.

"Guess that'd be my fault. I keep running from any kind of real commitment, I guess. Don't ever feel ready, mature enough, secure enough, you know, in myself."

She nodded her understanding.

"But there is this one girl," he confided. "If ever I'm going to take the plunge . . ."

She smiled knowingly, and they heard Eriq groan as he shook himself awake, terribly uncomfortable in the tiny space they all occupied.

Once on the ground, they all had jobs to do. Don refueled and filed their flight plan. Eriq contacted the Miami bureau of the FBI to let people there know their plans, and he also gathered drinks and sandwiches for the three of them, while Jessica contacted the MPD, leaving word with the chief of police and talking to Dr. Andrew Coudriet, who had information from Moyler in England.

One of Allain's prints which earlier had been sent to Moyler had found a match with one taken for an insurance policy in England for a schoolboy named Warren Tauman. Moyler's fax, according to Andrew Coudriet, was most definite: Allain and Tauman were one and the same.

"Jackpot," said Jessica over the phone to Dr. Coudriet. "Now if we can only corner the bastard."

"I have a feeling that if anyone can, you will, Dr. Coran."

Now, a little over an hour out of Miami International, Jessica watched Cuba appear and dissolve below them, as they had to fly above Cuban airspace in order to safely avert any problems there. Once across Cuban airspace, they descended. All of this gave Jessica a great opportunity at the controls, and Lansing seemed pleased to allow her to enjoy herself.

Below them sprawled the glittering, sun-dappled east Caribbean Sea on their southward tack for the three British islands which together formed a crown colony.

They'd stayed on this course for an additional few hours when suddenly the lush islands came into view. They were as breathtaking as when last Jessica had seen them in the company of a past love, Captain Alan Rychman, now Commissioner Rychman of the NYPD. She recalled their having dived the crystal-blue waters off Grand Cayman, a twenty-two-mile-long island, eight miles at its widest point, located some two hundred miles northwest of the west end of Jamaica and a hundred miles south of Cuba.

Still, even the gorgeous sight of the Caymans below couldn't dispel the fact that Jessica had become frustrated, as had Eriq, who remained silent in the rear. She could sense his seething. They had seen nothing whatever of the fleeing *Tau Cross* and their fugitive. Lansing, too, had gone silent, sensing that the mood inside the small space they occupied had soured considerably.

With the wind at their backs, they had made good time and fuel consumption had not been a problem. Their having had to fly over Cuban airspace at a safe distance had, however, presented one problem: It had taken them to such altitudes that their eyes were for a time useless in attempting to spot Patric Allain's boat, if it was down there. By the time they were able to return to eye level, hundreds upon hundreds of nautical miles had gone unsearched.

There had been so much to cover the man's tracks; so much in nature had conspired against Jessica that it angered her.

The other two islands here, located approximately eighty miles northeast of Grand Cayman, were Little Cayman at ten miles long and two miles wide, and Cayman Brac, twelve miles long and one and a quarter miles wide. The islands looked like jewels spread across the satin-blue water from this distance up; created of coral, the soil was fertile, and Jessica recalled a people of grace and good cheer and beautiful features.

Jessica knew from her previous visit that fishing, ship-building and stock raising were the chief industries here. The place was also good for thatch rope, mahogany, turtle shells, green turtles, shark skins, cattle and ponies. She'd done a bit of research back then, learning that Genoese-born navigator Christopher Columbus had discovered the islands in 1503 and had named them the Tortugas—Spanish for Turtle Islands. The place still literally "crawled" with turtles.

The Cayman Islands were colonized sometime around 1734 by the British, the records not being exact, and before becoming a separate British colony in 1959, the island government was a dependency of the Jamaican colony, and as recently as 1962, it had maintained status as part of the Federation of the West Indies.

With but a hundred square miles of land, the island population was crowded at twelve hundred permanent residents, and during peak holiday seasons, when the big cruise ships brought in the tourists and the grandiose sea-hugging hotels were full to bursting, the island could hardly bear the burden of people.

Jessica was disappointed that they'd seen no sailing vessel that might approximate the one they were looking for, but it made sense. They were a day ahead of the sailing vessel now, despite its having had a six-hour head start on them. Then again, perhaps nature had taken its vengeance on Tauman; perhaps he was floating hundreds of feet below the surface somewhere in the Gulf of Mexico where his ship had gone down in bad weather. One could only hope, but such a death was too good for the man. Perhaps, Jessica mused, there was no death other men could design that was not too good for him.

She would inquire when she arrived at George Town, the capital of the Cayman Islands, if there had been any reports of ships in distress in the Caribbean Sea, the Yucatan Channel or the great Gulf.

They were within sight of George Town now and she saw banners strung across one port, perhaps there to welcome an incoming cruise ship that they'd witnessed easing toward the island at what appeared to be the pace of a snail. Yet the floating building with its Norwegian markings had moved surprisingly far by the time they'd turned into the wind to make their final approach, Lansing having studied the air currents to make his determination.

He was a good pilot; Jessica silently congratulated herself at having found him back in Tampa, but she was too busy admiring the island below to verbalize her good fortune. From up here, the entire island blinked with white houses and orange-tiled roofs.

Earlier, Jessica had asked Don Lansing to radio ahead to have authorities meet them at the airport, specifically Ja Okinleye, if possible. The tower at the quaint little airstrip below had radioed back that their message had been forwarded to the ''correct Royal authorities.'' Now aligned with the airport in the distance, one single, long black strip and a small building in typical British Isles architecture, they quickly descended under the assault of the wind at the nose of the ship.

Jessica asked Lansing to again radio ahead to ask for the chief investigatory officer, Ja Okinleye, to meet them at the airport, and it was relayed back to them that Okinleye had been contacted. Now Lansing told them to ready for landing as he got his final clearance, although at such a late moment in the landing that he could only laugh and wryly reply, ''Thanks, guys!''

The approach was smooth and effortless, despite a brisk, buffeting wind which threatened havoc. Lansing laughingly said, ''The wind's a funny animal, like Huey, Dewey and Louie: You never know what they're going to give you.''

"Sounds like a Gumpism to me," said Santiva in the rear.

"Call it a Donism," Lansing replied.

Out her small side portal, Jessica could see an official-looking vehicle with a Cayman Island flag on each front bumper and two officers in dress whites—which amounted to long pants in this subtropical heat—standing nearby. One appeared to be Okinleye. In a moment the tiger-striped plane bounced shakily on and along the runway, their speed decreased to nil and they turned to taxi onto a side strip.

Moments later, they deployed from the plane directly onto the asphalt, where Ja Okinleye personally met them, his hand extended in a warm gesture of greeting. "Dr. Coran! It is a wonderment to see you, and we are so pleased to have you back with us again in our paradise."

"I wish we were just here to enjoy your paradise, my friend." Jessica saw that Okinleye's man had gone directly to the plane, ostensibly to see to their bags but with an obvious eye to any cargo aboard. Finding neither cargo nor bags, he was stumped, so he raised both shoulders to his smiling boss.

Jessica turned to Santiva, who had weathered the trip well by sleeping much of the way, and added for Ja's benefit, "This is Chief Eriq Santiva, the man I work for nowadays, Ja."

"I am so pleased to make with your acquaintance, sir." Okinleye looked about for their bags as he vigorously shook Santiva's hand. "My aide, Kili, he will see to your bags. Where are you staying, my friends?"

" 'Fraid we haven't any bags, Ja," confessed Jessica, a frown puckering her lips, "only what's on our backs. We left in something of a hurry." Jessica noticed the pained expression on Don Lansing's face. "And as for reservations . . . well, we have none."

"Oh, not good . . . it is the height of the season . . . You will then stay with me and my family in my humble abode?"

"We couldn't put you out, Ja."

"Please, it is not a bother."

"Well . . . first things first," said Santiva. "Have you had any word or inkling on the approach of this boat we're chasing?"

"No, none whatsoever. I only hope you are correct in assuming he will be coming this way."

"We're ahead of him, Eriq, but he'll be along," Jessica assured Santiva and Ja Okinleye at the same time.

Ja smiled and said in a mirthful tone, "Is that what your instincts tell you?"

"Yes . . . yes, it is. That and the difference between nautical miles and air flight."

"Well then, Chief Okinleye," Eriq interrupted, swallowing hard, "maybe we'll take you up on that offer of hospitality, after we stop at one of your local stores to pick up a few essentials?"

"Not a problem. We will drive you to wherever you need go, right, Kili?"

The silent, uniformed Kili eagerly nodded.

With this settled, Jessica turned to Don Lansing and thanked him for his help, paying him three times what his normal fee would have been. He stared at the cash as if it meant an operation for his kid sister or dog, his eyes sparkling. "Maybe this'll help me make that commitment we talked about."

She gave him a crooked smile. "I rather doubt it."

"This kind of dough . . . you sure you don't want me to hang around for a flight back, maybe?"

"What I'm going to need here is a helicopter, and I think Okinleye will point us in the right direction for that. Again, many thanks for getting us here so quickly, Don."

"Don't mention it; my pleasure."

"You heading straight back?"

"Yeah . . . my boss—partner—is going to be wondering what'n hell happened to me and his plane, so I'd better move it, yeah . . ."

Jessica, Santiva and Okinleye rushed now for the waiting official car which would take them from the broiler plate of the asphalt. *It must be one hundred thirty degrees in the shade,* she thought.

A glance back showed Jessica that pilot Lansing still could not believe he had been a part of all this. Maybe the little Cayman Island flags on Ja's official car were too much for him, she mirthfully thought.

· TWENTY-TWO ·

Appearances are not held to be a clue to the truth.
But we seem to have no other.

— IVY COMPTON-BURNETT

"So, now it has become a game of cat and de mouse, hey?" Okinleye asked Jessica and Santiva where they sat across from one another at his backyard patio table. There, they enjoyed a view of the ocean in the distance, the sun, the hibiscus trees, the birds chasing one another, the trade winds and the bright orange daiquiris which Ja's wife, Aliciana, had just prepared for them. The Okinleyes' home was, by island standards, a Grecian mansion, but Ja laughed uproariously when Jessica made mention of its grandeur.

"This . . . this old place? It is our little hut." Ja drew two of his three children into his arms while the third and oldest was ordered to answer an incessant door chime filtering out to them.

Ja had done well for himself and his family, perhaps too well to be above suspicion of graft, Jessica thought. It was well-known the islands over that graft was the rule of law and order in most dealings here. However, middle-class American standards of right and wrong seldom applied in foreign countries, where a man had to be concerned first for his family, and besides, here as in America, a complete absence of crime would mean people would have to go without food, clothing and shelter. Some just knew how to play the game better than others, it appeared. Jessica withheld her judgments of Ja for the time being.

"It was a foreclosure, this house. The old couple died owing a great deal of money to the island government. It was put on auction. I was highest bidder." It sounded good.

"Were you able to find anything helpful in your records here about the disappearances, the deaths, any possible connections with our man Tauman?" asked Jessica.

Ja sadly shook his head. "Very little of help, I'm afraid. We used both names you supplied, but nothing comes as result. Some notion here and there about some strange fellow. I have my men working on it still."

It didn't sound promising, and Santiva gave Jessica a frown.

"In the morning, we'll want a helicopter, very early, say six," she told Ja. "Can you provide us with one?"

"Ours is a small government agency, Dr. Coran, not like your FBI, no . . . I can only recommend to you my most talented cousin who operates a tourist line from George Town Airport."

"That will do just fine, but we'll need a combat-ready pilot for what we need. If we get lucky."

"Combat-ready? Henri, he is such a man."

"He has flown in combat conditions?"

"Bad weather, yes . . . combat, no," confessed Okinleye.

"Well, he'll have to do," said Santiva.

"I'm certified on fixed wing and choppers," came a deep voice from the patio doors. "I also flew a chopper in Desert Storm. Let me help you," added Don Lansing, who had been shown through the house by Okinleye's oldest boy. The boy had a wide grin on his face as though he had performed a miracle in making Don appear.

"Don, I thought you had to get back," Jessica replied.

"I'd like to help out any way I can, now that I know what you people are trying to do."

"And now you know how much we pay?" added Santiva.

"Well, yeah . . . that, too."

Lansing stepped closer, his hand out for Eriq to take. Eriq pushed up from his chair and the two men shook hands.

''But what about getting back? What about Pete?'' Jessica asked.

''Are you kidding? I'm in no hurry to see Pete. Besides, this may be my only chance in this life at ever doing anything . . . well, heroic. Hell, we pull this off and we're going to be island gods to these people, right, Chief Okinleye?'' Lansing smiled down at the chief. Obviously, Don had done some checking around.

Jessica raised her eyebrows, confused for only a moment. Then, her eyes boring into Ja, she said, ''It's all over the island. Everybody knows about us being here and why we're here, don't they? Don't they, Ja?''

''Oh, good Christ,'' moaned Santiva, whose eyes joined with Jessica's to bore into Ja Okinleye's.

''It is a small island,'' he weakly replied. ''Word leaks out.''

''It could leak out over the water,'' Eriq complained. ''Suppose a radio dispatch happens to say something to a ship out at sea.''

''All the more reason to go out hunting tomorrow morning,'' replied Jessica, ''bright and early. Make it fiveish.''

''How're we going to know it's him—his ship—when we see him?'' asked Eriq.

''We will . . . we just will . . .''

''Only boats we know of between here and Cuba are the racing ships,'' said Ja.

''Racing ships?'' asked Eriq.

''What about reports of any ships down at sea between here and the Gulf of Mexico?'' asked Jessica.

''Nothing reported, no,'' Ja replied, pursing his lips in thought.

Lansing joined them, taking a seat and accepting the offer of a drink from Aliciana. He found himself amazed to be involved in the FBI operation, and quickly settled in.

''What race?'' repeated Eriq, his voice revealing his irritation with Ja.

''Ahh, yes, that would be the Jamaica Run Sailing Boat

Race. Our port is a stopover for them, you know.''

"No, I didn't know. When do they stop over?" he pressed.

"Sometime tomorrow morning.''

Jessica, Santiva and Lansing glanced about at one another. "You don't suppose he's going to come in with the others, do you?" asked Lansing, voicing what was on Eriq's mind.

"Would he know of the race?" Ja sipped at his drink.

"He knows the islands," Jessica said, raising her free hand. "He has a state-of-the-art sailing vessel; he reads the sailing magazines. We know that. He has radio equipment. He may be listening to the other sailing ships and in communication with them and their whereabouts.''

"Where are they now?"

"They rounded Cuba at between noon and two today, I am told.''

"Rounded Cuba?"

"Her northern tip.''

"We'll know the boat when we see it," Jessica tried to reassure them, raising her daiquiri to the others, indicating that they should all drink to it.

Lansing turned to Ja and asked, "Do you think you have room for one more here tonight?"

"Oh, most certainly, Mr., ahhhh . . .''

"Lansing, Don Lansing.''

"Ahh, yes, with the Tiger airlines. I have heard of your services to and from the islands. Perhaps we can speak of more business for you and your partners here, after this trouble is complete.''

The two men exchanged a knowing look. Jessica and Santiva glanced significantly across at one another, but both kept silent. Then Eriq said, "Look here, Chief Okinleye, it's imperative—I mean imperative—that nothing goes out over the radio waves about our being here or about the possibility of the Night Crawler's coming this way. Do you understand this? If he is communicating with the racing ships, if he is intending to be a sheep amid this flock, then no one on this island can convey these facts to the racing teams or anyone out at sea.''

"Such as the cruise ships," Jessica added. "I wouldn't put it past Tauman to tap into the signals sent them."

Aliciana acted a mute to all this talk of a killer coming to the island and a trap being laid for him. The children listened in rapt awe. Their mother told them to go into the house and complete their chores and homework and say nothing to anyone about what they had heard. She then offered up another round of drinks.

Jessica looked about the lovely island setting. "It's so beautiful here. I don't recall ever seeing such vibrant, alive colors anywhere on earth save Hawaii, Ja. You've got such a place here."

Ja grinned wide, showing his white teeth, nodding his appreciation and grabbing at his boys as they ran past for the house.

Later that evening, during a lavish meal prepared for them by the Okinleyes, news came from Ja's headquarters that an important break in the Night Crawler case had come about back in mainland America. The *Pensacola Democrat* was the recipient of a letter from the Night Crawler, the letter having been postmarked St. Petersburg, Florida.

Ja announced the information after having looked it over thoroughly himself in a separate room when officers dressed in white uniforms—shorts and long socks—had interrupted him at his meal.

Ja brought the news and the facsimile of the killer's note back into the dining room with him, but he allowed everyone to finish eating and drinking before bringing up the disturbing news. "I fear perhaps you have come a long way for nothing," he said after his bombshell.

"Let me see that," demanded Eriq, staring down at the facsimile, then announcing, "It's him all right. The final verse in his perverse poem, Jessica." Eriq could not control the glare he gave her as he passed the letter to her. Jessica stared down at the verse, which read:

When audience cries,
lungs full with venom
and foam and lies,
moments before she dies,
an applause, a bow, arise!
for t smiles down
from taunni's distant eyes!
as t deems them all to be
flush with his breath,
so washed by his empowering
hand they will be flowering
and cleansed.

"This could be just another ploy to throw us off, Eriq."

"You really think this creep is that clever?"

"Yes, he has been."

The others slowly, quietly vacated the room to allow the two FBI people to hash out this latest wrinkle in the case.

"If we're down here on a wild-goose chase, Jessica, it's going to be damn near impossible to explain to D.C."

"It was my call, Eriq. I don't expect or want you shielding me again on this case. You got that?"

"What're you saying? That we go through with our plans as if this"—he lifted and tossed the facsimile of the killer's note back onto the table and continued to worriedly pace— "that this didn't happen? That it doesn't exist?"

"I'm doing exactly that."

He fumed a bit and then said, "You mean *we* . . . We're doing exactly that."

"Thanks, Eriq."

"For what?"

"For hanging in with me . . . for trusting me."

"I'm going to turn in early . . . Get some sleep," he advised. "We'll see what dawn brings."

Eriq gathered up the information provided by Ja and disappeared for his room upstairs. Jessica sat alone until Ja's two youngest children crept into the room and begged her to come play with them. She knew she would be spending a restless night filled with questions she had no answers for, so the simplicity of a children's game and perhaps a bedtime story held a tremendous appeal, and Ja's children were lovely.

Jessica allowed the children to pull her by her fingers away from all thought of the Night Crawler.

Jessica had been up before dawn, and she'd had one of Ja's sons—also up and watching a crude local television show for children—roust his father. Ja contacted the port authorities and asked if there had been any sightings of the ships racing toward Grand Cayman. There had been none.

"Ask if there have been any ships to come in overnight, any at all," urged Jessica.

Ja asked in his native tongue, a crude concoction of old French, Dutch and pidgin English. He listened politely after asking the question, then turned to Jessica and replied, "Only another cruise ship standing off the island."

"What news have they on the race?" she asked quickly.

Ja smiled at her and again in his native tongue asked her question of his port authority man. Jessica watched her friend as he unnecessarily nodded several times into the phone, when he then finally told her, "You may relax, my good friend. They are hours yet away."

She did relax, taking a walk about the garden which overlooked the ocean far below. It was a wondrous, ever-surprising place, this patch of sand lying in the Western Caribbean between Cuba and Belize—one of thirty-four island nations. The children had taught her how best to pronounce it the night before, training her to say *Kay-Monn*, and they wanted to know when and where she would be diving in the brilliantly green sea, as diving was done by everyone who came to Kay-Monn. She could only wish for the time.

Before the famed and legendary six-thousand-foot drop to the ocean floor called The Wall, with its extensive barrier reef, had been discovered, no one had ever heard of the Caymans, but word had spread among divers the world over. As a result, divers were always arriving and dive outfitters and excursions were one of the island's leading tourist industries. Every other shop along the wharves sold to or outfitted snorkelers and divers.

Jessica, on her earlier visit to the island in the company of Alan Rychman, had become familiar with the busy retail enclave here called Coconut Port and she and Rychman had outfitted themselves out of Aquanauts. Everywhere in Cayman you heard the expression, "Sorry, mon, can't help you tomorrow, 'cause I'm doing The Wall."

She recalled her own sense of freedom forty and fifty feet below—over the legal limit for these waters—as friendly black-and-yellow angelfish, electric-orange fish and others of many colors swam past stalk after stalk of elkhorn coral and wave-spreading fan coral. There were dry alternatives to exploring The Wall, like booking a seat on the Atlantis submarine, which carried tour groups on dives to one hundred feet—eight hundred if you wanted the deluxe treatment, which she and Rychman had opted for, at about what it had cost the two of them to learn to dive over the years. But The Wall was wondrous, magnificent, worth it, and Cayman—especially for the underwater enthusiast—was truly one of the few places on earth where the hype was not overkill and the reality disappointing. Still, to the naked eye and raw spirit, reality here seemed unreal, a mirror held up to another time, place, dimension—a colorful dimension like that of a cartoon. It was spectacular and breathtaking, reminding her of Hawaii, and of Jim, which all seemed now an illusion as well.

Had Hawaii ever happened? she silently wondered.

Only the wind coming in from over the ocean had an answer. It might be a wind that had traveled here all the way from Hawaii, she thought as she walked the lovely gardens where Aliciana had planted literally thousands of flowers of all color and variety.

Yes, the wind affirmed to her . . . Hawaii had felt real, Jim's touch and his love for her had certainly felt real, regardless of its near-magical qualities, its seeming like an illusion, just like this dreamworld place called Grand Cayman. It was quite as terribly real as it was beautiful. Nowadays, in fact, the orderly, tidy and superficially wealthy British colony was considered the Caribbean's best place for an underwater getaway, and how much further from ugly reality could one get than to become a fish?

Ja's home and grounds were beautiful and ugly, double-edged remnants of a time past, when the colonials ran things here and no native such as Ja stood a chance at capturing a brass ring like a good job, a career, a well-

fed family and, least likely of all, a mansion, Jessica
thought. Her walk at an end, she returned to the house to
find Aliciana, still somewhat sleepy, preparing a native
breakfast with much attendant fruit for them all. It appeared obvious that Ja had clamored until she climbed
from bed and went to work in the kitchen, to fulfill her
duty as a well-kept wife, but she was a kind lady, gra-
cious and easily giving; she extended a genuine and
lustrous smile for Dr. Jessica as she, Ja, and the children
had come to call her.

Soon the others were finding their way downstairs from
their various rooms, enticed by Aliciana's cooking, the
sweet, luring odors enough to brighten even Santiva's day.
Still, Jessica was anxious to get down to the airport and out
over the water in search of their prey, and to this end, she
hustled the others through their breakfast, despite Ja's in-
sistence that one couldn't hurry an island meal.

Sunlight buttered the island and the bays and the
wharves. To get to the airport, Jessica and the others had
to drive by George Town Port, where they saw a crowd
milling about the boats moored in the heaviest tourist district. The floating docks were mobbed with reporters, pho-
tographers, tourists and what Ja told them were friends and
family.

"Friends and family of whom?" asked Jessica.

"The racers, of course—the sailboat racers who stop
here today. They are touring the entire Caribbean Sea and
now they stop over here, later today, tonight, depending on
the sea and the condition of their sails, of course."

Jessica now realized what she was looking at, so she saw
that not everyone on the docks and wharves were idle on-
lookers, that many were shore-crew personnel, people
struggling to prepare for the arrival of the boats. Amid the
crowd she saw the bustle of business. She saw hoses,
vacuum cleaners, water jugs, crates of food, folded sails,
lines piled high, saws, drills, marine sealant, flats of card-
board, all shining in the blood-orange glow of morning sun.

It looked like the contestants had quite a welcoming committee on deck.

"How many contestants are in this race of yours, Ja?" she asked.

"Oh, it varies now. Some have given up. It may look calm out there in the Caribbean, but there are surprise storms, problems no one can plan against."

"An approximation then."

"Hmmmm, maybe one hundred twenty, maybe more."

"That many?"

"They will be spread about from here to Cuba this morning."

"Damn, that's going to make our guy hard to spot," Santiva complained.

"The Caribbean Classic is larger, but this one means big money, too," said Okinleye with a wide grin. "And it brings in de money to de island, as they say." His gesture was that of a penny-pinching banker or Scrooge as he said this.

"Well, we've got our own little welcoming committee for the Night Crawler," replied Jessica. "Let's get airborne, gentlemen."

Okinleye told the driver to "rush rush," and soon they were at his cousin's helicopter hangar, where a large sign read PARADISE FLIGHTS. But there were immediate problems. His cousin Henri would not release his best helicopter—he had two machines—to "no udder man" without a signature on an insurance form and twice his double fee. Okinleye nearly took the man's head off, and he settled for the usual fee and the signature, with Lansing taking up the better of the two birds.

After the haggling, Don Lansing took the helicopter up with Jessica beside him and Santiva in the rear. It was a large bird, with hatch doors on both front and rear seats, and Santiva's view was almost as good as Jessica's. They circled the island once on takeoff and then headed due north toward the incoming fleet of racing ships. Within an hour, they came into view of the racing ships, their tall masts and sails like miniature fingernails on the horizon at first, soon enlarging to half moons. The sun and shimmering emerald-blue waters here created a blinding effect of beauty and brilliance against which the sailing ships existed like cartoon cutouts.

"Fly in low over those boats. Let's be sure our guy hasn't gotten smart and is camouflaging himself among them," said Jessica over the headphones.

"Why would he bother?" asked Santiva a bit sullenly, still feeling jarred by last night's revelation that the killer might well still be in Florida. "He doesn't know we're here. If he has come to the Caymans, he's got no reason to suspect we know that, right?"

"We know he's outfoxed any number of port authority agents, Eriq," she countered. "We know he's cunning. Maybe he'll take the race for a way for him to slip into the Caymans unnoticed."

"And maybe he knew about the race all along?"

"Maybe . . . either way, we best not take any chances. Go in lower, Don, please . . ."

Don did as Jessica instructed, and together they studied each boat for any sign of perversion—a ragged sail, a weathered-the-storm appearance, any sign of death, as if it would leave a pall over the ship. What they found on closer inspection was that there were many ships in the race with torn and stripped sails and a beaten-up look. It appeared they had all seen some rough weather since their last stop-over.

The brilliant yellows, oranges, blues, greens and reds of the boat markings only added to the needle-in-the-haystack feeling of the search.

"If he has chosen to hide among this flock, he couldn't have selected a better one," Jessica said, a sigh releasing some of her pent-up frustration.

"There're too damned many . . ." complained Eriq.

"Look for a large ship, larger than sixty feet," she suggested.

Lansing added, "A schooner class is sleek, smooth-lined, but I gotta tell you, most of those below are schooner class. You gotta be to be in a race like this."

Santiva said through his teeth, "There're too damned many. If he is among them, how can we know?"

"He's got to be farther out than this. If he's trailing the race, he'll be due north ahead, and he'll be standing alone. Take us up and northward, Don," Jessica suggested.

The ships below were beautiful, the sails flapping in the wind, their brilliant colors winking up at the sun and the passing shadow of the helicopter.

The trio moved onward, northward out to sea and toward Cuba, looking intently at those straggling, losing boats at the end of the race line. But none called out to Jessica or to the others as the killer ship.

"God, I hope we're not out here on a wild-goose chase, Jess," complained Eriq.

"Whataya want to do now?" asked Lansing, the chopper continuing due north, no sails whatsoever on the horizon.

"Keep going forward for another ten or fifteen minutes," Jessica suggested.

"You suppose he was among those boats back there, Jess?" asked Santiva. "Maybe we should just return to port, wait at the dock and keep our eyes peeled there."

"No, he's out here somewhere, and we're going to find the bastard. Don't you see? If we can take him in international waters, before he gets to Cayman—"

"Then he's our prisoner free and clear, sure . . . I see, Jess, but it's not worth it if we miss him altogether. Trying to see from up here, well, it has its drawbacks."

"Give it a little more time, Eriq, please."

"Ten minutes, then we head back."

"Agreed."

They spotted a stranded ship on the horizon. The mast was down, and looked like there had been a war aboard the craft. They flew in low and closely examined the markings and the overall appearance of the lame ship. It was a sixty- or seventy-foot schooner, exactly what they were looking for, but there were three crewmen aboard, all waving life jackets. Their engines seemed damaged and they'd jerry-rigged a small sail, but it wasn't getting the job done.

Lansing dipped the chopper from side to side, an international sign that their distress was duly noted and that the pilot would send back help. They thought the chopper was very likely an official checker for the race.

"Now, turn us around and let's head back for George Town," Eriq told Don.

Lansing frowned and raised his shoulders, waiting for Jessica to give him the word. When she did so, Lansing turned the bird around, and they headed back toward Grand Cayman, the cockpit thick with disappointment.

"I want you to fly in lower over the boats as we come on them again," Jessica instructed Don.

"How close do you want to be?"

"As close as we got to that disabled vessel. I want to see the crewmen aboard, the names of the boats, the registration numbers, the tattoos on their biceps."

"What's the use, Jess?" asked Eriq. "Can't you admit defeat? He's not out here; he's most likely back in Pensacola, for God's sake."

"We've come too damned far for defeat."

Lansing brought the chopper down, skimming just above the water, and as they came in sight of a racing vessel, they buzzed it, making crewmen either shout or curse—it was difficult to tell which. Some likely thought them a camera crew trying to get some footage for the evening news, while others likely thought them race spotters or thrill-seekers.

They passed boat after boat, and each had multiple crew members. "We find a boat with a crew of one aboard, we'll have Tauman, Eriq," she promised, sounding like the psychic detective Dr. Desinor, "and if we find him soon enough, he's ours free and clear."

"Are you that worried the Cayman government will cause us problems with deportation?"

"I just got an uneasy feeling about Ja's plans for cashing in on this whole affair. He's a good man, but he's also into taking care of himself."

Lansing brought the bird up a bit and wheeled to the left, spotting a ship off in that direction. He glanced over his shoulder at Eriq to see if he was all right with everything.

Eriq shook his head and said into his headphones, "Go, do as she says."

Lansing lowered and came in hard toward the lone craft, and Jessica became excited for a moment, seeing a large *T* figuring in the lettering of the name. But it was the *Trinidad*, and there were two men above deck and a third who came rushing out when the chopper careened by.

More racing ship crewmen were alarmed now by the buzzing chopper, as if it were some enormous albatross that had invaded their space, a few of them sending up hand gestures to make their minds known. This only made Lansing more daring, and he began driving the chopper between boats that were a mere fifty or so yards apart.

While Lansing was having his fun, whooping like a cowboy, Jessica saw a ship to their extreme right which Don had not seen. The boat moved swiftly and its sail was clean, bright, a beautiful sundial image reflecting back at her. There were no rents in the sail. It looked different from the other ships only in that it was in too good a repair.

"Don, turn us around. There's one at just past three o'clock you missed, and I want to go in low over it."

"The sundial?" he asked.

"Yeah, that's the one."

"Give it up, Jess," Eriq said into his headphones.

Lansing did a complete turnaround and circled high over the craft.

"Bring us in," she instructed as Eriq now studied the clean, teakwood lines of the sundial ship, his eyes growing larger.

"She's got the teakwood veneer we've heard so much about," he granted. "Get us in a bit closer, Lansing," he unnecessarily added.

"Will do."

They lowered at an alarming rate, causing Eriq to grip the back of Jessica's seat. "Damn, take it easy," he shouted.

They came in fast and low across the bow of the ship

and sped by her. "You see anybody aboard?" asked Jessica.

Lansing shook his head. "Not a damned soul."

"Take us around again. This time approach the aft. I want her name."

Eriq's curiosity was piqued, but he cautioned Jessica with regard to the scarcity of crew members, saying, "They could all be below, eating or ill. Don't get your hopes up."

Coming in low again, they saw someone poke a head from the cabin and appear to shout back down to others. Then this figure waved for his comrades to come out and have a look, and next he warmly waved up at the folks in the chopper in a friendly gesture, unlike the angry other boaters they'd seen. Jessica could not clearly make out the man's features, except to say his hair was a sandy-blond shade. She instead concentrated on the stenciled name of the boat at the rear, as did Eriq, who read aloud, "*Smiling Jack* and blond hair. That's a far cry from the *Tau Cross*, Jess."

They buzzed off from the boat again, Lansing saying, "What now?"

"Take her around again for a closer look. I only saw one man."

"Jessica, I could swear I saw someone below. This manhunt is getting us nowhere. It's simply futile."

"It's the name: *Smiling Jack*! Remember Kim Desinor indicated we should take care to look as much for the symbolic as the literal meaning in things dealing with the Night Crawler?"

"I seem to recall something of the like, yes."

"His Union Jack and Smiling Jack could be one and the same. What symbol is as strong as a flag? And Jack has, over the years, been used to refer to the Devil, and a smiling Jack could well mean the Devil's grin. And C. David Eddings told us that if the killer is into e. j. hellering's poetry, he might well also begin to quote e. e. cummings."

"I don't get the connection."

"I took a little time one night with cummings and stumbled over a particularly nasty little limerick called 'jack hates all the girls.' ''

"You think he's gone to all this trouble to change the name of the boat only to leave such glaring Freudian slips behind?"

"I don't know, but I want another look. Besides, there's something queer about that boat and about the man's behavior."

"What?" asked Eriq.

She shook her head. "I don't know what. I just have a feeling, an instinct." Her darkest instincts, she thought.

"Bring her around for another look, then, Mr. Lansing," Eriq relented.

"Aye, aye, Chief."

TWENTY-THREE

Logic is the art of going wrong with confidence.
                        —JOSEPH WOOD KRUTCH

Back on Grand Cayman Island, Ja Okinleye, taking no chances, ordered his entire force to be on the lookout for any suspicious-looking ships entering the ports around his three-island nation. In the easy rhythms of the Dutch-French language which Ja and his men often reverted back to when talking with one another, his officers crowded the airwaves with questions: "What is meant by suspicious-looking boat?"

"How is a boat going to be looking like that? To look suspicious?"

"What do you mean, Chief Inspector?"

"I never heard of no seventy-foot boat being operated by one man."

"Fully automated ship?"

"Wouldn't someone in port authority know about such a ship?"

Ja angrily stared at the radio mouthpiece where he sat in his car, still at the airport in front of his cousin's island helicopter business. "Do I have to think for all fifteen of you? Anyone new coming into port, particularly alone, a lone visitor. *That* is suspicious. What kind of man is he who comes to Cayman without a woman? A ship with a registry outside our waters. Use your heads! Use your eyes and ears! Damn your lazy asses."

Ja Okinleye had never been involved in a case as large, and with such international roots, as this: a killer who was wanted not only in America but in Great Britain as well. Whenever he did have a bigger than usual case to coordinate, he found it best to be on hand, at the forefront, and so he operated now out of his limousine. This case could cement his career.

It had occurred to him that catching the now-infamous Night Crawler would mean a great deal to him politically, and he had for a while been giving some thought to running for higher office—to get away from being so directly involved in law enforcement. It would make Aliciana and her whole family happy. It would mean more time with his children, not to mention his own sanity and peace of mind. Over the years, he had managed to engender a lot of enemies who would be only too glad to see him placed in higher office, where he might do them less harm.

The island was teeming with underworld activity, much of it stemming from various gambling casinos and smuggling and money-laundering operations, especially in the drug trade. Cayman intermediaries helped mask the route of shipments pouring into the U.S. from such places as Colombia. Customs officials were notoriously easy to bribe, and replacing them again and again hadn't changed the "island habit" or the morals of the men involved. In the midst of such expected third-world palm greasing, Ja was all too well aware of certain facts of island life. In order to coexist, law enforcement, as much as Ja personally hated the drug trade, pretty much looked the other way save for the occasional good-faith show of a raid now and then, typically as a result of an informant in the drug trade wishing to quell a move by newcomers to the business. It was all so sordid, and Ja was sick of police work, where the investigator's hands were tied by the very people who charged him with doing his duty. It was, he assumed, the same in most third world countries and communist countries and cities across the world, including America.

Being a cop in Cuba must be the worst kind of hell, he imagined. Handcuffed by one's own bureaucratic nightmare—like here, he thought. Here the balance wasn't set so much by a corrupt government as by the powerful men of the island who ran everything, both legitimate and illegitimate and everything in between, including some of the giant casinos and tourist centers. Such powers expected Chief Ja to keep the peace for them and to know where certain lines were drawn, to know where his jurisdiction ended. Sometimes it was at a given door, sometimes at a given street, sometimes at a given level of intervention. It all depended upon the who— the players. He must be ever vigilant about whom he was dealing with and what their connections were and how much political clout they brandished.

Ja now opened another line to bark orders in his native tongue to other subordinates, telling them to be in place. "Nothing is to be left to chance," he insisted. "Now be certain to cover every slip at every wharf. Coordinate with the port authorities at each port." Even as he said it, he knew the meager resources of the PA here meant everyone working for it—maybe six men for the three islands—was so grossly underpaid as to make graft as common as tipping in a restaurant. He thought of bringing every damned one of these men in, grilling them until one of them gave him information on the killer's first visit to the islands. They— one or more of them—had to have known something, seen something. If all else failed today, he would look into this.

Another of Ja's men was now asking, "Are you certain, sir, you want to be including the hotels and restaurants?"

"*Especially* the hotels and restaurants."

"But, sir," replied the voice at the other end, "that will draw attention. What about the tourists?"

"And the casinos?" asked another of his men.

"To hell with the tourists and the casinos. I will worry about the tourists and the casinos." And worry he would have to. After this was over, he'd deal with the Tourism Council and the local money-making interests as best he might. They were both like natural forces he had to always enter into any equation if he wished to survive, and he had already worked out a script they could both easily understand, one that meant more money for them as well as for many islanders. But for now, he hadn't the time or the inclination to spend explaining his actions to anyone.

"But we will get complaints," the young officer at the other end of the line bemoaned. Ja realized that complaints translated into threats.

"I will handle all complaints! Just distribute the sketch I forwarded you last night, and the information, and do as I say!" Ja slammed down the receiver of his car phone and looked out over the sea in the direction Jessica and the others had flown. He trusted they would be unable to pick out a single sailing vessel amid the morass of ships out there and heading this way. It seemed only too logical to him that the killer would camouflage himself amid the racers, if he was indeed as crafty and cunning as the U.S. papers had made him out to be, and if he was indeed actually on his way to the Caymans.

Ja momentarily thought of his children, what their adult lives would be like on the island. No more living off sunshine and air and sea. The island economy was in a horrid state of affairs. His children were likely to turn into chambermaids and waiters in the casinos. There was so little opportunity for a native-born child. What would be the fate of his children? What kind of changes were coming with the trade winds?

He locked up his vehicle now and joined his cousin Henri, who had fired up his second, more aged and battered, whirlybird. Shouting over the rotor blades, he said, "Let's go, brother!"

"What do you hope to gain, Ja?" asked his cousin.

Ja spoke in his native tongue, saying, "I want to be in a position to see what transpires, when it transpires and where it—"

"Happens, yes, but if they are taking care of this business . . ." Henri fell quickly and easily into their home language as well, adding with a quick wave of his hand, as if disgusted by and dismissing his prominent cousin, "It has always been just the way with you, since the day of your birth, Ja." He finished with a laugh as both men clambered aboard the triple-bladed, battered island helicopter, found their seat belts and put on their headphones, and readied for takeoff.

"What do you mean, since my birthday?"

Henri was some eight years older than Ja. He now smiled and shook his head, and placing Ja Okinleye's fist over the stick control of the chopper, he said, "You always must be with your hands here!" shouted Henri, grinning from ear to ear, his stained white teeth in need of capping. Henri's meaning came clear to Ja.

"I suppose you're right, but sometimes it is a curse."

"How well the family knows this."

They were about to lift off the tarmac when what appeared to be a madman ran out in front of them, waving his arms and hands, a brilliantly shiny gold badge held high over his head, proclaiming the American-looking, well-dressed man as some important official.

"Damnit to hell!" cursed Ja.

"Who is it?" asked his cousin.

"More FBI, no doubt. Cut the engines."

Ja popped the door and leaned out, taking the tall, good-looking American's hand in his own and giving it a vigorous shake. The man introduced himself, but Ja was unable to catch the name beneath the rotor blades as they wound down. Ja caught only the badge and a quick glimpse at the ID, which told Ja only what he had suspected.

Obviously, the FBI had sent additional agents to the island to back Jessica Coran's move. Jessica, no doubt, had alerted Peter Kylie, the resident undercover FBI operative whom everyone on the island knew, a man who lived the good life here while ostensibly on the lookout for bad guys. Now there was no telling how many other FBI agents were crawling about the island. This man standing before Ja could hardly be heard above the still whirring rotors, but after introductions, he made himself quite clear. He was desperately seeking Jessica, wanting to know her whereabouts. Something about information that could not wait.

Ja breathed deeply and realized that this could be a stroke of good fortune. After all, with an American agent aboard with him, when the sailing vessel carrying the Night Crawler came within Cayman's watery jurisdiction, the FBI's own agent could attest to the fact that the monster—

who had murdered young women on the islands as well as in the U.S.—was, technically speaking, a prisoner of the Cayman Island government, and so he would become the bargaining tool with which Ja could further his own personal and professional ambitions and help his community in the bargain. This tack might lose him some favor with Jessica and the FBI, but it could gain commerce, industry, money for the islands and his people—legitimate money. After all, it seemed the U.S. wanted this bastard badly enough to make some assurances . . .

Using the Night Crawler in this fashion seemed the preeminent path to take. It could open economic doors now closed to his island nation; it could mean more import/export trade, perhaps reduced tariffs. There was no end to what it could mean for the Caymans, and it would all be due to his excellent investigatory work.

And as for a witness to this, who better than the tall, suntanned American whom he now invited along with him—Mr. Upstanding American Police Officer.

"We are following Dr. Coran's footprints now. You are fortunate. Please, take a seat aboard." Ja indicated the back hatch and the grateful agent climbed aboard.

Through their headphones, as the chopper lifted and took off, Ja and his pilot cousin spoke in their Dutch-French tongue. "If they take the Night Crawler in our waters, we can claim him as our prisoner," Ja confided.

"Do you want this scum to dirty your prison cells?"

"It would mean great things for us, Cousin. Trust me . . ."

Ja's cousin pursed his lips and nodded, accepting his kinsman's words as gospel. Ja had never guided him wrong. "But I thought these people—the Americans—were your friends."

"Friendship is important, not to be denied, but so too is blood; besides, I do not make the laws in Cayman. I can only enforce them."

"Ahhhh," the other man said, nodding, smiling as they made their way north across the emerald mirror below them.

• • •

James Parry, fresh out of Miami, where he had jetted to from Hawaii in search of Jessica, had gotten as comfortable as his tall frame would allow in the small rear section of the cockpit. Seeing that the other two men were talking, Parry donned headphones. He only caught the tail end of the conversation, but he knew enough Dutch and French and innuendo to make out the tenor of what was being discussed.

He wondered where Jessica was at this moment. He'd come halfway around the world to find her, to take her in his arms and to profess his love for her. In Miami the morning before, he'd been told that she and Santiva had left for Grand Cayman on a small plane. He'd managed to book a jetliner for the next morning, the flight requiring only seventy minutes. He had been in Cayman for hours, but had been unable to locate Jessica. He had tried the various hotels when finally he called the authorities, who had informed him that she and Santiva and their pilot had stayed overnight with the chief of the police department here, a man Jessica had spoken highly of—and here he was, Ja Okinleye, plotting to rip Jessica's prisoner out from under her. What a guy, what a friend, James thought now.

"How far out are they?" Parry asked over the headphones.

"We are not sure. Be patient, Mr., ahhhh . . ." Okinleye's voice trailed off. "I am most sorry. Did not catch your name over the noise of the helicopter. You are?"

"Agent Parry, Chief Okinleye."

Okinleye's neck almost came off as he twisted to look at the stranger once again. "Parry? Jim Parry of . . . of . . ."

"FBI's Honolulu bureau chief, Hawaii."

"Yes . . . yes, I have heard from Jessica of you." He was in a state of shock. "Did she know you were coming?" Okinleye's mind raced. This meant Parry had likely come alone, that he was on a lover's quest and cared little or nothing about the Night Crawler case. "Does she know you have traveled here?"

"No, no, she hasn't any idea."

"Aaaa . . . But she had to know you were in Miami? You flew in from Miami?"

He nodded, saying, "Yes, but she didn't know I was in Miami. Our paths crossed there yesterday, but I missed her, so here I am."

"It is a strange thing to imagine . . ."

"What's that?" Parry was confused.

"Imagine: Jessica Coran without a clue." Ja laughed good-naturedly, even clapping his hands like a small boy who has learned a naughty secret. His laughter and enthusiasm was infectious, and the pilot caught the giggles, too. As for Parry, the contagion only brought on his bright smile.

Finally recovering his composure, Ja added, "It will please her! Your surprising her here in our lush tropical paradise, Mr. Parry."

Parry threw up his hands. "I can only hope so."

"It will be a shocking good surprise for her, one which will benefit you both, I'm sure. Do you dive as well?"

"Yes, as a matter of fact."

"You must take her to The Wall."

Parry, like all divers the world over, had heard of Cayman's Wall. He had never been to the Caymans before, and he knew he would love someday to make the dive down the sheer face of The Wall, but for the moment, Jessica alone was on his mind.

"She, I think, loves you very much, Jim Parry." Ja's smile was catching and Parry settled back, smiling in return, giving his attention to the horizon now. There appeared nothing and no one out there, but just as he thought so, his eyes registered the tiny dots of movement over the water—sailing vessels running before the wind like so many dolphins.

At his feet, Parry now saw what it was he was kicking— a coiled rope ladder half hidden beneath the seat ahead of him. Rolling about also was a flare gun, fully loaded.

Damn fools're going to blow us all up, he thought, reaching down for the flare gun and making sure the safety was on. He snatched the flare from the weapon, rendering it harmless and placing it and the flare back into a metal container jutting from the bulkhead over the seat to his right. He then stared out toward the sailing ships again. Some were taking shape now; but there was no sign of the helicopter Jessica was supposedly out here in.

· TWENTY-FOUR ·

Her beams bemocked the sultry main,
Like April hoarfrost spread;
But where the ship's huge shadow lay,
The charmed water burnt alway
A still and awful red.
　　　　　—SAMUEL TAYLOR COLERIDGE

Despite the ship's teakwood beauty and its huge, golden-orange, godlike eye—a glowing sunrise against a silken white sail—Jessica saw that it was indeed now eerily deserted, bereft of human occupancy; it was oddly still and silent even as it ran before the wind at top speed. It presented a strange, sleek, modern version of a ghost ship, its colors bright and beautifully new—*too new*. The other ships in the race showed tattered sails by comparison. Something strange and unusual crept over Jessica as she stared down over the silent schooner. It was as if the ship had a secret life of its own, one which it wanted to tell Jessica all about. She felt a cold stab of ice like a knife blade at her spine. Something rancid skittered about the recesses of her brain. Something told her this was it, Patric Allain's killing ground, Warren Tauman's place of revenge on a world that had been too unkind to him.

"We all three saw someone on the earlier pass," said Lansing, a master of the obvious, Jessica thought.

"He's hiding below," added Jessica into her microphone. "We know he must have a fully automated ship to sail alone across the Atlantic. The weasel's hiding in the cabin below."

Lansing was approaching for a third pass now, but this time he brought the bird into a hovering stance directly over the boat, approximately thirty feet above the bow, then eased her downward. They buzzed about, circling like an enormous bee, each of them staring, searching for any sign of Warren Tauman, a.k.a. Patric Allain, but he seemed to be playing hide-and-seek with them for the moment. Had it been like this with Manley and Stallings out on that fog-bound bay? Jessica wondered. This time a clear sky and bright sunshine burned down on the killer, as if God had turned his eye on Tauman.

"Bring us in closer," said Eriq. "I'm going to board that ship."

"What?" Lansing asked, his amazement complete. "Are you nuts?"

"There's a rope ladder coiled at my feet, and I'm readying it to go over the side, and I'm going over after it."

"You ever do a thing like that?" asked Lansing.

Jessica knew that Eriq may have trained for such moments in his younger days, but she was certain he hadn't made such a maneuver in some time, and very possibly never in anything but a simulated situation. "Eriq, are you sure you want to do this?" she asked.

"I'm sure. I'm dropping the ladder over the side." Eriq kicked the small door wide while continuing to shout through his headphones at Lansing. "Take the bird in lower."

But Lansing held the bird in place, the noise from the rotors and the powerful wind filling the cockpit now. "I won't be responsible for your getting yourself killed, Agent Santiva."

"Hey, you're not in charge here, kid! I am! Now do as I say, now! Bring this chopper closer down over the boat well. I want that ladder kissing the deck. Got it?"

Lansing scratched at the back of his head, looked to Jessica for help and asked, "Why don't we just follow the guy into Grand Cayman?"

"We want to take him here, while we're in international waters," she reminded him. "Besides, if the guy thinks he's cornered, given our profile on this creep, he's liable to either attack or kill himself, if he hasn't already done so."

"But we would've heard the gunshot if he's committed suicide."

"Ever hear of cyanide pills, Drano, Tilex? Any of them will clean your clock," Jessica told Don.

Meanwhile, Eriq had managed to wrestle the rope ladder over the side. Jessica quickly and momentarily glanced back at Eriq, who'd remained frustrated at so many stages of the investigation. He'd had to wait on information to come available; he'd had to run interference for her; and he'd had to act as front man for the politicians throughout the case. He'd been equally frustrated by the killer's notes and his handwriting, which while it had revealed so much about Tauman had remained useless without a suspect to attach it to. Now, the possibility that Tauman would be taking the quick and dirty and easy way out was too much for him, as it was for Jessica. She understood his need—compulsion, rather—to simply take action.

Lansing began a tentative, downward spiral which was more like an awkward air-machine dance toward the moving boat, since the sea breeze was not cooperative in the endeavor to place Eriq aboard the *Smiling Jack*.

"Feed me any cover I might need," Eriq asked Jessica, who readied her Browning automatic, her eyes now on any movement below, riveted to the windows and the hatches, her weapon pointed. But as the bird hovered and was snatched in updrafts and downdrafts, she would lose targeted points and had to wait to refocus. It wasn't the best of circumstances by any means, but every minute was taking Tauman closer and closer toward Cayman waters, and she and Eriq both knew that Ja wanted custody of their monster.

Eriq tore off his headphones and started down the whipping ladder.

God, he's gutsy, she thought. Her memory led her to a fond remembrance of a strong-willed, determined, bull-headed old friend whose like bravado had gotten him killed some four-plus years ago in Chicago—Chief Otto Boutine, with whom she'd been in love.

She cared deeply about Eriq; she didn't want anything happening to him. She also wondered if she'd have the guts to climb out of this chopper while it remained in midair, hovering above the speeding boat. She wondered if it might not come to that should something happen to Eriq, and at the same time, crowding her mind was the question of where Tauman was lurking, if he was indeed on his back from self-inflicted wounds or was merely playing the trap-door spider, biding his time, preparing an ambush. Hadn't Kim Desinor called him exactly that? This seemed more Tauman's style, since he didn't care for the sight of blood and likely didn't care for pain of any sort either.

She shouted her fears to Eriq in a stream of warnings which he could not hear, since now he was without head-phones and the noise of the machine wind alone penetrated his hearing. Still she shouted, "Be careful! Go easy! Remember what happened to those FMP cops!"

"Your friend's damned crazy," Lansing, the only one who could hear her warnings, replied.

"The guy down there may've slashed his wrists or taken pills," she shouted in defense of Santiva, "and the more time we waste now, the more time he has to check out on us."

"The guy's got to be alive; he's steering the boat from inside the cabin."

"Could be on autopilot. That damned ship is so state of the art, it can likely run this course by itself."

"No, no . . . his course is keeping pace with the others, and he's corrected his helm more than once since we spotted him. No auto'll do that, not in these conditions, surrounded by other boats."

"I've been told differently," she countered. "That boat can set its own radar, respond to its own radar signals."

"Damn chancey to bet on it with your partner's life, Dr. Coran."

Jessica took hold of his arm and said, "You ever tell a Latino he couldn't do something? There's no way Eriq was going to listen to reason once he decided to go down that ladder. Right now, we have to do all we can to help him."

"I'm trying to get him down as quickly as possible, but part of my brain is asking, Should we do that or take him up? Better we all come out of this alive, even if you do lose your prisoner. You can have him extradited later. Get the State Department to threaten sanctions or something.''

"Maybe you're right."

"I know I'm—"

Suddenly, a metal rod slammed into the bubble top, creating a spidery web of cracks that began to spread over the glass before them. "Damn! What was that?"

"A metal part from the rotor, I think! Damn!"

"What's it mean?"

"If it's part of the rotor, we're going down. Something like a hundred moveable parts in that damned old rotor shaft, any one of which, if it gives, we sink like a stone. Helicopters don't glide down with the wind the way a plane does."

"I knew this damned old thing was old but . . ."

"Are you kidding? The glass isn't even shatterproof. We'll be lucky if it holds."

"Eriq! Oh, my God!" Over Lansing's protests, she tore off her headphone set and ripped her seat belt away. She then climbed into the rear, where Eriq had disappeared over the side. She stared down to see him holding so tightly to the rope ladder that it appeared now to have become a giant rosary upon which to plant a kiss and a prayer.

Jessica watched a dangling Eriq as Lansing fought the chopper for control, and she saw the dark, sinister shadow in an open hatch on the boat. She saw the metal spear rise like a bullet toward Eriq. When the ladder was snatched and whipped again by the struggling chopper, the spear missed Eriq by inches.

Jessica grabbed up the headphones she found on the floor and shouted into them, "Lansing! He's firing a speargun at us! It's not the chopper! Repeat, it's not the rotor!"

"Speargun!" echoed Lansing.

Jessica continued to monitor for any sign of Tauman, realizing now that Eriq was between her and the killer, but that if he showed himself at the hatchway again or at the entryway to the cabin she'd have a clear shot—if Lansing could get the damned bird stabilized.

Just then she saw Tauman—muscular, tall, ruddy-complexioned with wild hair blowing in the wind. He was armed now with a huge pistol.

"Damnit, it's a flare gun!" she shouted.

Lansing took the warning, instantly pulling up, but at the same time Eriq leapt for the boat, and as Tauman's fiery missile slammed into the chopper and bounced harmlessly away and into the sea, Jessica fired. But Lansing had jammed the chopper sharply to the right, sending Jessica's shot astray.

"Turn back! Get us around! Eriq's on board with that maniac, and he's got a flare gun!"

Lansing didn't hesitate, bringing the chopper back around in a tight arc, returning to the pursuit. "Now that sonofabitch's tried to kill me!" he barked.

The chopper skimmed straight over the water now, catching up with Tauman's boat. When they neared, they could see that Eriq had lost his gun in his mad jump onto the boat, but that he'd somehow managed to get hold of Tauman before he could reload the flare gun. The two men were fighting for control of the gun now, and it was pointed overhead.

Tauman viciously kicked Eriq in the groin, bringing him to his knees, but Eriq wouldn't let go of the gun, and Tauman, too, went to his knees, unable to free the gun and control it.

"Is it loaded?" Lansing wanted to know.

Jessica could not say. "I don't know. Get me closer, and I'll put a bullet in the bastard."

"You got it."

They dipped now over the boat, which the wind carried just ahead of them. The other boaters racing these waters had all slowed, staring, pointing, wondering what was going on and who were the good guys and who the bad in this confusing set of circumstances.

"Get on that radio and tell those others to stay back. Inform them we're FBI," she ordered Lansing.

"Good idea," agreed Lansing, who was about to find the necessary frequency when Jessica screamed and the second flare went sailing across the cracked glass bubble. "Sonofabitch!" Lansing shouted into the open frequency, the chopper rolling and banking again in response to his reaction to the near hit. But this time Lansing held on to his emotions and the controls, keeping the chopper fairly well in place.

Jessica again leaned far out over the side, trying to draw a bead on Tauman, but Eriq was all over the monster now, pounding him and pummeling him, looking as if he might kill him with his bare fists. Tauman wouldn't stay down, however. Then suddenly Tauman slumped into a heap, appearing either dead or deeply unconscious.

She watched as Eriq lifted Tauman by his hair and battered his head against the gunwale. Satisfied that the creature had finally been rendered harmless, Eriq went below to get the ship under control. Jessica took that as her cue to board the boat. She didn't want Eriq turning his back on this serpent.

She quickly holstered her weapon and breathed deeply in relief. It was over—finally over. They had the Night Crawler in custody, and the Night Crawler's boat deck was painted in the demon's blood. And somewhere aboard the boat, they would find incriminating evidence to prove this was indeed Patric Allain, indeed Warren Tauman, indeed the Night Crawler.

"God, we were right in tracking him here," she said as much to herself as to Lansing and the cockpit. "We've got him. We've really got him."

"It would appear so," agreed Lansing, smiling, breathing easier now. "I guess that's what you guys call probable cause, huh? I mean, the sonofabitch tried to kill us. So your boss had every right boarding the guy's boat the way he did."

"Carte blanche. Now we start the long process of prosecuting this bastard carefully, by the book, so that we don't violate his civil rights. He is, after all, innocent until proven guilty."

Her sarcasm wasn't lost on Don Lansing, who replied, "Like those cowardly mothers who planted that bomb in Oklahoma City in '95?"

"Yeah, how we had to look after their precious civil

rights. Provide them with defense attorneys, provide them with a judge and a jury and a forum—as if they still had rights as American citizens, as if they were human. Bastards deserved to be stripped of any and all rights. You don't give civil rights to murderers and baby-killers. They forfeit the right to be assumed human when they turn to taking human life, so far as I'm concerned.''

"You . . . you were part of the force that tracked those guys in Oklahoma down, weren't you?"

"Part of the BSU sent to Oklahoma, yeah."

"BSU?"

"Behavioral Science Unit, part of a larger division. We profile killers, try to get into their heads, track them through understanding them as best we can."

He nodded. "So, maybe if we shipped the cretin back to England it'd be better all around. Isn't he guilty over there until proven innocent?"

"You might have a great idea there, Don. Imagine the Menendez trial in England. The defense would've had to prove innocence, and all the prosecution would've needed to do would've been to burn incense, blow smoke and hold up mirrors, rather than the other way around. As it was, it was just the opposite in California."

"Why not extradite this guy to England then?"

"Good point. Maybe we'll consider it, but I doubt the American public will stand for it. Everybody wants him fried in Florida. Trouble with that is the electric chair's too good for the likes of this mother—"

"Death row food for how long?"

She shook her head, unable to answer.

"So, what do we do now?"

"We take the bastard back to the States to stand trial."

"Maybe we should let the Cayman authorities have him?" he wondered aloud. "Maybe their brand of justice would be swifter, surer?"

"You got a point, Lansing . . . you have a point, but once again the U.S. isn't likely to stand for it. Our government and the State of Florida'll be looking to control this one, not to mention *America's Most Wanted*."

Jessica took in another deep breath of the rushing, hurricanelike air all around her. "Bring the chopper in as low as you can. I'm going down to the boat."

Lansing was doing gyrations both in his seat and in his head, asking, "What? What'd you say?"

"I'm going down there . . . on the ladder."

"Hey, we're not talking child's play here, Dr. Coran."

"I want to be with my partner, and I want on that ship, now, Don!"

"But—"

"No buts! Just do it."

Jessica snatched off her headphones and looked out over the side. The straight drop gave her renewed respect for Eriq. Tauman was still unconscious, but she hadn't recalled his lying half on, half off the back of the boat where those thick, black nylon ropes were still draped. She wondered if any bodies dangled there now, but she rather doubted it. She also wondered if he'd moved, or if he had been moved. Had the boat simply shifted his deadweight? Had Eriq come back to kick him a few times?

Or had the Night Crawler, she wondered again, moved himself?

With the chopper lower now over the slowing boat, the bottom rungs of the ladder were loosely coiled aboard the ship when Jessica began her descent, doing so with one eye on the evil below her while the wind tore at her body, whipping wildly at her blouse and slacks. She thanked God she'd been wise enough to wear cotton pants and comfortable sneakers.

Each rung down the rope ladder brought her nearer Tauman, and she couldn't help but recall her father's long-ago words to her when they were on a hunting trip once in Minnesota. Her father had had to kill a snake, and she went to pick it up, curious to examine it as closely as possible. It was beautiful in its size, and variegated color scheme and surprising in its dead heft. She was thirteen at the time.

"Never assume a snake is dead until you cut off its head and feed on its heart," her father had warned.

"Oh, yuck, Dad. Whataya mean? Eat its heart?"

"Old Indian proverb—American Indian, Lakota, I think. If you don't cut off the head and eat the heart of your enemy, he will rise again to strike you when you least suspect it."

Another glance at Tauman told her this particular snake was stone still. Maybe Eriq had indeed killed Warren Tauman. It would certainly save the taxpayers a bundle if it were true; still, she wanted this devil alive. Florida had the death penalty, and she would conduct hundreds of hours of laboratory tests over the remnants of his victims to prove Warren Tauman more than just the "alleged" killer.

Jessica was two rungs from the boat deck now, twirling uncontrollably around and about over the deck of a still moving ship, dangling from the chopper overhead, holding on tightly. Maybe Don Lansing was right. Maybe she was a fool to risk life and limb in this manner, but for so long now they had tracked this beast, and so she felt she had to get a closer look and be certain that her partner was all right.

She didn't want to jump too soon, didn't want to lose her balance as Eriq had. In the meantime, due to the buffeting winds here, Don Lansing had had to bring the helicopter a bit higher, and looking down at her feet, she realized there were no rungs lying on the deck any longer. In fact, she had reached the final rung, and there remained a three-foot drop, with the boat still going at quite a speed. She took a final look at the snake whose blood was dripping over the gunwale and into the salt sea.

Tauman lay there like a broken granite statue; he hadn't so much as flinched. He was exactly as she had seen him from the top. Maybe he was dead; maybe Eriq had used deadly force, which would mean a review of every moment of every second of this past hour. The Bureau and the attorney general of the United States would be studying Eriq's behavior instead of the killer's, trying to determine if deadly force had been necessary, and the eyewitnesses to that deadly force would be Lansing and Jessica.

She saw Eriq coming up from below, his wild, adrenaline-fed eyes meeting hers just as she jumped on deck, and he cried out, "Nooooo!"

When she hit the deck, the momentum of the ship sent her directly back, and she fell into the grasp of Warren Tauman who'd gotten to his feet. Tauman snatched her gun from her shoulder holster before she could get at it, both of them fighting for balance, and now pointed her weapon at Eriq, focusing through blood that streaked from his forehead and half blinded him. Eriq, in that same instant, surged forward, trying to react, but froze in place when he saw the gun pointed directly between his eyes.

At that moment, Jessica half heard, half saw the flare which Lansing had suddenly fired across the boat; reacting immediately, she stomped on Tauman's foot with all her weight and forced both Tauman and herself back toward the aft, until both of them again lost their footing.

Together, they went over the back of the ship and into the water, the boat moving swiftly away from their falling bodies.

· TWENTY-FIVE ·

Do not take life too seriously; you will never get out of it alive.
—ELBERT HUBBARD

Hovering above the boat now were two helicopters. Jim Parry had had Henri contact Lansing, telling him who they were. Lansing recognized Okinleye's voice, Okinleye saying something to the effect that they were well within Cayman's waters at this point and that the prisoner below was his prisoner now. Parry was simply yelling at Lansing for having allowed Jessica Coran to take the dangerous step of climbing down onto the boat from the moving chopper. Everyone above had then seen the sudden standoff below.

Parry had had an instinctual feeling that Tauman was not secured. He saw no handcuffs or anything else restraining the man, and earlier, he, Ja and Henri had seen the two flares sent up from the boat at the helicopter. Parry had prepared the flare he'd earlier seen, and he had had it poised and ready to signal those on the boat of their arrival the moment they came over. Instead, he'd used it to disrupt the Night Crawler's plan when Parry saw him grab Jessica and take hold of her as his hostage. The distraction had worked, but only up to a point. Now it appeared Jessica was in the water with the now armed madman.

Parry shouted for Henri to get them in closer, over the water, and as Henri worked to do so, he tore at the rope ladder below the seat in front of him, and shoved open the door, which came immediately back at him, closing on him as if to deny him his plan. Ja Okinleye, too, meant to deny him, grasping him by the arm and shouting, "Don't be a fool! We already have two people in the water. Don't add to the problem!"

Parry snatched his arm away and pushed the door against the wind a second time, continuing with his plan, tossing the rope ladder out over the side.

"You will only add to the casualties if—" But Ja saw that he was talking to an insane man. He threw his hands up and ordered Henri to give him the radio.

Parry shouted through his headphones at Henri the same instant, "Locate her in the water! Bring us over Dr. Coran, Henri, until this ladder is within her grasp! Do you understand?"

"I will do my best, sir!"

Ja radioed Lansing, ordering him to pick up the prisoner using his chopper and rope ladder. Meanwhile, Parry tore off his headphones and his suit coat and climbed out onto the ladder, his body in the vortex of wind below the rotor blades now as rope and man swayed madly below the belly of the rattling old machine. He got a face full of exhaust and fuel from something that seemed abnormal, a leaking valve or fuel pump. Ignoring this, Parry worked his way down toward the surf as Henri and Ja searched the waters for any sign of Jessica.

When Jessica surfaced, she didn't know where Tauman was or where the boat was. Twisting about in the water, she located first the chopper and next the boat, both trying desperately to turn around and retrieve her and Tauman. She glanced around now for Tauman, fearful he might've held tight to her weapon. Even wet, it could do a hell of a lot of damage. But Tauman hadn't surfaced. Was he a nonswimmer?

The waves here were not terribly high, but Tauman, she knew, could easily be just beyond the next wave, just out of her extremely limited perspective and sight. Or he might at any moment pop up beside her and place a bullet in her head. She reached down to her ankle for her second gun, a .38 Police Special. Thus armed, she felt a bit safer, until she saw the huge, gray-blue fin streaking along the surface some seventy or eighty yards off.

Shark, she thought, her pulse racing, knowing Tauman's blood had baited the shark for some time now. She saw a second fin break the surface, a third and a fourth. Then she made out Tauman's head bobbing about in the sea some fifty yards from where she'd spied the first of the sharks, which for the moment seemed content with the morsel before them.

Jessica held more tightly to the gun than ever. She wondered if she'd use it to fire at the sharks as they neared or if she'd use it on herself before being eaten alive by the beasts. She recalled Islamorada, imagined herself—or part of herself—returning there through no fault of her own, found in the belly of a great white. She thought how mad her life had been, how much she had given up over the years to become who she was; she questioned who she was, what she was, and wondered if it had all been worth it . . .

Lansing and the chopper got to her much more quickly than she had thought possible, and far more quickly than Eriq possibly could with the boat. She waved and shouted, but Lansing went by her, going for Tauman, who was in far graver circumstances. Still, she cursed Lansing his choice.

Then she saw the second—and from this distance nearly identical—chopper and realized it must be Ja Okinleye. He'd come through for her after all. A rope ladder trailed below his chopper, too, and amazingly enough, someone was dangling on the ladder. Okinleye?

No, it was not Ja. The clothes were not island uniform or wear; rather, it was a man in a gray flannel suit. She could not make out who the man was, but she thanked God he was coming for her.

The second chopper and rope ladder were now her only hope, her lifeline. She grabbed out at the ladder once, twice, missing as the helicopter hovered above. She missed a third pass, then finally snagged the ladder and held firm with one hand until she could safely put the .38 into her shoulder holster. The man above her had descended almost to where he could reach down and help her up, but not quite. He was wearing expensive dress shoes—totally wrong footwear for this work—and having some difficulty holding on, and she began to fear for him. She was in no position to see his features, only his size and predicament. If he should fall over into the water, she knew, the sharks could easily feed on him, too.

She had not dared watch the sharks, but she still didn't feel completely safe so long as any part of her remained in the water.

Quickly now, Jessica tugged and pulled and powered her wet weight and the weight of her wet clothing onto the ladder. It was an exhausting struggle to do so, and when she slipped and fell back a rung, she felt a hand grasp her by the wrist, and then heard Jim Parry's voice repeatedly calling her name.

"Jim? Jim, it's you!"

He wasn't satisfied with her heels dangling in the sea, and so he dragged himself up, tugging her along with him until she was firmly on the bottom rung. The chopper was having trouble with the weight, first rising, then dipping, her ankles teasing the surf as it did so.

Parry remained calm, although he saw two sharks heading straight for them, responding no doubt to the slap and fray in the surf here. "Higher, Jess. Pull yourself up alongside me! Come on . . . come on . . . " he said, managing to keep the sheer terror from his voice. "Hell of a party you're throwing here."

Jessica fought against the weight of her own cloying clothing, which seemed in a conspiracy to keep her in the water, but with Jim's strong hand and help, she managed to pull her way to come alongside him on the ladder, panting wildly, finally able to breathe. Face-to-face with Jim Parry for the first time since she'd last left Hawaii, she said to him, "Hell of a way to surprise a girl."

Again the chopper jarred them downward, dipping their legs into the spray, and for the first time Jessica saw how close the pair of sharks were. They had come within ten feet. She involuntarily screamed while Jim shouted to God and waved madly at the chopper pilot, screaming, ''Get us the hell out of here!''

Henri gained control of the air and the weight tugging at his machine, lifting them all ahead of the hungry sharks, then speeding off.

Jessica heard gunshots. Tauman still had hold of her gun after all. Was he firing at Jim and her? At Lansing's chopper as Don tried to save him? Or was he firing at the feeding sharks? Lansing was in no position to know, but Ja or Henri must have radioed him that the shots were being directed, for the moment, at the sharks and not the chopper.

Jessica, glancing over her shoulder as she and Jim were hauled off, wondered if Don Lansing might not simply leave Tauman to the sharks. And why not? He had nervously moved a little off after the first shots had rung out. But now Lansing lowered in on the fugitive again.

Henri's chopper having risen sufficiently, Jessica had a better view of what was happening with the snake amid the sharks to the north of their position.

Tauman was pumping his bullets into the sharks. With each near approach, he would fire into one of the animals, the water now thick with blood, so that the number of sharks only increased.

Tauman would soon run out of bullets. Jessica wondered if he planned saving one slug for himself, as she had intended to do.

Ja's cousin Henri, seeming to have gotten the hang of this thing now, almost gently deposited first Jessica and next James Parry into Eriq Santiva's waiting arms aboard the killer's boat. Jim then took over from Eriq the duty of draping a blanket over Jessica. Parry and Jessica stood at the stern of the boat as it closed in now on the shark party and Tauman, who was finally responding to Lansing's rescue effort, reaching out and grabbing on to the rope ladder dangled before him.

James Parry had draped his arms about Jessica as they watched the unfolding drama before them. It looked as if

Tauman would be rescued, but Jessica recalled how difficult it had been to pull her weight and drenched clothing up along the rungs.

The boat was closing in on the scene, and now Eriq maneuvered the boat closer and closer in hopes of dispersing the sharks and possibly coming to Tauman's aid, but it was dicey, extremely so since their fugitive was armed with a lethal weapon. But then came the hollow click-click of the empty chamber.

"He's run himself out of bullets," Jessica said aloud.

"Move in faster!" shouted Jim to Eriq, who revved the boat.

Lansing's lifeline looked like Tauman's only hope, but Tauman had refused to let go of the gun and now slipped from the ladder, falling back into the waiting sea. Tauman had foolishly continued searching for a bullet in the chamber, obviously in a state of shock or knowing nothing about the type of firearm he'd grabbed hold of. They could hear the useless click-click-click of repeated attempts to bring a bullet into the chamber as if by some magic.

Eriq brought the sailing vessel ever closer and they watched as Lansing, using the rope ladder, tried his level best to place this lifeline over the now trapped Tauman, the sharks having circled and circled and tightened their circle as they'd done so. One of the sharks took a run at Tauman, who slammed the gun into its snout, deflecting the brute. A second creature took a run at him, tearing a chunk from his body somewhere below the surface, sending Tauman's scream to the brilliant blue heavens.

Warren Tauman's shouts could be heard across the water. But he was now shouting with a giddy happiness, for he'd latched hold of the rope ladder a second time, and now the chopper began to rise, tugging at his wet body, lifting him from the water. It appeared the snake would live to face charges after all, and would become the contention of three countries, the subject of extradition orders, mass interest and countless newspaper articles. It appeared the Night Crawler would stand trial before a judge and jury and a fascinated public.

Jessica and Jim looked into one another's eyes. "It's over," he said, trying to soothe her, feeling her tremble and shiver beneath the blanket and his embrace. He held her tighter still when suddenly the tone of Tauman's voice went from that of a cheer to that of a scream of horror and pain. This sent Eriq forward, and along with Jessica and Jim, he looked out over the bow to see Tauman's torso lifted from the water by Lansing's upward pull. But both his legs dangled loosely there, and were suddenly amputated by a duo of sharks who leapt from the water and took them off at the hip.

Lifted from the water, Tauman's torso and arms seemed wrapped up in the rope ladder, twisted and twisting like a frantic eel, clinging to life, his bottom half leaking blood like a busted oil can. Lansing continued to carry what was left of Tauman higher and farther away from the shark pool. Tauman's arms had become so twisted up in the netting of the rope ladder that his weight held there. Jessica had to turn her eyes away, as did Jim Parry, while Eriq, captivated by the sight before him, stared in amazement, for Tauman was still alive and in great suffering and pain.

Warren Tauman's final anguished, unholy wail, and his wide eyes, reached out across the water for a mercy that was not forthcoming. Then there was silence.

"The snake's head and his heart are gone," Jessica said.

"What's that?" Eriq asked.

"It's over . . ."

"It certainly is."

"But we need what's left of the body, Eriq," she told the others. "It will help tremendously to prove it's Tauman, that this guy is the Night Crawler, without the slightest doubt."

"God, he'd better be at this point," Eriq moaned.

Parry instantly got on the radio and got to Lansing, telling him to be as gentle as possible, that he was still carrying Tauman's body below on the rope ladder and that it was needed for examination and identification.

"God, mister . . . what do you want me to do with it?"

Jessica was beside Jim, having torn away the blanket,

and she snatched the radio from Jim. "Don, try your best
to lower it over the boat. We . . . we'll take it in from here."

"Aye, aye. I'll do my best."

Eriq shouted from the stern, "Damnit, we're losing
him!"

Jessica and Jim looked up to see that Tauman's torso
now dangled by one knotted arm and that with each second,
even this connection was loosening. Below the twirling ladder, a stream of blood had baited sharks to follow. The
remains were ugly and contorted in the Caribbean sun,
which beat down relentlessly and in stark juxtaposition to
the moment, as if God's awful, inscrutable reality had finally turned on Warren Tauman, the Night Crawler, and
had decreed all of him to be consumed by the sea.

Like a drunken, disabled diver, Tauman's remains awkwardly came loose, dangled, loosened further and sailed
heavily downward to the waiting sharks, who then fed vo-
raciously on them.

"Damn . . . damn," muttered Jessica.

Lansing came over the radio saying, "I'd like to say I'm
sorry, but I can't quite work myself up to sorry."

"It's all right," Eriq assured Jessica. "We know it was
him."

"But can you prove it?" contested Parry.

"Yeah, we can prove it, can't we, Jess?"

"There've got to be papers about. You can show it's his
handwriting, Eriq."

"That's hardly enough in a court of law," countered Jim.

"It's one nail in the coffin, then," she contested.

Jim nodded and asked Eriq, "Did you see any papers
lying about below?"

"Nothing lying out, no, but there're papers inside the
cabin somewhere, and possibly far more incriminating evidence aboard. The ropes, the taxidermy stuff, chemicals
maybe."

"Have you seen any of this?" Parry asked, continuing
to play Devil's advocate.

"No . . . but who's had time to search?"

"We'll need to search the boat from top to bottom."

Jessica said. "We've got to show, beyond any doubt, that it was Tauman who was killed here, that it was the Night Crawler."

"We'll have the boat returned to Miami, get the witnesses to ID the boat," suggested Eriq as if he'd just closed the matter.

"If we can get the boat out of Ja Okinleye's hands," hinted Parry.

"What're you talking about?" asked Eriq. "This is evidentiary property of the United States government now."

"Tell that to the Cayman Island government." Jim turned to Jessica and explained, "I'm pretty sure your friend Okinleye is interested in parlaying something out of all this. He's going to want assurances."

"Yeah, I sensed it earlier on," agreed Jessica.

Eriq asked, "What kind of assurances?"

"The kind the U.S. makes to all its allies all the time."

Eriq set his teeth. "That weaseling, black—"

"—national . . . He's looking out for the interests of his own. Can't say as I blame him—not too much," said Parry, who'd had a great amount of dealings with native Hawaiians over the years.

"We'll deal with Okinleye and the Cayman government fairly," Jessica said. "Meanwhile, they're in no position to do a complete DNA search. If we find any DNA evidence on the ropes, on the deck, anywhere, matching any single victim, including the murdered Marine Patrol officer in Tampa, we'll have incontestable proof."

Santiva was nodding during her entire speech, and now he added, "Well, at least *we* will have no doubt."

"Yeah, the SOB tried to kill us," Jessica said, chorusing Lansing's point.

"Whatever is decided and however it goes, Jessica here needs to be *off* the case," Parry said to Santiva, their eyes meeting.

"What are you talking about, Jim?" she replied.

"No, no, Jess, Mr. Parry is absolutely right," said Chief Santiva.

"Eriq! This is my case; has been my case from day one,

and now that it's over, that you'd even consider such a . . . such a . . . proposal is—''

''It's time, Jess, you got a little R and R, and I think Mr. Parry here is just the fellow to see to it you get all the R and R you need.''

''What about blood splotches, fingerprinting, the evidence search?''

''I have some authority, Dr. Coran!'' Eriq returned. ''I'll have a team sent down from Florida or Quantico if necessary. Meanwhile, you two can enjoy the Caymans. Go do that 'Wall' thing you all do here.''

''Try Rome and Athens,'' countered Parry. ''I have two tickets, Jess. Will you go with me to Rome and Athens? No work, just play?''

She looked stunned. She looked from Jim to Eriq and back again, finally turning to Eriq and asking, ''Are you absolutely sure?''

''Just do me one favor.''

''And that is?''

''Talk to Okinleye. Get us the best deal you can.''

''That pirate. Sure, I'll do what I can, of course, and by the way, he likes it if you can pronounce his name correctly.''

''I thought I had been . . . Okinlee, right?''

''No, Okinlee-ye; a bit of emphasis on the *ye* at the end, please. It might help in all the negotiations when it comes to them . . .''

''He knows you best; maybe friendship still counts for something in this world?''

Jessica smiled, Eriq laughed and soon the three of them were nearly hysterical. She hugged Eriq, kissed him on the cheek and hugged him again.

''I was so worried for you,'' she told him. ''That was the bravest thing I ever saw anyone do, climbing out on that ladder and jumping onto this deck at the speed this boat was going.''

''You did it yourself.''

''No, not at the same speed.''

''Let's get turned around for the island. I'm burning up

out here and sweating like a pig," complained Eriq, pretending he was uncomfortable with the flattering compliments. Looking back over his shoulder as he went for the controls, he added, "Hell of a schooner, wouldn't you say, Parry?"

"She is beautiful; yes." Parry again had his arm around Jessica, who had dried in the sun and wind now, her hair hanging in stringy ringlets about her brow. Overhead both helicopters had taken up a hovering position, and now both radioed down that they were running for George Town.

Eriq, using the radio, thanked the two pilots and Okinleye for their excellent assistance in what had turned out to be a treacherous raid on Tauman's killing ground. He then alerted George Town port authorities that they were coming in with the boat and to be prepared to place the boat under quarantine in order to keep any prying eyes and hands off. No one was to go near it. If there were any incriminating evidence aboard, he certainly didn't want it to be contaminated any further than it already had been. He then turned back to Jessica and Parry, calling up to them from the well of the cabin, saying, "Listen, you two, while I'm getting us back to shore, I think it safe to begin searching the boat for anything incriminating to help our case once we get back to the U.S. God, I sure hope Tauman didn't swap boats somewhere between here and the States."

"We'll start a search," agreed Jessica. "Meantime, everyone is to try as hard as possible to avoid the blood spatters. We'll take some of Tauman's blood in evidence, but unless I miss my guess, we'll find evidence of other blood spatters aboard this death ship. Look there." She pointed at a section near the starboard side center-rear. "Notice the pinkish hue where blood has soaked into the deck?"

"That could as well be fish blood," suggested Parry. "I've seen like stains on a thousand boats."

"Just the same, our boy didn't appear to do a great deal of fishing. I want that panel cut and raised for lab inspection, Eriq. It's a place to start. The material is porous enough that, even after cleaning—and it obviously has been cleaned—trace DNA evidence could quite possibly be lifted for the electron microscope.''

''Leave a list of instructions. We'll get a team down here,'' Eriq assured her. ''We'll get the best.''

''That's impossible, Santiva,'' replied Jim, ''because the best is leaving with me.''

''Get J.T., John Thorpe,'' she suggested. ''He and his team will do an excellent job. And you're right. I'll make a list.''

Together, Jessica and Parry began to carefully canvass the boat from the inside out as Eriq brought it in toward Grand Cayman.

· EPILOGUE ·

Fear on fear, like light reflected
from the dancing wave,
visits all places, but can rest in none.
                                    —ROBERT JEPHSON

Seven Days Later

Athens and Rome were stunning, and it was delightful to
get away from the profundity of both her work and the
horrors of the Night Crawler case. James had arranged
everything down to the last detail, and he had managed to
make her forget all about Warren Tauman and the atrocities
he had created in his wake. Their vacation was complete,
for she cleared her mind of what might or might not be
going on back in the Cayman Islands, Miami and Quantico.
She hadn't given a whit's thought to the collection and
delivery of evidentiary materials from Tauman's boat to the
microscopes at Quantico. She felt confident that John
Thorpe could do a more than adequate job in her place, and
besides, hidden away in a secret compartment was a book,
a diary of sorts which Tauman kept. It was mostly a captain's journal of ports of call, places he and his ship had
been, and on the surface of it, there was nothing incriminating there, since he spoke not a word about the killings.
He had put all his passion about the killings into his notes
to newspapers, apparently. There were, however, names of
every port he had visited, along with the dates, and this
placed him at every locality where some young woman had
disappeared. And there were vague references to his god,
his belief system, a belief system that was more than simply
scattered and confused and out of focus. There were vague

references to his having given "offerings" to his god. But
there was nothing whatever that pointed to what exactly he
had offered up or how he went about these obscure rituals.
However, there was one thing about the journal that was
most clear indeed—it was written in the same mad script
as the hand of the Night Crawler. Eriq Santiva was satisfied
about that the moment his eyes fell upon the script.

This alone was not enough, however, so the book was
also dusted for fingerprints, and several of them were lifted
from its leather coverlet. Tauman's prints were also found
on the consoles and on the speargun he'd left behind, the
weapon believed to have killed Marine Patrol Officer Manley back in Tampa. Other evidence would take more time
to construct and reconstruct at the microscopic level, and
Jessica was banking on the section of stain she'd noticed
while aboard the death ship, hoping that it might be
matched to Rob Manley's or Ken Stallings's blood type
and DNA.

It was a foregone conclusion that, in time, they would
prove beyond a shadow of a doubt that it had been Warren
Tauman aboard the boat they'd boarded, and that Tauman
was Patric Allain, and that both were one and the same as
the Night Crawler. Being the Night Crawler was perhaps
the only time he felt whole.

So it was with an easy mind that Jessica, after having
worked out some preliminary negotiations with Ja Okinleye
and several of the highest-ranking officials on the islands,
had left Eriq to his own devices in Cayman. That had been
a week earlier, and neither she nor James had been bothered
by headquarters, newspaper reporters, politicians or ghosts,
other than those that roamed the Aegean Sea and the ancient ruins of Greece.

Amid the beauty of Greece and the solitude of anonymity, which they prized above all else here, Jessica and James
rekindled their passion and renewed their unspoken vows
to always love one another, no matter the distance between
them or the circumstances they found themselves in.

Jessica now lay out at the pool of the Hilton in Athens,
beyond which blinked the gorgeous blue Aegean Sea. With

James beside her, she merely baked, soaking up the sun as if it were water, realizing that they'd both been absorbing its effects for over an hour. It was nearing noon and hunger had begun to bite, but Jessica felt a deeper hunger arising in her when she looked over at James, his body spread with buttery oil.

"Let's go back up to the room," she suggested.

"Already?"

"Trust me . . ."

He perked up at the tone of her voice.

"Trust in the doctor," she seductively added.

"You know you're the author of my desires," he replied. "It probably sounds like a corny cliché, but you know . . ."

She waited for his final words, but seeing that he'd swallowed them, she pressed, "Go on. I like corn."

"I'd go to the ends of the earth for you, Jessica."

"Seems you have . . . seems you have . . ." She took his hand in hers, tugging him to his feet and leading him across the pool deck as others watched the two American lovers, some quite envious of what they apparently shared.

They located the closest elevator that would take them up to their room overlooking the Aegean. In the elevator, she passionately kissed him and said, "You know, what we have is extremely rare, maybe as rare as emeralds and diamonds."

He breathed her in. "I couldn't agree with you more." He returned her kiss and they became even more passionate, the doors opening on an elderly couple, who both giggled and blushed before them.

"Bravo," said the old man in a European accent.

His aged wife pulled him past the young couple, a warm smile on her face as well.

Jessica and James made for the privacy of their room, and once the door was closed, they began to kiss and caress one another in a fumbling, less than well-orchestrated dance for the bedroom, their passion coming before the choreography. Falling, stumbling into a wall, trying to sidestep an easy chair and a coffee table, they simply were not going to make it to the bedroom. They silently agreed to this fact,

Jim allowing her to slide down onto the carpeted floor of the hotel room, where she began to fire his already heated passions even further.

Jessica, hungry for him, pulled him down beside her on the soft beige rug, and there they continued making love. Her hunger, the fire within her, raged and burned, and she found James equal to the task. He made her feel whole again; made her feel invincible and energized and strengthened and alive all at once. He made her feel safe from all harm and all ugliness in the world. His arms were like a corral into which she willingly, wantonly enslaved herself.

Out of passion's enslavement came a sexual fulfillment like none she had ever known before, like none she would ever know again.

"I want you, Jim, forever," she cried as he penetrated her.

"I'll always be yours, Jess . . . always . . ."

Always and forever . . . impossible notions, she knew, but love was impossible from its inception—like trying to see one's true self in a reflecting mirror only to witness the magic that was a mirror, the magic that never reflected back the same image as seen by others. Like the looking glass, love had nothing whatever to do with logic or science or intellect. Love mirrored only instinct, and her instinct for the moment was to love James Parry and to hold on to him for as long as God and James allowed.